To Amy.

Because I believe in destiny.

the most important little boy in the world

Dean Briggs

WORD PUBLISHING

NASHVILLE

A Thomas Nelson Company

Library of Congress Cataloging-in-Publication Data

Briggs, Dean, 1968–.
    The most important little boy in the world / by Dean Briggs.
        p. cm.
    ISBN 0-8499-4255-1
        1. Epidemics—Fiction. 2. Healing—Fiction. 3. Boys—Fiction. I. Title.

PS3552.R4556 M6 2001
813'.54—dc21

                                                                                        2001017663

Printed in the United States of America

01 02 03 04 05 PHX 9 8 7 6 5 4 3 2 1

Acknowledgments

I wish to thank my primary advisers, Dr. Thom Mohn and Dr. Drew Shoemaker, for their medical insight, direction, and willingness to brainstorm with me; my mother and father, Benny and Darlene Briggs, for training my heart in the ways of God; Bob and Jane Hodgdon for the generous use of their cabin as the deadline loomed; the many readers who were so encouraging of my first book; and the team at Word for the chance to write.

Most of all, I wish to honor my four sons, Hanson, Evan, Gatlin, and Gage, who continually ignite the father heart within me. Without knowing it, the gift of their lives transformed this process into a series of sacred encounters with God. As a result, it is my desire that everyone who reads be struck afresh with the devastating love of our Father in heaven, the One who did not merely read John chapter three, verse sixteen, but Who lived it. I am amazed and undone at His mercy.

"Phasing out the human race will solve every problem on earth, social and environmental."

—Dave Foreman, founder of *Earth First*

Prologue

The most important little boy in the world was born September 17.

He arrived much like the day that year, with little fanfare, save one regrettable parallel: not only was the seventeenth the hottest day of the hottest summer on record, but inside, in DR3, his mother ran a fever that nearly took her life. Across a four-state region—including the small town of Folin, Oklahoma—the shimmering heat and buttery thick air had become much like the sword of the angel of Eden, driving the inhabitants away from earth and sky towards the desperate hope of other comforts; in this case, air conditioning.

Cotton farming was the main living in these parts. Peanuts and vegetables did pretty well, though the soil was not nearly so rich as east and north, or further south into Texas. At harvesttime you could drive fifty miles in any direction and see nothing but field after field of soft, fluffy grayish-white as the ripened bolls split and thick tufts of fiber spilled. In the broiler which occurred on the day of the birth, however, not even harvest was possible. Heat swells rose from the flat earth like invisible streamers, stealing life and will. Folks were hardy in these parts; once upon a time they might not have noticed the heat. But several generations removed from pioneer stock, they had begun to grow soft. Come midmorning of the seventeenth, even the old ones who might otherwise cuss and fuss about the shiftless youth found themselves broken by the will of the thermometer. As the mercury rose, a silent, sweaty command went out, and people fled, searching for relief in a cool glass of lemonade or cable signals and a smoky-glassed plastic box, inside which a man named Jerry Springer and a woman named Oprah battled for the moral soul of the nation.

Folin itself was not a cotton town, but a mining town. Actually, that was like saying the Vatican was a "religious hub" for Catholics. Apart from a couple of small factories and retail operations, Folin was nothing but mining. Sure, a few farmers worked some large acreage in outlying farmlands, but the town's paycheck was rock. Located right off US 62 in between the state capital and the city of Altus, along the eastern foothills of the Quartz Mountains—a curious name for a string of glorified hills neither mountainous nor full of quartz, but possessing an abundance of rare and beautiful granite, called red granite, exported around the world—Folin was not known for much except rocks before Sylvia Chisom gave birth to a crow-headed lad she named Joshua.

As it happened (those who know are not afraid to call it fate), September 17 was also the day the world began to die.

Of course, none of this was known at the time, neither the coming plague, nor the significance of this child, Joshua Lee Chisom, 8 pounds, 5 ounces, 21 inches, who emerged screaming into the world at precisely 11:59 P.M.

But all would be proven in time.

1

I will speak plainly," the man replied. He was slender, hair slicked back, spectacles on his narrow face, clean-shaven. He sat calmly, eyes blue, cold, dressed in a $2,500 suit, smoking filtered clove cigarettes. His English was excellent, with only a thin Slavic afterbite on the *w*s betraying his native Ukrainian tongue. Nikolai was his name, Nikolai Petrinsky. Behind him, two horse-jawed men in shiny black suits and impenetrable sunglasses, quite a bit thicker than he, cradled compact, modified, Russian-made Groza 9-millimeter assault rifles in their crossed arms.

"We can get what you want," Nikolai continued, eyes narrowing. He poured himself another shot of Smirnoff, pushed the half-empty bottle towards Jean de Giscard. "But tell me . . . why do you want it?"

Jean didn't move, didn't blink; he downed another glass, his third.

"Because I want to destroy many, many people."

He said this with a faint, shadowy smile. Like kings in a chess match, the two studied one another. Their eyes, watery, inebriated, glowed in the dim light. At length, Nikolai wiped his chin.

"You wish to kill," he said, showing his teeth. "Do you want to kill *me*, Frenchman?"

The challenge was seductive—silk and razors. Jean leaned back in his chair, placed both hands behind his head, as if to give serious consideration to Nikolai's question. But the irony was too absurd. Spastically, drunkenly, he fell forward, slapping the table with his palm, coughing so hard a ball of spittle formed on his lips. The two thugs behind Nikolai jumped at the sudden motion and moved in protectively. All the while,

Nikolai regarded Jean as he might a cockroach on the tip of his polished boots: wary, curious, disdainful. Both assumed the joke was on the other man. Jean could not stop laughing and pointing. At length, even Nikolai chuckled, if only at the pitiful sight of such a refined man so foolishly out of control.

"You Frenchmen should hold your liquor better," he snickered.

Jean pounded the table harder, wheezing for air. Nikolai laughed, too, resting his palms on the table. It was all about money. What was not to laugh about?

"Tell me the price again," Jean mumbled, slurring his words.

"Fifteen million," Nikolai replied. "Ten for the goods, five for the service. Half up fr—"

He never finished. Catlike, Jean slipped a knife from his sleeve, plunged it through Nikolai's open right hand, pinning the flesh to the wooden table. The move, slippery with speed and far from accidental, had been rehearsed dozens of times in knifing duels at Saint-Cyr, then honed to perfection through the years as an expert fencer, though Jean could also display a half-dozen thin, white scars to prove the required learning curve. Nikolai gasped at the pain, wide-eyed. Blood immediately began to flow. Jean's drunken demeanor dropped like a deadbolt snapped with bolt cutters. He became instantly, terribly sober. "Now *I* will speak plainly to you, Nikolai Petrinsky. *Double* the fee. I will pay it. But stay out of my business."

Weapons scuttled as Nikolai's guards leveled their Grozas, but the thin man jerked his one free hand up over his shoulder, commanding them to retreat. They obeyed, sinking into the shadows. Collecting himself, he reached down for the haft of the knife. Blue veins popped from underneath the thin skin of his neck as his whole body tensed. In one swift motion he jerked the blade free. Defiantly, he turned his hand palm up, letting the blood pool and flow from the hollow of his palm to the table, which sloped toward Jean. Jean never took his eyes off the Ukrainian. As a winding rivulet of red rolled slowly toward him—was about to drip off the table—he simply scooted his chair away from the edge. The blood dripped onto the bare concrete floor.

Like a pressure chamber, the room compacted with silence. The staging ground was an old warehouse along the Thames in London's Southwark district, off the wharves east of the London Bridge. The place appeared to have once been a fishery, or at least smelled like one. Wooden cargo crates yet lined the walls, unused, many dank and rotting. The tin roof creaked in the wind. Jean sat across from Nikolai at a simple wooden table lit only by candles and battery-powered lamps. Outside the building, a black Mercedes waited to escort Nikolai to Stansted, from which he would depart for a rendezvous with his mistress in Kiev before rejoining wife and children, waiting eagerly for his return on the coast of the Black Sea. For his part, Jean would be departing from Heathrow for the States in a couple of hours. His "negotiations" with Petrinsky were in their final stages and had, from Jean's perspective, just taken a turn for the better. He could care less about the money.

Nikolai trembled; the muscles in his face were hard as bone, the skin as tight as a piece of Saran Wrap stretched over his skull. With his left hand, he pulled a clean white handkerchief from inside his suit pocket, pressed the cloth hard to his hand to staunch the flow. Careful not to show pain again, he poured the remaining vodka over the wound.

"It will take time to place one of our own on the team," he said, gritting his teeth. "It is very secretive work. I have heard reports that things are moving very slowly. There were no medical records, no church records, no government records. They aren't even certain the bodies match the profile."

Jean was impatient. "There are six to choose from, Nikolai. Six men buried in the permafrost of Longyearbyen, Norway. Take your pick. A few grams' worth of tissue and blood samples will be enough."

"You push me!" Nikolai snapped. "I need twelve months."

"No good. You have eight."

"Impossible."

"For thirty million? Nick . . . I think you'll find a way. You need the money, remember? Besides, securing the samples is only the beginning. I have other timetables."

"Ten months."

"Eight."

Nikolai leaped to his feet, cursing in Russian. He overturned the table with his unwounded hand, whipped a 7-millimeter Walther from the back of his pants, pressed the barrel point-blank to Jean's forehead. "Fifteen million dollars up front. No negotiation."

"Done. I already gave you my—"

"Next week! I want the money next week. No later."

"That will be difficult."

"Next week!" Nikolai raged, clicking back the hammer. "In my account. Or no deal."

Jean considered, shrugged. "I'll see what I can do."

He stood, slowly, ducking away from the line of the gun. Fingering their triggers, the musclemen moved in beside Nikolai, glowering. There would be no funny business. Jean was finished, anyway. Before leaving, he extended his right hand, held it there for a moment before catching the faux pas. Retracting, he offered his left hand instead. Nikolai snarled, took the hand, shook it once. Jean turned to go. As he walked away, Nikolai said, "If you ever strike at me again, Frenchman, I will kill you."

Jean didn't break stride.

• • •

Please, Jesus, Josh whispered, his long black hair flapping in the autumn breeze. He wasn't sure if God heard him or not. *Please help me.*

It should never have come to this, yet it always seemed to. All he had done was notice a problem. That's all he ever did: notice things, observe. This time it would cost him. Why hadn't he just left the kitten alone? Why Katie? Why Ronnie Wilcox? Why Ronnie, *again?* It didn't matter. What mattered was that Josh now chose to stand his ground.

It was mid-October. The weather was starting to cool, though the grass remained more green than brown. Overhead, the watercolor sky was a wash of fading periwinkle blue. Though Ronnie Wilcox's body blocked his view, Josh could see other children in the near distance playing at recess. Scores of happy, competitive, temperamental kindergartners joining with first and second graders in every conceivable game, laughing and screaming, kicking or throwing balls or Frisbees or sometimes rocks, working towards a fevered pitch of abandoned, sweaty glee. That's where he wanted to be. Over there.

Not here.

Ronnie snarled. His balled-up, meaty club lobbed sideways in the Arc of Pain and aimed straight for Josh's face. This was a familiar moment. All playground noise dimmed into a brilliant white-hot point of concentration as Joshua braced himself. He saw the fist coming, could have ducked sideways. Didn't. (For the life of him, he had no idea why he never ducked.) As the knuckles moved towards him, he even had the presence of mind to ask himself a question, *Why do you never move out of the way?* The only answer was a dull thud . . .

Fist to face.

Sharp, crunching pain.

Knees. Buckling.

Joshua dropped to the ground. Nope, God must not have heard. Maybe he should pray harder next time. Before he even landed, the skin around his left eye began to swell, discolor. He didn't cry. He *didn't* cry. But oh how he wanted to.

"Get out of the way, Joshy-boy!" demanded the seven-year-old, professional bully standing before Joshua like a miniature ox. Ronnie was already big for a second grader, practically a monster to any kindergartner.

Staring at Ronnie's feet from the flattened grass, Joshua couldn't help but remember the first day of school six weeks ago. His mother had dropped him off, waving good-bye through tears. He had stood near the front door and watched her disappear. Shy, with one missing front tooth and shoulder-length, raven-colored hair, his first day passed awkwardly, mostly alone. On the second, a girl named Emma invited him to play with her and two other friends. Then two more friends joined in, including Katie. By the end of the first week, Josh had gained a marvelous group of playmates, children who never searched behind his cautious smile for something hidden, some edge of fear or doubt or suspicion. In the six short weeks that followed, each friend had found his or her own special place in the group. Bart was the strong one. Scooter the fast one. Jenny, the pretty one. And Emma, well, she was funny and nice and goofy and smart all at once. But what made Josh proudest was that they all looked to him for the *answer*. It was instinctive. He knew he wasn't the loudest, the smartest, or even the leader of the group. Yet they trusted him to know what to do.

Most of all, what Josh loved about his friends was that they didn't notice his unusual eyes. His Granny Meem called them "old soul" eyes.

"My goodness!" she would say, shaking her head. "You're just full of years."

Josh never knew what that meant. When he stared in the mirror, all he saw were two circles sort of the color of a mug of frothy cocoa. Yet he knew there was something more to his gaze, something that made adults grow vaguely restless around him. He had seen it dozens of times. Once, at his grandma's retirement home, a crotchety old man had snapped at him in the dining commons, demanding that Josh quit asking so many questions. But Josh hadn't said a single word. He had merely watched the man for several long moments.

By age four, with a few incidents like that under his belt, Josh had developed a fairly sophisticated mechanism of avoidance. The catch was, if he looked away from a person, *even for their sake,* they inevitably thought him rude and snotty. And so he came full circle, back to Katie, a kitten, and a bully named Ronnie Wilcox. Because the danger in seeing everything was that you eventually got caught. And the only thing worse than getting caught was getting involved.

This time, Josh couldn't help it.

Behind him, Katie's angry, trembling fingers clutched a calico ball of fur to her chest. She scowled at Ronnie and stuck out her tongue, which did little to improve the situation. Joshua had seen the kitten before Katie ever did—a mere five minutes ago—bounding across the playground, chasing a grasshopper. Not a week earlier on this same playground Josh had caught the kitten wandering blindly through the mowed grass. He had touched its clouded eyes and made up a name for it. So of course he noticed when Katie began to play with it, and also when Ronnie grabbed the cat from Katie, swung the poor little thing around in circles by its tail, then dropped it and started poking it with a stick.

Katie had snatched the kitten off the ground and tried to run away. Ronnie chased her, trying to pry Katie's fingers loose, pulling on the cat's head. When Katie screamed, no one had heard except Josh. That was pretty much the whole story . . . he had been watching.

Now, as he climbed to his feet again and took his place in between Katie and the bully, his mind raced for whatever solution would involve the least pain. No one else on the playground had yet noticed the conflict. Nursing his cheek, Josh desperately scanned the swing set for Bart or Scooter. No sign of his friends anywhere. Behind him, the kitten made a soft, mewing sound.

Trembling, Josh tried to be casual. "C'mon, Ronnie, Katie was playing with the kitten first."

Ronnie mimicked him. "C'mon, Joshy-boy. I don't care."

Diplomacy wasn't going to work. Besides, no matter how much he tried to be calm, Josh could not stop panting with fear, and his eye hurt terribly. "C'mon, Katie," he said as evenly as he could, groping blindly behind him for her hand. "Let's go show Mrs. Tellier your kitten."

Ronnie stared at him, unmoving. Joshua's heart pounded. He knew he couldn't run fast enough or far enough. His body wouldn't let him. Within twenty steps he would be gasping for air in panic. He would have to walk this one step at a time and it already felt like it was going to take forever. He pulled on Katie's arm. Slowly, she responded. They both stepped around Ronnie, who had not yet touched them, and began walking toward the cluster of chattering teachers near the big, brown school doors.

Suddenly, with one leg swipe from behind, Ronnie brought Josh to the ground.

"Run, Katie!" Josh grunted as he fell, letting go of her hand. Katie took off. Josh rolled onto his back and saw Ronnie hesitate between chasing Katie or pummeling him. He chose the latter, falling to the spot where Josh lay.

But this time Josh *did* move. Scrambling to one side, he slipped through Ronnie's hands, climbed to his feet, and began what he knew would be a very short sprint. Being fairly quick, he grabbed a good lead, but his lungs simply wouldn't pay the toll for a full ride. His chest began to constrict asthmatically. Without his inhaler, his air felt as though it were filtered through the mushy fibers of a chest full of cotton balls. Heaving, fearing the loss of breath more than he did another pounding—and with Ronnie right on his heels—Joshua dropped to the ground, gasping for air. Awaiting the inevitable, he closed his eyes and braced himself, ready for the first punch to—

"Ronnie Wilcox, just what do you think you are about to do?" an adult female voice shrilled just a few steps beyond where Josh lay. Trembling, flooding with relief, Josh looked up to see Mrs. Tellier . . . and Emma! . . . stomping towards them with judgment flashing in Mrs. Tellier's eyes.

The short, slender teacher wasted no time. In about thirty seconds flat she had scolded Ronnie, cleaned him like a fish, and sent him to the principal's office with his tail between his legs. To Joshua, she was like the hero in a movie, surrounded by a halo of light, distributing justice as would an angel, setting all to right. As she swooped in on a stammering, suddenly penitent Ronnie, she was nothing less than a she-bear; but that done, quick as you could flip a switch, she became a mother hen, helping Josh to his feet, searching his bruised face for clues. As she had many times before, as few other adults could, Mrs. Tellier looked right into Joshua's ancient brown eyes and did not flinch. Emma and Katie also watched with care. Emma, watching from the junglegym, had seen the whole thing. She must have run to Mrs. Tellier, arriving long before Katie would have been able. From its perch in Katie's arms, the kitten mewed, seeming no worse for the wear. Mrs. Tellier stared at the little animal's face for a long, silent moment.

"Are you okay, Joshua?" she asked, her voice as soothing as warm milk. Joshua looked at all three of them, one at a time.

"He was going to hurt . . . kitten. Katie," Josh sniveled, pointing. Then, shuddering in her embrace, he began to sob.

Mrs. Tellier let Joshua go home early amid the gossip of the other teachers, who whispered—only among themselves—things like, "Probably had it coming" or, "You never can tell with that one," even though they knew good and well that Ronnie was the bona fide troublemaker.

Mrs. Tellier fumed at such nonsense but never had the courage to make a point of it. Instead, she sent Josh to the school nurse, who phoned Sylvia at her job at the local factory, a bottler for an off-brand cola. The factory employed about thirty people, mostly miners' wives, in a run-down sweatshop on the north side of town, in the shadow of the hills. The equipment was uniformly antiquated, probably circa 1962, lit by hanging fluorescent lights that reflected off yellow concrete block walls painted the color of three-day-old lemon rinds. The nurse had to wait for well over three minutes while Sylvia was paged and had arranged for a swinger to replace her on the line. Dutifully, Josh folded his hands in his lap, looking straight ahead. His breath had returned.

"Josh was in a little scuffle again," the nurse said curtly when Sylvia finally picked up. "You better come get him. No, no. None the worse. Just boys being boys, you know. Can you make arrangements?"

"Yes, yes . . ." Sylvia's voice trailed off. "Of course, yes. But probably not me. Hold on . . ."

The nurse held the phone, tapping absently on her desk with her fingernail. At length, she passed the phone to Josh, said, "They aren't going to let her off, Josh. Mary Beth's fibromyalgia is acting up again."

Josh took the phone. "Hi, Mom."

"Hi, Joshy? Are you okay?"

"Yeah, fine."

"Good. Good." Sylvia's voice trailed away.

"Mom . . ."

"What, honey?"

"I can stay at school if I need to."

"Why would you say that, Josh? Mrs. Tellier said you need to come home, didn't she?"

The little boy shuffled his feet. "I just figured, you know, you probably couldn't get me."

"Josh, *I'm* going to come get you. One way or another. You just sit tight."

Josh hung up. Twenty minutes passed, then thirty. Finally a woman walked through the door and smiled. Josh didn't bother to look up, just stared at the floor.

"Hello, Josh. Ready to go?"

After fifteen minutes, he had known it wouldn't be his mom. Sure enough, it wasn't. He had known the moment she hung up. This time the designated driver was Mrs. Etheridge, a friend of his great-grandmother's. She came dressed in a baby blue–and–white plaid print skirt and jacket, with a full string of fake pearls around her neck and her hair perfectly coifed.

"Josh?"

Her question lingered, an unwrapped present nobody wanted. Josh did the only thing he knew to do: stare at the ceramic tiled floor, nod, finally rise to his feet, walk away.

It wasn't Mrs. Etheridge's fault. She was a perfectly nice lady. Wonderful really. One of the few adults that Josh could hug and really feel them hug back. More to the point for this occasion, she got around just fine, which Josh's great-grandmother could no longer do so well. Josh's Granny Meem was the only extended family Josh had, or knew of anyway, apart from Uncle Rick, whom Josh adored. Uncle Rick dropped by only about once or twice a year, usually around Thanksgiving, even though he just lived a couple hours away in Oklahoma City. Meem was Josh's father's grandmother, his only living relative except for a sister that lived in Baltimore. Meem still lived in Folin and was willing enough to help, but fairly limited in her ability to get around. Since moving into Red Hill Retirement Community she had become dependent on the facility's shuttle schedule for transportation. Mrs. Etheridge, (the elderly Mrs. Chisom's neighbor) who was not only younger but quite a bit more stubborn, refused to yield either her driver's license or her 1983 Buick Regal to the encroachment of age and was all too glad to come to Josh's rescue when Sylvia called.

Together, old lady and a young, crestfallen boy departed, leaving nurse Ruth to her paperwork and nail file. Josh picked up his backpack and dragged it behind him, pursing his lips as near as he could into the shape of a polite smile. He dared not look Mrs. Etheridge in the eye, lest she see his disappointment.

All he wanted was Mom. No one else. Mom.

Mrs. Etheridge didn't say a word until they reached the school's main front doors. With a twinkle in her eyes, she said, "I just simply don't know what to do here. Simply don't know . . ." and then she fussed and made a scene of fumbling with her purse and pulling on her chin.

Josh was curious. Her tone had just enough genuine perplexity in it to hook him. But he didn't want to bite, at least not out loud.

"I mean," continued Mrs. Etheridge and she laid a wrinkled hand on Josh's shoulder. "It's just not fair. The only thing worse than being sent home after a rough day is being sent home without ice cream! Don't you think? I wonder if you have any ideas what we can do about that?"

For the first time that day, Josh smiled.

After ice cream, the two of them spent time in the park and Josh got to play on the junglegym and feed the ducks stale crumbs of bread. It was a lovely day, the sort that makes you forget school bullies and parents trapped by jobs. The park was empty, except for two mothers and their toddlers, whose laughter made Josh think of the sound of spoons clinking in his mother's silverware drawer. Overhead, a flock of gray-bellied Canadian geese triangled southward, early defectors looking for warmer climes. Their distant squawking call floated to the ground as whisper-soft as wing feathers. Josh watched them for a long time, as long as he could, before they slipped between the cracks of the treetops and were lost to the fading sky.

"What do you think it's like to fly?" he asked.

Mrs. Etheridge smiled. "I don't know. I suppose it's kind of like being set free. Like you can go anywhere, do anything, see everything."

"I want to fly," said Josh.

The earliest Sylvia could get home was after four. When she arrived, she found Josh fast asleep on the couch. Mrs. Etheridge clutched her purse to her chest, touched Sylvia's arm, and said fretfully, "Poor dear. Don't you worry. We had a fine day. He was just fine." She looked lovingly at the little boy sprawled in all directions on the sofa. "I must say, it kind of surprised me when he just up and fell asleep. I wouldn't have said we did *that* much, but maybe school frightened him more than I thought."

Sylvia nodded. Of late, tiredness in Josh wasn't so unusual. Two days ago she had stolen away from work at four o'clock, much like today, and taken Josh to the doctor for a checkup, precisely because of unusual and persistent fatigue. The doctor was *supposed* to call her today with lab results. She glanced at the answering machine. No messages.

"Thank you, Mrs. Etheridge. Thank you so much for your help."

As a matter of ritual, Sylvia reached for her purse, knowing that Mrs. Etheridge would refuse. True to form, Mrs. Etheridge held up a gloved hand and waved her away. "Stop that, Sylvia. Before long you're going to hurt my feelings."

Sylvia put her purse down, silent, grateful. She couldn't have afforded to pay Mrs. Etheridge, anyway. The older lady bustled to the front door, turned. This too was part of the ritual. Every time—every single time Mrs. Etheridge was around Josh—she would say the same thing to Sylvia, a reminder, almost a solemn warning. She would point to Josh, as she did now, and say in a voice barely above a whisper, "That's a precious little boy, Sylvia. He's special. You know that, don't you? You can see it in his eyes."

Sylvia nodded. Anyone who looked, who dared to look, could not help but see.

• • •

"We are incapable of transformation, don't you see?" Jean said. He was back in the States, tired but comfortable, having arrived a couple of hours ago from his London encounter with Nikolai Petrinsky. This time, though the tones of his voice were no less subtle, they were noticeably warmer. As he spoke, he gestured to his companion, painting the air.

They sat amid the understated elegance of Rover's, overlooking the soft pattering waves of Lake Washington. This part of Seattle, known as Madison Park, was strictly upper crust. With the lights low, the warm waxy smell of candle fire mingling with the aroma of sautéed shallots, lemon, and basil, Jean was relaxed, suave, hypnotic. His peppered hair was coarse, with long bangs and natural curl that kept swooping down over his low thick brows. His eyes were fierce, hawkish; his accent velvety and unmistakably French.

"Man bears the awful and singular burden of his own existence, and this fact alone means we are utterly and forever incapable of innocence. Self-awareness will not cohabit with virtue of any sort. Why should we pretend? Only the animals are free." He sighed, disgusted. "We are wretched creatures."

Alyssa, his attractive, twenty-eight-year-old companion, was free of his spell, or so she thought. She and Jean shared a chalet a few blocks away. "No, Jean. *We* are the saviors. *They* are wretched."

"No, no. All of us." He swirled his arm in a circle, as if wrapping a cord around the entire restaurant. "I hate you as much as I hate myself, love."

Dressed in plain blue jeans, black turtleneck, and thin, black wire-rimmed spectacles, Jean de Giscard was every bit the French intellectual, nursed from childhood in the revolutionary traditions of French enlightenment. At the University of Paris twenty years ago, Jean had drunk deep of Voltaire, Rousseau, Hugo, Zola, and the poetry of Valéry. He could speak at length on the progression of French literature, from the dramas of the Classical Age—Molière, Corneille—to the "liberty in art" movement of romanticism, to realism's scornful insistence on "sincerity in art." From there it was only a short journey to modern surrealism, the theater of the absurd, and postmodern nihilism. During these years of intense intellectual shaping, Jean found his most ardent allies in the poetry of René Char, the prophetic ardor of Rousseau, the philosophies of Sartre. Albert Camus's *The Stranger* was a devastating, month-long epiphany.

Jean de Giscard was extremely well connected. The son of an ambassador, who was himself the son of a man of considerable means, Jean had lacked for nothing all his life. He had served his required time in the French military and further time, at his father's insistence, at Saint-Cyr, the national, elite military school of France. That proved to be a fateful decision; it was there Jean learned both strategy and deceit and made many of his early connections with mercenary intelligence services in the emerging post–Cold War black market. He was unmarried, had traveled in the right circles, gone to the right schools, been trained in the necessary protocols and groomed for influence.

The lovely woman sitting across from him was more than his companion. Alyssa was his protégée, a willing disciple. Very willing. "You don't hate me, Jean. You hate how much you want me."

A waiter passed by, refilled their water with lemon slices, cleared away the vegetable plates. Amused, Jean leaned across the starched white tablecloth, touched her hand sweetly. "I love your body, yes?" He touched her face. "And I love the vigor of your mind. But you are a fool if you think I do not hate everything your *soul* represents." He said these words as easily as he might have read the menu, or asked for dessert. He led her, of course, though she did not know it; had never known it, in fact. One thing was true: Jean de Giscard was *always* in control. "Do not be offended, love. Every arrow I loose at you I have already died upon a thousand times. Your soul, that of another, the billions of souls which have brought us to this misery—I curse them all, yet none more severely than the curse I place upon my own."

"God, Jean!" Alyssa protested, jerking her hand away. When Jean bruised, it went to the bone. "I'm not a pet project. And I'm so tired of the circles! What does any of it matter? You and I both know that whatever you say, the bourgeoisie have no power and the money barons have no interest. They haven't listened in the past and they won't listen now. Curse all you want. Your arrows aren't finding their mark."

"True."

"You waste yourself. You waste your emotion. And you toy with me for sport."

"Of course it is a waste. But you, a toy? No. Besides, the nations are spellbound. What do you want me to do?"

"They are fools, Jean. They will never believe you and you know it. You know it better than anyone. They will continue to believe that all is well until all is lost."

Jean opened his palms, helpless. "What do you want me to say?"

The woman sighed impatiently. "Nothing! Don't say anything else." Her voice grew hard. Jean was in control, but she knew the language of his inner circle. She had proven her willingness time and again, faithfully molding herself to the contours of his image. Jean had proven remarkably patient to the task, never pushing, only drawing her further in, as he did now. Alyssa continued, "Jean, the time has come. Strike deeply, unforgettably! Irrevocably. Make your mark!" Her voice grew soft again, soft and wild. "The time for quiet words is over. Now you must shout—

shout so loud the whole world hears. Do *that,* or be still, and let us love one another in a single night what a year of love would require."

"Unfair. You know I am powerless when you speak in poetry."

Alyssa lowered her head, a coy gesture. "I only want to help you."

"Help me? Do what?"

"Take your place."

"Where?"

"Among the greats. Of all history."

He knew she would offer such praise. Jean leaned back in his chair and gravely observed, "You very much want my approval, don't you, dear? Even more than my love."

Alyssa raised her eyes, stained with dark mascara. Jean did not wait for an answer. Low under his breath, he cursed. "Sheep and fools, spoiling the earth." But even as he said this, he watched her carefully, calculating her response.

He signaled the maître d', who approached, dressed in crisp black and white. They exchanged a few words in French, and the maître d' departed. A moment later he returned with a bottle of ten-year-old Chateau d'Yquem Bordeaux, sugared scones, and a platter of fruit and cheese. Four hundred dollars and a whiff of cork later, Jean was tilting his glass toward the light.

His voice grew distant. "I think it was 1855. In that year, this lovely wine was afforded the unique prestige of *Grand* Premier Cru. Did you know that? It is French, of course, one of the most consistently remarkable wines in all the world. Truly, nectar. Not even Lafite or Latour were honored so."

He swirled the wine, smelled its fragrance, drank deep. The corners of his lips played with an unaffected smile. "Ahh! We are a contradiction, you and I. We enjoy these things, these fine things. But our hearts are full of lawlessness."

"Words," she answered, unimpressed with his self-reflection. "I am tired of words. I want action. You are up to something. You have been for years. You have support in the underground. Now is the time. I want in. No more games."

Jean showed his teeth. "No more games?"

Alyssa leaned forward. "In America, we say it like this: show me the money."

"Ahh, the money . . ."

"Not the *money*. What have you been doing overseas? What's going on? I know you, Jean. The wheels are turning."

She had come a long way in just a few short years: seasoned, cynical, loyal. She would have to travel further still. Much further. Jean raised an eyebrow, stroking the rim of his glass with the smooth tip of his finger. He chose his words carefully, pushing a piece of scone towards her, pouring her a second glass. It was a perverse sort of communion table they shared . . . an initiation ritual for another zealous disciple.

"Then you are ready," he said, teasing.

"Ready?"

"For the next level of commitment."

Hungrily, the woman leaned forward, eyes narrowed. "Name it."

"You have named it yourself: *action*. Irreversible action."

• • •

As Folin settled in for the evening, trails of cobalt-hued altocumulus clouds streaked across the sky, practically exploding from the horizon, rimmed with orange, like steel cut with a welder's torch, climbing to ten thousand feet overhead as if shot from a cannon. For Tim Chisom, sunsets on the Oklahoma prairie were nothing short of breathtaking. Heaven bent low, kissed the featureless earth; the sky shredded with color.

About this time every night in the Chisom home, a ritual usually transpired. Come six o'clock (give or take a few minutes), the front screen door would slam, triggering a loud pronouncement—"Daddy's home!" as Joshua would scamper from his room. Framed in the open doorway, Tim would stand with shoulders half-slumped, hair dark and matted, clothes stained, but arms outstretched.

No matter what.

"Hey! How's my boy?" he would say, or something similar, and then regardless of how dirty or worn out, father would grab son and squeeze—not too hard—but rough enough to be men together.

Tonight, however, the clouds rolled, the sun set, and the door slammed, but Josh neither ran nor yelled. At first, he did not come at all. Tim noticed but didn't press the point. Instead, he went about his business, kissed Sylvia, pulled his boots off, wiped his eyes. He could tell by the look on his wife's face that something was up, though he figured it was just another factory thing. Common enough. Preferring a little more time to settle in, he didn't ask for details.

After a few moments, Joshua wandered in. His posture was timid. Tim immediately recognized the swollen, crescent-shaped discoloration curving from high up on his cheekbone around to his eyebrow. Taking a deep, silent breath, Tim faced Josh.

Josh pointed at his dad's chest. "What's that?" he whispered, drawing nearer to get a better look. His nose wrinkled. "Smells yucky, like tomatoes."

Tim held out his shirt for inspection. He spoke in measured tones. "What you're smelling are *sweaty* tomatoes. See, I'm wearing some of your mom's soup."

"Messy day."

Tim lightly poked him in the belly. "Not as messy as your room, I bet."

Josh didn't move. His nervousness was apparent. Tim studied him for a moment, then craned his neck forward. At first what he did made no sense. He *sniffed* in Josh's direction, purposefully imitating the way Josh had sniffed at him only moments earlier. The sniffing grew gradually more exaggerated in a houndish sort of way. If Tim knew anything, he knew his son needed him, at this particular moment, not to be an authority, but a playmate. Right now, he needed a moment of random joy from his father, a spark of foolish, wild fun. It was part of the privilege of fatherhood, to preserve life from the curse of solemnity. The black-eye story Josh dreaded to tell could wait.

Josh wasn't so sure. "I asked Jesus to help me—," he began to explain.

"You know," Tim interrupted, his voice growing thick and conspiratorial, "you said *I* smell funny. But I'm not so sure"—*sniff, sniff*—"I think it may be you that smells kinda funny. Not like tomatoes. Kinda strange, kinda funny, like a little *boy* or something." It took several moments for Josh to realize that his father was giving him a gift, that this was, after all, play mode and not the time for scolding. He was being offered a way out. By now, his father was clapping his hands, pointing, howling out, "That's it! That's what you are, a *little boy*. A little boy with a *big* problem!"

Unsure, Josh said, "My eye?"

Tim shook his head emphatically.

"School?"

"No, no, no! Your problem is that I've been home for almost ten minutes and still haven't gotten my hug! What do you say to that, little boy?"

"No, Daddy, wait. I'm not a boy, okay? I'm a . . . *bug*." Josh held up his hands and tried to make a scary face. "A big slimy bug!"

"A bug? Hah! *I'm* an even bigger turtle and I eat slimy bugs." And with that, Tim threw Josh on the sofa, tickling and chewing softly on the skin of his neck. Josh squealed with delight.

Sylvia, watching, smiled, though Tim noticed the tight set of her lips. What he didn't see was that only a few seconds earlier she had stuffed several five-dollar bills in the old red-and-white oatmeal tin on top of the fridge.

"Better wash up, both of you," Sylvia said. "You first, Josh."

Tim tousled his hair, "Okay, Mr. Bug, you heard your mom."

"But Mom—"

"I said now, Josh. Please."

Scowling, Josh stumped off. The room fell quiet, except for the sound of the creaking wood beneath Josh's feet, then water running in the bathroom up the hallway. Sylvia didn't move.

Tim asked, "Who was it this time?"

"The Wilcox boy, Ronnie. Josh said he was chasing a little girl, hurting her cat. He tried to help. The nurse sent him home early."

Tim clenched his jaw. "How convenient. They better have sent Ronnie home, too."

"I doubt it. Probably punished him at school."

"Oh come on—"

"Tim, they send Josh home for his own sake. You know that. It was Mrs. Tellier's decision and I don't think that's the way Mrs. Tellier is."

Tim smirked. Sylvia said, "Besides, that's not really the point."

"What's not? You mean the way they act nice to cover their tracks? He's just a boy, for crying out loud. Why can't they grow up and be adults."

Sylvia lowered her voice. "Not so *loud,* please. And no, that's not what I mean. I mean that none of that stuff matters to me right now. We expected this sort of thing from school and we'll deal with it like we do everywhere else." She tucked a strand of hair behind her ears, adjusting her Sally Jesse–style glasses, about ten years out of style. "It's Josh I'm concerned about, Tim. He's not behaving normal. You've seen him. He's very lethargic."

Tim waved his hands. "C'mon, Sylvia. It's probably just another growth spurt."

"I don't think so." Her words trailed away. Tim was about to respond when the telephone rang. Sylvia grabbed the portable. "Hello? *Yes,* Dr. Perkins . . ."

Tim arched an eyebrow, listened. For about five minutes, Sylvia and the doctor spoke. She asked several questions, mainly repeating phrases like "Uh-huh" and "Okay" or "What's that mean?" As she spoke, her posture visibly loosened. She asked, "What should we do differently?" Apparently, it wasn't much; moments later she thanked the doctor and hung up.

"Good news," she announced with relief. "No big deal."

"Growth spurt?"

"No, but everything looks fine. Josh's blood work came back iron deficient. Borderline anemic. Apparently that's the problem."

"That's all?"

"Well, that's not necessarily good. But that's all, yes. That's what he said. He also said we might as well go ahead and get Josh on the rolls, like I've asked. There's just no reason not to."

"The Comanche rolls?" Tim sat up. "Good grief. You must have been really worried about this."

Sylvia tried to be stoic. "I just had this ache inside. You know, the big 'what if?'" She sighed. "But anemia is nothing at all."

"And that explains the tiredness?" Tim asked again.

"Dr. Perkins seemed pretty sure. He said to make him eat more vegetables and maybe take an iron supplement and watch for cuts and

bruises. If that doesn't take care of things, we're supposed to get back
with him, but—"

"Otherwise normal?"

Sylvia reached out a hand to the coffee table, knocked twice. "Otherwise . . . perfectly normal."

2

Eight Months Later

Can't . . . do it!" the pilot shouted, fighting for control. His hands, white-knuckled, gripped the stick. The helicopter felt like a kayak in choppy water—bucking up, down, side to side. "The wind shear coming over that ridge is about like hitting a wall. If I try to land this bird, we're going to get hammered."

The man in the backseat surveyed the ground some fifty feet below with cool disdain, watched the snow peeling back in concentric circles from the blast of the chopper's blades. A couple hundred yards east he glimpsed a chain of five glowing tents. Base camp.

"How far to Longyearbyen?"

"Ten miles," the pilot said, pointing. "That way."

That way looked like every other way: white. The terrain was nothing but vast, undulating sheets of ice, jagged here and there, lying like giant hunks of broken ivory, then rolling away in smooth, blinding stretches of snow. Beyond, dimly visible through the haze of unbroken miles and wind-whipped snow, lay the ice-capped ocean. At this point, only eight hundred miles from the North Pole, the oil in the helicopter could easily freeze, even while running. They had exceeded the danger zone.

Seventy-eight degrees north, fifteen degrees east. The man in the backseat repeated the mantra over and over again, clutching a single black bag in his lap, frowning. He did not well tolerate complications. Landing in town would no doubt be safer, but it also meant a two-day delay to put together a sled team to get back to this point.

"Here," he said firmly. For a moment, his accent nearly leaked through.

"No chance, Jack," the pilot repeated.

The passenger glanced around irritably. "How about over there? If we move a bit closer to that swale of ice, on the southern side, we should get some protection, eh?"

The pilot followed the sweep of the man's hand, his pointing finger, and saw the lay of the land. At first he shrugged, then shook his head. "That'll *maybe* get us twenty feet closer to ground. Listen, I've flown this before, but not often. Nobody comes out here. The cross winds are like a woman on PMS, angry all the time and always changing their mind. I'm here thanks to ten grand from you, but I'll refund your money before I touch down."

"Twenty feet," the passenger declared. "Agreed. You can lower me by ladder the rest of the way. I will walk."

The pilot's eyes widened. "You're a fool. You'll get flung around like a rag doll."

"I have many skills."

"Not at forty below you don't!"

"Move me into position!" the passenger snapped.

The pilot scowled. Banking left, he began a slow, even descent towards the dry powder and ice, positioning the chopper over the location suggested by the passenger.

"Open the door and throw down the ladder," the pilot yelled, as thirty mile-per-hour winds whipped through the helicopter.

Freezing temperatures sliced through the passenger's coat like steel blades. He grabbed the rope ladder coiled in front of the hatch and did as the pilot instructed. The ladder flopped in the air like a string in front of a fan. He also grabbed an extra length of rope with a cinch hook on the end.

"Good luck," the pilot called, saluting.

The passenger clutched his single bag and nodded; without a word, he scuttled down the rope—surprisingly quick and agile for a scientist. At the bottom of the rope, with a good twenty feet of empty air remaining, he secured the single strand of extra rope by hook to the last rung of the ladder. The pilot could see none of this, but if he had, he would have known this was no scientist. The passenger scuttled down the rope with expert rappelling skill, landing softly on the frozen ground. He moved away and signaled the chopper with a wave of his hand.

The helicopter set off, as did the lone figure on the ice, toward base camp. He had hired the chopper ten miles away in Longyearbyen, a town on the island of Spitsbergen, in the Svalbard Archipelago of Norway. Just off the north coast, Svalbard was a land of primitive, frigid conditions that seemed more consistent with its five-thousand-year-old Stone-Age history than the requirements of modern civilization. A mythical Svalbard was mentioned in ancient Norse sagas, suggesting that Svalbard may have been officially founded in 1194. But none of that mattered to the passenger trudging doggedly over the rough ice. No, what mattered were the bodies of six young miners, buried for over eighty years in the permafrost of this little unsuspecting corner of the Arctic Circle. Six men, each felled by the notorious 1918 influenza pandemic, a strain of influenza so virulent it claimed the lives of nearly 40 million people worldwide.

In the years that followed, the history and structure of the 1918 virus had provided endless fascination for virologists, microbiologists, and other clinical professionals. The allure was obvious: even with the primitive state of medicine factored into quality of life at the turn of the century, how could a single pathogen cause such devastation? Yet it had. The 1918 influenza was both modern plague and historical fact. Scientists and historians had pieced together the birthplace, incubation centers, methods of transmission, and body counts. But the element that transformed the virus into a terror of mythological proportions was the critical gap, namely, the composition of the virus itself. For eighty years no known specimens of the contagion existed. Critical labs maintained samples of killers such as Ebola, hantavirus, typhoid, malaria, tuberculosis, polio, and others for examination and decryption. But the extreme lethal effectiveness of the 1918 flu ensured its very scarcity, until Professor Sally Donaldson, a geographer from Canada, made the Svalbard discovery.

Such knowledge did not come easily. At the time, there were no medical records, since the local hospital had been destroyed; no church records to investigate, since the first pastor did not arrive in Spitsbergen until 1920; and no governmental records, since Svalbard only became part of Norway in 1925—all too late to be useful. However, she discovered that diaries had been kept by the coal company's head engineer, diaries that recorded the names, birth dates, and dates of death for six men between the ages of eighteen and twenty-nine. All six perished during the winter of 1918 from complications related to influenza. The volumes were now owned by a Norwegian schoolteacher who had volunteered to translate the work for Donaldson. After finding the account of the miners, Professor Donaldson shocked the academic community by putting together an international, multidisciplinary research team to uncover the virus. Her sole purpose was to enable scientists to study its particular strengths to better prepare the human race for another onslaught, whenever such an outbreak might occur, from whatever source. Little did she know the events she would set in motion.

The man trudged on. Up ahead, the warm lights pulsating inside the base camp tents beckoned him. As he walked, battling the biting wind, he muttered words, spoken in crisp, practiced British English, but in his brain, his thoughts formed in Russian. He was being paid very well by Nikolai Petrinksy to do this work.

As he drew near to camp, a single figure emerged, bundled in a thick, goose-down coat, carrying a flashlight.

"Dr. Stafford!" she called, but the shriek of the wind snatched away her voice. "We were concerned . . . you wouldn't make it!"

She knew further words were futile, so she motioned him inside the main tent. It was mercifully warm inside. Though trained for difficult conditions, Stafford—one of many aliases he employed—was nonetheless grateful for the heat. Two hundred yards of sub-zero is a herculean task. He should have dressed better.

"You must be Dr. Donaldson," he said, extending a gloved hand.

"Yes," she replied, shaking it, glancing at his clothes, his bag. "Is this all you brought?"

"All I need," he smiled.

Two other individuals, a man and woman, also sat inside the tent, sipping hot tea at a table. At Stafford's arrival they both stood, walked over, shook his hand, and introduced themselves: a virologist and bio-chemist, both from the United States.

"We're grateful you could come on such short notice. We did not expect Dr. Helmut's early departure, but there was a family crisis—totally unexpected. You come highly recommended."

"Only believe half of what you hear," Stafford grinned. "It's amazing what you can forge these days."

They all chuckled. The other two returned to their seats.

Donaldson said, "I don't know how well you've been briefed, but six months ago we completed our final noninvasive ground-penetrating radar study, which revealed the most probable location of the victims' graves. The radar confirmed that the graves are well below the active layer and should therefore be well preserved. As you probably know, we're funded by a grant from the National Institute of Health, so the GPR study enabled us to secure Phase 2 investigation."

"Excellent," Stafford replied, licking his lips. "Current status?"

"We've successfully exhumed two bodies."

"Any samples?"

"Yes, actually, just within the last week."

"Confirmation?"

"Positive. Tissue samples have proven to be a plague popsicle. Or at least that's the consensus. We want you to take a look, obviously."

Stafford did not want to appear too eager. "What about contamination? What's your layout here?"

"Well, you'll have to take a prophylactic influenza antiviral," Donaldson replied. "We all did. The exhumation is conducted two units down from here, inside a barrier tent. We call it the 'Dead Ringer' because there's a bell inside that we ring if there's a breach of safety or other trouble. Though we're limited in our ability, we try to keep security pretty tight, as I'm sure you would expect. For obvious reasons, only a few people have full access, and for the sake of accountability, there's always at least two in the ringer at the same time, never just one."

"What about my gear?"

"Don't worry." She grinned. "We've got a couple of extra portable safety suits with respirators. One's just about your size. Dr. Helmut was built very similar to you."

"Yes, too bad that, with his family and all. Never can tell when something's going to happen." He sighed for effect. "Now how about a look at those samples?"

3

Present Day

It was a normal, humdrum day, much as any other in Josh's life recently. Inside the classroom, probably along with every other kid, Josh felt restless. The sky was gray, scattered with gloomy clouds. Barometric pressure was low. A perfect mix for low attention spans and high mischief.

Several weeks ago, on the first day of school, Mrs. Tellier had explained to her new class how much she had looked forward to a new year and the changes it would bring. After logging seven good years with kindergartners, she told the principal she needed new challenges and older kids.

"Who can tell me what eight times four and a half is?" she asked her third graders, pointing to the numbers on the board.

A half-dozen hands shot into the air.

"Emma?"

"Thirty-six?"

"That's right. Good, Emma."

Josh glanced at the clock on the wall: 1:13 P.M. After math would come writing. He was supposed to concentrate on answering the questions, but he couldn't. Math was worse than Sunday school or a Sunday morning communion service. To his left sat Emma, smiling, looking at Josh in the row next to her as if to say, *I got the answer right and at recess I'm going to kiss your cheek*, while sketching hearts in her notebook with Josh's name inside. In response, Josh rolled his eyes teasingly, feeling nervous. A yellow mockingbird outside the window noisily and beautifully interrupted the stillness. The sun, radiant with heat, passed behind a scarf of clouds before shuddering free to shine again.

The past three years had been good for Josh—years of positive change. For all practical purposes his asthma had disappeared. He hadn't used an inhaler in months. The change in diet had taken care of the anemia. Within a month of taking iron supplements and a dreadful dose of spinach every evening, he had regained his energy. He had also settled into a nice rhythm at school. Though still regarded with a certain suspicion on occasion, those times were far less frequent, less vigorous. To help things further, he never positioned himself where provocation was likely. All in all, he'd worked out a tolerable series of compromises. He still preferred his small circle of friends to bigger groups, and still flustered adults with nothing but silence, but the passage of time had done for him what it does with nearly everything, stones and memory alike: erode resistance.

In practical terms, that meant less teasing. Less ostracization. In fact, Josh hadn't been picked on for a fight since the first grade. Best of all, here he was, in his favorite teacher's class. To Josh, Mrs. Tellier was one of those teachers every kid deserved to experience somewhere, somehow, at least once in his life. Josh got her twice.

She wrote another problem on the board: 8 x 9 =

Hands shot up, including Josh's. But an answer never came. Instead, like shattering glass, an agonized voice shrieked from the hallway.

"Help! Please, help! Get it out!"

Mrs. Tellier jerked at the sound, dropped her chalk, glancing at her class sitting frozen in their chairs. The screaming continued, almost simultaneously joined by a second, terrified wail. Both sounded young and male, though it was hard to tell at that pitch. Their voices clamored up and down the corridor.

"Wait here," Mrs. Tellier commanded before dashing out the door. In just a moment she returned. The children awaited, breathless. Mrs. Tellier hesitated a moment, then said, "Joshua Chisom, come here, please."

A room full of wide eyes turned to Josh. He touched his chest, a silent question. Mrs. Tellier nodded. Slowly, Josh slid from his seat, feeling the weight of everyone's stares bearing down on him.

The sounds of activity outside in the hall increased. A jumble of voices: "Call 911!"

"Apply some pressure . . ."

"Where *is* the nurse?"

Standing near the door, Josh couldn't see a thing, but he and all the rest of the class could certainly hear, though by now the yelping had diminished a bit. Mrs. Tellier took Josh by the shoulders, looked him in the eye.

"Am I in trouble?" he asked.

"No, of course not. I normally wouldn't do this at all, Josh. I don't know why I'm doing it now. I know this sort of thing makes you very uncomfortable." Josh could tell she was nervous; he, more so. She said, "Will you come with me?"

Josh glanced back at the class. No one said a word. Twenty-three faces stared at him. Mrs. Tellier stepped outside the door and held it open for him.

Josh stepped through.

In the middle of the hallway, a handful of adults formed a tight, bustling knot: principal, nurse, teachers. Blood splattered the ground, quite a bit of it, bright red, forming two thick puddles. There were two boys as well, both older, maybe fourth or fifth grade. Both were terrified, one on the perimeter, watching fearfully, the other in the center, prostrate on his back. The nurse bent over the one on the ground, along with another teacher, pressing bandages to his right eye. He moaned and squirmed.

"We were just playing," the one on the perimeter said over and over again. "We were racing to class. I tripped Marty. Just a joke, I promise. I promise! He fell and—"

"Would somebody get him out of here!" the principal demanded sternly. "For the last time, get him out! Where's the ambulance? Are they on their way?"

Another teacher nodded. "They're coming. Shouldn't we move him to the nurse's station?"

The nurse traded one blood-soaked towel for a fresh one. The front of her blouse was smeared red. "I can't stop the blood!" she whispered frantically.

"Why don't we just pull the pencil out?"

"Get it out. Please, get it out!" the boy whimpered. "It hurts."

"No! That would be worse. Just keep the pressure on. And hold him *still!*" Then to Marty she said, "Please, don't jerk, honey. Everything's going to be fine. *Somebody hold his head!*"

Mrs. Tellier squeezed Josh's hand. After allowing Josh to see, she drew him aside, looked him in the eye. "You can help him, can't you, Josh? You can help Marty."

Josh took a deep breath, startled. He said nothing.

Mrs. Tellier said, "I have a secret I need to tell you, Josh. Actually, two secrets. I've kept them for quite a while, but I'll tell you both of them now if you like. Do you want to know?" Mrs. Tellier didn't wait for an answer. "Three years ago, there was an incident during recess. I'm not talking about that time with Ronnie . . . the fight. This was before then. But I saw you with that same kitten. Do you remember? I saw you playing with your friends, out on the playground, and when that one little kitten came by and your friends weren't looking, you touched its face." She bent down, whispering. "That's my first secret. *I saw you touch its face.* But I've got another secret, too . . ."

Josh waited. His face was blank, revealing nothing.

". . . that kitten was my neighbor's."

Immediately, Josh turned back to Marty. Mrs. Tellier pressed in.

"I saw that little kitten when it was born, Josh. I saw its eyes. They were all messed up, weren't they? But then you touched them. You did something. When Katie had the cat that day, after the fight, they were fine. I noticed then. And they've been fine ever since. I've checked myself. My neighbor has never been able to figure it out."

Time was running out. "I don't even know what I'm asking you, Josh. I've never mentioned a word of this to anybody. And if I'm wrong, I'm going to feel more than a little foolish. But I'm betting you can help Marty, and right now he needs it. Josh, listen to me. I'm afraid Marty could lose his eye if something doesn't happen quickly." She nudged Josh forward, into the circle. "Don't be afraid," she murmured.

Josh wanted to resist. Too much was happening. But the knot of activity loosened. For some reason, the press of bodies made way for him. Guided by her hand, Josh slipped through. Almost . . .

"What in the world is he doing here?" the principal thundered, glancing up. "Get the kids in their classes! Josh, move it, now!"

With Mrs. Tellier's hand on his back, Josh held firm. Marty was weeping, terrified, struggling time and again to squirm free of those restraining him and get his hand up to his bloody right eye, where a thick yellow chunk of pencil protruded from the outside rim, deeply embedded in the soft pink tissue. Josh flinched. Because of all the blood he couldn't tell if the white part was punctured, but it didn't look good.

"Josh—!" the principal demanded.

Mrs. Tellier said calmly, "Josh, go ahead. Do . . . whatever you need to do."

Josh didn't blink, didn't move, didn't breathe. He just stared. He saw everything, the panic and fear and worry. The sense of helplessness in the nurse. The anger in the principal. Gingerly, he began stroking his hands in rhythm, inching forward, never taking his eyes off Marty. Gradually, the other adults realized he was there and yielded, almost magically, succumbing to a sort of shimmering stillness, the way a thousand sparkles of water can hypnotize when the sun is setting. Bewildered by his presence, even Marty calmed. For some reason, the nurse made room. It was as if nobody knew why; they all just grew still. Whether from sheer confusion or by some force of presence . . . Or maybe it was nothing more than the way Mrs. Tellier seemed to be fixed on the little boy before her, the little boy she apparently believed could make a difference.

As he drew near and bent low, achingly slow, Josh stretched out his hands. Even then, every single person thought of protesting; even then, none did. Open-mouthed, they watched as he laid the warm flat of his palm on the boy's wounded eye, careful not to touch the shard of pencil. As he connected with the boy's skin, the muscles in his arm convulsed slightly. Josh wrinkled his face, scrunched his eyes, almost as if in pain. At first it was like the strain of a hurtful memory, then it progressed to a level of physical effort, as if he were lifting something heavy. Then came a jolt, a wounding, like a bee sting. He panted once, twice, felt the hair on his arms, on everyone's arms, stand up. Suddenly, a fragrance of flowers filled the air—lilacs in full bloom. Josh relaxed. A few seconds later he pulled his hand away.

In stunned silence, as one person, every head turned from Josh to Marty's face. Josh heard the nurse gasp first. Everyone could plainly see that the blood had stopped. Completely. The swelling had shrunk. And though still bruised, the flesh was much more its natural color. Even the white part was cleaner. Basically, his eye looked almost normal, except of course a stub of pencil was sticking out, which seemed strange but no longer seemed to matter. The damage appeared contained.

"Oh, my God," the principal whispered.

Mrs. Tellier put her hand over mouth. No one appeared to notice the sound of the sirens approaching outside, or the grating sound of the heavy double doors at the front of the school building swinging open. Marty reached up and touched the bulging skin around where the pencil was lodged.

"Am I gonna be okay?" he asked.

"Does it hurt, Marty?"

He shrugged. "I don't feel anything."

A bed wheeled around the corner. Two paramedics rushed in, calling out, "Make a little room, folks. Give us some space. Everything's gonna be all right."

Since nobody knew what else to do, they numbly complied. Josh stepped back and attempted to hide in Mrs. Tellier's skirt. She rested her hands on his head, speechless. Even though she had requested it, had seemed to have known or at least suspected what might happen, the look on her face proved she was totally unprepared for the fact of it.

Josh glanced towards his classroom. Up and down the hall, from every class, students were crammed near the door, watching. Every face, every single eye, was on him. Nothing could have been worse. He hated it, wanted to crawl away.

"Can I go now?" he asked quietly. Not a soul spoke. Patiently, he waited for an answer; he didn't ask twice. No answer arrived. Cheeks burning, he lowered his head and shuffled slowly towards his classroom.

"Josh," Mrs. Tellier said softly between breaths. "That was . . . beautiful."

Josh pushed gently through his classmates, found his seat, and began scribbling math problems.

Later that afternoon, exhausted, Josh struggled to stay awake during class. At home, he fell asleep on the floor of his bedroom with his favorite airplane in his arms, a gift from Uncle Rick.

His mother woke him. "The bus driver said you fell asleep on the way home," Sylvia murmured, touching his forehead and cheek. "You don't have a fever, though . . ."

Josh yawned, stretched. Heavy-lidded, he sat up, attempting to focus. As he gained his wits, he chose not to mention anything about Marty, knowing full well his mom would get word soon enough and come to him. It was just a matter of time. Probably not the best way, of course, but he was too embarrassed to tell her face to face.

"Sorry, Mom," he said as another yawn seized him. "Just tired, I guess. I'll be fine."

Josh *did* want to tell her about one thing: his report card. Progress reports were passed out after school and Josh had done well. He was eager to share his secret at dinner.

"Wanna go outside and play?" Sylvia asked.

Josh shook his head no. His mother kissed him and left him playing quietly with his planes. Many were models he and his dad had spent hours and hours together assembling, painting, detailing. Others were gifts from Uncle Rick, whose own fascination with flight had first fired Josh's imagination of all things skyward. Before long he was flying his planes and rockets round and round in imaginary trips to China or the moon or some faraway planet. Every night, he flew his planes until Dad came home.

Sylvia left him alone and wandered towards the kitchen to begin preparing supper. Fifteen minutes or so passed—stolen moments of peace for Josh—the calm before the storm. From the way she acted, he could tell she didn't know yet, but it didn't take a genius to figure that sooner or later someone was going to call and spill the beans.

By the time the phone did ring, he had almost managed to forget the whole thing. He jumped to his feet and leaned against the doorjamb in the hall so that he could hear the conversation better. More than her words, Josh was interested in his mother's tone. That would be the giveaway.

It didn't take long.

Josh didn't want to hear any more than he had to. Closing the door, he sat on the floor, feeling desolate, exposed, as if he had suddenly been caught doing something wrong. He took a toy jet fighter and shot it straight into the sky, dreaming he was inside, headed for the darkness beyond the blue veil of earth's atmosphere.

A few moments after the phone call ended, Sylvia feverishly began preparing her hamburgers. However, rather than forming the beef into patties, she pummeled it.

Not now. Not now, was all she could think, over and over again.

It was of course the principal who had called—called from home, even. Without so much as a "hello" or "how are you?" to soften the blow, like verbal napalm in guerrilla warfare, he struck from nowhere, blundering through an explanation of earlier events, stammering along in stream-of-consciousness fashion, unaware of the burn of his words. His tone ran the gamut: short, quick, angry, awe-struck. Even his awe caused Sylvia to wince. To be fair, she knew how he felt. She had known the man for years and liked him. He was a reasonable person who had witnessed an unreasonable event; the struggle was obvious in his words.

"Mrs. Chisom, I don't know how to explain it," he said. "It smelled like flowers. Out of nowhere. And then Marty was fine. Had a pencil sticking out of his eye, but he was fine . . ."

Ah, the flowers! Sylvia could not help but swallow hard. From that point on she listened as well as she could, as politely as she could, but his words might as well have been from another world. That single word—*flowers*—was a tripwire for dozens of half-formed emotions and carefully contained memories, colliding now within her suddenly like lottery balls on jackpot day. Her stomach lurched. The principal talked several moments more. Asked questions. No answers. Silence.

"Thank you." He hung up quickly.

She knew, of course, all too well—knew the wonder and fear, yet didn't know at all what to think at this moment, with all she had ever feared suddenly made public. So as she stood in the kitchen, she pounded the soft pink flesh harder, as if perhaps some sort of muted violence might halt the memories.

How do you casually listen to something that makes the walls of your heart crumble? If she had only known five minutes earlier, she would have torn the phone out of the wall rather than answer that call; would have rather torn her own heart out than have to listen, all of a sudden, to the unraveling of the thin-strung faith she had held onto all these years, knowing, hoping that the fears themselves would pass away or be forgotten. Still the memories came: three stark, wonderful memories, the briefest of moments, almost footnotes to the last eight years. Yet the profundity of those experiences had altered her, forced her to look at her son and forever realize he was not just any ordinary boy.

Now, with a single phone call, the tide swelled, unrestrained, and burst open upon the present. It could not be stopped. It would roll on from this moment to whatever point destiny ordained.

The first time was years ago. Sylvia first caught a glimmer of Josh's "ability"—is that what you *call* it?—when they were outside together on a nice sunny day. Josh was only two at the time, barely speaking, when the prissy little poodle from the mean old lady next door came wandering across the lawn. Sylvia already held a grudge against the woman for often scolding Josh for no reason at all and always looking at him suspiciously. Almost as bad, her dog, named Muffin, would regularly lay fecal treasures in Sylvia's yard.

On that day, as Muffin stared at the two of them, it was obvious she had a terrible case of pinkeye. Both eyes were swollen, full of pus, dirty, and veined with red. But Josh, who only the day before had celebrated his birthday, just giggled and said, "Duggie bar! Duggie bar!" and reached out happily to pet the dog. Sylvia, being a young mother, had frantically interrupted him, told him to wait, wait right there, and don't touch, as she ran into the house to get a pair of old gloves or something, something that would keep his hands protected. After all, she didn't know if animal pinkeye was contagious or not.

When she returned a moment later, it was to the potent smell of flowers, maybe lilacs. The odor was thick and oily in the humid air, almost making her choke. But Sylvia had no flowers, only shrubs—nor did the neighbors on either side. One more thing she noticed: the poodle's eyes were clean and white. Josh stood there wiping his hands on his jeans, where the muck of the dog's eyes had touched his skin. Baffled, she sank to her knees, stared at her son, at the dog.

What's a two-year-old going to say? But he watched the dog, smiling, as if he knew a secret. Thirty seconds later, the neighbor noticed Muffin missing and yelled angrily at the poodle to come home, scowling at Josh and Sylvia the whole time. The dog wandered off. Healed . . .

Another time, Sylvia herself had contracted a fever, and by some fluke the virus had spread to her eyes. The doctor put her on antibiotics and gave her eye drops, but she was very ill and uncomfortable, unable to go to work. On the third day, she fell asleep on the couch, only to awake about an hour later to Josh standing before her, expressionless, with the same smell of lilacs lingering in the air, less intense this time. She never had the eye problem again. A few days later as she sat to read the paper, she discovered she no longer even needed her reading glasses . . .

And then, the last time anything like that had happened as far as Sylvia knew was when a friend had given them a hamster for Josh as a pet. Josh immediately loved the animal, played with it every day. He must have been four at the time—was it four?—anyway, within a month, wouldn't you know it, the hamster developed a big mole or tumorlike thing growing over its left eye. It was so big and ugly, every time Josh would look at the hamster he would cry. Every day the tumor got worse, and every day he cried. Then one day, Sylvia found him cradling the animal in his hands, stroking its face with his little fingers; he wasn't crying anymore. She picked up the hamster, this time suspecting a miracle, because the air in the room was unmistakably sprayed with the scent of a full bouquet of fresh-cut flowers.

Sure enough, the tumor was gone.

What was this gift? She didn't understand it, didn't have a clue what it meant or where the power came from. She hoped it came from God but was afraid it didn't since the pastor at their church mistrusted miracles. They were for the early church, he said, not for today. In fact, he had just wrapped up a four-week series warning his flock not to get caught up in searching for signs and wonders. His teachings had sparked quite a bit of thought in the Chisom household, at least with Sylvia. She knew where Tim stood on the issue. His opinions generally ran parallel to the pastor's, though it wasn't nearly as big a deal to him. In other words, it wasn't a theological crisis, as apparently the pastor believed it should be.

Sylvia sighed. Par for the course. Tim's unflappable sense of equilibrium had been charming, at first. As their relationship progressed, it became admirable, then critical. But it could also on occasion be quite maddening. His level head made him the rock of the family, while Sylvia served as the heart. Tim had been a believer since he accepted Christ at church camp years ago and had always approached his faith as he did every other facet of his life—analytically, methodically; committed to the core, but with an introvert's natural reserve. Nothing over the top was necessary to convince him further. Over and over he had told Sylvia that faith made *sense*—the Word made sense—meaning it could be examined logically for purpose and benefit. The question was not whether the supernatural realm was real, but what it had to do with everyday life.

So after the pastor preached, Tim had told Sylvia flat out he wasn't looking for miracles. He didn't need them to be able to believe. He just wanted to know what was true and how to obey.

"Sure, God can heal," he had told her during lunch on the final Sunday of the pastor's message. "But he also gave us brains and doctors. They didn't have that stuff back then."

"They didn't have brains?" Sylvia teased.

"You know what I mean. The world has changed a lot. God works in other ways."

Sylvia disagreed. She thought the Bible talked an awful lot about a God who *did* perform miracles, and all the arguments the pastor made for them ending seemed quite arbitrary to her mind.

"So you think when science came along, God thought it was such a good idea that he just sort of surrendered the power to heal to medicine, and then what . . . moved on to more important things?"

In contrast to her husband, Sylvia had not grown up as a believer. Quite the opposite. Yet she remembered well the day she gave her heart away. It was the day she found out she was pregnant with Josh, the beginning of wonders in her life. Every doctor had told her it would be impossible for her to bear children, so she knew a miracle when she saw one, when nine months later she held him in her arms.

"It's just as wonderful when God heals a person through a doctor's hands."

"How can you say that?" Sylvia whispered. "You know what happened with your mother. That wasn't healing."

Tim put his fork down. "Do we have to talk about this? Now?"

"I just want you to see that your experience contradicts your beliefs. You know the damage firsthand. But you still say no to miracles. It doesn't make sense. Science is the one who has hurt you."

"I don't know what else to say, Sylvia. I have reservations."

"About God?"

"About the hoops people expect God to jump through before they are willing to believe. About the process of healing in general—from both ends, natural and divine. I think God wants us to be sensible, to take advantage of the advances of modern technology. At the same time, I know darn well that only miracles come clean and free. Drugs and medicine are preloaded with a sheet full of side effects. Awful stuff . . ."

"But you're more willing to give science the benefit of the doubt."

"That's not fair, Sylvia. You know that's not fair."

The conversation ended, but Sylvia remained unsatisfied, wanting desperately to believe there was more. She had *seen* more, in her son. Was her son's power unholy?

Just thinking about it made her insides knot up. She found herself aching for Josh one moment, and the next, as his mother, soaring with him in her imagination. But the truth was, she had no idea what she was supposed to do or how she was supposed to feel—how could she? For eight years she had suffered fear and insecurity, wondering how to protect a boy with magic hands. Sylvia had no idea how to nurture a gift, only how to nurture a *child*. Not just any child. *Her son*. There was only one thing she knew, and she knew this as deeply as the belly of the Earth knows heat: Josh was not going to become some spectacle or research project. Watching Josh heal the hamster, so long ago it seemed, Sylvia had sworn to herself that her son would be a child as long as he could be, as long as she had any control at all or breath in her lungs.

Afraid of what he would think, Sylvia never informed Tim of any of the miracles. Now she would certainly have to. What had once been her secret alone had gone public. The "miracle healing" was probably dinner fodder for half the population. And that made Sylvia nervous.

Dinnertime came and went. Tim wasn't home yet. Josh still played in his room, silently traveling the smooth, cloudless skies of his mind. Finished with preparation, Sylvia sat in the recliner, staring through the house, looking for comfort. Something with roots.

The Chisom house was a simple ranch design: two bedrooms, a single bath, cozy kitchen, and stove-heated family room, set on half an acre in a well-kept little neighborhood right off the main street in the northwest of Folin, which is to say, not far away from anything: five or so blocks away from one of the two town stoplights, near the IGA grocery store, five minutes from the school, and a couple of miles from the bottler.

Inside, everything was neat and tidy and showed pride. Though the carpet was a bit old and the color of mud, it was in good shape. Three summers ago, Sylvia had decided the carpet made the house too dark, so she spent all her evenings painting the walls a color called "milk cream" and then carefully stenciling little flower or crosshatch patterned borders along the tops of each room. It paid off nicely, adding plenty of personality to offset the drab. (Josh's room was definitely the most feisty, with airplanes stenciled using a World War II motif.) For Christmas last year, they made another upgrade. Their present to each other was a new recliner. This year Sylvia was pulling for a new dishwasher, since their old one hadn't worked in more than six months.

All in all, not much maybe, but more than enough to get along. Better still, it was theirs, not the bank's, owned free and clear. Tim and Sylvia weren't poor and would have never thought of themselves as such. They simply had to work hard for everything and didn't often get the chance to take a breather.

It never occurred to them to complain. Even now, sitting in silence, pondering her son's fate, her first reaction was not to complain, but to adjust. Do what was necessary to make the best of it. She wanted to be angry with Mrs. Tellier for interfering, but she knew that wasn't right. She wanted to be happy for Marty, but concern for Josh overshadowed even that.

All she could think, over and over, was, *What will tomorrow bring?*

• • •

West of Folin by two time zones, Alyssa sat cross-legged in her bedroom in Seattle, sipping bottled water, munching baby carrots, and listening to Tori Amos wail away in fit after fit of existential angst. She was freckled and pale, her jewelry simple and silver, her makeup dark— the color of purple mud. Pensive, distracted, she flipped channels, attempted a nap, squirmed and fussed, finally gave up and reached for the clothbound journal beside her bed.

October 3, 3:12 P.M. —

I am so restless. Jean is back! Well, he's in the air at least. He should arrive at Tacoma in just a few hours, and I will be there waiting. Tonight we will drink wine and make love and talk until the sun rises. At least I hope so. He will probably want to work, but I won't let him. Not tonight, when we've been apart for so long! He has been relentless for the past six months. I can't wait to hear his voice, to see him.

Okay, be realistic. He will be tired. Will he be tired? Will he share with me? Let me hear his thoughts? Oh please, Jean, don't be in one of your moods. Not tonight. And don't let this rash of traveling wear you out. You made a promise to take me to France and I expect you to keep it. You must know how important promises are to me.

Silly man. He called from Munich to make sure I could pick him up. Did he think I would forget? Men are so strange. Anyway, I was glad for the call. He seemed in good spirits. Apparently his contacts at the lab in Germany are having much success, though at what Jean refuses to say. He simply calls it "new and improved." Whatever the plan, it seems to be coming together. All I know is that, at long last, after many years, we will make our voice heard. Jean has been hesitant to give too many details. I've asked, believe me. I've even begged. He just winks and smiles and a wild fire lights his eyes. It's almost scary how committed he is. But he promised a closed meeting with top-tier GPS soon. No doubt that's ground zero.

My stomach is in knots. I can't write any more. I think I will go on to the airport.

P.S. I hope Jean is happy to see me.

• • •

When Sylvia heard Tim stomp his steel-toed boots on the welcome mat at 6:30, the house was full of the smell of mouth-watering, fatty beef and grilled onions.

"Ah yes," he said, his voice tinged with nostalgia. "Love that smell."

Inhaling deeply, he stepped inside, set his metal thermos on the table underneath the coatrack in the entry. Sylvia watched him as she finished setting the table. Even with a million thoughts tangling in her mind like seaweed, she couldn't help but smile at the sight of her husband. The years had been good to him. He was handsome the way a pair of weathered leather gloves are comfortable. Lean, angular in face, unable to hide the mild scarring of adolescent acne, Tim Chisom wasn't so much attractive as ruggedly, comfortably appealing, with a mellow voice as smooth as the soft white scar along his left jaw.

By contrast, Sylvia, though dark-skinned like Tim—a bit more olive to his Comanche—was smoother, with almond-shaped eyes the color of aloe vera and a small, round beauty mark on her cheek. They had always made a nice pair. Sylvia knew she wasn't pretty in a cover girl way and would have been the first to admit it. She wasn't Ginger and would have done well to be compared with Mary Ann, but she was all woman. Not in a 36-24-36 sort of way, but in manner and sensibilities.

"Do you remember that smell?" Tim asked, wrapping his arms around her waist. At first, Sylvia responded stiffly to his touch. Relaxing a little, she tried her best to lose herself in the moment. At that moment she would have loved more than anything to follow Tim where he was trying to take her.

"Are they as good as Mickey's tonight?" he asked, grinning.

Sylvia bit her lip. "Maybe better."

She couldn't hide the dread in her voice. After all the years, Tim would know. He could tell whether she had laughed or cried by the shape of the creases of the soft, thin skin around her eyes. He knew the slight, downward curve of her lips when she was afraid. He knew everything about her, not the least of which was how rarely her mood darkened. Sylvia was normally the anchor of joy in the Chisom home, the bright one, the cheerleader.

If there was fear, he'd know it meant Josh was involved. As ever, Tim was patient. There would be plenty of time to discuss. No need to rush. Ever so slightly, Sylvia calmed in his embrace.

"Time to eat," she said.

As ever, this particular meal brought back memories for Tim, memories of the first time he and Sylvia had met years ago during his high-school senior year. The place was Mickey's Eatery. Entering late one night, young Tim had kept his head low, silently searching for a table in the back.

An hour earlier, he had stood in the end zone of the grassy field at Folin High, helmet removed, covering his eyes, chugging great gray gusts from his lungs into the chilled autumn air. Tendrils of steam radiated from his sweaty head as if he were on fire. Only seventeen years old at the time, Tim had just blown the big game, the game the Folin Miners were picked to win on their way to the state tournament, by missing a beautiful spiraling Hail Mary deep into the end zone. With less than a minute left, the ball hit him in the numbers, in both hands. He tried—Lord, how he tried! Couldn't hold it . . . couldn't grab hold. Juggling, dancing, fumbling, time ran out and the Miners lost by three. The Oklahoma 2A Regionals were over.

Unlike all the other young studs from Folin High who marked the occasion of both victory and defeat with drunkenness, Tim usually preferred to pull away, to mull and stew. That night, more than ever, he had wanted to disappear. And so he found himself up the road a bit at Mickey's Eatery, wearing his green-and-white letter jacket, unable to stop his mind from replaying the pass over and over again.

When a young waitress approached his table with her hands on her hips, smacking her lips, Tim had no idea how everything was about to change.

"If you're wanting to sit in here and mope, you probably ought to order something," she told him. Her tone was churlish, even rude.

Tim didn't even glance up, just mumbled, "Cheeseburger and fries." Not much was fancy about Mickey's, but the man fixed a great burger, loaded with sautéed onions. And cheddar cheese, not American. That was the key.

The waitress put the order in and took her time attending to a couple of other customers who were ready for their check. When she finally returned with his food, she introduced herself.

"I'm Sylvia. Mind if I sit?"

Tim could only grunt. "You probably don't want to be anywhere near me tonight." Glancing up, he cocked his head. "Say, I know you, don't I? Isn't your brother a couple years below me?"

Apparently Sylvia considered that a yes. Taking a seat opposite him, she went straight for the jugular of his self-pity.

"It's just a game," she told him, resting her chin on her hands.

That was not a good way to start with an athlete. Of all the things to say—patronizing, sympathetic, mocking—Tim despised that line the most because it somehow managed to be all those things at once.

"A few old men in Folin who don't have anything better to do come down and holler and make you guys out to be the heroes they never were," Sylvia continued.

"That's not the point," Tim countered.

"Fine. Then tell me: What is the point?"

"I could have caught it."

In tone and posture, his body language said "back off" loud and clear, go away, or at the very least, shut up. That should have ended it right there. Sylvia was intruding, perhaps with kinder intent than Tim was willing to admit, but her delivery was rough and the last thing he wanted was to have her polish her sales pitch on him.

Instead of retreating, however, Sylvia did a magical thing: she laughed. Reckless and wonderful, the sound had cut the heaviness in the air clean in half, causing Tim to blink, as if awakened from sleep.

She then told him something unusual, at least for a pep talk. "Tim Chisom, both my parents died when I was four years old. Four! You know what, though? I'm going to college next year. Life goes on. My life didn't end then and I don't plan on it ending anytime soon."

With the pump now primed, Sylvia launched into nearly five un-interrupted minutes of life story, the kind Tim knew was supposed to make a point. Make him feel better. It was a tough story for sure. Tim could understand how she had grown bitter. Surprisingly, she also informed Tim that she knew of him, pretty much the way everyone knew everyone in a small town. So when he stepped through the door—cocky little senior, wearing his jersey, crying about his little foot-ball game—she got mad. What did he know about troubles? But then she thought about her own dreams, and how far away from Folin they took her, and how stuck she often felt. In that light, seeing Tim so sad about what happened made her giggle, made her laugh at herself, too. She had survived. Survived!

Tim remembered well how much he wanted to be irritated with her, but Sylvia never gave him a chance. Poking at the table with her finger, she explained to him how she served stiff, rancid coffee all night, every night. She told him that for several more months she would have to endure spills, leering truckdrivers, low tips, and greasy pork steaks—until she earned enough money for college. But she also told him it was worth it. She had two years of reasonable savings in the bank and figured she could begin school the following fall, assuming her application was approved.

"That's how you make the most of something," she concluded. "You wipe the dirt off and stay focused."

She was spirited, feisty; that much was obvious. In spite of himself, Tim found himself drawn to the edge of fascination. Sylvia seemed so . . . mature. An older woman.

"Where'd you get that little scar?" she'd asked in a distracted voice, pointing to his cheek.

"Helping my Grandpa out on the farm," Tim replied, touching the fleshy white line, as he did even now. He remembered his answer, how he had coughed lightly, deepened his voice. "I was just a kid then."

"You should be more careful," she chided, laughing for the second time, but with an obvious sparkle in her eyes.

From that point in the conversation, it hadn't mattered what she said. All Tim wanted was to hear her laughter. He had made it his mission for the rest of the night. Before long, he forgot the game, the burger, the fries. Sylvia, more devoted than ever to finishing her "Buck up, camper" speech, had come back to it again and again, finally saying, "It may feel like it, but I don't think the whole world hangs on that one moment for you, Tim, and probably never will. If it does, chances are you won't drop the ball next time people need you. You'll remember this moment and you'll make sure all is right."

Though Tim started out thinking the rude waitress from Mickey's rather waifish—thin, gangly, with cocoa-colored hair pulled back into an unflattering ponytail, oversized glasses sliding down her nose—he ended up wondering what she would look like with her hair loose. Smiling, he stole a glance at Sylvia as she ate. Beside him, Josh munched quietly.

The rest, as they say, is history.

In honor of that first encounter, Sylvia fixed Tim a Mickey's-style burger once a month, never letting him know exactly when, always keeping a bit of surprise in the mix, though never veering from the essentials: sautéed onions and melted cheddar, not American. All things considered, tonight probably *was* a good night for a memory. As the Chisoms ate together, conversation slowly emerged. Sylvia tried to hide her sadness, at least from Josh, but Tim noticed.

Josh didn't speak much, except to brag about his good grades. He proudly proclaimed, "Five A's and two B's!"

Tim grinned and pounded him on the back. "Nice work, Son. Very nice."

But glancing at his wife, watching Josh, he saw the sadness on her face grow inexplicably deeper.

• • •

Later that night, Alyssa's journal entry was rushed, written with gouging strokes.

October 3, 10:32 P.M. —

Why do I bother? Why do I let him do this to me? Jean was mean, cruel, and distant. I hate him. All he talked about was his plans—fine enough—but even then he would tell me nothing. After all this time, all my devotion, I am still kept dangling on a string from a distance. Everything is big, something big in the works, but I am left out. Doesn't he know this has become my passion, too? He has shown me so much. He has shown all of us so much. It's beautiful. It must become true. But why can't we dance along the way, he and I? When I picked him up, he did not even pretend to see me. He didn't say a word in the car. For dinner, he drank, talked in fragments, kissed me once, laughed at me, insulted me, and then left me to find a taxi because he "needed my auto."

Why does he treat me this way? Doesn't he know I would do anything for him . . . anything to help him succeed? I believe in him, in his passion. He rescued me. I cannot ever forget that.

I suppose it does no good to whine. I am tired of writing the same stories, page after page. I must choose. That's it, really. I must choose. Either leave the movement, which I cannot do. Or leave him, which I cannot bear. Or stay and abide, and somehow . . .

October 4, 1:16 A.M. —

I can't sleep. My pillow is wet and the tears won't stop. But why bother with tears? As I consider the alternatives, the choice is easy. I simply will not lose Jean, and that is final. Nor will I allow him to lose me. So I will become whatever it is he needs. It seems so simple really. Obviously, I have not yet met his needs, or he would not treat me this way. I will become what he cannot live without. That is the answer.

Even if I lose my soul in the process—if I gain him, it will be worth it.

4

Days passed. Days turned into weeks. Following a good hard frost, the trees gushed of orange, red, and yellow. Fat, ripe pumpkins began to appear on the front porches of homes all over town. Shortly after the browning leaves fluttered from the trees came Halloween, and the chill weather turned cold. In the days immediately following the big event, Folin was briefly and fiercely abuzz with news of Joshua Chisom's miracle at school, but as winter settled in and Thanksgiving came and went, the buzz faded and life returned to normal.

For the most part.

In the immediate aftermath, Sylvia feared old patterns would flare up again: bullying, insulting. It never happened, perhaps thanks to the many trembling prayers she offered in search of gentle grace for her son. Many town folk continued to maintain their distance—especially superstitious old men and women and a few churchgoing parents, some from Sylvia's own church, who feared the chance for wrong influence on their kids. Wherever the Chisoms went, a trail of whispering followed, but that had always been the case.

The new wrinkle was that, for many people, the effect had actually proven positive. If they stared at Josh, it was with a new tilt to their head, a new appreciation in their eyes. Some even befriended him or his parents, though it became clear most of these preferred favors to real friendship. In those few weeks, Sylvia discovered bits of gypsy or carpetbagger in nearly everyone, scheming for the divine lottery ticket in whatever form it might appear. Whatever would help or amuse or profit *them*.

She sheltered Josh from these folks as best she could, though at a public school such a task wasn't always easy. She hung up on strangers who called, turned down a newspaper interview, and tried her best to keep Josh in sight. But Sylvia couldn't keep out the jokes. At the bottler one morning she found a small poster advertising a healing evangelist who was coming to a local church for revival services in a few weeks. Underneath his name in big bold marker someone had scratched Josh's name over the real name.

Amazingly, word didn't spread much beyond Folin. Probably no one would have believed it anyway. Sylvia knew Tim caught some flak at the quarry. She also knew most of the men were wiser than to scrap with him. That first week, he informed her that a few of the guys honestly had a question or two, which he reluctantly tried to accommodate. Thing was, Tim was more embarrassed by what he *didn't* know, rather than what he did. That was the big issue. Having intentionally kept him out of the loop all these years, Sylvia knew she had placed him in an unfortunate predicament: that of a father discovering something remarkable about his own son after much of the town already knew. Her mistake triggered more than a little tension in the Chisom home in the days following Sylvia's a priori confession.

Then came forgiveness, sort of, or at least a truce, along with the relief of minimal community backlash. Everything settled in nice and easy. Nothing really stung until the week after Thanksgiving, when Emma's birthday party arrived . . . and Josh was not invited.

Like most all news, word of the rebuff came from the grapevine, which only doubled the insult. When Tim heard, he immediately flew into a quiet, fuming rage. Sylvia listened from the kitchen as he called his grandmother, knowing Meem would fume with him, indignantly reminding Tim how Emma's mother had grown up not a block away from Tim, and though a full two years younger, and not even very well behaved, mind you, she had been invited to *every one* of Tim's birthday parties through the fifth grade. Why, they had attended Sunday school together! On and on . . .

Sylvia didn't know how to be angry. She didn't have the heart or the will for it anymore. All she could think to do was hold on to Josh and hurt for him. Strangely, by all appearance, Josh didn't need it. He didn't cry, whine, or ask why. The night they heard the news, he took the snub without a single question, retreating to his room full of airplanes.

Sylvia followed, prodding him. "Josh, are you okay?"

"Uh-huh."

"Are you sure? If you aren't, honey, that's all right. We can talk."

Josh stared, unblinking. Sylvia caught her reflection in his hazelnut eyes. She could not fathom how far they fell—yet it seemed deep enough to scrape the soul of the earth.

He said, "I'm okay."

Sylvia tiptoed forward. "So this doesn't hurt your feelings?"

"You mean that I don't get to go to Emma's party?" he asked. "Or that they don't want me?"

Sylvia stroked her son's face with the back of her hand. "They're just adults, honey. Adults can be very stupid sometimes. They don't know what they're missing."

Josh ran his fingers through the carpet. Sylvia hoped he understood. At the very least, she hoped he knew it wasn't Emma's fault. But she could tell it wasn't fun for him to think about.

Taking his chin in her hand, Sylvia guided her son's eyes to meet hers. "Know what? *I* wanted you even before you were born. I really did. I wanted you so much I could taste it. But I didn't know how much I wanted you until *after*. Sometimes people just don't know what they're missing."

Josh closed his eyes, thinking big thoughts. "Mom?"

"Yes?"

"I'd like to just play now, if that's all right."

Sylvia rose to her feet. "Of course."

As she was about to leave the room, Josh asked a final question, phrased in passing as he glanced around the emptiness of his toy-strewn room.

"Mom, why am I the only one?"

"What do you mean, honey?" she asked weakly. She knew what he meant. Why did it seem that fate had singled him out for rejection? The question might as well have worn boots and kicked her in the stomach.

Josh repeated. "You know . . . why am I the only one?"

Sylvia stared down the hallway, searching for a faraway token of grace as the soft, failing light of the western sun warmed both the window sill and the salty sheen of her eyes. What she wanted most to do was pretend not to hear, to make up an excuse—do anything but face her son's unflinching gaze. For a mother, however, flight is never an option. So she stood, and as she stood, something fierce swallowed her more timid compulsions. Some need for justice, for mercy; some need to bury a stake in the heart of all the little injustices her son seemed destined to endure. She almost dove towards Josh, like a rescuer returning into a burning home.

"I'll tell you why you are the only one, Joshua Chisom. Because you are special, that's why. Because God only makes so many *special* people. Everyone else is just the same, but every now and then God requires angels to turn into humans so that everyone else can see how to live. Don't you ever forget that, Joshua. You may feel like the only one, but you are the lucky one, and all the rest of us are just trying to figure out what you already know. Whenever God has big plans, he will always need someone very special to make them happen. Only a few of those people are ever born, and you're one of them." She caught her breath and leaned back. "Do you understand, Son? Does any of that make sense?"

Josh didn't even try, just shook his head. "Nope."

Sylvia sighed, spent. "What don't you understand?"

"I just want someone to play with. You know, another kid. What does all that stuff about angels have to do with me having a brother or sister? Why am I the only one?"

Sylvia stared, blank-faced. Then she touched hand to head, eyes screwed shut, desperately processing the conversation up to that point. Suddenly she understood, sniffling and bursting into laughter.

She grabbed Josh and held onto him and wept.

• • •

A couple miles east of Atlanta, just north of the main campus of Emory University, Stuart Daniel Baker of the Centers for Disease

Control idly checked his e-mail, cursing. He sat in an office in Building 16, the newest and nicest of the CDC pantheon. Building 16 was in fact the recently completed administration building. In contrast to the sea of cubicle partitions he faced, Stu's windowed, glass-plated office was clear evidence of his position. Rows of thick venetian blinds blocked Stu's view of the maze and the underlings' view of him.

The day had been hectic so far, this being his first chance to actually sit. Piled on his desk were requisition forms, field reports, and about half a dozen requests for assistance, two within the U.S. and four abroad. As chief of the division of Epidemic Intelligence Services, he had to review these cases, weed out the nonessentials, and then assign priorities for the sake of investigation. EIS officers were the famed medical detectives of the CDC.

At his door, a square chunk of man appeared, blocking out the light. The man knocked and, in the same gesture, opened the door. He plopped yet another manila folder on Stu's desk.

"Downtown Minneapolis, chief," the man sniffed. "County hospital thinks it has three or four cases of whooping cough."

"Thinks? What about lab results?"

"Presumptive at this point, but I think we've got clinical compatibility."

"Our lab or theirs?"

"Theirs."

"No good. Tell them to send samples and we'll make our own diagnosis. We aren't going to take just anyone's word, you know."

"Already told 'em. They say one of the cases is the mayor's daughter. They're requesting a team."

Stu sighed and picked up the folder, absently leafing through the pages; the words blended one into another like thin lines of black paste.

"You know, Frank, I used to be in the game." He pushed back from his desk. "I'm an M.D. I've got a Ph.D. in epidemiology. But now? I'm nothing but a human paper clip. I gather papers here and file them there."

Frank grinned. "That's what you get for being so darn smart."

Stu didn't smile, didn't find the humor. "I've been doing this job for five years now—division chief—and I think I realized just today that I've regretted every day of it. Every single day."

"C'mon, Stu. For crying out loud, you're a walking, talking promotion. Quit your whining. You should be used to the drill."

"Not this," Stu replied, tapping the stack of folders. "I didn't do it for this."

"Well, cheer up. When Ebola takes over the world, they'll yank you out of here so fast it'll make your head spin." He backed out the door, calling over his shoulder, "In the meantime, let me know about Minneapolis. Can you handle that, *old man?*"

He enunciated the last part with a little snicker. Stu watched him depart, cracking his knuckles one at a time. In five days, he was going to turn the big five-o, a fact he fastidiously avoided thinking about, though everyone else in the office seemed more than willing to remind him.

Supposedly, it was all in good humor. Stu suspected a bit of spite mixed in, perhaps even revenge. He was not easy to get along with, was like a piece of sandpaper—flattened wood pulp covered with glue and grit—made to rub a person raw. Which was fine with him. If his particular brand of nihilism bothered a friend or colleague for some reason— no big deal, no huffing or puffing, just wave good-bye and hit the door.

He could afford to be that way. Stu was something of a minor legend at the CDC, having been one of the lead researchers responsible for isolating the rod-shaped bacterium responsible for legionnaires' disease when it erupted at the Bellevue-Stratford Hotel in Philadelphia in 1976. He was in Sudan later that year for Ebola, commanding the field crew; was part of the 1978 and 1981 campaigns in West Africa; and as recently as 1993 was a nearly singular voice calling the world's attention to the tinderbox of AIDS sparking in the red-light district of Bangkok. He could smell diseases before a microscope could identify them. His instincts were uncanny—part scientist, part analyst, part bloodhound. At forty-nine and counting, it seemed he had always been thus, trusting intuition. Thirty-plus years ago, fresh-faced from high school, he figured his skills would best serve him as a profiler for the FBI, but within a matter of weeks he had joined the army. It was three more years before a college biology professor had turned him on to a different kind of killer. Stu was hooked immediately. Now, balding except for salt-and-pepper side panels and a neatly trimmed triangle of chin hair and mustache, Stu was spring-loaded for the field, not the desk. There wasn't a twenty- or thirty-something in the entire CDC who would dare argue otherwise, much less try to keep up with him.

But the Peter Principle was alive and well at the CDC, and soon Stu was promoted to his level of incompetence or, rather, disinterest. He was out of fieldwork by late 1993, formulating opinions based on other people's work, watching with envy from a distance as virologists at the CDC nailed the Muerto Canyon Hantavirus in Arizona and, in 1997, the new Hong Kong flu, H5N1.

Minneapolis, huh? he thought idly.

He grabbed the phone, started to dial, set it down. He simply wasn't in the mood for phone chatter right now, whooping cough or no. The computer beeped at him, politely alerting him to a completed batch e-mail download. On-screen, fifteen new messages showed up in his box. He scanned the subject lines. Three or four were immediately recognizable as either spam or junk, the kind you get every day from net sales or well-meaning people who have nothing better to do than send a nifty little poem or joke or inspirational trivia to everyone on their contact list.

Tap, tap, tap. He deleted them, unread.

Half a dozen more he clicked through quickly, allowing only a cursory review of the contents, documents that would require much more time and study—interoffice reports and such—as well as responses from colleagues at various university medical departments and private research facilities. A couple of personal notes were thrown in the mix, an invitation to lunch from a doctor friend in town. Basically, an average day of e-mail.

Except for message number thirteen, down at the bottom, simply titled "Sleeper."

Stu almost wrote it off as more spam, but the name intrigued him, so he clicked on it. When he did, a simple little message appeared on-screen:

Virus environs are not as you think.

Let all partake the bitter drink.

Five more days, you'll see the link.

Stu read it again. *Five more days,* he mused. *My birthday?*

Hardly a coincidence. *Another office joke, I suppose.*

He studied it further, searching for the punch line. If it *was* a joke, he didn't quite get it. The bitter drink? Virus environs? Seemed a bit oblique. Even dark.

Let all partake the bitter drink . . .

He scanned the file directory and carbon copy list to see if he could nail down who in the office had sent it to him. The list was ridiculously long—probably 150 names deep, minimum. Out of all of them, Stu didn't recognize a single name. He strummed his fingers on the table, almost ready to hit delete, but then he noticed something. The cryptic message included an attached file.

Ahh, the answer to the riddle . . .

He pointed and clicked. The attached file must have been an executable, a mini application, because something obviously sprang open. The small Microsoft Windows hourglass flickered briefly, signaling some sort of processor activity . . . but that was it. No new screen. No funny cartoon illustrating the bitter drink, making sense of it all. Stu frowned. What kind of attachment was that? No document, no nothing.

"Whatever," he muttered, pressing delete.

The message named "Sleeper" disappeared.

Picking up his coffee mug, he inspected the oval ring of black grinds stuck to the bottom, like psychic portents capable of revealing his future. Stu hadn't lived a day for nearly twenty years that he didn't down at least three cups of coffee, and it was high time for number three. He rose, stretched, shook his right leg to work out the stiffness.

Arthritis at fifty, he grumbled to himself.

Then, leaning on his cane, he strolled down the hallway in search of a warm coffeepot, the blacker the better.

Behind him, in his office, as if waiting for him to leave, his computer began to crunch with internal activity. The little scrap of computer code Stu had launched—focused with missionary zeal—signaled an internal timer, and the virus Stu inadvertently welcomed onto his hard drive aggressively commenced its single mission: to replicate. The program ran transparently and would utilize his computer once and only once as a launching pad for transmission of the same message to everyone Stu's computer knew, just as Stu had received it from another unwitting victim. In a matter of seconds, the virus code had scanned Stu's e-mail directory, logged every name, composed a new message identical to the one he had received, and begun transmitting.

Only this time, on this computer, the catch was greater. Instead of a mere 150 names, it managed to find over 350 names—Stu's e-mail list was quite large—and all of them were scheduled for instantaneous, exponentially increasing delivery via the World Wide Web.

• • •

The next day an invitation came in the mail, addressed to Joshua. Sylvia opened it. It was from Mrs. Tellier—actually her son, Paul. He was a grade ahead of Josh. In bright colors, the card announced that tomorrow he would have a birthday party. And Josh was invited.

Ahh! Sylvia thought. *Bless you, Mrs. Tellier.*

"Josh!" she called out excitedly. "Josh, come here."

A moment later Josh drifted in. "Yeah, Mom?"

"Josh, Paul Tellier is having a birthday party tomorrow and you're invited."

"Paul Tellier? Oh, he's cool."

"Well he must think you're pretty cool, too. Wanna go?"

"Sure!"

"Well go grab your jacket. Wal-Mart closes in half an hour and we need a gift."

• • •

Next morning, the weather turned bitter, forcing Paul's party indoors. Happily, there was plenty of room. The Tellier home was a nice, middle-class, two-story farmhouse, with white vinyl siding and cherry red shutters. It was situated on the upward roll of about three acres just west of town, in the middle of a circular subdivision with a trickling seasonal stream that, at the moment, happily chortled with water, though the water was by now only about five degrees shy of freezing.

Upon entering, a few of the kids greeted Josh warmly. Josh said hi to Paul and a couple of other kids he knew. Most of them were a grade ahead, about ten or twelve of them total. Josh timidly stepped in, mumbled a few words, tried to make a joke, and gradually insinuated himself into the culture of the older boys. Since a year doesn't matter much at that age, all was soon lost in a haze of games and fun and activity. Sylvia lingered behind, watching, with Mrs. Tellier.

"Thank you," she said.

"For what?"

"Most of these kids probably got their invitations a week or two ago. I suspect you sent ours last minute . . . after you heard. I just want you to know I know what you've done here. And I'm grateful."

Mrs. Tellier sipped a large glass of heavily sweetened iced tea. She set the glass down as if to reply but, caught on a word, thought better of it. Finally, she said, "I knew he would be hurt. Emma is one of his best friends. It just didn't make any sense. This isn't much—"

"But it's more than most people do, at least for Josh," Sylvia said. "And it's more than you had to."

Mrs. Tellier held her hands palm up. "Better late than never."

Both women stared quietly into the living room, where a dozen kids jumped and hollered. Each woman wanted to tease information from the other but did not want to presume, leaving the fragile silence as their only real connection—that and their love for Josh. Sylvia observed the huddle of children, how Josh fit and didn't fit.

"Do Josh and Paul even know each other?" she asked.

Mrs. Tellier sipped her tea again, pointing. "They do now."

Sylvia looked. Paul sat beside Josh, crafting a paper airplane for him, instructing him in the proper folds and creases, showing him how to hold his hands.

"I'll bring him home later," Mrs. Tellier said. "Don't worry about him. He'll be fine. You go home and enjoy the afternoon."

"I'm sure you know, but try not to let him get all moody. He's such a serious child. He needs to play."

Mrs. Tellier touched Sylvia's arm. "He'll be fine. I'll take good care of him."

After a Kool-Aid break and a birthday song, presents were opened. Mrs. Tellier had a piñata for the kids to swing at and an organized game or two, including an old game of Twister that everyone thought was just a hoot. Then it was time for cake and ice cream, and then Nintendo.

As the party entered its final stretch, Josh quietly watched from behind the cluster of children in front of the TV. No one excluded him; they all just sort of closed ranks. After all, *they* were classmates. It wasn't that Josh was the outsider; he just wasn't an insider. Even Paul, carefully instructed by his mother to be attentive to Josh, was caught up in the action on-screen. Josh didn't mind, had learned not to notice. If anything, he hated it when adults tried to force something. That only accentuated the difference. Still, when Mrs. Tellier took a step forward and put her arm around him, he felt comforted. She seemed tense, hesitant, as if she were not exactly sure how to comfort discreetly.

From upstairs, Josh heard a slight, shuffling sound. He glanced at Mrs. Tellier. She had heard it, too. Leaving him, she hurried up to check on the noise and came back down a moment later. Out of the corner of his eye, Josh saw her staring hard at him, somewhat reluctant, almost fearful, as if a small battle was taking place within her. Josh could see on her face that something won. And something lost.

"Josh," she said softly, squeezing his shoulder. "I want you to meet someone. Could you come with me for a moment?"

Curious, Josh slipped away with her, as Mrs. Tellier led him upstairs to a room at the end of a hallway. Gingerly, she pushed the door open and tip-toed inside. Josh followed. On a queen-size bed in the center of the room he saw a girl a few years older than himself—twelve, maybe thirteen, he guessed. Dressed in a white gown, she lay on her back, staring toward the ceiling. Even from where Josh stood, he could see the girl's vacant, glassy eyes. He swallowed hard. The room felt creepy. It had a powerful odor, like the clash of a moldy, acrid bathroom laced with newly sprayed air freshener. All of a sudden he wanted to be anywhere but there. Mrs. Tellier's firm hand on his shoulder prevented him. What was she doing?

Walking over to the eastern window, she threw open the lace drapes and opened the glass. A fresh breeze blew in. The girl on the bed moaned, perhaps in response to the cool air. When the girl tried to speak, however, an unintelligible string of slurs and half-formed vowel sounds came out. Her left arm jerked, and Josh saw the impossible angle of the wrist—the gnarled bones and knuckles.

Terrified, fixated—all at the same time—Josh could not squelch the dread rising in the pit of his stomach. But Mrs. Tellier bent over the girl and kissed her forehead, whispering in her ear. The girl moaned again, louder. Her torso arched spasmodically. To Josh it seemed she was more pleased than pained. He even would have sworn that at one point he caught the hint of an awkward smile on the girl's twisted mouth, though from his angle at the foot of the bed, it was hard to be sure.

Mrs. Tellier motioned for Josh to come closer. Josh's eyes widened. He took a single, silent, timid step forward, then stopped cold. She motioned again, reaching tenderly for his hand. The smile on her face was sad, patient. Josh shuffled awkwardly to stand beside her.

"This is my daughter, Elise," she said, stroking the girl's hair. Elise was turned on her side, helpless to adjust herself, yet it appeared she was trying hard to focus on Josh's face. A wide, silly smile split her face. One of her teeth was missing, and there were two long, thin white scars, one creasing her eyebrow and another curving across her jaw toward her lips.

Josh stared in silence for a moment. Gesturing with his wrist, he murmured two words: "Hi, Elise."

Elise made another sound, loud and snorting, thumping the bed with her free hand. Her eyes rolled to her mother's face, attempting to refocus. Josh stepped back.

"Don't be afraid. She likes you," Mrs. Tellier exclaimed. "Five years ago, Elise was in a terrible car accident. She almost died. It's a miracle she's with us at all. And I'm so thankful."

Mrs. Tellier continued combing her daughter's hair with her fingers, speaking in a soothing, loving tone, full of memory and echoes of joy. Elise wagged her head to the rhythm of her mother's touch.

"She can't understand what I'm telling you right now. She is severely brain damaged. But once upon a time, she danced. She wore ballerina shoes and she danced and all the world was her stage."

Josh felt the pounding of his own chest, heard the ache in Mrs. Tellier's voice, though she never let the smile fade from her lips while Elise looked on.

"Josh . . ."

"Yes, Mrs. Tellier."

"I have no right to ask you this . . ."

Josh's heart pounded harder.

Mrs. Tellier fumbled for words. "I shouldn't do this. It isn't right. I know you are special. I don't want you to feel . . . like I'm making you do something." She turned and took Josh's hand in between both her own. Her lips trembled. "Your mother would probably think I'm a horrible person for asking this of you, for putting you on the spot like this. I . . . I just want to see my girl dance again."

She lowered her head, ashamed, hiding her dry eyes from hope. "I guess what I'm asking is . . . is there anything you can do? Please. Is there anything? I know you have power I don't understand. Can any of your power help my little girl?"

Elise lay quietly, and for a moment it appeared she was listening for the answer, except that her mouth remained fixed in a huge smile. With one finger Josh brushed the skin of the girl's twisted hand. He stared for a long time, quietly—a liquid, molten flow of watchfulness—tracing the girl's face with his eyes. Something in him from a great distance drew near to the surface. He was no longer afraid.

"I can't explain it," he whispered. "But it only works on eyes. And not all the time, even then. I don't have any power besides that. I'm sorry."

Mrs. Tellier's shoulders heaved a single, quick, controlled sob. She stood very quickly, pressed her blouse, regaining composure. For her daughter, she smiled bravely, but, without turning, she addressed Josh.

"I'm the one who is sorry, Josh. I never should have asked. It wasn't fair. Forgive me."

Even as a nine-year-old, Josh could recognize the fading shades of disappointment in her voice. What surprised him, even as the color drained away, was the persistent love that remained, like a sail catching wind and holding fast though the wind died down. Afterwards, resignation, like a sedative taking effect, finally settled in.

"Josh, please," Mrs. Tellier murmured. "I would appreciate it if you wouldn't tell your mother."

She drove him home in silence. Josh was grateful, and weary to the bone.

"I've asked God why," he told Mrs. Tellier, before she pulled away from her driveway. "Why only eyes? But he hasn't told me."

He felt heavy, sad, empty, as if he were a jug full of water that had been drained clear to his feet. He was thirsty. Having drunk punch and water like a horse at the party, he still wasn't satiated. As he climbed the steps to his home he heard, strangely, the sound of angry voices coming from inside. Swinging the door open, all voices hushed. Mom, Dad . . . and Uncle Rick.

"General Josh!" Uncle Rick exclaimed as he turned, forcing a new expression onto his face. "How's my boy?"

That was Rick's nickname for him—General Josh; Josh didn't mind. Uncle Rick was brutish and loud, but fun. And a great storyteller. Pretty much what you'd expect from an uncle. Josh loved to hear Uncle Rick tell stories, usually about wars and flying and heroes.

"What was all the shouting about?" he asked.

"Nothing dear," Sylvia said hurriedly. "We were just discussing some things. How was the party? Did you have fun?"

"We played Nintendo. When can I get one of those, Mom?"

"Your father has answered that plenty of times, Josh."

Tim reached out his arms. "Let me give you a hug and then you run on to your room, okay? You look beat."

Rick stepped in. "I believe I better be first in line for a hug," he said as he whisked his nephew up into a rough embrace, squeezing so hard Josh started to cough. Rick had a thin, trimmed, two-day-old beard and blond shoulder-length hair pulled into a ponytail. "I mean, how long has it been, General?"

Josh coughed again and grinned. "A while, I guess."

"One year," Sylvia said precisely.

"It's been too long; that's all I know," Rick answered, winking at Josh. "Too dadgum long. Hey, I can talk to your parents more later. Maybe you and I should take a ride."

"Yeah!" Josh exclaimed, shaking off his lethargy. Rick's vehicles of choice were cool motorcycles. Ever since Josh had turned seven—following a vigorous and prolonged series of beggings—he was allowed to ride behind, at least on side roads, and feel the wind in his hair. It was practically tradition.

"Not a chance," Tim countered. "What are you thinking? You've got beer all over your breath!"

"Whoa," Rick waved his hand. "I didn't say right *now.*"

"Don't even try, Rick. That's exactly what you said and exactly what you meant."

Rick made an exaggerated motion of surrender. "Fine, no problem. I can give him a ride tomorrow."

Sylvia exchanged a quick glance with Tim and put out a feeler. "What do you mean, tomorrow?"

"Too . . . mor . . . row," Rick said with a smirk, drawing out each syllable, gesturing with his hands as if Sylvia were a child. "It means not today, but the *next* day. Not today, but the next—"

"Where you staying, smart mouth?"

"That's the best part." Rick grinned. "I figured I'd kick back with you guys for a day or two. You know, spend some time with the fam. I don't mind the couch."

Sylvia covered her mouth. "You got fired, didn't you?" she whispered.

Rick was, or at least had been, a civilian analyst at Tinker Air Force Base in Oklahoma City, stationed at the famous Building 3001, the massive hangar and administrative complex responsible for such craft as the KC135. He had explained to Josh once that they also did maintenance and repair of numerous engines, including F-16 and F-15 fighter jets. Josh didn't know many particulars about his uncle's job, except that he got to be around some really cool planes. Supposedly, after high school, Rick had wandered for a couple of years before joining the army, getting some discipline, some skills, finding a real knack for math, crunching numbers, systematic thought. He spent six years in the military before an honorable discharge and a good recommendation gained him a spot at Tinker on the civilian side of things. But his career had proven tumultuous thus far.

"What?" Even in his stupor, Rick could not hide his surprise. "'Course not."

"Yes, you did. I can tell. You're trying too hard. Either that or you're on probation. Again."

"Would you stop playing the big sister!" Rick shouted. "Just once in my life, would you stop? Is that too much to ask?"

Tim immediately turned to Josh, calmly said, "Son, why don't you head out to the front yard and play. Maybe ride your bike. I'll come out in a minute and we'll play catch."

"But, Dad—"

"Go," Tim commanded. Josh, still wearing coat and cap, obeyed.

Behind him, the voices of the adults continued, low and terse. Josh was too tired to play. With the full sun of late afternoon having warmed the day quite a bit, the previous bitter cold now felt merely chilled. He sat on the steps of the front porch and, having nothing better to do, blew hard into the air, watching his breath billow and rise, grayish white, blending into nothing. Breath after breath he watched disappear, until finally his lungs ached and his head was light.

At one point he heard his mother shout, "How dare you!" muffled though it was through the wall; after which the voices turned low again— low, lethal, incomprehensible. Josh could pretty well guess what they were saying. Mom and Dad had problems with Uncle Rick. Seemed like they always had. Things were always tense whenever he was around, even when his name came up in conversation. Uncle Rick was a perpetual boy, they would say. Josh had heard his mother on a couple of occasions, talking with his Dad, calling Rick's problem the Peter Pan syndrome. Josh knew the story of Peter Pan, but didn't know what a syndrome meant. When he asked one time, all his mom would say was, "Uncle Rick is a good person, but he doesn't want to grow up." Then she ran to her bedroom and closed the door.

Josh liked Uncle Rick. Always had.

By now, he was starting to get cold. He figured he probably hadn't been sitting outside long, so he considered his options. Maybe he could just slip in the back door and sneak into his room. That way he wouldn't get in anyone's way. He took one more breath, blew, watched. Inside, he heard his dad say something strong, couldn't tell what. As Josh was about to rise, the front door ripped open. Uncle Rick stormed out.

"Fine!" Rick shouted back. "It's no wonder I only come once a year!"

He slammed the door, swearing. Neither Tim nor Sylvia bothered to open it again. No retractions were offered, no soft words spoken. Rick clenched his fist, turned a half circle, eyes darting here and there as if looking for something to punch. Finally, he started kicking and scuffing the porch with his boot.

"Man!" he said, plopping down beside Josh.

Josh didn't know what to say, so he sat very still.

Rick pressed both palms against his eyes, moaning. His gaze settled on Josh, beside him on the steps. As if sparked, he grinned and cocked his chin towards Josh. His eyes narrowed to thin slits.

"Looks like I'm not staying this time, General," he said. In his voice there was a hint of danger.

"Heading back to the city?"

"Yeah, yeah. Heading back. I really hate it, though."

"Hate what?"

"Well it's brand-new and all. We haven't even broken it in yet. For our tradition."

"What's new?"

Rick pointed. Josh followed his finger. He couldn't believe he hadn't seen Rick's brand-new motorcycle sitting there, a Honda Shadow Sabre—all black and chrome and cool. Uncle Rick put his arm around his nephew and shook him gently. He *was* acting funny, Josh knew. He also knew he shouldn't even consider what was about to happen. But the inevitable offer was simply too tantalizing to resist.

"Wanna ride, General?"

Fifteen minutes later, the front door to the Chisom home burst open. Clamoring for help, obviously panicked, Rick pushed his way in, limping quickly along, supporting Josh with one arm around his waist. Josh was screaming, holding up his left hand, gone limp at the wrist. A second later everything degenerated into chaos. Sylvia rushed from the back bedroom down the hall, saw Josh, dropped to her knees, began scouring for clues.

"What happened?" she demanded frantically. "How did this happen!"

Tim took one glance, turned fiercely on Rick. Everyone started shouting at once. Josh's arm was badly scratched, streaked with blood. Sylvia dashed to the kitchen, returning with a handful of wet rags. After a few gentle wipes, she determined the cuts were superficial. Josh's coat was torn and the left knee of his jeans shredded. The skin beneath had already bruised.

"I'm so sorry," Rick moaned, releasing Josh to fall into Sylvia's lap, pushing his hands against his temples. Dazed, he was unable to pay attention to Tim's questions, just kept hovering over Josh. "It's not serious. I just thought a little ride might be fun before I left. I'm sorry, Josh. You know I didn't mean it . . ."

Tim stomped his foot and shouted, "You did what?"

Rick's cheekbone was bruised. His pant leg was torn. Tim stared wildly, eyes wide and hard as granite. He curled his fists in Rick's jacket collar and shoved him against the wall. "What did you do to my son?"

"We were riding," Rick stuttered. "He had on his helmet, I promise! I was showing off a little bit. I took a turn pretty sharp and the bike slid on the gravel, but it wasn't that hard of a fall. He must have hit just right."

Sylvia tried to touch Josh's wrist, to move his hand, but the motion brought a howl of pain.

"I think it's broken," she told Tim worriedly. Hearing that only made Josh cry harder. "We'll need to take him into the emergency room."

She scooped Josh up into her arms and headed for the door.

"You're going to be fine, honey," she whispered soothingly. "Everything's going to be fine. It's just a broken bone. These things can be fixed. Shh . . ."

Uncle Rick watched her walk away, his face pained. He stretched out his hand toward her.

"Just an accident," he kept saying. "There's no way it should be broken. No way."

Hoping to find Tim, to explain further, he spun around. From two inches away, Tim's knuckled fist crunched into his jaw. Rick toppled to the floor. Tim grabbed his coat and headed out the front door.

"I'm sorry, so sorry," Rick murmured, still reaching towards the door, a drowning man in search of a lifeline. Outside, the Chisoms loaded into Tim's beat-up old Chevy and cranked the 350, accelerating so fast the wheels screeched. Behind them, hazy through the screen door, Sylvia saw Rick, still reaching towards her.

5

Early the next morning, before most staff arrived, with the winter sun rising cold and pale, Stuart Baker sat in his office, flattened the center crease on a fresh, inky edition of *USA Today*, and scanned the headlines. True to form, page one was nothing but breezy, brightly hued coffee fodder. Stu read with half a brain.

Stu Baker was a relic Deadhead who still collected old bootlegs of Jerry Garcia in action and thought marijuana should be legalized. He was not some time-warp poster child, just a one-bullet gun: fighting to preserve life, but caring little for people. When the human inventory was threatened by soulless, microscopic, biological entities—well, that was almost fun. Kinder souls would try to preach to him from time to time, tell him he ought to care about something for a change. Care for *someone*. Most learned to avoid him altogether, unless a signature was required. Even the sentiments of those who openly admired him were usually conducted from a safe distance, and for purely technical reasons.

All this from a man who daily bore the irony of being named after the car he was conceived in. It had always been something of a joke, even to Stu, but that was about as far as his sense of humor went. The first of four siblings, he was the smartest and most successful; had been married once, but his wife passed away years ago; was estranged from his adult daughter, who several years ago had retreated into the Pacific Northwest and practically disappeared. He had a dog. Had three computers: a desktop, a laptop, and a Palm PDA. That was pretty much Stu D. Baker's life, and for all he knew, it was as good as life was meant to be.

Page two, flip, scan. Page three, flip, scan. Another presidential scandal. Partisan bickering. Human rights violations in China. A movie star with a cause. And—at what must be number 21,834 in an ongoing series—yet another painstaking analysis of what the latest sixteen-point shift on Wall Street meant for the nation's collective portfolio.

Nothing, nothing, nothing. Pretty colors and pop journalism.

Draining the last of his cup, he wiped his eyes and was about to toss the rag in file thirteen when a little blurb on page eight caught his attention. The headline was simple:

"SLEEPER" LATEST IN RASH OF NEW COMPUTER VIRUSES

His interest piqued, Stu skimmed the article: four paragraphs describing what the experts had determined was a curious, nonthreatening virus, discovered only two days ago. The one thing that alarmed the experts was how effectively the virus replicated itself. Replication served no real purpose, it seemed, other than to display a cryptic countdown message, which changed daily. A quoted FBI source called it an anonymous college prank. The article ended with the simple recommendation to delete the file and forget about it.

Stu stared at his computer thoughtfully. Unjuiced, the screen was flat black. He punched the power on button and waited for boot up. A minute later he was staring curiously at the Windows desktop. Nothing looked different. Where was Sleeper? He continued staring. Finally, he reached for his mouse. The moment he moved the cursor the entire screen faded to black and a message appeared. The letters were plain, nothing fancy, white on black, fifteen-point Courier:

In 68 a vision famed,
Four remain until the same.

When he moved the cursor again, the message went away. The Windows Start screen reappeared. In fact, no amount of movement or clicking would bring the message back. Stu stroked his chin thoughtfully. He jotted the words down on a corner of the newspaper, tore the strip of paper off, and stuffed it in his pocket. His Palm beeped at him. Stu pulled it out and read the reminder: *"Call Josie this morning."*

Stu groaned. He didn't want to call his daughter. Actually, he did— but it hurt to think she might not answer. Again. For nearly a decade, correspondence had consisted of two postcards, both from her, listing a new address or phone number, nothing more. They hadn't actually spoken in years. He tapped the thirty-minute-delay option on his Palm, pushed it aside, wiping his eyes. Stu was a morning person by nature, but not without a little help. He grabbed the balled handle of his polished cherry wood cane and aimed for the office coffeepot.

Black, no sissy stuff.

• • •

Midmorning, Sylvia hung around the phone, waiting for the doctor to call. She had used a vacation day to stay home with Josh. X-rays from the night before had revealed a clear fracture in the smaller of the two wrist bones. He was put in a cast and, some two hours later, sent home. None of the three Chisoms had spoken on the way back from the emergency room. Josh was wiped out, not even bothering to change his clothes for bed.

Still tired this morning, he forwent breakfast in favor of a couple more hours of sleep. Rick was there, too, having begged for the chance to make sure Josh was all right. He had spent the night and was now sitting in the living room, shirtless, reading the paper. It didn't seem as if he even heard the ringing phone beside him.

Sylvia picked up from in the kitchen.

"Hello?"

"Hi, Sylvia. This is Frank."

"Dr. Perkins, hi. Is everything all right?"

"Oh, I think so. How is Josh?"

"Fine," Sylvia replied. "He's sleeping."

"Good. Let him rest. Listen, would you mind bringing him in later today for some additional blood work?"

Sylvia hesitated. "I'm not sure I follow. Is something wrong?"

"No, not necessarily. Don't get all worried. I've just been studying his x-rays and have a couple of routine exams I'd like to run. I want to cover all the bases. Is that all right?"

"Are you concerned about something?"

"Not at the moment. That's why I want to run more tests. To eliminate doubt."

"Umm, Dr. Perkins, we don't have the kind of money to just throw on extra tests if it's not—"

"I'd like to do these tests, Sylvia. I think we *should* do these tests. We'll worry about the money later. I'll make it right with you, somehow."

"Okay . . ."

"Could you bring him in? My nurses will make room in the schedule today."

"Today . . ."

"Yes."

"Fine."

"I'll transfer you to the front desk, then."

"All right." Sylvia gulped. Before she knew it, a receptionist was asking her polite questions in a soft voice and Sylvia was answering them, scheduling a one o'clock slot for unknown blood work. When she hung up, she could think of nothing else to do but sit in the easy chair.

"More tests for Josh?" Rick asked.

Sylvia nodded and said nothing.

"Any problems?"

"Don't know."

"I wouldn't worry about it," Rick replied, sounding cool. He never even lowered the paper. "Probably nothing."

Going to the doctor was never fun, even if it meant missing a day of school. So when Sylvia told Josh of the afternoon appointment, his feelings were mixed. He didn't much care for needles. They ate lunch together—PBJs just like Josh liked with strawberry jelly and slices of banana—though he still didn't seem too hungry and played Yahtzee on the carpet beside a floor vent. The warm air reminded Josh of the feeling of hiding under his bed sheets with a flashlight, until his own breath made it so hot and stuffy that he had to throw back the covers for a gulp of cooler air. By contrast, in the summer, he loved nothing more than to come in from the heat and lay his face against this vent, letting the chill of the air conditioning curl through his lengths of hair, billow down his shirt, and graze the skin of his back.

He got Yahtzee twice, and whooped and hollered. Uncle Rick joined in the second game, under Sylvia's watchful eye. Josh beat them both.

Rick asked if he could tag along to the doctor's office. Sylvia acquiesced. The ride to the clinic was quiet, and short. Sylvia signed Josh in and sat down, reached for a magazine, and began flipping pages. Josh could sense her unease. Uncle Rick grabbed *Sports Illustrated* but didn't sit long. In short order he excused himself to the rest room.

"No big deal here, Josh," he said, tapping his nephew on the shoulder as he passed by. "They poke you with a needle and give you a sucker. Easy money."

Josh slowly surveyed the room. There were old people, wrinkled and worn; young mothers with babies, fearful of their responsibility. A few women his mother's age—tired, tense, terse. But mostly old people. Since the clinic served the region beyond the city of Lawton's reach, primarily attracting a rural, aging population, the need for specialists was few and general practice, great. Like Dr. Perkins, most of the physicians were family practitioners.

Hands folded in his lap, Josh watched the people: coming, going, fussing to get comfortable. He saw the teenage boy in the back with the headphones, bobbing his head slightly to the silent rhythm. He saw the two old women whispering, neither very happy. He saw the old man who stared at him with a look of complete disgust, though Josh had a feeling his disgust was likely the reason the old man was visiting the doctor. At eight years old, Josh just knew these sorts of things. Whenever he settled upon something, he did not care so much about visually processing the object, as most do, but rather the shape, texture, and feeling of the space it occupied. Joshua hardly ever *looked* at anything. He *studied*. Others calculated, analyzed, drew conclusions. Josh absorbed. So when he giggled, perhaps at the flight of a butterfly or a funny looking snowman—any distraction, really—though his laughter was every bit a child's, his eyes would brim with something very much like memory, as if he were drawing out of the well of his own soul some secret history, some intimate connection to the object which he himself had not yet encountered.

"Joshua Chisom," a nurse called, standing in the doorway with a clipboard.

Josh hopped up. Sylvia dropped her magazine. Both followed the nurse to an examination room. Josh jumped on the cushion covered with a fresh sheet of noisy paper.

"Okay, let's see what we have here. You must be Josh?"

The nurse was young and pretty, blonde. Josh smiled.

"I have a few tests I need to perform, Josh. Are you a brave boy?"

Josh shrugged.

"Well, I need to draw some blood from your arm. Some kids think that hurts a little, but some like to make it a game and see how tough they can be, especially little boys."

Josh shook his head doubtfully. "I'm not very tough."

"Oh, I bet you are. I bet you're stronger than you think."

"What are these tests?" Sylvia asked.

"Looks like I've got a chem profile and CBC and . . . also a biopsy. But I'll send you to a pathologist at the hospital for that."

"Biopsy?" Sylvia repeated, alarmed.

"Bone marrow. I have no idea what all this is for. Could be anything. Didn't you and the doctor speak before you came?"

"I'd like to speak with him now. Before you do anything else."

The nurse clucked her tongue. "Sorry, he just got called to the hospital to deliver twins. If he had known you wanted to see him, I'm sure he would have stopped in." She smiled, but it was the kind of smile that discouraged further discussion. Instead she focused on Josh. "Well, little man, how's your wrist healing?"

"Fine," Josh said.

The nurse rolled up his sleeve past the elbow. As she applied an alcohol cleaning pad to Josh's skin, she said in a matter-of-fact voice, "A bone biopsy is a little unusual, but the other stuff is pretty standard. Mrs. Chisom, I could hazard a guess, but that's all it would be, and I'm really not supposed to speculate with a patient. Sorry I can't help more."

She threw the pad in the trash and tousled Josh's hair. "I wouldn't worry, though, right, Josh? Are you gonna be tough?"

Swinging on her heel without waiting for an answer, she departed, then came back a moment later with two syringes and some other equipment. Softly, so as not to frighten, she held up the needle.

"Now let's get some of your precious blood. Be strong for me . . ."

• • •

While the nurse prodded and poked, Tim was a dozen miles from the clinic, hard at work in the Quartz Mountains, a rough, low-lying range of foothills that erupted oddly from the ground in the middle of an otherwise vast flatland. To someone flying overhead, it would no doubt look as if a great giant had flung a pile of huge rocks to the ground and then walked away. The gnarled outcroppings once scraped the heavens at over twenty thousand feet tall—or so the story went. Now the tallest point was Granite Rock, at just over nineteen hundred feet. Nature lovers flocked to the preternatural beauty of the surrounding wilderness, but it was Cambrian-age stone—red granite, a beautiful rose-colored rock speckled with grays and oranges—that kept Tim busy day in and day out.

Still, the wilderness had a way of touching him, both in spirit and mind. He had always figured it was his Indian blood. Wildlife roamed freely in the refuge bordering the mountains: sixty-thousand-plus acres of buffalo, Texas longhorn cattle, elk, and deer, supported by strings of small, man-made lakes and below the outcroppings and sparse vegetation, fertile, sandy soil.

Down in the quarry, on the eastern rim of the Quartz, Tim eyed the rock, shading his eyes against the keen sunlight. Both up on the ridge and down below, the sound of equipment echoed loudly through the high rock walls: drills, concentrators, crushers, haulers. A paunchy, bearded man named Jackson stood beside him, transit and tripod in one hand, lit cigarette in the other. He and Tim were surveying the land for the next expansion of the quarry pit. Both wore old blue jeans, sweatshirts, and lined Windbreakers, hard hats and goggles.

"It looks like there's a line of smut there," Tim shouted over the noise, running his finger in a horizontal line along the southern face. His breath curled in the air. "But it's got some pretty natural cleavage vertically."

Jackson grunted, idly puffing his Winston. "Just tell me where to shoot, Chisom."

"Well, what do you think?"

"I don't see it, man. I never do. But I know you do. You're the money man."

Tim shook his head. "You're smoking the wrong stuff, my friend. In case you haven't noticed, I just make *other* people money. Or should I introduce you to my truck?"

Jackson chuckled. He set up the tripod, lining up the transit. Tim pulled out the survey maps and made a few marks. The air was chill, the quarry floor dusty. Forty feet up on the ridge, a crew was busy cleaning away the overburden to expose the granite core underneath. Tim had learned to tune out the noise, but a sharp voice grabbed his attention.

"Hey Chisom . . . catch!"

He glanced up, shielding the sun with his eyes. One of the crew above, some young punk out of high school, heaved a rock the size of a small melon up into the air and over the ridge. It was a stronger throw than even he expected. And the wind was stiff.

Tim observed the trajectory, almost out of body, incredulous at the crewman's foolishness. He didn't have time to think, only react.

"Jackson!" he shouted, diving towards his friend, propelling him out of the line of impact and toppling the transit in the process. The stone hit the quarry floor with a dull thud behind them; fragments flew. With a rock falling from forty feet, a hard hat would have done nothing.

"What the—?" Jackson roared, shoving Tim to one side and scrambling to his feet. He made a fist, shook it at the ridge. "Was that you, Max?" he shouted to the man. "You piece of . . . You better be gone before I get topside!"

At his side, Tim's walkie-talkie buzzed. The team leader on the ridge was waving at him from above. He was an older man, older than Tim.

"You fellas all right down there?"

Tim grabbed the walkie-talkie and put it to his mouth. "We're fine, no thanks to your boy. What kind of a show are you running up there, Morton?"

"Believe me, I'm about to start chewing. I just wanted to check on you first. It's the kid's first week on the job."

"It'll be his last if I have anything to do with it."

Morton dropped the line, which turned to static. On the ridge, Tim saw him take three strides, grab the kid named Max by the collar, and throw him to the ground. Another voice crackled from his receiver.

"Chisom. Tim Chisom. Location, please. This is HQ."

It was Steve, assistant supervisor for Red Rock Corporation.

"I'm in the floor of quarry three, making lines," he yelled into the receiver.

"Can you come topside anytime soon? The boss wants to see you."

"Give me ten, Steve. I'll be there." He replaced the walkie-talkie on his belt and handed the survey maps to Jackson. "Take a breather, Jackson. I'll be back in a few."

Jackson nodded silently, still shaken. "Good thing you were looking, Chisom. Good thing . . ."

Tim had to walk the quarry floor, climb the ladders, and head by jeep to the office a mile away. When he arrived, a hot cup of coffee was waiting for him.

"Thanks, Steve."

David Tellier, the husband of his son's teacher, came out of the office and shook Tim's hand. "Tim, come on in."

Tim followed him in and closed the door behind him. He was dirty, so he didn't sit. "What's the story, Dave?"

"I'll get to the point, Tim. We've had some personnel shifts . . ."

Instantly, Tim's stomach sank. He sipped his coffee slowly. Personnel shifts never seemed to be a good way to start a conversation with your boss. Tim had seniority over at least half the men, though. He should be safe. Besides, what else could he do? It would be just his luck . . .

"I'd like you to be overman of quarry three, Tim. Would you consider that? That'll be a salaried position with paid vacation and benefits. Thompson has some family problems and needs to transfer immediately to be with his family. Plus the work's been getting kind of sloppy."

Tim stared. He didn't move. Did he just get offered a promotion?

"Well, Tim?" David said, smiling. "I know you're the right man for the job. I didn't even bother trying to figure out a second choice, so don't put me on the spot here. Will you take it?"

"I will," Tim replied slowly. As if through a fog, he heard his own words. An overman was a foreman position, basically number three on the chain, right beneath the supervisor and his assistant. A huge grin split his face. "I will."

"Good, you can start immediately. I'll let the boys know tomorrow. Anything you would like to do officially to start your new job?"

Tim didn't hesitate. "First I'd like to call my wife. After that, the new kid, Max, is out of here."

• • •

Stu walked the perimeter of the CDC campus, sipping on a latte from the cafeteria he had spiced with a shot of Puerto Rican rum from the flask in his desk drawer. The ground under his feet was hard but dry. No snow so far this year.

The main campus of the CDC was jumbled and uninspiring. The single six-story red brick building overlooking 1600 Clifton Road could have just as easily been the Department of Agriculture, rather than the front office of the legendary disease-fighting institution. Behind the main building, unseen, the land fell away. Down this hidden hillside lay a broad complex of buildings, more than a dozen total, all interconnected, tangled evidence of the rushed pace with which the CDC had been forced to expand to accommodate the growing biological threats to world populations. It was like a hidden city, a labyrinth of laboratories, specialty divisions, animal shelters, and office and administrative space. Seven other minor facilities sprawled across Atlanta proper, a secondary network that encompassed regional centers across the United States and a multibillion-dollar annual budget.

The CDC had a colorful history. In 1942, after the Japanese attacked Pearl Harbor, the sole purpose of the agency was simple: control the spread and influence of malaria in the southern United States, home to numerous military bases and training grounds responsible for making

American troops fit for war. The agency originally bore the awkward name Malaria Control in Defense Areas and, after that, Malaria Control in War Areas, then the Communicable Disease Center and, finally, the present-day Centers for Disease Control. Ostensibly, the CDC owed Coca-Cola, of all institutions, a huge debt for its current influence in world affairs. After distributing a barrel's worth of quinine pills to protect local farmworkers from the ravages of malaria, the head of the soft drink company donated fifteen acres to his alma mater, Emory University, to convey to the CDC for development. In 1947 the CDC purchased the land for a token ten dollars, but the project languished until the mid 1950s when the same Coca-Cola boss made a call to his friend President Ike Eisenhower with plans for a building.

Now, with eight facilities in Atlanta alone, the seven thousand employees of the CDC remained distinct from all other government agencies in one critical respect: in spite of a typically bloated government bureaucracy, each staff member carried a burning sense of mission. Everyone—*everyone*—was there for one reason: they believed in what they were doing.

Although Stu was on lunch break, he wasn't hungry. Something about that Sleeper virus nagged him, but he didn't know what. Adept at computers, he nevertheless resisted geekdom, though the anarchistic lure of the dark side appealed to his libertarian instinct. Pulling the crinkled piece of newsprint out of his pocket, he read the message again for the hundredth time. He couldn't get it out of his brain. It said *something*. It was more than a prank.

In 68 a vision famed,

Four remain until the same.

What in the world happened in 1968? Or was it 1868? Did some famous psychic with a predilection for headlines grab the country's attention? Perhaps this was the anniversary of the big event?

Think, think . . .

When did the Beatles sing "Imagine"? Around then, wasn't it? What else? Man was on his way to the moon, but that didn't seem to fit.

He was suspicious that the whole thing would prove to be little more than New Age psychic drivel perpetrated by some half-crazed devotee of a wiccan priestess sitting somewhere on a sand pile in Sedona. If that were true, the very idea would ruin the chase. Anything esoteric was distasteful to Stu. Visions and such were foolishness, at least if intended literally. He had grown up in the Methodist Church and learned quite well to hate God there. But when his younger sister was sick and dying from lupus, he had prayed every night, with all his heart, for weeks on end, all the way up until the very hour she passed away. From that point on, at ten years old, he had decided there could not possibly be a God who deserved another moment of his time.

Science, however, seemed a reasonable pursuit. It offered measurable results and a predictable set of logical rules to follow. Religion, inherently immeasurable, never again gripped his heart, except in moments of scorn. Yet bitterness was never so simple. Along with religion, relationships of every stripe suffered. Stu had adored his sister, loved her deeply—unusually—for a sibling. The pain of losing her had left a deep and lasting scar. The simple choice he made was to shut down, to create a bubble, a buffer zone between his heart and intimate involvement. He could actually remember the day he made the choice. Like flipping a switch, he shut off the energy flowing to one part of his life and redirected that energy to another. Done deal. No surprise he landed in medical research. His job was perfectly suited to his crutch. He could maintain the illusion of involvement without the burden of caring.

Others paid dearly for his detachment. He married a woman who truly loved him, then proceeded to kill her with neglect. He never cheated, was never unfaithful. But there was no spirit in the marriage, no connection of souls. Within a year of their vows, she found herself searching desperately for companionship, eventually becoming rampantly unfaithful herself, a lighthouse on a shrouded beach, ever casting her beam across the dark waters toward an iron-clad vessel who never cared to respond or draw safely to shore.

She spent every day of their life together looking, listening for a signal from Stu that he cared even a little. Stu never gave that signal, because he didn't care. His wife died more lonely than if she had remained single, though she had a dozen other lovers while they were married. Their one daughter, conceived that first year of marriage, grew up in the cold shadow of her father's obsession with work and the pain of her mother's haunted eyes.

Only recently, as his career began to fade and his daughter's bitterness drove her from home, had Stu begun to even consider that most of his life might have been misspent. Old habits are difficult to break, however. To give credence to such a thought required returning even temporarily to that switch, diverting energy to the possibility of loss, and therefore regret, and therefore pain. Stu hated emotional pain.

Sitting alone on a wooden bench under the bare branches of an aging sycamore tree, he finished the last of his coffee, lit a cigarette, and considered his life. Seven years ago he was offered the position of director of the viral and rickettsial diseases division, a bureau with four hundred professionals under his command. Against his better judgment, he took the job, mainly for the money, though he convinced himself otherwise, self-righteously insisting that his office remain in Building 15, near the troops. Two years later he was promoted again to his present position. More money, more prestige. Less thrill. Nothing but downhill ever since.

His Palm beeped. He pulled it out of his pocket, tapped the teal-colored screen.

Another reminder: time to call Josie.

• • •

Later that evening, Tim arrived at home and announced that he was going to take Sylvia out to dinner, a treat, just the two of them. Since he hadn't been able to reach her by phone from the mines, he knew the promotion would yet be a surprise. Sylvia's reaction was decidedly mixed.

"I'm worried," she explained. Tim could tell there was more.

"I don't much like the idea of leaving Josh with Rick, either," he said, touching her hand, taking his best guess as to her worries. "But I want it to be just the two of us tonight."

Sylvia frowned, still hiding secrets. Tim shifted his approach away from solemnity. With winks and smiles, he kissed her deeply, declared that, by golly, they were going on a *real* date, and furthermore, there was nothing she could do about it.

So they went. Rick promised to be responsible and Josh waved them good-bye. When they climbed into Tim's old Chevy, Sylvia figured they were headed to the KFC buffet. Instead they sailed right by it on their way to Lawton about a half-hour up 62, to a nice sit-down Italian restaurant named Luigi's. As they settled in, Tim couldn't help but swallow at the prices.

"Tim, we don't have to stay," Sylvia whispered.

He stared hard at the menu for a few more minutes before laying it down, his face relaxing into a smile. "This is perfect."

When the waiter arrived, Sylvia requested the Caesar salad. Knowing she was trying to be frugal, Tim quickly canceled that. He ordered her chicken parmesan instead; he knew she loved it.

"And a sixteen-ounce prime rib for me, rare," he said proudly. Then he asked the waiter to bring a decent bottle of champagne. As he popped the cork, poured, and held out his glass to Sylvia for a toast, Sylvia could not help but giggle. She hadn't seen her husband this excited in a long time.

"Tim, what is this all about? This is more than a date."

"Maybe," Tim said, eyes sparkling as much as the drink in his glass. "Or maybe I just woke up this morning and realized I'm the luckiest man alive."

Tim stared lovingly at his wife, noticing how her eyes pulled from the color of her winter-green sweater—a thick, turtlenecked fluffy thing. For a brief moment, he was enchanted all over again with her; gratified as well to see that she had finally begun to relax, respond, anticipate. He held up the bubbly. Not knowing what else to do or say, she held up her glass. Tim poured it half full. Dozens of little bubbles in the honey-colored champagne broke free, slipping to the surface. They clinked rims together and drank.

"To the life God has given us," he said. "And . . . to a big promotion at work."

It only took Sylvia about half a heartbeat to process what he said. She had always been remarkably quick. Leaning over the table, mouth open, she squealed, clapped her hands, then jumped up, scooted around to where he sat, wrapped her arms around his neck, and squeezed.

"I ran the numbers real quick this afternoon," Tim said. "It may be a little tight, but I think, if you want, you could stay home with Josh now."

"Are you—?" she gasped, her lips near his ear. Suddenly serious, she sat back and grasped his shoulders, "Exactly how *much* of a promotion is this?"

"Enough," Tim said modestly. Then he grinned. "Actually, pretty big."

Sylvia squeezed her husband's muscled arms and said, "Tim Chisom, I am *very* proud of you." He knew she was. He also knew he had worked hard for this moment.

Tim said, "If the factory can give you a part-time job that fits with school hours and you want to see if that can work, that's fine by me. But you don't have to do anything at all. I'm overman of quarry three now."

"Ha, ha! That's wonderful!" Sylvia exclaimed. Suddenly self-conscious, she returned to her seat. Tim watched her shake her head in disbelief. "You know, I was just wondering how I was going to manage taking another day off to talk to the doctor tomor—"

Midsentence, she clipped her words and ducked her head. Too late. Tim set his glass down and asked a reasonable question.

"What's up with the doctor? It's not the wrist thing again, is it?"

Sylvia could not cover the slip, nor play it down. She had never been good at hiding her true feelings, at least from Tim. Inevitably, they leaked out. True to form, Tim saw the shadow of sadness pass over her gleaming eyes.

"Is something wrong with Josh?" he asked.

"I'm sorry, Tim. I didn't even mean to mention anything. At least not yet."

"Not yet? What's that mean?"

"Well, I was waiting for the right time. I really don't know anything yet."

The waiter interrupted them, arriving with two plates of food, steaming hot and garnished nicely. Tim cut into his prime rib and took a bite. It melted in his mouth, sweet and tender. Sylvia took a bite of her chicken parmesan and let out a soft sigh.

"Talk to me, Sylvia," Tim resumed after chewing. "What's the deal?"

"I don't know, really. Dr. Perkins wanted to run some tests on Josh.

And then when I got there, I found out he had requested a bone biopsy, but I don't know why. Really, it's probably nothing. We can talk about it later."

"But you think it's something more than his wrist?"

Sylvia brushed a strand of brown hair out of her face and pushed her glasses up on her nose. "Tim, I said I don't know."

Tim cut his steak more aggressively. There was a long pause.

"I suppose I should be thankful," he said. "Sounds like this time, at least, you were going to tell me. Or were you? When you said you didn't want to say anything *yet,* that meant what exactly? That I was only going to have to wait a week after the fact, instead of a few years?"

Sylvia closed her eyes. "No, dear. I'm sorry. You came home and had this wonderful evening planned, and were so excited, and we left in a whirlwind. I didn't know when to tell you. And I didn't know what to say. Please, can we just—"

"Biopsy," Tim mused to himself, considering the word for the first time. "That doesn't sound good at all. Isn't that the test that checks for cancer?"

He said it without thought or malice. Breath and air formed the word and left his mouth, lingering in the space between them like a pinless grenade, or the dangling fruit of the Garden of Eden.

Cancer.

As is the case with forbidden knowledge, both withdrew, subtly, one from the other. Tim felt almost ashamed he used the word or heard it or even considered it. To speak it was to validate its potential. He had bitten the forbidden fruit, and there was no escape, no spitting the bite out, pretending nothing happened. Tim wounded himself with the word, but sensed that somehow he had wounded Sylvia even more. He did not know how she had considered the word all day, yet had carefully walled off such thoughts. She was like a little girl who walks by the fence of a cemetery, knowing what is inside but never looking over the fence just the same. In the secrecy of her mind, she hadn't dared to actually enunciate the word. Now, however, it might as well have been a coiled snake on the table.

Cancer. Biopsy. Lab tests for a broken bone.

Neither said another word. They ate the rest of the meal in utter silence, hearing only the sounds of their forks clinking against the plates and ice melting in their drinks.

The drive home was long and lonely for both of them.

• • •

Etched on a small placard made of new copper—about as tall as a man's hand—in clean, Roman typeface, the sign read simply: GPS Industries. The raised letters easily reflected the blue glow of moonlight hanging over the bay. Inside the building, the front office was spare: two desks, two chairs, a computer, phone, and fax. No other decorations or furnishings of any kind were present. The air smelled salty like the sea, and stale. On the back wall, another door led down a wide hall to a much larger space, a warehouse capable of holding a great deal of inventory. Here, on the bare floor, empty of product, huddled a group of twenty people, dressed casually but monochromatically, tending towards blacks, dark browns, dark blues. None of these people was on the GPS payroll, these followers of Jean de Giscard, yet they remained fully devoted ambassadors of the GPS mission. With two exceptions, they fell between the ages of eighteen and thirty-four: prime demographics for a radical cause. Jean was the exception to the stereotype, along with another man with a long ponytail, pushing fifty, who could have been George Harrison's missing twin if he were to shed thirty pounds.

In the front office, the window blinds were pulled, preventing prying eyes, as did the darkness. The sounds of waves and boats drifted through the walls—mainly commercial vessels. GPS made its headquarters in Fishermen's Terminal in Seattle, which was located on what is called Salmon Bay. Fishermen's Terminal was home port for the vast North Pacific fishing fleet. As a regional backbone for the commercial fishing industry, the terminal annually supported more than seven hundred fishing vessels and work boats.

Lots of boats coming in and out. Paperwork. Cargo in all shapes and sizes.

Surrounding the terminal were the various neighborhoods of Seattle—Ballard, Magnolia, Queen Anne. Dozens of industries had their offices at the terminal and had done so for years. GPS Industries was an exception, having paid rent for less than two years on a five-year lease.

"What time is it?" Jean asked. He was founder, chairman, and sole employee of GPS Industries, or would have been if GPS were listed on any federal registry. But Dun and Bradstreet had no record of GPS, nor did Wall Street. Nor, for that matter, did the city of Seattle. GPS had no revenue stream, sold no product, owned nothing, marketed nothing. It rented an office and a phone line and, on three occasions in the last six months, had received cargo, either smuggled, or mislabeled on another vessel's manifest, then diverted to GPS for a fee. The third and final shipment sat on the concrete floor beside him.

"Time is 10:30," someone answered.

"Everyone's here who's going to be. We've got more than enough."

Alyssa was there, of course. She knew the plan by now, was awe-struck, terrified—had in fact developed three ulcers from the plan in the last two months. Her brain couldn't stop thinking, couldn't let go. It chased her into sleep, greeted her when she awoke. Everyone knew. Everyone feared. But they were committed. They were gathered together because the plan was unlike any ever conceived, because somewhere between wild abandon and precise logic, the plan made terrible sense. In the end, Jean's personal labor of nearly a decade boiled down to a simple question: Are you willing? Whether victim or hero of their belief system, none of the assembled men and women could refuse to consider the question.

They stood together in the overspill of a single sixty-watt bulb hanging from the ceiling, speaking in hushed voices, each sporting a carrier of some sort—backpack, paper sack. Beside Jean two cardboard boxes were stacked on top of a much larger wooden crate, stamped in black with Cyrillic letters. On the corner, in English, smaller, incomplete letters read "Sturgeon-Kiev." Regardless of whether they spoke, listened, or were silent, each face continually returned to the wooden crate, some eager, as if it might contain some rare archeological treasure, some with dread, as a primitive might look upon the statue of the god he worshiped. Jean could sense the trembling range of emotions.

"Lewinda, did you secure the tickets?" he said confidently.

"Right here," Lewinda whispered, handing over an unmarked envelope of nineteen tickets. Each was stamped for the same day of departure from Seattle-Tacoma International Airport, three days from now.

"I saw a blurb in the paper on Sleeper," someone murmured.

"Yes, I did, too."

The youngest in the crowd, a flannel-shirted, ragtop teen, said, "Check this out. I heard this radio dude mention Sleeper this morning. He was like, 'Dude! What's up with the poetry?' and I was like, 'All right, dude. Airtime.'"

Ethan was a clown. He was also the actual programmer of the computer virus. Everyone snickered, but it seemed impolitic to laugh. Jean began passing out the tickets to each member. He also pulled small travel bags from the cardboard boxes, along with watches synchronized to the second.

"Let's see the goods, already," someone said eagerly.

"Patience, friends. Patience."

Jean took a crowbar, slipped it between the slats of the crate cover, shifting his weight against the bar. He groaned and pushed. Nothing happened. The older, ponytailed man stepped up to help. As they worked together, the wood splintered and creaked and finally came loose. Inside were layers and layers of dried, smoked fish. Jean took hold of one shelf, then another, pulling out several palettes. He handed these to the people standing around him. After a few minutes of labor, the crate was empty. Puzzled, Jean studied the outside, the inside. He leaned over, ran his fingers along the bottom, exploring by touch. He found a thumb-sized nook, looped his finger and popped the bottom board open to reveal a hollow cavity underneath. From this cavity, surrounded by straw, he extracted a sealed, insulated metal box about the size of a large suitcase. The group held their breath as he spun the numbers on the combination lock. The tumblers fell into place, popped two mechanical clasps . . . and the lid opened. Artificial coolant billowed from the box.

No one moved.

"This is the real deal," Jean said, glancing up. "Everything's here."

Ethan peered over the lid and whistled softly. "Dude!"

"Brilliant," another said, as Jean shifted the container so that everyone could see. "No one will ever know."

6

On day three of Sleeper, word spread nearly as fast as the virus. A handful of major media outlets, newswires, and Internet e-zines had begun taking turns spinning the mysterious messages, alternately blowing the thing out of proportion or belittling it. Estimates of over twenty million affected computer systems in the U.S. were leaked by one source, though not a single instance of actual damage had yet to be reported, apart from loss of productivity thanks to the water cooler buzz it inspired. Even so, IT staff were working overtime to purge their corporate systems.

But the virus was sneaky.

". . . Not only does the mysterious Sleeper virus follow the recent trend of reading the host computer's e-mail records, then using that information to infect everyone in that list, it also does something more," explained the talking head on CNN. "The explosive nature of the virus is actually due to a much more insidious technique. Rather than traveling only user to user, in itself a highly effective technique utilized by the infamous 'Melissa' and 'I Love You' viruses, Sleeper also disguises itself as an e-mail attachment at the server level and is included with every mail the server transmits. The net result is that each infected server becomes a massive channel of distribution. Computer experts at the Federal Bureau of Investigation call the tactic 'flawless' and, therefore, a clear danger if repeated by a more hostile virus . . ."

Stu flipped off the channel, yawned. Though it was nearly 10 A.M., he was still waking up—rather abnormal for a workaholic. After rising with a pounding head cold and low-grade fever, he decided to call in sick and take the day off. He half considered skipping right through to the weekend, robbing everyone of their birthday plans.

Might be a good idea, he mused.

Dressed in his bathrobe and slouching in his favorite recliner in the den of his home, Stu sipped his second cup of French roast and stared out the window. Thin, gray drizzle shook in the air. Not far beyond the pastel fog, a few faint, smudged angles traced the outline of the Blue Ridge Mountains rising above the barren, knotty elms. His home was situated comfortably in Scottsdale, a couple miles east of the 285 loop, thirty minutes from the office. It was the same home he had lived in for twenty years, the same bed he had slept in, the same lampshade in the living room, the same throw rug on the hardwood floor. The only new item was the refrigerator.

Stu never took days off work, but for whatever reason, he just didn't much care today. What he wanted to do, he decided, was talk to his daughter. He looked the number up on his Palm, dialed the phone, hoping to catch her. It would yet be early there.

Two rings, three, then the answering machine: "Hi, it's me, not home. Remember, if you can't be with the one you love, love the one you're with. That's what I'm doing. Leave your number. Peace."

Three short beeps, one long. Stu cleared his throat, started to leave a message, then abruptly hung up. So much for family. Probably just as well. He marked the reminder in his Palm, "Done." Forget Josie. She never tried to call him anyway.

With nothing else to do, Stu felt free to do what he actually wanted, which was pursue Sleeper a bit further. He could surf, read up, and brainstorm. Logically, he knew the computer bug shouldn't be this big a deal, but it was. Using his laptop to log on, he downloaded the day's e-mail. Yesterday, he had purposely e-mailed something to himself so that he could snag the virus with his portable. Sure enough, there it was, listed number four of nine messages.

As before, viewing the e-mail triggered the small string of code. A new snatch of poetry appeared on screen, like a screen saver. Day three's message:

Come the purging, soon begin.
Three more days, no more sin.

Stu cussed, read the note, cussed again. Computer viruses fascinated him because of their remarkable similarity to the real thing. But what was Sleeper all about? Nothing about it made sense. Why would anyone go to the trouble to create something so successful in delivering an otherwise pointless message? There had to be more. It just didn't bear the tone of a prank. Stu remembered well enough the rush of collegiate mischief. And yes, much of it was purposefully dark and meanspirited, such as the time he had his friend call the girl he was dating to inform her that Stu had been in a motorcycle accident and was being taken to the hospital. All a lie, a foolish lie designed to take a person's emotions hostage through clever language and the risk of unbelief. At the time, his girlfriend didn't buy it, but Stu's friend was persistent. The big question was, What if?

What if . . .

For Sleeper to wrap itself in enigma and riddle made it that much more mysterious. But what if Sleeper *appeared* to be a harmless college prank by design—and that was its brilliance? What if it purposefully made itself publicly suspect, laughable, and therefore able to be dismissed by default? *Three more days, no more sin*—who could buy into such a maudlin plot? What if the irony was that Sleeper did just what its name implied, dulling people's fear with implausible braggadocio, essentially closing the world's minds only to actually follow through come day five with a total shutdown of the global computer grid? Or whatever.

The purging.

In 68 a vision famed . . .

Hard to swallow, even for Stu. Impossible, really. But the thing that kept nagging him, like a chigger bite on his brain, was the buildup. Why the clever suspense, unless there was full intent to deliver? Stu couldn't believe he was the only one thinking these thoughts. Grunting, he took his cane, stiffly stood, and made his way to the kitchen.

The coffeepot was empty. Stu reached for his cigarettes. At work he allowed only four or five a day, but at home, he didn't even try to suppress his addiction.

He dialed a friend in the IT department of a large Atlanta advertising agency. "Hey, it's me. Listen, are you guys infected with this Sleeper thing?"

"Oh, man," his friend groaned. "We have our own mail server, and the bug nailed the thing the first day. Now every computer in the place has got it."

"What's your plan?"

"Well, we're trying to clean 'em up. Thing is, Sleeper breaks its code base into four or five chunks scattered on the hard drive and randomly assigns a naming scheme to each chunk. So every computer has three, four, five chunks, with no two pieces of code bearing the same name. Remote administration is impossible. Each system has to be manually serviced."

Stu knew enough to be impressed. "What a nightmare."

"Oh, that's just the beginning. If you don't get every chunk, the overlooked chunk will regenerate the others, so you have to be incredibly thorough. We learned that the hard way."

"Okay. But what's the point, do you think? Is it dangerous?"

"I don't know, Stu. It's a pain in the rear; I'll tell you that. All its resources seem to be directed toward delivering those stupid messages, but I just can't quite . . ."

His friend sighed. Stu waited while he struggled for words.

"It's probably nothing, I suppose. Like mosquitoes in summer. There's a whole lot of 'em, and you swat for a long time, but at the end of the day all you've got is a little bite or two—no big deal. That's the buzz coming from my colleagues, anyway."

"But . . . ?" Stu urged. He heard more in his friend's voice, a hesitancy.

"Heck, I don't know, Stu. If you ask me, this thing is bad news."

• • •

December 14, 11:09 A.M.—

I cannot believe what is about to happen. It is right. I know it is. I simply cannot believe it has come to this. Jean is talking to no one, not even me. He is in seclusion. I have seen a few of the others. They look like ghosts, wandering the streets with bare expressions, wolfish and hungry. They look upon their prey with self-inflicted loathing, and yet I see penance in their faces, too. Some just wander. Others prove the virtue of the cause through their own lack. It is odd that a person can pledge their lives to order, become militant in zeal, and then explain our very purpose with the debauchery and rage of their last few moments' freedom. How ironic. We are all on the Titanic and we know it, but some of us pray while others feed the flesh. I don't mind the boys chasing a last moment of pleasure, except that there is no love in their hundred-dollar whores.

At times such as this I wish I were aboriginal. I would go to my sweat lodge, put fire to the sage . . . or perhaps pine needles . . . and in my tent of cleansing let the smoke wash me, fill my lungs until I choked. I would let it choke out the empti- ness, stinging my eyes until they bled pure tears. It is called smudging, I think.

I need to be smudged.

I know the plan is right. Even so, I am afraid and I do not know how to be free. Everything seems to be falling apart. This is what I said I've always wanted. Jean made me to want this.

I know nothing anymore. I wish I were a man and could find love so easily. I would go to the streets at once and lose myself in five minutes' passion. But I am not. I am a woman. I love a man who promised me France.

You lied, Jean. I think you knew it all along.

• • •

Reveling in her freedom, Sylvia helped herself to another scoop of no work, knowing she may in fact never have to return to the factory again. She and Josh visited the grocery store to pick up a few items. At the checkout counter, she noticed a small plastic container with a slit in the lid and a photograph taped to the side. The photo was of a little girl, three years younger than Josh.

"Please help my daughter," read the message beneath the picture. "She is five years old and has been diagnosed with leukemia. Her name is Sarah May." The address of the family was in Altus. The can was prac- tically empty. For the first time, Sylvia dropped in her spare change, plus a dollar bill or two.

Staring at the can, Josh said, "Why does God help some people and not others?"

"He's always helping," Sylvia answered. "Sometimes the help just comes in unexpected ways."

"Like your money?"

"Like my money. Exactly. That family can choose to thank God or thank the money."

"But *you* gave the money."

"All right. But God blessed us with it and just now put it on my heart to give some of that back."

She loaded a full plastic bag into each hand and headed for the automatic doors. Josh didn't say more. Plastered on the glass exit, among many other community announcements, was the same handmade poster Sylvia had seen in the factory, announcing the revival service "only two days away!"

"Bring your sick," it said. "Friday, Saturday, Sunday." Sylvia's heart fluttered.

On the way home, Josh played with his toy plane. He asked her a few questions about Uncle Rick, which she successfully evaded. Earlier that morning, Rick had left for Oklahoma City. Said he couldn't afford to take too much time off of work.

"I still have a job, you know. Can't use *all* my vacation time down here."

Liar, Sylvia thought. Her brother had done fairly well for himself, was ranked GS-13 with the operational base, and therefore trusted with some pretty sensitive stuff. But he ever seemed to teeter on the edge thanks to that huge chip on his shoulder.

Always has. Since he was a kid . . .

It was three o'clock by the time they returned. A single message awaited her on the answering machine. Josh ran in first and punched the blinking button while she struggled with the bags at the door.

"Sylvia, this is Dr. Perkins. I'd like for you to come to the clinic, please. I have some very important things to discuss with you about Joshua. If possible, bring Tim with you. Anytime this afternoon, no need to schedule a time."

"Mom, what's that all about?" Josh asked.

Sylvia shuffled to the kitchen, pretending not to hear the question. Josh persisted.

"Mom—"

"Nothing, honey. I don't know. I imagine it's about those tests they ran yesterday."

Josh put his hands at his side, watching her. "You're acting upset."

Sylvia cleared her throat. "Don't be silly. I'm not upset."

They unloaded the groceries together. The only sound was the hum of the open refrigerator. At length, Josh grabbed Sylvia by the hand. "Am I okay, Mom?"

She covered her trembling lips. "I don't know, sweetie. That's what I'm going to find out."

She didn't bother calling the mines. Instead, she drove directly there, leaving her son with Mrs. Etheridge, who was delighted to help, as usual. Tim made quick arrangements with David Tellier and departed. They were at the doctor's office by 4:00, ushered into Dr. Perkins's office immediately. His face was grave.

"Mr. and Mrs. Chisom . . . Tim, Sylvia, I have serious news. Please sit down. This won't be easy."

They sat. Sylvia reached over and clutched Tim's hand.

Oh God, she thought. *Not my son.*

Dr. Perkins asked, "Have you noticed anything abnormal about Joshua's behavior recently? Maybe fatigue or loss of appetite?"

Sylvia tried to remember. "Maybe a little. I don't know. Nothing too unusual."

"What about thirst, persistent thirst?"

Sylvia shook her head, trying to assemble a single distinct thought. Every feeling, sensation, and memory of the last eight years suddenly congealed in her brain. She couldn't focus, couldn't think of anything, could hardly breathe.

Tim said, "Just cut to the chase, doc. If you don't mind."

Dr. Perkins took off his glasses, searching their faces in turn. "I strongly suspect, based on test results, that your son has an unusual type of cancer."

Nothing, *ever,* could be worse for a parent to hear. It was like a bullet through the brain, only you kept living. What little air remained in Sylvia's lungs, or energy in her body, siphoned out, dripped from her fingers, from every pore, stolen away. She did not move. A fist to her gut could not have felt any different.

"Cancer?" Tim choked, his voice unsteady. Color drained from his face. For Sylvia, it also drained from the room, from the blue sky outside.

"Please listen," continued Dr. Perkins. "It's a condition called multiple myeloma and it *is* treatable, though with difficulty."

"Multiple what?"

"Myeloma. It is a cancer of the plasma cells."

"Plasma." Sylvia repeated. "Blood plasma?"

"Actually, plasma cells are found in *bone* marrow, which is where they are produced. As you probably know, bone marrow is the soft, spongy blood-producing tissue that fills in the porous spaces inside our bone core. Bone marrow is the factory of a person's blood supply."

Sylvia stared past Dr. Perkins's face to the window behind him, on out, into the parking lot. She felt cold. *I'm dreaming. This is all a dream.*

Dr. Perkins continued. "Part of the function of plasma cells is to produce antibodies, substances that help the body fight infection. Usually, plasma cells make up about one to two percent of all cells in bone marrow. In a person with multiple myeloma, however, a group of abnormal plasma cells, called myeloma cells, takes over and multiplies."

Dr. Perkins explained more. The symptoms of multiple myeloma varied from person to person, he said. When red blood cells, which transport oxygen, become displaced by myeloma cells, anemia resulted, leading to tiredness and fatigue. He asked again about Josh. Again, Sylvia couldn't remember, though it did seem to ring true. Also, the large number of myeloma cells in bone marrow could cause pain in the back, ribs, or other bones. Unexplained bone fractures were a sign of myeloma.

"His wrist . . ." she whispered.

"Exactly. I had no reason to suspect from the break, per se, but the x-ray of the break was my first alert."

He turned to the lightboard and flipped a switch. Hanging from the clip were three pale negatives of Josh's wrist from different angles. Dr. Perkins pointed. "You see here the unusual texture of the bones, as compared to"—he pinned up two other x-ray sheets—"these bones, from unaffected patients."

Tim peered closer. Sylvia knew he was growing frustrated. With good reason. She couldn't see any difference between the x-rays herself. The bone break was clear enough, but everything else looked like ghostly white globs. She turned away.

"In and of itself, an x-ray is inconclusive," Perkins was saying. "At best, it raised a red flag, telling me to look deeper. That's why I wanted to run those other tests, hoping the x-ray was flawed for some reason. You see, as bone tissue becomes affected by the disease, calcium from the bones dissolves into the blood, yielding a high blood-calcium level. Your son's urine sample and blood profile confirmed this: high calcium, low hemoglobin. And then when we saw the unusual protein spikes, besides albumin, well . . ."

"Well?"

"The likely cause is Bence-Jones," Dr. Perkins said, matter-of-factly.

Tim clenched his jaw. "Would you please speak English?"

Dr. Perkins shut off the lightboard and sat down slowly. "The fact that a person's body is producing myeloma cells instead of red blood cells is one problem. That facet of the disease causes a definite lack: oxygen levels, low calcium in the bones. But that's not all. Complicating matters further is not just what the myeloma cells steal, but also what they produce: large amounts of what we call a monoclonal protein. Some of these monoclonal proteins are fully formed, naturally occurring antibodies, targeted at nothing, serving no real purpose. Many are just fragments, called Bence-Jones. These fragments are a random, essentially useless chemical by-product, which the myeloma cells slough off. Neither the monoclonals nor the Bence-Jones are necessarily hostile. They just get in the way. In large enough numbers, they make it much more difficult for other important body functions to succeed. Primarily, the danger is that monoclonal protein levels will become severe enough to form excessive deposits in the kidneys. If untreated, these deposits will eventually prevent normal filtering of the blood's waste products and may damage the kidneys themselves."

Sylvia buried her head in Tim's shoulder and began to sob. Dr. Perkins clasped his hands together and spoke as tenderly as he could.

"The long and short of it is that Josh's body will have fewer and fewer resources to fight off attack. It will become unable to oxygenate itself because of the lack of red blood cells. And all the while, more toxins will develop inside from the protein buildup." He sighed. "I won't lie to you folks. My heart breaks to have to tell you. But this is a dangerous disease."

Tim's shoulders drooped.

"Isn't there a chance you're wrong?" he asked.

Dr. Perkins shook his head. "I wish that could be true, Tim. That's why I went ahead and asked for the biopsy at the same time as the other tests. I didn't want to put you all through the ringer twice. The biopsy doesn't lie."

"But the anemia. A few years back—"

"That's the thing. I checked his history. It helped clue me in, since we had his previous profile to compare to. But the anemia was not in any way related to this. Tim, you just have to accept that we're talking about a different animal now. The hemoglobin count was rock solid back then, and the calcium levels were normal. Iron was the only problem and you all addressed that."

"But the symptoms," Tim said. "They don't sound like they match. Sylvia knows that boy inside and out and what you're saying doesn't ring true."

"I agree. I wish I understood it. I wish to God I was wrong. But you've got to understand, only three people per one hundred thousand are affected annually by this disease. It is very rare. The average age of a person with the disease is around seventy. That's what baffles me the most about Josh. He doesn't seem like a candidate at all. Maybe the strength of his youth is compensating well or mounting a vigorous response. I simply don't know."

"Is it contagious?" Sylvia asked in a dull voice, pulling her hands away from her face. Her eyes were swollen, red.

"No," the doctor replied softly, handing her a tissue from the box on his desk. "And it cannot be inherited. As Josh receives treatment, if he conquers it, he will have no reason to fear that it will pass on to his own children."

"So it can be fought?"

"Absolutely," Dr. Perkins emphasized. "And with Josh's age on his side, I believe it can be won, though I must tell you such victories are rare. That's why the sooner we begin, the better. I have taken the liberty to schedule an immediate consultation with a specialist in Oklahoma City at the children's hospital. Use her as a second opinion. She will probably need to run a few more tests, but she will be much better equipped to diagnose the stage of the disease and to prescribe a model of treatment. She's very good."

Husband and wife sat together, staring vacantly. A gaping hole opened in the air between them. Tim looked like a fish in a fishbowl, suddenly vulnerable to all the world. Sylvia knew he hated to be the object of pity. He was probably trying to figure out how they would afford the treatments.

For her part, she felt like a failure, felt afraid, felt excruciating pain for her son. Somehow, it seemed like it must be her fault. Tim rose first. Collecting herself, clutching her purse, Sylvia followed.

"I'm so sorry," Dr. Perkins said as they prepared to leave. "We should all be very, *very* thankful for that broken bone."

7

The last thing Sylvia remembered before finally drifting to sleep were Tim's words, whispered across the darkness in their bed. "He's our only son. We'll find a way."

Sylvia had never considered herself much of a prayer person, at least in any formal, eloquent sense, but she talked to God—never more than in the last couple of days. Usually she just gabbed, plain language, highly conversational, though she usually felt lacking as a result. Half the time she didn't even make sense, rambling along, venting emotion. Leaking otherwise private thoughts.

At present, she couldn't have cared less how polished she sounded. Staring at the ceiling above their bed, with Tim snoring softly beside her, she whispered desperate words, unconcerned with fluency. She prayed to a God she had grown to love deeply for many reasons, not the least of which was the way he had mended her wounded heart. After believing for so long that no one cared, such affection was no small feat.

As she prayed, a thought struck her, so clear and yet so familiar that she wasn't sure if it was her own, or some sort of divine reply. She realized Josh was *the promise God never overtly made to her, but kept anyway*. It was a striking revelation, and hardly arguable, since the impact could be clearly seen in her life. From the moment the gift had been given—a child, Josh, but also so much more—she had embraced her new role with both fierceness and gratitude. This in turn triggered a deep process of healing from the sorrows of her childhood, the loss of her parents, and the particular and secret pains of being a foster child. In spite of an otherwise vivacious personality, the fact was that Sylvia had struggled with bitterness most of her life. Yet in her love affair with Tim, realized most fully in Josh, God had slipped through the hardened cracks and found her with unseen strokes of grace and truth. Like snowflakes on warm skin, he had gently melted the pain. How? She didn't know, except that in the past ten years she had grown more feminine, less abrasive, than she ever thought possible.

Now, all she could think was, *Not my son,* and she kept thinking it, repeating it, over and over. It was her simple, singular petition on the ride home from the clinic; through a silent, brave-faced dinner; on into the night. Lying in stillness, breathing hard, with tears streaming down her face, she pleaded with God, plagued by fear. She prayed and prayed.

You gave your Son. Please don't take mine.

Couldn't the God who healed her heart heal her son? Around four in the morning, exhaustion overcame her. She fell asleep believing the answer was yes, hoping she believed enough, that her pastor was wrong, that miracles still happened.

At seven, she awoke, fixed breakfast, made ready for the whole family to leave. She and Tim both agreed she should let the factory know she was quitting before leaving for the city. If Josh were in for the fight of his life, there was simply no point in messing with the job. Likewise, Tim called Red Rock, taking Thursday and Friday off, using vacation days. Tellier could have barked on such short notice, but instead he was sympathetic—a pleasant relief.

Though she would slip for a few minutes at a time, Sylvia refused to allow herself the luxury of grief or self-pity. Perhaps it would have been therapeutic. In the face of a disease like cancer, however, such expenditures of time and energy must give way to many more pressing concerns. All she knew to do was to switch to battle mode. After leaving Dr. Perkins's office and drying her eyes, she knew she faced the choice: cry or fight. She chose to fight.

It was Thursday. By the time Josh awoke, the house was bustling. At a little past eight o'clock, husband, wife, and child loaded two bags with a couple of changes of clothes into the old truck and set off.

That morning, Sylvia had woken with a brief thrill of hope in her heart. But as their '85 Chevy pulled out of the driveway and she looked back on their home shrinking in the distance, lost amid the trees, she could not resist the sinking feeling that, somehow, they were driving away forever. Whatever kind of life they had lived up to this point would soon be no more.

They were en route to Oklahoma City. Dr. Perkins had successfully arranged for an immediate consultation with a pediatric oncologist there. Some of Josh's data had been faxed direct; the rest he sent in a folder with the Chisoms to hand-deliver.

Pointed towards the eastern horizon, curls of vapor trails, like paper shavings, hung low in the sky, playing games with the pale winter sun. One by one those few clouds skittered briefly across its burning smile. Like moth wings, each would ignite around the outer edges first, then the whole belly of the cloud would glow incandescent white.

The engine in the cabin of the truck was loud, open-throttled; the buzz of the tires skimming over the concrete was hypnotic. It was a new day. Despite the somber sense of mission with which Tim gripped the wheel and the empty longing with which both he and Sylvia watched the yellow slashes blur past on the road, their mood, while far from light, was surprisingly composed. For whatever reason, whether because each was unwilling to speak for fear of stealing hope from the other or because the scripture was true—mercies *are* new every morning—the silence was not unbearable. Quite the opposite; for Sylvia it was a relief not to speak.

Beside her, Josh did not seem so inclined. Sandwiched in the middle of the bench seat between her and Tim, he had complained three times about how hot it was. Wiggling out of his coat, he announced, "I don't *feel* sick."

It sounded to Sylvia as if he was trying to make a point, to put their minds at ease even more than his own. Sylvia placed her arm around her son. "I know, honey. We're going to double-check some things and see what the doctor has to say. This doctor is a specialist for kids. She might know some things we don't."

Tim stared straight ahead. "You just keep on feeling good, Josh. You feel as good as you want to."

And then they were quiet again. Sylvia found herself yearning to know Tim's thoughts. In the silence, she needed to feel joined to him. Husband, wife—at the same time, mother, father—together, they were as blind men groping in the dark, feeling for the right tone to take with Josh, but also with each other.

After an hour or so of driving, Josh yawned and fell asleep, his head against Sylvia's shoulder. Though it should have been a nonevent, both adults were solemnly aware of the fact that their child was sleeping—never mind that they themselves were tired, that road trips can knock a person out, especially a child. They watched the road, left the radio untouched. If they spoke it was only a word or two at time. As the sun climbed higher in the sky, they joined I-40, and their course began to edge as much north as it did east, towards the state capitol. Tim drove with a heavy foot. Josh snored.

When Josh awoke, he asked a single question. "Mom, why don't you and Uncle Rick get along?"

Taken aback, Sylvia stumbled over her words. "There are things we disagree on."

That had always been enough in the past. Not today, though.

"I think there's more," Josh said. "You just aren't telling me."

"What do you mean?"

"Well, you and Dad sometimes fight, but you don't treat him mean like you do Uncle Rick."

"Ha!" Tim snorted. Sylvia reached across the bench seat and poked him lightly in the ribs.

Josh pressed in. "I'm serious. I think you and Uncle Rick *try* not to like each other. I don't know why. He doesn't seem so bad to me."

Feeling put on the spot, Sylvia fidgeted. She wasn't really in the mood for a conversation about Rick. "Josh, it's a long story. The only thing I can say is that things get messy sometimes. Brothers and sisters don't always treat each other as nice as they should."

"So is that why you didn't have more kids? Because you figured we might not get along, either?"

"Not at all. I was *lucky* to be able to have you. Remember, Josh: you were born special. How many times have I told you that? Born for a reason. A gift from God. I wish I could have had more, just like you, but my tummy hasn't always worked as well as it's supposed to—"

"Why?"

"Do you mean how is it supposed to work?"

Josh nodded.

"Well," Sylvia said, measuring her words. "It's supposed to be able to bear children. That's what makes a girl's tummy special."

She hoped that would suffice, that the questions would die down— that Josh would become distracted by anything: the road, the clouds, the cast on his wrist. He did not.

"You and Uncle Rick should stop hurting each other," he said flatly. "We're all supposed to forgive, *remember?*"

"Watch your tone, Son," Tim warned.

Sylvia said, "Josh, we should forgive. I don't know what else to say. I know it's hard to understand, but some things happen to folks that cannot ever be changed. Ever. Even when there is forgiveness. That just seems to be the way of it."

"Things can always change," Josh countered. "You just have to want it bad enough."

He withdrew into silence after that. In her heart, not even thinking of Rick but the boy who said the words, Sylvia thought, *I want it more than you can possibly know.*

Tim said, "Looks like we're almost to the big city . . ."

Finally, a suitable distraction. Josh sat up in the seat, eyes wide and excited.

"Oh boy!"

The doctor's name was Sung Li and she was Korean. As she explained it, she was actually from Brazil, the daughter of missionaries. Slender, attractive, a youngish fifty if Tim were guessing, she told them to call her Sunny. She was one of nearly four hundred staff pediatricians and pediatric specialists at the hospital—the only freestanding, full-service pediatric facility in the state. Like the majority of the staff, she was also a member of the faculty at nearby University of Oklahoma's College of Medicine. The three exchanged quick greetings, then Sunny bent down to Josh's level.

"You must be Frank."

Josh's eyes fell to the floor. He shook his head no, dark bangs tumbling over his forehead.

"Charles? Tom? Alexander?"

More head shakes. *No, no, no.*

"Salvador? Mazula?"

Josh giggled, refused to look up. Sunny reached out, fingering his shoulder-length hair. "Not many boys come in here with hair as dark as my own," she said, holding her own hair out for inspection. It was straight, thick, the color of sable. Strands of gray sparkled here and there like delicate, silvery waterfalls. "Nor is it ever as long. But I will tell you a secret, if you like."

She waited for Josh to respond, or at least lift his face. As soon as he did, she offered him the warmth of her smile, eyes wide, inviting him into her world. As she interacted with his son, Tim studied her, forming his own first impressions. He saw how Sunny nearly gasped when she discovered for herself how far she could fall into Josh's gaze. He saw Josh, standing before this unknown woman—dutiful, wary, unfazed by her adult poise—displaying a crooked grin that was more for her sake than his own. Josh looked to Tim like one who, if told he must, would do his best to hoist the world onto his back. Sunny obviously felt this and tried to look away.

Not what you expected, is he? Tim thought. *Not just another kid.*

The last thing he would have expected was for Josh to try to make it easier on Sunny. Perhaps he sensed that she didn't really want to be afraid of him. Whatever the case, in unusual fashion, he reached out and attempted to pull her back.

"Sunny, right?"

"Yes," Sunny said, breathing deeply.

"Sunshine makes things grow."

Dr. Li smiled, waiting.

"You think you can help me grow healthy, Dr. Sunny?"

Sunny touched his face, rose, and met Tim's and Sylvia's broken eyes. "I will try my best."

The plan was straightforward. After reviewing the fax from Dr. Perkins, personal comments, and the information in the folder they gave her, Dr. Li had a battery of additional tests she wanted to run that would take much of the morning and early afternoon. There would be more blood work—complex chemical analysis beyond the scope of Dr. Perkins's lab—an MRI, and other stuff Tim and Sylvia didn't understand.

Dr. Li allowed both parents to stay by Josh's side the whole time. She tried to be gentle. Tim watched as Josh was poked, prodded, hooked up to wires, stripped of his shirt, planted with electrodes, then poked, bled, and prodded some more. Josh cried at a couple of the pricks, but generally toughed it out.

Sylvia did not fare so well. As morning dragged into afternoon, her gaze grew more dull.

"It's like my insides are being torn away one piece at a time," she whispered into Tim's ear.

Tim just held onto Josh's hand and kept repeating, "I'm here, Son. I won't leave you. I'm here . . ."

If the word *cancer* had never been said—if Dr. Perkins would have just said, "multiple myeloma, problem with the blood, serious, but treatable"—none of the tests would have caused such anguish. Even the word *disease* as a generic term, though terrible, was not so lacerating to the soul. But no, the word was *cancer*.

Josh bore it well. He had not heard that word yet, was largely free to remain a kid, playing with his plane, even though strapped to monitors and junk. Tim could tell he was uncomfortable and tired. At one point, when Sylvia began to whimper, Tim led her into the hall and admonished her, telling her that Josh would become frightened if he saw her drifting into fear. Back in the examination room, Tim tried to feed Josh with distraction, attempting a joke a time or two. Sylvia forced a laugh. Even for Tim, the humor tasted stale. Late in the afternoon, Dr. Li told them to go out and get some air, take a break, take a drive around the city. The majority of the next phase was lab work and analysis.

"In fact," she said, "if you're planning on spending the night in the city, you might as well book a hotel and get some rest. Our labs are staffed round the clock, so we'll push this through. I'm traveling tomorrow myself, but I want to see to this before I go. How does midmorning sound?"

They agreed to meet back together at ten o'clock the next morning. In the truck, the Chisoms flipped a coin to see whether it would be the Motel 6 or Super 8. Motel 6 won, and Tim was glad; it was probably cheaper. The motel wasn't far away, so they swung by, scheduled a room for one night, and dropped off their bags. Tim asked Josh what he wanted to do next. The choices were movie, mall, or zoo.

Of course, the answer was zoo.

Tim didn't hesitate. It wasn't as though they had money to burn, but he had decided early on that the last thing he was going to do was count change when, from this point on, potentially every moment counted and should be savored. If the prognosis came back favorable and all the dust and worry settled and life returned to normal, then so be it; he will have blown twenty bucks. Maybe a hundred. But he simply wasn't going to bring his son to the city, have him prodded like a farm animal, and then drag him home to await his fate. The least they could do was have some fun. *Make* some fun. Lemonade from lemons.

Sylvia begged off the trip. Tim pulled her aside. They talked. She *wanted* to fight for this moment, this chance. She told him so. She wanted to be a part of every moment. But she simply couldn't. Not right now. It was all too much, too soon.

He left Sylvia behind to grieve in her own way, which would likely be to hide in their rented room, fling herself on the cheap, stiff bedding, and search for God.

There was nothing more Tim could do for her. Off to the zoo went father and son.

• • •

Day four of the growing infamy of Sleeper. Had the Chisoms read the local weekly, *The Folin Dispatch*—printed faithfully for Thursday morning delivery "for nearly seventy-five years" as the banner line proudly claimed—they would have found that news of the virus had even made it to their neck of the woods, though tucked away on page seven behind such items as hog futures, Edna Thomlin's blackberry cobbler recipe, and the all-important price of cotton.

On the pages of *The Daily Oklahoman,* however, the story was by now front-page material.

CURIOUS SLEEPER VIRUS THWARTS EFFORTS TO
REMOVE: NONDESTRUCTIVE CODE REINFECTS 50
OF ESTIMATED 200 MILLION AFFECTED SYSTEMS

In much-more-hip Seattle, Alyssa read a different headline in the opinion section:

TO READ OR NOT TO READ: SLEEPER MAY
NOT DAMAGE YOUR CPU, BUT HAIKU HURTS EVEN WORSE

The story described the latest riddle and made a tongue-in-cheek appeal to all hackers to dip into Shakespeare next time when searching for inspiration. Alyssa didn't have to read or check the day's e-mail to know the message. She knew it by heart:

Death, they say, is the color gray
The skies are blue . . . today

Tasting the riddle over and over again, Alyssa felt the chill of it on her lips. Deep within, she smiled—a hollow gesture at best, bringing little pleasure and no comfort. Rather, like standing on a dark precipice staring into the unknown depths, dropping a pebble and waiting for the splash, Alyssa flung the shape of the destiny she had chosen into the void, waiting for its impact.

Nothing.

Even in her thoughts, where imagination took flight, even in that place she heard no echo for all she had spent, would spend; saw no ripple, found no evidence or assurance that she had ever lived, ever mattered. Alyssa was many things—compulsive, angry, needy—but rarely dishonest, at least with herself. As she contemplated the inevitable reality of the plan, the only thing she felt was fear, and that mainly for herself. After all, when a light bulb burned out, did anyone bother with wistful memories of its brilliance? No, they reached into the cabinet and got another bulb. A replacement. Easy and done.

A terrible realization hit her for the first time: *What if the plan fails?*

It was a terrifying epiphany, especially to come so late in the game. Was she the only one losing spine? Others, surely, struggled with similar thoughts, though none had yet been confessed to her. In fact, not a soul had bothered calling on her at all, whether in penitence, rage, or plain old common curiosity. Quite the contrary, the GPS crew was living as if they each planned to die. Realizing this, Alyssa felt the blood rise to her face, ashamed. She was a silly girl—weak, foolish. This was no time to be selfish. No one could back down. They wouldn't; she couldn't. It would jeopardize the plan.

Still, she had yet to hear from Jean, the voice that watered her soul. If honesty was the requisite of the moment, Alyssa could only admit that she was plagued with misgivings. At the very least, on their last night, she had hoped for more, for a kiss, a clinging—if nothing else, a tangle of flesh so that for one brief moment their souls could collide and she could hear the splash of her life, flung into the abyss, crashing on someone else's shore.

Impact.

Alone, completely alone, she turned the lamp off, sat in darkness. Husky harmonies rose from the floor—the Indigo Girls, a decade past. Their voices mingled with the jasmine sizzling softly in the brass dragon on her coffee table: *". . . spent four years prostrate to the higher mind, got my papers and I was free . . ."*

Alyssa listened, but listened more to the whispering dampness in the air. The pall that ever hung over Seattle, thick and gray, was especially wet tonight, the night especially cool. Having nothing to lose, she picked up the phone, dialed. Her fingers trembled. Jean answered, full of intensity.

"Jean?" Alyssa whispered.

"Yes."

"Jean, what are you doing?"

"I am alone. I am quiet."

"I thought we might spend this night together."

Jean breathed into the phone rhythmically, voiceless.

Alyssa said, "Doesn't that seem right? Don't you want to be with me?" Nothing.

"I want to be with you," Alyssa said bravely. "I will never be with you again."

"Stay the course," Jean murmured. "Do not call me a second time." *Click.*

Alyssa knew she would never speak to him again. In a few hours— so short!—she would be flying. And that would be the end of it. The end of all.

• • •

From its perch midsky, the late afternoon sun caused long, spindly shadows to leak across the asphalt and grass like oil spilled from a can, in vermicular shapes that occasionally resembled trees, automobiles, pedestrians. Downtown Oklahoma City was a maze of concrete and glass, like every other city. Where the money flowed it was humanized by treelined parkways, street lamps, and cobblestone. Where the money trickled there were cracked sidewalks, fading murals, chipped paint, and slums. Sometimes the contrast was only blocks apart, rich from poor.

Tim drove with a heavy heart, wishing for a flat tire.

The last thing I want, the last place I want to be . . .

They weren't on the way to the zoo after all. Just out of the parking lot of the Motel 6, Josh had decided he would prefer to visit the bombing memorial, instead; the one Mrs. Tellier had described in class. Tim attempted to talk him out of it, but Josh would not be dissuaded. Reluctantly, Tim agreed.

"But can you tell me why?" he asked.

Josh's answer was simple. "Mrs. Tellier said if we ever got the chance, we should."

So they went. Tim knew the way—knew it all too well, as many central-Oklahomans would. From the Motel 6 he managed to connect to U.S. 77, then south, then west on Northwest Fifth. They parked and slowly made their way to the reception area, full of photos, history, speeches, and essays. Tim moved skittishly through the room, herding Josh along.

From there they moved onto the broad green commons of the memorial itself, the very site where the Alfred P. Murrah Building once stood before being cut open by a truck bomb. Several other folks were there, milling about alone or clustered together, dressed in coats and gloves, snapping photos, writing, touching, talking in hushed whispers. Tim preferred to get as far away as he could from this place. But Josh tugged on his arm, leading him forward.

Hesitantly, father and son stepped toward the center, where water flowed in a long, shallow reflecting pool lined with black granite. At opposite ends of the pool stood two monolithic walls of glimmering polished bronze, called the Gates of Time—one marked 9:01, the other 9:03. Like sentries on guard, or perhaps more like the covers of a book, the gates framed the entire story of tragedy, heroism, and death. Adjoining the pool parallel to its length was a gently sloping belt of grass, and on the grass nine rows of thin, straight-backed chairs, oddly fashioned of bronze and glass.

"They look like tombstones," Josh said solemnly.

"I think they're supposed to."

One hundred sixty-eight protruded from the ground, one for each person killed.

"How many were kids?"

Tim put his hand on Josh's shoulder. "Nineteen, Son."

Together, they stared down the muted rows. For Tim, the symmetry, the austere lines, were an invitation not only to beauty, but pain and memory. Reconciling the purposeful order of the memorial with the stark reality of the event it symbolized was a difficult task. And that was the point. Strolling the length of the memorial, pausing, reading, holding Josh's hand, Tim felt the struggle within himself. He remembered all too well the broken bodies, children pulled from the rubble, weeping rescue workers, the tangled carnage of rock and steel. Here, on this very plot of earth beneath his feet, the Murrah Building had stood, and in between the bronze slabs, in the middle of the reflecting pool, where Northwest Fifth Street once ran, a Hertz truck had parked.

Loaded with an explosive, organic compound, it detonated at precisely 9:02, April 19, 1995.

Living souls. In a moment, snuffed out.

It seemed so long ago. Now, to be present, all over again, to view the earth and know the history, to gaze upon the stillness of the water where the bomb exploded, to touch the massive bronze walls and then peer down the neat rows—simultaneously beckoning the thoughtful to draw closer, yet warning them to keep their distance—the experience was provocative and unsettling. As they walked, in the way Josh clung to his father's hand and the questions he asked, Tim knew even he could sense something sacred about the place.

What Josh could not sense, at least fully, was how with each step, each question, Tim withdrew more and more. His son had cancer. Life was changing. The paradigm of the future had been irrevocably altered. And he was here, here of all places, standing in a memorial, where . . .

Press on, he reminded himself. And he did his best to press on.

After drifting below, they made their way beyond the memorial, up sloping grass to the periphery, where an American elm leaned to one side and spread its empty branches over the earth. A sign told the story of the tree. It was nicknamed the Tree of Life. Though scarred and burned, it had survived the blast. It lived, even thrived, turning green again and blooming with each new season, giving shade to visitors and serving as inspiration to those still struggling to cope with their loss— even after all the years. Josh was immediately fascinated with the tree, rubbing the bark of its thick trunk gently with his palm.

Tim watched him move his lips silently. *Tree. Of Life.*

The name obviously triggered remembrance of the story of the Garden of Eden. As the rambling trails of his imagination led him away, Tim found himself wondering what it must have been like, to not know sin. How did that feel? How did it feel for Adam, as a grown man, to live from his heart in complete innocence? Stuck on the other side of carnal knowledge, the very possibility was nearly impossible to fathom. What was it like when the sweet taste of the fruit dripped down his chin, and his glory was suddenly stolen? What was it like for the first lingering sensations of death and impermanence to creep through his bones, his muscles,

his blood? What did it feel like for the eternal to surrender to the tempo-
ral within his own soul, bowing low, tarnished in disgrace? Standing
beneath the Tree of Life, gazing over the hillside, Tim was eyewitness to
at least part of the answer. It meant bombs and killing. Disease and death.

Even for children.

Many whose lives were stolen at this very site were younger than Josh.

Father and son found seats together on the retaining wall near the
tree. From that place, elevated above the memorial, both grew still.

At length, Josh spoke. "So you get a memorial for dying?"

"Not always. Not everyone."

"Just if you're important?"

Tim thought for a moment, then said, "This was different. Bombs
don't usually go off in a place like this, Josh. Everyone was shocked. It
wasn't supposed to happen here."

"I get that. But people die all the time."

Tim grasped the difficulty his son was experiencing. Beholding a
shrine for the first time, Josh needed to understand why it mattered so
much that *these* people died.

"Maybe it's because they were innocent victims and didn't deserve to
die," he said softly. "Maybe because of that they are heroes. Maybe this
is all here, and all this money spent, because sometimes people just
know that we can't ever allow ourselves to forget . . ."

They lingered a few moments more, neither speaking.

Tim said, "We should get back to your mother."

And so they wound down the slope from the tree, past the pool and
the chairs carved with names, into the reception area, retracing their
steps to the parking lot. Sharp-eyed, Josh stopped in his tracks as they
passed by a wall laden with photos. He stepped closer, closer again.
Then he whispered: "Dad, is that *you?*"

Tim closed his eyes and swallowed. He had hoped, so fiercely hoped,
to escape. Peering more closely at the photo, he sighed.

"That's me."

In the photo he looked younger. Wearing official rescue worker garb,
he had a miner's helmet on his head, with the light shining. It was dusk
in the photo, but the torn rock of the fallen building was unmistakable in

the background. It looked like a war zone. Tim's face was covered with dust and soot, his hair matted, his body obviously weary. In his arms he carried a young boy about Josh's age. Underneath the photo were the words *"An anonymous volunteer saves a young boy's life."*

"You worked *here?*" Josh whispered, eyes fixed on the photo as if it were a magical talisman and he, lost in its spell. His voice held the kind of wonder only a son can muster, and for which only a father is worthy.

Tim's answer was flat, simple. "I work with rock. They needed people with experience. When officials called around looking for help, I figured I'd done that sort of thing before, at the quarry." He stared at the photo once more, his voice low and strained. "I'd never dealt with this, Josh. And I never want to again."

As his son stared into his face, Tim couldn't hide the haunting, the pain.

"We can go now," Josh said softly.

8

They did not carpool. They did not look for one another or wave or pretend to know. But if anyone had a reason to notice and the ability to survey the whole airport at once, he might have thought it strange that during the early morning hours, right around five o'clock, some seventeen or eighteen people, dressed in black jeans, black pants, black T-shirts or turtlenecks or sweaters, all drifted anonymously into the airport—a ragamuffin band of nobodies, each carrying a simple bag of identical looking carry-on luggage.

Of course, the many strangers drifting about, standing, reading, checking their watches, would have no reason to notice one more stranger passing through the glass doors, making his or her way to the first available check-in counter. The entire process had been carefully scripted for months to appear completely unscripted, casual, typical. Each went to a different terminal, serviced by a different airline, headed for a different destination. Each carried a unique ticket, traveling under his or her own name. No observer would suspect that a wholesale invasion of the planet was underway.

And so, while the custodians slowly walked the floors, pushing the motorized, red-wheeled buffing machines, leaving the broad floor shiny behind them, scuffless for thousands of new feet to scuff; and sleepy business travelers made last-minute phone calls to spouses, lawyers, and partners; and the steam rose from the gratings in the street like foam washing ashore; and the cafés and grills prepared big, fresh, stiff pots of coffee; the loyalists of GPS slipped unobserved into Seattle-Tacoma

International Airport with tickets in hand, like grains of sugar melting in water. Some smiled; some were grim-faced; some glanced furtively over their shoulder as if they feared being followed. Some had a loopy, drugged look in their eyes. Nothing strange at all for an airport, really; not by a long shot.

By all accounts it was just another day of work: for the shopkeeper selling the magazines, the cart vendor with the soft, doughy pretzels and fake cheese sauce, and the uniformed lady behind the computer, smiling graciously, checking baggage. Just another ordinary day.

At each terminal, at each checkpoint, the invaders were asked the standard security questions: "Do you have any knowledge of dangerous materials in your bag, has your bag at any time left your person since your arrival here, and/or have any strangers asked you to carry foreign materials in your bag?"

At each terminal, the foot soldiers of GPS politely shook their heads, "No, nothing, thank you," and moved on.

At the x-ray machine, each dutifully surrendered his or her bag, which was properly scanned and shown to contain—if anyone had been able to correlate—pretty much the same stuff. Three changes of clothes, basic toiletries, some paperwork. Not much else. A couple of overzealous security workers asked to open the bags, a request to which Jean de Giscard's disciples readily complied. Inside, the metal tube under suspicion proved to be nothing but a can of brand-name deodorant. No big deal. Just another ordinary traveler on another ordinary day.

One and all passed easily through security, to their respective gates, awaiting their 747s or 777s or, as in Alyssa's case, a DC-10 bound for Vienna in two short hours. Though many would not depart for hours yet, others were scheduled to leave immediately. As they waited, each wondered fervidly exactly how he was supposed to feel, but none knew. So they sat, resigned, committed, some even joyous, holding that custom-sewn stretch of reinforced canvas with a handle—ordinary looking "luggage" that contained a poison, and a plan, to set the world free.

By a long shot, this was no ordinary day.

• • •

After McDonald's for breakfast later that morning, the Chisoms went shopping for a new winter coat for Josh, calling it an early Christmas present. Josh's spirits were high. At ten o'clock, they were back at the hospital. The metal placard above the double-doored entrance to the west wing read: Center for Cancer and Blood Disorders. Inside, everything was scrubbed and sanitized—even the air. The walls were cream, the floor white-and-gray-flecked tile. Since the facility maintained a staffed playroom for children, Dr. Li requested that they please leave Josh under supervised care so that she might be allowed a private consultation with just the two of them. Nervously, they acquiesced.

With the door closed and seats taken, Dr. Li's message was grave.

"I must sadly confirm Dr. Perkins's diagnosis," she said, leaning forward in her leather-backed chair. "Josh does indeed have multiple myeloma. I'm very sorry."

Beams of saffron-hued light streamed through the venetian blinds; dust pirouetted through the air, like the shimmering flakes in a child's snow globe. From that point in the conversation, everything was just details. Something deep inside Sylvia had hoped against hope that it was all just a big mistake. No such luck. Tim reached over, squeezed her hand. Her fingers were limp in his grasp.

"Go on . . ." Tim said.

"Josh's case is remarkable for a couple of reasons. First, it is extremely rare to see this disease in a child. Almost without exception, the elderly are the likely victims. The second point of note is how nominally Josh seems to be affected."

Sylvia's ears perked up. "Could you say that again, please?"

Sunny smiled softly. "Don't get me wrong. On a scale of one to ten for this disease, with ten being the worst case, I would say Josh is at about a six or seven. And in truth, it's not unusual for myeloma to hide awhile before symptoms become evident. It *is* rare for it to hide this long. All I can say is that his body seems to be compensating remarkably well. That should give you both hope."

Tim and Sylvia said nothing. Dr. Li continued.

"Even so, the numbers don't lie. The disease is very much there. And because it has gone undetected for so long, we are now actually facing the advanced stages."

"But he's fine," Sylvia protested. "He's acting fine."

Tim joined in. "We're around him every day. You couldn't tell a thing was wrong."

"I understand . . ."

"No, I don't think you do," Tim said. "I'm hearing you say it's worse than it looks, but then you say it's better than it seems."

"That's actually a pretty good way to put it, Mr. Chisom. I can only speculate that his youth is working for him in this regard. But that's only one side of the equation." She held up one hand, as if weighing truth in her scales; then she held up the opposite hand. "On the other side it basically boils down to this. Even though Josh shows only mild clinical signs—things like fatigue, soreness, thirst—your son has a life-threatening form of cancer inside him. That cancer is at work even as we speak, and likely progressing. I can prove that with a bunch of charts and numbers, but in the end you have to trust me, because as far as his apparent health is concerned, Josh seems to be no worse off than if he had a bad head cold."

Sylvia let out a gush of air and touched her hand to her mouth. "Wait a minute," she said, her eyebrows digging in toward her nose as if to scrape her brain for an answer, then leaping towards the ceiling with hope. "I just want to know if you're telling us good news or not. To my ears, no clinical signs *sounds* good."

"I said minimal clinical signs," Dr. Li corrected. "And yes, it does sound good. But as difficult as it is to accept, you should regard his good health as temporary. Eventually, that too will falter. This is a very serious disease, and difficult to treat."

"So what do we do?" Tim asked.

Sunny removed her thin, round spectacles, regarding Tim with unblinking eyes. "I recommend we begin treatment immediately."

Guardedly, Sylvia said, "What kind of treatment?"

"I don't think we can afford to go soft," Dr. Li replied, holding up her hands. "I recommend we begin what we call combination chemotherapy immediately."

Chemotherapy was another tormenting word, much like *cancer*. Tim wiped his jaw, smoothing the rough cut of his unshaved whiskers. "Dr. Li, you've been very nice to us. But you need to know something about me. Shortly before Joshua was born, my mother died of breast cancer. I watched her struggle. No doubt, the cancer might have killed her. Probably did . . . we don't know for sure. But I know one thing absolutely certain: that chemo stuff took her life. Just plain took her life."

"Fair enough," Dr. Li replied. "I should have been more clear. The majority of treatment involves chemotherapy at some level, because our choices are pretty limited for this type of disease. However, it's not unusual for patients with few clinical signs to opt out of treatment until they absolutely have to." She paused, choosing her words carefully. "However, most of those patients have *already* lived a long, full life."

She was stern, but tactful. The most common reaction for those caught in the storm, as the Chisoms now found themselves—especially if they were parents—was to become so stricken with emotional paralysis that they ended up drowning in fear and indecision.

"Do we have any options?" Tim said sullenly.

"A few. Conventional chemotherapy will yield a standard range of results. By contrast, aggressive combination chemotherapy, while notably more physically taxing, has also proven more effective. You may decide that is not necessary at this time, and that is your choice, especially considering your son's relative health. But I must tell you, it is dangerous to wait until things get worse before committing to a treatment plan."

Sylvia swallowed hard, found her voice. "What . . . what are his . . ."

She was unable to finish. Dr. Li picked up her failed string of words and formed an answer.

"I will be honest with you: I don't know. Based on his lab work, I think we have two, maybe three years at the most to turn this thing around. His calcium levels are very high, the monoclonal proteins in his urine are dense—known as a high titer—and his bones are broadly affected. His hemoglobin levels are low. The sooner we start, the better."

"But what are his chances?"

In an emotionless voice, Dr. Li said, "Chemotherapy has proven nearly 60 percent effective in adults."

"Dear God in heaven—"

"Mrs. Chisom, that is six out of ten."

"My boy is more than a number," Tim warned. "Before it was over, the doctors treated my mother the same way. I won't stand for it."

"But numbers are good, Mr. Chisom. Imagine how wonderful if he could be one of the six saved! That's a good number to be part of. And the ratio gets bumped slightly higher if you combine complementary treatments. There is a wide range of clinical trials going on all over the nation even as we speak and all of them are in pursuit of the best combination of treatments. Trust me, multiple myeloma is receiving a lot of attention."

Tim took a measured breath. "What else do we need to know?"

There was always more. Dr. Li told them about recent work to provide the equivalent of a DNA-level vaccination for the disease, though those efforts weren't quite ready for market. She said the most common direction was to combine bone marrow transplantation or something called "peripheral stem cell support"—which, she claimed, helped replace blood-forming cells destroyed in the process of treatment—with high-level chemo, though the side effects could be unpleasant. Then there was radiation therapy, with its complications. Another very interesting area of exploration, she said, involved the use of thalidomide—

"Thalidomide?" Sylvia gasped. "*The* thalidomide?"

Sure enough, Dr. Li said it was the very same drug used by mothers in the fifties and early sixties for morning sickness, which, they soon discovered, caused terrible birth defects and was stripped from the market. Apparently now, in other controlled applications, it was proving to be something of a miracle drug, though researchers didn't quite know why or how. Dr. Li seemed quite impressed with some recent studies coming out of Arkansas. But she was cautious.

"Please, Mr. and Mrs. Chisom, I do not want to be coy with you. I'm not trying to convince you the glass is half full. I realize the risks and the physical discomfort associated with chemotherapy. In my professional opinion, however, the greater risk is to do nothing. Your concerns for his welfare are legitimate, but you need to be considering his life. With your son's obvious resilience and age, his chances may well be higher for successful, permanent remission."

And that was that. As her voice trailed away, Tim and Sylvia stared stone-faced at the floor, each lost in a pain that was, in the same moment, both private and communal. Dr. Li folded her hands, waiting, unhurried, as did the Chisoms, loath to commit to anything. The room grew still—still enough to notice when the low and steady white noise of the air conditioner lapsed and the drafts from the ceiling vent ceased. From the hallway, distant voices and the sound of soft-soled shoes padding along the floor leaked underneath the door. Inside the office, in the awkward stillness, fear and worry amalgamated into something thick, sticky, like molasses, impossible to get away from, leaving a sulfurous residue in Tim's mouth and an ache in Sylvia's chest. Yet even with so much turbulence inside them, at the very same moment, a great *nothing* stretched before them, a vacuum of emotion, thought, even a prevailing sense of reality. With a few brief words, their oasis of hope, even life itself, had become a dry and thirsty crevasse, with every corner of rock sharp enough to draw blood if they moved even an inch.

Tim searched for strength. Soft as butter, speaking to himself more than anyone else, he uttered a single word. The sound of his own voice surprised him.

"No."

It was a surgical cut, a simple word, but pus flushed from the wound. Because underneath both the emptiness and fear lay something more true: unyielding resolve. *It's not the end of the world. Not a death sentence. We'll make it.* With his voice, Tim set his own resolve free, for both Sylvia and him to latch onto. Like the roots of an oak or the shout of a madman, coming from deep within, the word willed itself up from the silence of his soul. Sylvia heard the courage and joined the defiance. Launched into the dark void, that simple word hung in the air ragged with love, adrift in space, hopeful that someone, somewhere, might hear and know their torment, and being moved with compassion, remunerate the stolen life of their son. Yet if not, they would find another way, fight another way. They would not take Josh's life, if life was still in him. It was not an easy decision. Nevertheless, in an instant, it was made.

Dr. Li knew all too well the nature of their choice.

"Please reconsider," she said. "We have an excellent staff. There are drugs that can help minimize his discomfort. Only give it a chance—"

"What chance?" Tim asked calmly, feeling the strength of his mate beside him. "You are asking us to give our eight-year-old son a treatment in the name of healing that will actually make him feel much worse than the disease itself has made him feel so far. I saw my mother die every day for six months, with her hair in a pile on the floor. One day she finally stopped breathing. But she had died a long time before."

"We can't be sure how long his strength will last. By the time his fortune turns, it may be too late."

"What about alternative medicines? Natural stuff. Other medical techniques."

"Mr. Chisom," Sunny said, bearing in her voice equal notes of sadness and disdain, "the whole world will promise you a cure, sell you a bottle of hope, if only you are willing to believe. And pay cash."

"You just said the same thing about yourself, that we should trust you. What's the difference?"

Eyes narrowing ever so slightly, the dark-haired woman said, "I am not a salesman, Mr. Chisom. I am a doctor, a good one. I am doing my best to tell you the facts and to prove my case, but the choice is still yours."

Tim struck his knee with his fist. "Can you *prove* to me that the disease is advancing?"

"No, not yet. Dr. Perkins's lab results and mine follow each other too closely to be certain."

"So it may be holding steady?"

"That does happen. We call that a case of smoldering myeloma. He may have hit a plateau, but I doubt it."

"Can you prove that his body can't win on its own or fight better than the chemotherapy?"

"I can assure you—"

"No, can you prove it? I mean, Dr. Li, what if his body is actually fighting this thing and winning? What if that's why he's not showing more symptoms?"

"Because that doesn't happen. This disease is a killer, Mr. Chisom. It is not a head cold, regardless of how Joshua feels."

Tim rose from his chair and reached for Sylvia's hand. She was timid at first but followed his lead.

"At the very least, we need time to think," he said tersely. "What can be done in the meantime for my son?"

Dr. Li sighed and began scribbling on a pad of paper. "I can prescribe some medication for secondary symptoms, if they get worse, but that's about it. Erythropoietin is a hormone produced in the kidney. That will help. Iron supplements and antinausea medication such as Phenergan will strengthen his appetite. At some point I might prescribe Prednisone, which is an immune suppressant, to keep his system stabilized and not expend too many resources fighting the Bence-Jones proteins. Of course, all of those are merely managing the symptoms. They contribute nothing to the cure. You understand that, don't you?"

Tim poked his arm through his jacket sleeve and took the pharmaceutical sheet offered by Dr. Li.

"We understand. We'll be in touch."

He and Sylvia headed for the door. Dr. Li said, "I'll be gone for a while. My mother's birthday is in a couple of days. I'm leaving tonight for Brazil. I'll call you when I get back. Maybe that will give you time to think."

"Maybe so."

Josh slept half the trip home. The other half he sat and stared. There was little exchange between Tim and Sylvia. Both were too busy reviewing every last detail of the day, of their lives, wondering how they had come to this point. Tim kept thinking of Dr. Li's last warning, ringing like a bell in his brain, that if Josh should begin to complain of back pain, they must call her immediately.

"Acute, chronic back pain is the surest sign the disease has reached critical mass," she'd said in a low voice.

By late afternoon, the Chisom truck was pulling into Folin. Passing the IGA on the way home, Sylvia ran in to grab a gallon of milk for cold cereal in the morning. A man stood outside, passing out flyers. She took one, didn't bother to read it, and stuffed it in her purse. As they pulled into their driveway, the first thing both noticed was a familiar motor-cycle parked on the curb.

"Uncle Rick's back!" Josh exclaimed, stirring to life.

It was true. Rick had helped himself to the front door, and the fridge. They found him reclining comfortably on the couch. When woken from his nap, he appeared sheepish.

"Got here about an hour ago," he explained. "You all were gone and it was cold sitting on the porch, so I found that key you keep on the backside of the downspout and helped myself in. Hope that's all right."

Without waiting for an answer, he faced Josh, touched his arm. "Josh, I am really sorry about your wrist. It was just plain stupid of me to give you a ride. I wish I never had."

Sylvia caught Tim's eye. Neither spoke.

"You can still give me rides. I don't mind."

Tim spoke. "How long you in for this time, Rick? We normally don't see this much of you."

"Not sure. I'll probably be in and out."

Sylvia was not interested in playing games. She took a deep breath. "Rick, give me a straight answer. Did you get fired?"

The question surprised Rick. He glanced at Josh, as if embarrassed to have to answer in front of a kid. He dropped his head. "There were cutbacks."

Tim coughed. Rick became defensive.

"Hey, I've been looking for work for a couple of weeks, you know? Nothing's coming together. Gimme a break!"

"You low on money?"

"A little."

Sylvia pulled out her checkbook. "I can't help you much."

"I need a place," Rick said. "I lost my apartment."

"Don't you have some friends in the city?"

"I got a couple buddies, yeah. But their wives were getting tired of me hanging out."

Sylvia closed her eyes. "You can stay here for a few days, until you find some work. But you do things our way while you're here, got it? That means not a drop, Rick. Not a drop."

She meant liquor, and by her tone of voice and the guilty look on Rick's face, she knew he got the picture.

It was a little after three o'clock. The family slipped out of their coats and unpacked their bags. Josh plopped down on the couch and turned on the TV, unmoving. Sylvia put the milk away. Tim lingered in the bedroom.

"Josh, how do you feel?" Sylvia asked nonchalantly.

"I'm okay," he answered, but his voice was dull.

"Are you hungry?"

"Nah."

Of course he wasn't. It was midafternoon and he had eaten a decent lunch. But everything was now a checkpoint, a cause for worry or hope, depending on which direction his answers leaned. Sylvia turned away, willed herself to stop. Rick could feel the strain. Cautiously, he moved into the kitchen, spoke softly.

"What's up? Where've you guys been?"

Tim had yet to come out of the bedroom. Sylvia glanced sternly at her brother, though he used an appropriately hushed voice.

"Why don't you and I take a ride?" she announced, with false volume. "I'll show you some of the new sites in town." Like it or not, Rick was family. He would know sooner or later, might as well be now. Grabbing her coat once more, Sylvia breezed past Josh.

"Tell your father we had to run some errands. We'll be back soon."

They drove in silence for a while. Sylvia didn't know where to start. All she could think, over and over, as the sky rolled and the streetlights changed and the cars passed by, was that at some point she would have to carry on this exact conversation with her eight-year-old, terminally ill son, and she dreaded it. She would rather fall on swords a thousand times than have to look into his eyes and utter the judgment of nature against him. What she feared even more was that some part of his soul, she knew, would accept that judgment with a serenity, a surrender, that would seem like wisdom. If that moment ever came, she was not sure she could withstand the force of his vulnerability. She wasn't afraid that Josh would hear and not understand, but rather that he would hear and accept, leaving her alone to grieve.

Tim would stand with her, rise to the occasion, but at the same time turn increasingly inward. Josh would dutifully bear the burden on his shoulders. And Sylvia . . . what would she do?

Run and hide. Run and hide and die.

That was what she wanted, what she felt like. It was also the last thing she would ever do. With anything concerning Josh, Sylvia was a bear wrapped in the body of a German shepherd, dressed like a woman; a soft clay vase, kiln-fired, built for pressure. Like it or not, disclosure was unavoidable and must come soon. Rehearsal, therefore, became a practical necessity, but the effort required for her to gather her thoughts felt like a belly crawl through a field of barnacles. Not much ground could be covered, and it all hurt.

"Is this about Josh?" Rick asked, when he could wait no longer.

"Yes."

"Is it about his arm? Did I mess it up pretty bad or something?"

"No."

Rick regarded his sister with rare concern. Rather than feel frustrated with her silence, he saw a woman with a mole on her cheek and green eyes the color of a wide open field, humbled now with worry. He saw the smooth skin, the caramel hair, the too-large glasses pressing against her nose. She had changed much since they were children, but her smile and the warmth in her eyes were the same.

"What's the deal, Sylvia?"

Sylvia pulled the truck over and parked on the curb. "We just got back from a specialist in Oklahoma City."

"And?"

"Josh has cancer."

Rick physically jerked. "What?"

"It's treatable, we hope. It's in his blood."

"Cancer? Oh, Sylvia. That's awful."

She quickly briefed him. All the while, Rick sat stunned, his breath stolen. Sylvia had no idea what his thoughts were, but when he finally spoke, his voice was a mixture of wonder and dread. "Good grief. My scope actually warned me this would happen. I don't believe it. This is just terrible."

"Your *scope?*"

"Yeah, just this morning. It said, 'Today will bring bad news. Strive for peace.'"

Sylvia bristled, turning ferociously. "I just told you about my son and you're telling me about your stupid horoscope!"

Rick held his hands up. "No, Sylvia. I didn't mean for it to sound that way. It just popped into my head."

"Well, pop it out! Those things are stupid. This is about Josh's life." Angrily, she fired up the truck, jerked it into gear. "I never should have brought you here. I never should have tried to be serious with you. You can't handle it. You've never handled it. And apparently you don't ever plan on trying—"

Rick didn't wait for another punch. The gloves were off. "What, Sylvia? Go on. Trying to what?"

"I don't want to talk about it."

"Don't pull that start-and-stop stuff on me. We're out here. Let's talk."

"No."

Rick jerked the wheel. The truck careened into an open parking lot. Sylvia slammed on the brakes. Both tempers flared.

"What am I supposed to be trying to do, Sylvia? Huh? Tell me!"

"Let go." She slapped at his arm. He was stocky, strong. "You could have killed us."

"Tell me one more time what I'm not doing right, Sylvia. What am I supposed to be doing?"

"You're supposed to be—"

"What? Who? You?"

"An adult! For once in your life, would you please just try to act grown up! For a change."

"How dare you!" Rick hissed. "You've never cared about my life. Don't pretend to start now."

Sylvia wiped her eyes. She didn't want to go through this again. "Are we back here, already? Everything isn't about you, Rick. Don't you see?

Can't you get that through your head? *Adults* figure that out. They learn to think about others. Has your horoscope ever told you that?"

"It was just a stupid comment, Sylvia. I love that kid! I'm sorry, all right?"

Sylvia glared at her brother. Deeper still, she felt sadness. He still didn't get it. "My son is sick, Rick. That's bad enough. Talking about it is even worse. But let me tell you what you just did. You basically implied that fate, in some small way, has decreed that my son be sick, maybe even die. The stars have predicted it, right? Did you ever consider for a single moment how that would make me feel?"

Rick swallowed. Of course, he hadn't considered it. "You just said you don't believe that stuff."

"No," Sylvia returned. "But *you* do."

She refused to say another word. The drive home was locked in a silence more painful, more resentful, than the one in which they began.

· · ·

While Rick and Sylvia argued, in Oklahoma City, Dr. Sunny Li made hurried, final preparations for her departure to Brazil. Plans had already changed once, tickets had changed; not a big deal, except that she would now arrive much later, around midnight, rather than afternoon. All thanks to Joshua Chisom. In fact, it was his case—one nagging doubt she simply had to allay before leaving—that caused her to reach for her cell phone. Riding beside her husband to the airport, trunk full of bags, she dialed the lab. The chief microbiologist answered.

"I want you to do me a favor," she said. "The Chisom blood samples. Run the numbers one more time."

"We've already done it twice," came the flat reply.

"Then let's make it a third. I don't want this family worrying if we've missed something. I really want to confirm the titer on the monoclonal antibodies. There are so few Bence-Jones fragments, but such a high concentration of fully formed antibodies. It's unusual. Almost too dense to be real. Maybe we didn't calibrate correctly."

"Dr. Li, the monoclonals *are* packed, and the numbers are real. I know what you're thinking, but you saw for yourself. There was an extremely strong band on the gel electrophoresis."

"I've never seen numbers like that, Jack."

"Especially not in a kid."

"Exactly. It's probably that simple. The high concentration may explain his health, his natural resistance. But like you said, this is just a kid. I don't want any mistakes on a cancer diagnosis."

The voice on the other end sighed. "I've got some time after lunch."

"Great! E-mail me. I'd like to hear something by the time I land."

She hung up, thought quickly, resigned herself to waiting. At the terminal, after checking their baggage, she used a pay phone to check her e-mail. As she hoped, there was a new message from an old colleague, Dr. Terrance Alexander. Sunny smiled. She and Terrance had served their residency together at the same hospital in Chicago years ago. They had become good friends, even romantic friends. One windy spring day, underneath the shadow of the Sears Tower, Terrance had actually bent his knee and asked for her hand in marriage. At the time, Sunny was deeply in love with her career and slightly suspicious of commitment. She decided her feelings for Terrance, though sweet, were nowhere near deep enough for marriage. In subsequent years, after a difficult cooling-off period, they had resumed their correspondence. Both had since married others, but they still kept in touch. Terrance was now a leading expert in blood disorders, allowing Sunny fairly regular occasion to draw upon his expertise. At this point she owed him so many favors she would likely never catch up.

Hi, Sunny. I received your message earlier this morning. Very intriguing. Only eight years old? If you can get it to me quickly, I'll include the Chisom sample in a broader assay I'm running. Also, if you don't mind, I'd like to include his blood in a specialized series of tests I've undertaken. I think I might have mentioned this to you before, but earlier this year I treated an elderly MM patient suffering from a concurrent illness, lupus. Her condition was severe enough that I decided to test whether correlations exist between MM antibodies and other autoimmune diseases, such as systemic lupus, rheumatoid arthritis, pemphigus, etc. My

hunch was that in rare cases, the monoclonal antibodies of certain individuals end up targeting the host, actually binding to certain cell types,
thus creating the concurrency. As you know, systemic lupus erythe-
matosus is caused by polyclonal and antigen-specific T and B lympho-
cyte hyperactivity. Not so in my client. Her MM monoclonals were
precisely structured pathogenic autoantibodies, causing vast tissue and
cell damage.

In the end, her body became a virtual drug factory, only in her case,
the drug she produced was killing her. There was nothing we could do.
What are the chances? We've never suspected that monoclonals served a
direct purpose other than to get in the way and clog the system. But, it
seems, every key has a lock that only that key will open. So now we're
looking for as many locks as we can find. With your permission, I'll add
Josh to the key ring. If you want to read up on the research, you can find
it in the May issue of the Journal. The last few months have taken us in
all kinds of unexpected directions.

The letter ended with a final flourish.

Get me the samples, Sunny, and I'll try to give you some answers.
They're always in the blood.

Terrance

9

After Sylvia and Rick returned, Tim slipped out the door without explanation. Josh seemed sluggish, though he perked up a bit when Rick offered to play airplanes. Rockets and planes fascinated Josh largely thanks to Rick. It was a part of her brother Sylvia had never really known, since it developed later in his life. It made sense, though, this love of planes and flying. As a cost analyst for the air force, Rick had plenty of exposure to military war birds. Being something of a history buff, as well as a collector, he had over time acquired an impressive mental repertoire of famous air battles, particularly from World War II. To this day, Josh would drop whatever he was doing when Rick began to tell a story. Josh's favorite toy was a die-cast, F-16 Falcon replica, about the size of a man's hand, which a "blue-suit"—a uniformed officer, in this case, a pilot—had given Rick and Rick had passed on to Josh for his sixth birthday. Owing to his rank and prior military service, Rick also had access to the BX, the commissary, and the Officer's Club, where he could hang out with pilots and pretend, if only for a few moments every day, that he was the one up in the air. Or that's pretty much how Sylvia imagined it. As far as she was concerned, all the aviation stuff was one more opportunity for Rick to avoid the realities of his life and growing up.

He had tried to tell her otherwise. In a moment of rare vulnerability two years ago, he had tried to explain that flying was not some abstract fascination. It was more than a historical pursuit, he told her—more than a hobby, more than curiosity. It was who he always wanted to be.

He even admitted, strangely enough, that his desire to be a pilot was why he drove a motorcycle. If he could not soar fast and unfettered through the sky, he would at least skim fast and unfettered along the ground. Since he was a teenager, he had longed to sit in the cockpit and feel the engines burn. Sylvia was able to connect the dots from there. Unable to fulfill his dream—and for whatever other excuses he could produce—he found regular solace in both booze and the token lifestyle: collecting planes, working around planes and pilots, ever attempting to live the *Top Gun* life on the ground, brash and daring, and often drunk.

It drove Sylvia crazy. That was exactly the kind of behavior she feared would get him fired one day. Or lead to a fatal crash.

She watched her brother grab Josh and swing him through the room, ripping and snorting, telling lavish tales of the Battle of Midway and Guadalcanal; of the famous Black Sheep Squadron, of Spitfires and Hurricanes, the evil German *Luftwaffe*, the legendary P-47 Thunderbolt, B-1 bombers, and F-51 fighters; of bombs and explosions and aerial kills. He was living the adventure himself. And though it was more violent than she preferred, Sylvia took consolation in the fact that Josh was learning about real-life heroes, like British Flight Lieutenant James Nicholson, who, during the Battle of Britain, was attacked by four German fighters. Telling the story again, Rick pretended to be Nicholson, wounded by a cannon shell, yet fighting on—with his cockpit engulfed in fire—long enough to destroy another enemy ship before abandoning his Hurricane.

"Zooooom . . . crash!" Rick hollered, making noises with his throat.

It was all Sylvia could do to not dig her fingernails into the wall. With great forbearance and a cool voice, she called from the kitchen, "Easy, Rick. The kid is only eight."

To her surprise, Rick calmed down.

Later that afternoon, Tim returned. They ate supper together, the four of them. When the meal was finished, Sylvia put away the dishes, washed her hands, reached into her purse for her lipstick, and pulled out the folded sheet of paper from the man at the grocery store, declaring,

Two More Days Remaining!
Bring Your Loved Ones Who Are Sick and Unwell!
Revival Services with
Bagwell McComb, Noted Evangelist and Healer
Ministering at the Folin Pentecostal Holiness Church
7:00 P.M.
Everyone Welcome!

The flyer was newly printed—probably that morning by the looks of it. Underneath the block-lettered invitation were three different testimonials of locals who had attended and been touched or healed, or so they claimed. The third photo grabbed her attention: Mary Beth Watkins, from the factory. The quote beside Mary's picture read, *"I've suffered from fibromyalgia every day for seven straight years. A friend asked me to go hear Brother McComb the first night and I reluctantly agreed. He prayed for me. I woke up the next morning and, I can't explain it, but I don't hurt. I can hold my coffee cup without pain. Praise God!"*

It was a strange moment of epiphany, bordering on surreal, of the type and flavor only the desperate ever taste. Sylvia read the sheet three times, breathing in gulps, then crumpled the paper to her chest. What did she have to lose? She usually laughed at the stories she had heard about Pentecostals, but there was Mary Beth, and Mary hadn't fallen off the turnip truck anytime recently. Apparently these folks believed in miracles, and that's what she was looking for. Mary Beth had always been about as big a stick-in-the-mud as they came. Sylvia couldn't count the number of times at work she had heard Mary Beth wince, seen her stiff, painful movements and the pills she would pop for relief. Now, on a crumpled piece of paper, Mary Beth sounded like a believer, claiming her fibromyalgia was gone.

Sylvia glanced at her watch: 6:43. She hesitated, wondering if she should tell Tim. He might not approve. Feeding false hopes. Putting God on the spot. Putting Josh on the spot.

"C'mon, Josh," she said. "Grab your coat. We're going to church."

The small church was packed like cellulite into spandex. Fortunately, two fans kept the air moving. Better still, someone had resorted to leaving the back door ajar. Nevertheless, winter's chill did very little to freshen the sweaty, stuffy room.

No one seemed to mind. People were shouting, waving their hands. The mood of the place bordered upon electric. Standing on the very edge of the raised platform, near the pulpit, Bagwell McComb made dramatic gestures with his hands, raising his voice from the peaks of a shout to the depths of a whisper as easily and suddenly as one might lift a stone or drop it. Young men and old women would stand occasionally, point with their fingers, and say something like, "C'mon now!" or "Tell it!" and Brother McComb would charge like a rhinoceros into another sweeping declaration of the mercy of God or the terror of sin.

"Moses the deliverer came, but God still had to pour judgment upon Egypt before his people were set free," he roared. Then, as if he were sharing a secret (though it couldn't truly be called a secret, because it was loud and hoarse), he pointed his Bible at the congregation. "It is a *paradox!* 'Behold the kindness and severity of the Lord,' Paul said! And friends, I have news for you: they are one and the same. Kindness to the heart of faith, yet severity to the heart of unbelief. Mary had a sword pierce her soul, but she said the Mighty One had done great things for her and holy is his name. She watched her Son hang on a tree, but then was witness to his resurrection. Friends, listen. If you want to believe in God to take you higher, you have to learn to thank him through the severity until that trial becomes revealed to your heart for the kindness it truly is."

Sylvia and Josh sat in the back, behind rows and rows of straight-backed pews on a makeshift string of folding chairs lining the back wall. Around the perimeter, many folks were forced to stand. She was hot, but listened as best she could, even though they had been there for an hour and a half, including a good forty-five minutes of foot-stomping southern gospel during the worship time. Unaccustomed to long Pentecostal services, she was growing weary. Josh was restless. Everywhere, people fanned themselves with church bulletins or scraps of paper from their purses.

Something must be happening here, Sylvia found herself thinking. *Otherwise, no one would put up with this.*

Even so, she decided that something had better get rolling soon or she was leaving. She hadn't come to hear a sermon; she had come in search of a miracle. Despite his oratorical skills and obvious passion for the message, Sylvia had trouble recalling five minutes' worth of whatever point the preacher was trying to make.

Then she heard it.

"So come . . ."

That's all anybody needed. Nearly as one, dozens and dozens of people stood, filed into the aisle, began pushing forward. Sylvia's heart jumped; she clasped Josh's arm, leaned over, and said, "Josh, honey, we may be going up front together. Is that okay with you?"

"Are you going to have that man pray for me?"

Sylvia swallowed, nodded.

Josh studied his mother's face, then said, "It's only 'cause I'm sick, right?"

"That's right, Josh."

"I don't want to say any prayers."

"No one's going to make you do anything. Will you go?"

Josh sighed. "I'll go if you go."

Sylvia saw the reserve creep over his features. He was hedging his bets on what this was really all about. It gave her pause, made her wonder one more time if she was doing something wrong, something that might actually push him away. How much did he truly understand? How much was necessary to cross that critical line? Oh, he knew the stories from church and Sunday school, knew who Jesus was and what he'd done. She *knew* he knew. Together, she and Tim had gently, persistently soaked him in their faith, she hoped without drowning him in it. Josh had heard his parents' prayers over and over again—had even said a few himself on occasion. He had asked good questions, right questions.

The one thing he had never asked, however, was to take the step for himself. Neither Tim nor Sylvia wanted to push it. It should be natural, they agreed. In his time. But when they did talk to Josh about how to go to heaven, and how to believe in God, and what Jesus did on the cross, Josh would withdraw, say he was embarrassed, that he didn't want to have to do things like be baptized with a bunch of people watching.

Now he was going to have to walk down this aisle. That would be terrifying enough.

People sitting in the pews had crammed together to make as much room as possible in the center aisle for the seekers to pass through. The floor congested instantly; a low hum of prayer filled the room as gray-haired men and women looked on kindly, hoping to see one more miracle.

With all the hoopla, Sylvia found herself surprisingly unaffected by the energy in the room, except for the fact that her legs trembled slightly and her palms were clammy. Not so much because of what was happening, nor the particular style. Her weakness was something much more elusive, yet no less fundamental. She was about to take the proverbial leap of faith, defying the all-too-familiar jokes and cynicism surrounding faith healers. The question was, who would catch her fall? More to the point, this leap, this obligatory song she must sing, was for her son. How would the song end? Would anyone, any power, catch *Josh*?

Up front, above a sea of heads, Sylvia barely glimpsed the preacher, no longer red-faced from shouting, but soft-spoken, almost timid, perhaps even moaning, as he laid his hands on the heads of person after person, asking God to move mightily. Folks were old, young; some limped; one was pushed forward in a wheelchair, while another person put a hand to her head and swayed; behind both, yet another, a middle-aged man, pointed to his back with difficulty.

"Save them, Lord!" McComb would say, and many would shake when he touched them. "By the blood of Jesus, heal them. Deliver them from the enemy of life! Make their bodies well and strong."

Sylvia watched and listened to each prayer, anxious for some measure of faith to rise in her own heart. She held Josh's hand, feeling lost beneath the rolling tide of bodies on every side. They waited, inched forward, waited, prayer by prayer progressing to the front of the line. Every so often a sort of shock wave would ripple through the crowd, pressing those in front of her backwards, and herself into those behind. At nearly the same moment, from the front, a new voice would shout, "Hallelujah!" or merely sob. Many would fall to the floor, apparently overwhelmed. Sylvia figured the falling to be the source of the ripple effect. Each time, recovering her balance, she would strain to see over the heads of those ahead in line—she wasn't very tall—and might see a figure hopping, pointing to a body part and beaming an amazed smile, or stretching his arms above his head, eyes wide. Each time, others in the audience, family or friends, would cover their mouths, moved with emotion, or shout.

"What's happening?" Josh asked, holding Sylvia's hand loosely, trying to peek around the backs of people.

"I don't know, honey . . ."

The whole thing definitely carried the scent of the Pentecostal stories she had heard. It was a free-for-all, but not nearly the free-for-all Sylvia had imagined. The mocking stories did not convey the genuineness of the moment. And for whatever reason, whether it was the emotion of that moment, or the creeping drama of the line ever moving forward, or simply the mystery of the unknown, Sylvia found herself growing more hopeful. Some walked away. Many danced.

Sylvia wanted to dance.

Oh God, please . . .

Then the line parted. Sylvia stumbled forward, with Josh in hand, face to face now with Bagwell McComb. The low hum of prayers continued. Some three or four bodies were laid out on the ground, a linen cloth thrown over the laps of the women. Sylvia glanced nervously around, squeezing Josh's hand tighter.

"What can I do for you, ma'am?" he asked gently. His silver hair and heavy jowls were damp, and his breath came from deep within his barreled chest.

"I've come . . . for my son."

Fervidly she hoped no more information was required. Bagwell McComb's eyes fell on the boy, and a flutter of noise passed through the folks up front assisting the preacher—those who were to pray and those who were to catch those who fell under the power. Though Sylvia had not heard it before, someone at the piano was playing and singing softly, "Oh the Deep, Deep Love of Jesus." Strange as it was to notice such a thing, she found the song especially lovely.

The preacher reached down, smiled warmly, put both of his big, meaty hands on Josh's upturned face. Their eyes met and, for just a moment, man and child stared deeply into one another's soul. Sylvia waited for a prayer, some motion or movement, but the silent connection between Josh and the healer persisted. Something passed over the man's face. Sylvia didn't know what it was, but it looked like recognition, the way an idea or concept, once realized, works its way from the brain to the countenance. Suddenly something came to life in Bagwell McComb's eyes, and he raised his voice with authority, though he only dared whisper.

"I see healing all over this child," he said, transfixed. "Tremendous healing."

Only a few people heard. Sylvia was one but strained forward as though she had not. Was that the prayer? It didn't *sound* like a prayer. Had he made a promise, from God to her, a promise of healing? Sylvia didn't understand these things, but a quick shiver of whispers passed among the others who heard. Beside Sylvia, an older woman watched with twinkling eyes. With awe in her voice, she murmured to her companion, "Spirit of prophecy's come on Brother McComb."

"God's a-movin'," the reply came back. "That boy's being called to ministry."

But they did not know. Josh did not know, nor did he move. As ever, he stood his ground. The preacher finally broke free, removed his hands, and turned to Sylvia. Almost pleading, he said, "You must take care of this child. God has something special for his life. I cannot say more."

And he did not. Instead, his last words dropped to the floor, crouching like the Sphinx between Oedipus and Thebes with her great and perplexing riddle. That moment might as well have been an out-of-body experience. Sylvia had taken a plunge into the dark abyss and found only darkness. Fumbling for Josh, they clasped hands and began picking their way through the crowd. Seconds earlier, she had brought a heart lined with a strange and wary hope. She would leave with that same heart, threadbare.

Out into the cold air, into the truck, she knew nothing but to flee.

The evening crept forward on dark, padded feet, slipped away, present to past. The Chisoms retired to bed—Sylvia wondering through tears how God could tease her with riddles at a time like this; Tim muscling his wandering thoughts away from pity for Sylvia, and frustration for stealing Josh away without his approval. Instead, he tried to consider the work due come Monday. With care for Josh lingering behind every consideration, it proved hard to stay focused. Josh fell asleep easily, thankful no one bothered to ask him how he felt, because he didn't know.

But it wasn't hard to figure that something was quite wrong.

Around the world, darkness deepened even further, in the capital cities of the Earth: Tokyo, Singapore, Moscow, London, Paris, Vienna, Rome; in Sydney, Cairo, Bombay, and Jerusalem; in the transportation centers of Central and South America: Mexico City, São Paulo, and Buenos Aires; and finally, Houston, Los Angeles, Toronto, and New York City. The major arteries of planetary traffic and population density were about to be assaulted by a handful of high-minded ecologists, swayed to plain-clothed subterfuge by the philosophical conceits of Jean de Giscard, who himself, aboard a DC-10, was even now descending the skies to his native Paris. Many of the members of GPS had already arrived in their designated locations, were simply waiting, sitting on a bench, drinking in a bar. They were alone, had no bags to claim, only the single walk-on, which they hovered over protectively. None left the terminal. Every so often they would glance at their watches, synchronized across the globe to one minute before midnight, Greenwich Mean Time.

Time for planet Earth was running out.

• • •

On the kitchen table, a dozen black roses, along with a bouquet of black balloons, teasingly offered grim benediction to Stu's fifty years. His big day had come, and he was none too happy about it. He thought he had robbed his office staff of their perverse pleasures. By avoiding work on Friday, Stu figured he'd dodged the bullet of their mockery. Not so. They simply hired the FTD florist to bring the joke to him over the weekend. Today was actually the big day, anyway. No escaping the punishment, it seemed.

Stu flipped the channels in agitation, dragging distractedly on one cigarette after another. Talk of the Sleeper virus was everywhere: *Nightline, Charlie Rose*, CNN.

Day five. The big finale.

Predictably, the buzz was hot, made hotter by the fact that no one knew today's message. In a departure from the previous four days, infected computer screens had remained blank and sullen all day. Since the virus had yet to hinder computer operations, work had progressed as usual for a Friday. No systems crashed. The stock market had not plunged. Yet that did little to keep the social prophets from dire warnings of malice and foul play, claiming the sky was, indeed, dropping. They offered theories of massive conspiracies of such complexity that Stu found himself wondering at the mental acuity required to concoct them. Most "respectable" outlets dismissed the whole thing as a hoax that had finally, mercifully, run its course.

In either case, the media had a field day.

On the *Tonight Show*, Jay Leno yakked it up about how, if the virus had a gender, it would almost certainly be male, because it promised more than it delivered.

"My wife gave me a list of chores for the weekend," Leno began. "I told her, 'Sure, no problem.' Friday night she reminds me again. 'Count on it,' I tell her. I'm thinking, *Hey, this is my time to show off, really accomplish some things.* Saturday comes, the big day, and what do I do? Get out my tools, strategize the best course of action . . . and take a nap." The audience laughed. "Face it, men. We are Sleeper."

A few channels away, with characteristic sobriety, Judy Woodruff on CNN reviewed the history of cryptic messages thus far, trying to piece together the clues. Local Atlanta outlets had headlined Sleeper in print and on the evening news. The Discovery Channel reran a previously aired documentary delving into the culture of hackers and their legacy in a paranoid information age. Network news anchors and metropolitan journalists alike chased leaks and leads to be the first to break the *real* story as to who the culprit might be, and what the big joke was all about. Wishing to remain anonymous for the camera's glass eye, outlaw hackers and crackers spoke boldly of anarchism, and admiringly of Sleeper's charisma, but only from the safety of shadows and silhouettes. David Letterman took a different track. His top ten for the night was "The Ten Worst Imaginable Sleeper Computer Disasters." Number one on the list: "You get bored to death." If only as a curio or novelty, the virus had succeeded in capturing attention. Like a bite from the Tree of Knowledge, eventually everyone was affected.

Stu sniveled into a Kleenex, tapping his finger on the remote. Out of all the messages, the one that continued to haunt him was that of day two: *"In 68 a vision famed, four remain until the same."* Today was that day. What did today have to do with anything? He had spent most of yesterday ignoring the work he should have accomplished so that he could chase this thing in private, all based on a nagging suspicion. Deep down, gut level, he just knew that something major was up. This was not a joke, not at all. Whether snide or patronizing, the media's analysis had yet to dissuade him. Yet after scouring the Internet for several hours, and searching the Encyclopedia Brittanica for any historical relevance to this day, Stu had yet to come up with any tangible evidence or realistic scenarios. Numerous chat groups and Sleeper sites had sprung up in the last five days, each claiming to have the skinny on the virus; theories proliferated on-line with greater, more bizarre voracity than the predictions that surfaced in print. None rang true.

He reached for the ashtray, put the Winston to his lips, inhaled, and blew curling gray smoke. Disgusted with his own failure, he flipped the channels. David Letterman blinked off; the Atlanta Superstation, TBS, blinked on. A male voice-over reviewed the evening's schedule, announcing the upcoming second in a trilogy of Clint Eastwood classics, followed by a commercial for Ford trucks. Stu stared at the screen numbly. He wasn't interested in movies or trucks, was tired of flipping channels, and was tired of sitting in this chair.

Rising, he muted the TV and began pacing the floor in circles, his house robe trailing behind him, his slippers sliding silently across the hardwood floor. Nearly three days old, his beard was scruffy and rough. His knee was acting up again, so he leaned a little more heavily on his cane as he finally settled on the direction of the kitchen and a cup of plain yogurt for a snack. After a bite or two, breathing deeply, he realized the yogurt tasted sour, though he couldn't tell if it was spoiled or simply the aftertaste of a fresh smoke. Leafing through a few documents he had brought home, along with others he had printed off the Internet, he thumped the table in frustration and powered up his computer, knowing it was futile.

It's not just going to magically appear.

Stu was a Vietnam veteran, the son of a preacher. His father, an ebullient showman with a fat Bible and full visitation schedule, successfully danced through four affairs before the ladies in the church finally started comparing notes. He was defrocked immediately. Never one to quit, Reverend Baker loaded up his little family, moved to another town, changed denominations, and started all over in another church, promising his wife he would be good. Didn't work. Stu's mother endured five more years of humiliation before leaving, dragging Stu and his younger sister with her. One year later, his sister was dead from lupus, and Stu was done pretending. He hated school, he hated family, he hated politics, he hated God. First thing he did when he turned eighteen was join the army, just so he could get as far away from home as possible, and maybe shoot some people in the process. The army happily sent him to Vietnam. Stu survived the jungle in a haze of marijuana smoke, before a bullet to the leg sent him stateside early. By then, he had a GI bill to put him through college, where his great disdain for convention proved brilliant in deconstructing microbial life. Cynicism can be a useful ally.

The flickering light of the TV caught his eye. Muted still, the last round of commercials was over, the movie about to begin. Stu instantly recognized the film. It was, indeed, an Eastwood classic. Caught in a daze, eyes unfocused, Stu found himself drawn to the screen for some reason. There, before the opening credits, for a few brief seconds, the film displayed a stark reading from the Bible. The passage revealed the movie's namesake:

"And I saw, and behold, a pale horse, and its rider's name was death, and hell followed him . . ."

Stu's mouth literally dropped open as he read through to the very end of the quote. The answer he'd been looking for was plain as day. The passage was found in Revelation 6:8.

"In 68 a vision famed . . ."

Stu dropped his cane, bolted for his office, fumbling through his reference books searching for a Bible. Where, where? He found one, barely used, nearly tore it open, to the very back of the book, to the most famous vision in history. Part of that vision was recorded in chapter six, verse eight: "And I looked, and behold, a pale horse; and he who sat on it had the name Death; and Hades was following with him. And authority was given to them over a fourth of the earth, to kill with sword and with famine and with pestilence and by the wild beasts of the earth."

Reeling, Stu placed both hands on the back of the chair to steady himself.

Authority to kill . . . with sword . . . with famine . . . with pestilence . . .

All at once, the prior daily messages flickered through his memory like ticker tape, one by one. Worse, they made sense: *"Let all partake the bitter drink . . . Come the purging, soon begin . . . death, they say, is the color gray . . ."*

It had to be. How could he have missed it? How could the whole world have missed it? Stu didn't have a clue to the details, nor the plan, but a terrifying recognition struck him: Whatever person or group had launched the Sleeper virus had achieved an incredible duality, warning the populace while at the same time distracting them. The computer virus itself was mass delusion, essentially inoculating the crowd around the water cooler by diverting their fear to a nonevent, a computer collapse or some such nonsense, while cleverly promising a different reality at the same time.

But what was that reality? What did the engineers of Sleeper have in mind? Could it possibly be on a global scale, as the reference to Revelation 6:8 implied? The very idea seemed entirely doubtful, if not outright fanciful. Who could pull something like that off? It would take billions of dollars, massive stockpiles, a full-scale assault. Cutting edge technology. World powers? No way. Rogue nations?

No, no . . .

Fact was, this clearly wasn't a nationalistic effort, nor was it politically motivated. It didn't have the right feel for that. Terrorists, renegades, rabid dictators with biological weapons—the Saddam Husseins of the world—didn't launch a public relations campaign before striking.

They simply struck. Terror, more than destruction, was their goal. Sleeper's dreamy patience and double entendre had a certain terrifying elegance, a finesse, which suggested a much more careful strategy. If he was right at all, there was purposeful and deliberate genius at work.

Stu shook his head at the thoughts ricocheting through his brain. Was he crazy? The biblical passage riveted him. The insidious language of the riddles seemed to eliminate "sword," which struck Stu as denoting a military operation. Likewise, famines could not be scheduled with such precision . . .

But pestilence.

Which brought the question back to biological weapons. Stu had to admit they were still a possibility, though doubtful. But weapons just didn't seem to fit the profile of the puzzle so far, unless . . .

Swords are weapons.

Stu pursed his lips. True, true. Maybe it was all three. What fit? Was it meant to be literal? Was the whole verse the message, or merely the pathos? Maybe it was something like a crop-destroying biological poison capable of creating world food shortages.

Get a grip.

Stu was wildly speculating now and he knew it. The very thought of such a crisis sent terror through his bones. He was overreacting; it was like being alone in a dark room and imagining, suddenly, that a serial killer is in the room with you. But there was another problem. In spite of the moral pang it produced, the idea of such calamity held a certain dread fascination. He couldn't help it. It was how he was built.

Didn't matter. Fact was, nobody would believe him anyway.

No, he corrected himself sternly. *The fact is, you've done nothing all day, you're on a nicotine high, and you're sounding more slipshod than the freaks on the Net. You don't have two hard facts to rub together, just one more crazy computer prank, so stop trying to start a fire just so you can maybe put it out. Nobody's dead. Nobody's dying. Just go to bed. You're going to feel foolish enough tomorrow as it is.*

He felt a bit foolish already. Whole thing probably was a hoax. Some clever kids with a deep sense of irony and way too much free time had concocted a way to lead the all-too-willing to a place of undiscovered genius within, where a person believes he can solve the riddle no one else has yet unraveled. The kids told their tale through the perfect postmodern vehicle, the computer; using the perfect medium for maximum paranoid impact, a computer virus; in the process drawing upon the deepest seeds of existential angst a millennial society can produce: "we're all gonna die."

Stu almost had himself talked out of the whole thing. Yes, he felt pretty foolish, all right. Right up until the point he turned—ready to shut off the lights, the TV, the computer—glanced at his color monitor, found there a final, fateful declaration, synchronized to the hour, having mysteriously appeared only seconds before, as the clock struck 11:59 P.M.

Sleeper has awakened. Bye-bye.

• • •

By the time Stu read that message, it was too late. Five hours earlier to the minute, while he was still surfing the Internet in search of answers, the GPS plan went into effect with terrifying simplicity. Along the prime meridian in Greenwich, Great Britain, midnight struck.

The final minute of day five.

A few minutes prior, seventeen people had emerged from the rest room facilities of cities around the world with small bags strapped to their backs. Inside each of these bags was some loose clothing, other miscellaneous articles, and a single, upright can of otherwise ordinary aerosolized deodorant spray, precisely positioned and secured in place so that the contents could be emitted through a special opening in the back of the luggage. Though physically indistinguishable from brand-name packaging, the cans were custom crafted so that a single press of the button on top would yield an uninterrupted flow until the entire contents were emptied. This flow was premeasured to last approximately three minutes.

Solemn, sober, anxious, exhilarated, at two minutes to twelve each person had obediently pressed the button—they had not come this far to fail—and then began a reasonably quick jog down the crowded terminals. Any casual observer, if he noticed at all, saw only a rushed passenger trying to catch a flight. They did not yell or flail their arms.

They simply ran, with purpose, weaving back and forth, making *S* patterns to cover the wide hallways. There would be no return flight. Each person's ticket went one way. It was all perfectly rehearsed; no airport personnel or tourist en route had any cause for suspicion. No guard tried to stop them.

Death, however, lingered in the air. Trailing behind the GPS runners, a colorless, odorless gas diffused silently from each can, which was pressurized to nearly double the normal capacity, and fitted with a specialized tip to ensure microaerosolization. The angle of the can, like every other detail, guaranteed maximum air penetration; the extra-light vapor, maximum suspension, and therefore transmission.

And the runners ran.

Some, with tears streaming down their faces, ran as if from grief, feeling their hearts collapse inside as, at the last minute, literally the last, they realized it was too late to repent, to turn back. Others ran with something akin to personal revelation, free-flowing with the rancor and venom they had nursed within, manifested in their hard strides and dark faces, in the vigor with which their retribution would fall on the unsuspecting. Nearly all felt, at long last, that their lives now had purpose. Though brief, their barbaric yawp would be heard by millions, even billions.

For once, they mattered. Their ideas counted.

In São Paulo, Brazil, one ran down the terminal, weaving past a woman hunched over her computer with a cord strung to the modem outlet on a pay phone. Dr. Sung Li turned, saw the commotion, saw a man with a backpack jogging to catch a flight. She was weary but smiled at the determined look on his face. Returning to her computer, she read the e-mail from the States a second time. Again, it confirmed the original diagnosis. She jotted a quick reply, requesting the lab to immediately forward Josh's case and blood samples to Dr. Terrance Alexander. Then she dashed off another e-mail to Terrance herself, folded her notebook, and aimed for the baggage claim, her husband trudging along beside her.

And still the runners ran.

Three minutes came and went. Most had covered a significant number of departure and arrival gates. Though they did not reach every gate, they had each zigzagged between hundreds of passengers from all over the world.

At the end of their trek, as Stu idly munched a potato chip, as Josh played war hero in the living room with Uncle Rick, as families ate meals and children were born and old men dreamed of their youth, each runner withdrew a small pill from a pocket, broke it open, popped it in his or her mouth, and chewed quickly . . .

"Do not pause to think at this moment," Jean had warned softly, steel-eyed, as they had gathered on the docks in Seattle, *"lest you fall prey to the burden of empty social virtue and lose the courage of your final triumph. Embrace your solemn end, be meek, and the earth will become your inheritance."*

With their last conscious breaths, they swallowed the pill, unfolded a piece of paper, and lay down on the ground . . . as if to sleep.

Seventeen people dead. The air poisoned. Planes coming and going. In their hands or under their heads or on their chests, the paper bore a single message:

Gaia must be set free from her cruel taskmasters.
We pass first as penance, loosing Sleeper,
That Mother may dream again.

10

The world continued, uninterrupted. On Sunday morning—which, of course, took twenty-four hours to unfold, time zone by time zone—the headlines slowly unraveled the bizarre conclusion to the Sleeper saga. In Folin, as in much of the heartland, news took a clumsy, circuitous route. It would hit the airways before it showed up in print, though in Oklahoma City, even NBC and ABC were silent. Simply put, weekend news was nobody's priority.

Sylvia awoke that morning to find Rick still asleep on the couch. Usually she didn't sleep this late, though it felt nice for a change. She started to get dressed for church but found a note on the table, with a quick scrawl from Tim: *Took Josh to McDonald's for breakfast. Just want to spend time with him. Sleep some more!*

But she was awake by now. Quietly, she dressed, poured herself a small glass of orange juice, wondering how best to spend the day. It wasn't easy. She must make each day count. Mornings now arrived with a dull pang—a sickening sense that something more should be happening, something valuable or emotionally connective or healing or meaningful. After mulling it over, Sylvia decided that tonight the Chisoms would immerse themselves in family tradition. Sure, they were three weeks late putting up the tree, but they could enjoy it for at least a few days before Christmas. Besides, it would be fun.

Not all things are so easily decided or cleanly divided. Even as she promised herself the monotony of worry would not consume her, the process had already begun. To distract herself, she spent much of the morning sifting through the attic, pulling out boxes of ornaments, unwrapping the artificial tree, then piling everything in a heap in the living room, which, oops, woke up Rick. She set popcorn out for later, lit a cinnamon-apple candle, and dug up some old Christmas records, feeling better, lighter, with each new discovery. If only it would snow.

She had worked up a bit of a sweat by now, so she decided to rest for a minute. She sat on the arm of the recliner. Bleary-eyed, Rick stared at the pile of Christmas goods in the middle of the floor. Neither volunteered to speak first, which was fine with both of them. Rather than sitting idle, however, a new thought struck Sylvia. She grabbed her keys and, without saying good-bye, headed for the county library.

• • •

On the heels of a difficult night and a stressful week, Tim decided time with Josh one-on-one was more important than church. He hoped it would give Sylvia a breather, some needed rest, and he knew enough about grace to know that God would enjoy the occasion as much as Tim would. If there was one thing Tim believed, it was that a lifestyle with God was meant for the market as well as the pew. Time with family was a sacred rite.

As they stood in line at McDonald's, made their order, found a booth seat, he reflected on how like him Josh was. They both walked with a hunkering gait. Though Tim's hair was cut close to his head and Josh's was long and wavy, both were dark, thick, coarse. The connection went deeper than appearance, though. Josh tended to be watchful, silent, as did Tim—though they rarely needed to be this way with each other.

As Josh bit into a sausage biscuit, Tim sipped his coffee, regarding his son with pride and heaviness. He and Sylvia had talked last night. Or rather, he had listened as Sylvia cried and poured out her heart: what prayers were said at the church, the healings all around, the brief words spoken to her about Josh—and then all the hope and fear, and somehow even shame she felt when she fled the church.

Tim had felt anger churn inside him on her behalf, though he wasn't sure precisely at what. Actually, he did know. Part of it was at her own naiveté. Tim would love nothing more than to believe his son could be magically healed. Apparently it was possible, because his own son had healed others (though Tim preferred to skirt that issue). Josh's malady, however, could not be so easily dismissed as his unusual gifts. A major illness would likely require major medical treatment. Plain and simple.

Intellectually, that made sense. Emotionally, Tim recoiled at the prospect. He had watched chemotherapy ruin his mother, couldn't bear the thought for his son, especially when Josh seemed to be holding his own—at least for now. So why push it? And why had Sylvia decided to chase a spiritual ambulance—or in this case, a traveling faith healer? It would be miracle enough if Josh got better, no matter how it happened.

Even if it meant chemotherapy.

Tim blew steam from his coffee, fearfully considering that perhaps he had overreacted against the idea. He and Sylvia might not have a choice. As a father, he knew his personal demons should not be allowed to interfere with Josh's best shot at well-being. Perhaps radical treatment did make sense in the long run. Certainly, the worst thing would be to wait, afraid, until it's too late.

In spite of himself, Tim thought, *Of course, I'd take a miracle if God wanted to give us one.*

It wasn't that he didn't believe God was capable. Power wasn't the issue. At gut level, Tim simply had to admit that miraculous intervention struck him as unjust. All the pomp and circumstance inherent in certain brands of religious hype, where the supernatural becomes routine, where faith somehow becomes both a channel and indicator of divine favor—with God directly inserting himself into the human equation—offended his sense of order and fairness. If God helped one, why not all? Why pick and choose? Why the Chisoms and not the Smiths or the Weinsteins or the McCormicks? Why did some of those kids at the Murrah Building die and some didn't? The reality of the answer left God looking capricious and arbitrary.

God promised strength, courage, not instant solutions. Sin had bruised the whole world, Tim figured. Unfortunately, that meant sickness was now part of life from time to time. Yes, God could help and was willing, but man's obligation was to *accept* the terms, not define them—certainly not to the point of requiring God to perform parlor tricks every time something went awry. That's why faith was nothing if not sensible. Faith was about the realization of character, which kept a person on the safest possible path. Faith was based on a reasonable progression of spiritual benefit—on God's terms. The proverbial "leap" of faith was fundamentally a rational decision.

Not some outlandish contradiction and certainly not some divine tease, he mused. *Just show me the plan. I'll follow. But for Josh's sake, show me . . . show Sylvia, soon.*

Such were his scattered thoughts as Sylvia had sobbed with confusion over what had happened at the Pentecostal church. Tim did not try to share his conclusions; he sensed it wasn't the right time. All he could think to do was hold her. They fell asleep clutching one another.

Now, with Josh, he cleared his head and asked, "Think you'll catch up okay in school? You've missed a couple of days, you know."

Josh thought a moment and chewed. "Sure."

Other folks came and went. Tim wanted to say something funny or happy, something reassuring. He knew his son. He knew Josh had already picked up on plenty of body language, snatches of conversation, tone of voice, not to mention the repeated visits to the doctor—all obvious enough. Still, Josh had yet to ask about any of it, which concerned Tim. Was Josh trying to protect *them?* Was he trying to carry this alone? Was he too afraid to talk? And what was Tim to say, anyway? What sound did a heart make when it was torn? What words could be spoken, what breach of silence could be tolerated, that would not cause a further rending?

"What's your favorite color?" Tim queried. He had asked the question a dozen times before, but Josh always changed the answer.

"Blue," Josh replied instantly, mouth full.

"Any reason why?"

"Nope. Just like it."

He was distracted, eyes darting here and there, studying the faces of folks sitting at their tables or new people coming through the doors. Tim watched his son watching others, following his line of sight to a well-dressed older lady with styled, frosted silver hair. She was thin, prim in posture, comfortable, but refined. Dressed for church, no doubt.

"What do you see?" Tim pressed in gently.

Josh kept his eyes focused on the lady.

"A pretty lady. She looks lonely." He paused. "I think she is very brave."

Tim didn't see it. "What makes you say that?"

Josh didn't try to answer. "I bet she has kids that live far away and never visit."

As sometimes happens, the restaurant cycled through one of those hushed moments when everyone seems to lose interest in conversation at the same time. Josh, quite finished with speaking, seemed uncomfortable with the exchange, as if he had given away a gift and would rather have it back. He shifted his gaze, glanced to his half-eaten biscuit, and pushed the rest of it toward the center of the table. Tim eyed the gesture warily.

"I thought that was your favorite."

"I'm not very hungry." He held his cup in the air towards his father. "Could I have some more to drink?"

Tim took the cup, refilled it from the metal water cooler near the front. It was hard not to feel as if all of that meant something.

"Josh," he said when he returned, thinking, *Be direct; play it light.* It's all he knew to do. "The doctors, Sunny and Dr. Perkins, have figured something out . . ."

Josh drank deeply from the cup and adjusted his gaze to the angle of Tim's face, waiting patiently. Tim knew he must establish an unwavering visual lock, must not look away. To do so would send the worst possible message. It was easier to say than do. Tim's heart raged for his son. He was, after all, a father, and this was his child, a child whose eyes were ever open to him, unguarded, waiting to hear the truth. Josh's eyes, for him, were never closed.

"They say you have . . . a sickness, Josh. It's a sickness that may take a while to fix."

"Like my asthma?"

"Kind of like that, yes. There are things they want to do to help you feel better."

Josh grew cautious. "I don't feel so bad."

"I know, and we told them that. But you have been pretty tired, haven't you? And you aren't eating like you usually do."

Josh didn't respond. Tim dropped his line of sight to the sausage biscuit, making his point. Josh shrugged.

"I'm glad you feel okay, Son, and I don't want you to worry about this. Not one bit. You go to school and do your stuff and live and be a kid. Your mother and I just want you to know what's been happening. We told the doctor that as long as you are feeling pretty okay, then we don't see any reason to do differently."

That seemed to make Josh happy—a minor vote of confidence.

"Thanks, Dad."

"But," Tim said, holding up one finger. "If you don't feel well, for any reason, you don't hesitate to let us know. All right? This isn't something to mess around with. I don't want you hiding anything."

Josh nodded thoughtfully. "I guess if you drove me all the way to Oklahoma City, it must be . . ." His voice trailed away.

Tim's reply stuck in his throat. "It . . . could be a big deal, Son. I don't know." He was careful to avoid weighty words. This was not the kind of conversation a father and son were ever supposed to have. "How's that make you feel?"

With those words, a window opened—a brief window into Josh's soul. "All I've ever wanted was to be a kid," he murmured. "Just a normal kid."

Tim reached over, grabbed his hand.

Josh kept his hand safely under his father's and lowered his head. "That man at the church said he saw healing all over me."

"Your mother told me about that."

"That'd be pretty nice, wouldn't it? If I just got better all of a sudden?"

Tim took one last, long sip of coffee and swallowed hard. "I can't imagine anything better."

Christmas, which had been simmering in the air since before Thanksgiving, was now running full throttle, splashed across store windows and downtown banners and glowing from the lights and trees decorated in homes all over town. Somehow, magically, the chores of life in December seemed less like work and more like fun, or so Josh thought. Smiles were taken at face value and returned; perhaps usual fare for small-town folk, though at Christmastime the usual seemed that much sweeter.

Tim and Josh left McDonalds, ran errands together, talked together, and sat together for most of the morning and early afternoon. Tim asked Josh if he wanted lunch. Josh said no.

"I have a place I want to take you," Tim told him, when the other errands were finished. "Something I want you to do. I think you'll like it."

Josh was curious. They went to the quarry, bundled in heavy coats and gloves, and stood together on top of the cliff overlooking the rock bottom forty feet below. Tim told Josh about his promotion and Josh whooped and gave him a high-five. Gazing across the expanse, Josh saw a neatly carved cavity several hundred feet in diameter, with heavy equipment clustered in three different work areas. He loved to visit Red Rock, to pretend it was the Grand Canyon, though for safety reasons, he was rarely allowed.

"Is this my surprise?" he asked.

"No," Tim said, reaching behind the seat of his truck, pulling out a long, wrapped package. "This is."

Josh's eyes lit up. He tore into the package, pulling out a Styrofoam glider kit, the kind with extra-long breakaway wings. It only cost about five dollars at Wal-Mart, but Josh instantly understood the prize relative to the place. This baby would fly!

They quickly assembled the kit. Held in his father's grip, Josh edged to within four or five feet of the skirt of the cliff for maximum viewing distance. The quarry was huge. Josh imagined the plane would likely glide forever.

"This is awesome, Dad," Josh said, gripping the plane. The air was cold, but windless—perfect for flying.

"Let her fly, Josh. You're in command."

And so he did. Clutching the thick Styrofoam belly of the plane, he hoisted it behind his back, thrusting it out and over his head. The plane slipped over the edge of the quarry, suspended midair, then lofted even higher as a gentle, sweeping updraft rose from the floor below.

Then it sailed. And sailed, hanging in the air as from a string dangled by the finger of God, diving, swooping, angling left and right. It was beautiful. Josh watched, as long as he could, awe-struck. It was a sea gull taking wing, a jet hovering in that cloudless belt of breath between earth and space, an angel dancing in heaven. Finally, just a speck of white, the plane touched softly at the far end of the canyon floor.

"I felt that," Josh said. "Way down in my belly. I felt it."

Tim smiled. Together they rested on top of the rock and told stories. Tim told of his high-school days, mainly because Josh begged to hear of it, again. That, and how he and Sylvia met. It was too cold to be comfortable for long. As the day wore on, Josh wore out. By two-thirty, he was depleted. When they returned home, the first thing Josh did was collapse on the sofa.

• • •

On Monday, the media began to piece together the initial fragmentary reports related to their own national or continental boundaries, but a random suicide in an airport barely made the evening news, even in the target cities. Once the media realized the notes left by each victim matched, apparently solving the riddle of Sleeper, word sizzled up and down the information highway. Come Tuesday, newswires, networks, and Internet were replete with front-page material:

SLEEPER NO JOKE: SEVENTEEN DEAD

COMPUTER VIRUS CAUSED BY SUICIDE CULT

DEATH PACT SPANS GLOBE WITH STRANGE FINAL MESSAGE

In Atlanta, Stu read the headline and accompanying story in the *Constitution* with a critical eye. It was obvious no one expected lucidity from such obvious madness, though the *Constitution*'s reporter, among others, did find the message curiously haunting. The accompanying editorial, however, was nothing short of bizarre, going so far as to offer a strange sort of tribute. It read:

Death is never fashionable, regardless what the euthanasia enthusiasts would have us believe. Nevertheless, when life's fragility is so shockingly demonstrated, it gains our attention. The net effect is that we are forced to consider evidence to which we might otherwise remain deaf. When you see someone willing to perish—for the sake of the entire planet, no less—at the very least you must pause and wonder what kind of people these were, this as-yet-unnamed group of co-conspirators. In this circumstance, you are likely to even recoil, discounting them as lunatics.

But maybe, just maybe, you and I will also stop and think, and in the process become an incrementally more sensitive citizen of the ecological web. Voluntary public suicide is, at minimum, rude. But is such a violation of our sensibilities really the question, or as the Sleeper clan asserts, is the primary offense against the earth herself? What life are we taking, every single day? Is it not our own? Viewed as caretakers of ourselves and future generations, we too are committing suicide, though much more slowly.

Still, it seems such a waste. After the flurry of publicity is over, will their deaths have accomplished what they dreamed? We truly wish, first, that they had not employed such drastic measures, that they could have creatively employed other means and spared themselves this tragedy; second, failing the possibility of persuading them otherwise, that they might have chosen a date other than two weeks prior to Christmas, the one season usually reserved for hope around the world. But maybe that too was part of their plan. Perhaps these were freaks. But maybe their message is one we should hear, sooner rather than later.

Blah, blah, blah. Very few of the other stories he read on-line at *Newsweek* or Reuters found any compelling connection to the larger question of the previous computer messages. As a whole, initial speculation viewed the series of messages as a twisted, though intriguing, public relations machine hinting at the macabre way in which the group would push its radical environmental message, much like the Buddhist monk who set himself afire to protest the war in Vietnam.

Stu knew better. What he didn't know was how to prove it. Though the various reports contained interesting, similar details—the same time tables, same strange running pattern according to eyewitnesses, same luggage, same cyanide pill in the stomach—instead of proving a point, they painted an image from which the rational mind recoiled. As a result, the details were more likely to feel creepy than compelling to the average Joe, something on par with Heaven's Gate: each person in bed, fully dressed, with shoes and bag ready to depart for the spaceship in the comet's tail.

From behind his desk, surrounded by paperwork, Stu cursed loudly. His phone rang; he ignored it. Rang again. He turned the ringer off. On his computer screen, thirty-four e-mails were still stacked up for review from the weekend, carried over to Monday, awaiting Stu's attention. As were about a dozen colleagues and subordinates, and numerous requisitions. Though the morning was bright, Stu's mood was foul. He hated messing with inane bureaucratic buzz, which kept him essentially swatting at flies instead of uncovering the real hornet's nest, Sleeper. The raw feeling in his gut urged him to keep going, keep investigating. He picked up the phone, pondered for a moment, then dialed.

"Put the director on the phone," he requested. As he waited, he realized he had yet to sample the morning's grinds. The thought only annoyed him further. "I don't care what he said about interruptions. Get him on-line."

At the same moment, after lightly scratching on the surface of his door with her fingernails, Stu's secretary cracked it open and poked her head through. "I think you should take a look at this," she said gravely.

"I need the file on Miami, Marge," Stu demanded, without glancing up, "and I want a status report on the rubella outbreak in Prague. And another thing: I want every clipping you can find on this Sleeper thing that's been happening—"

"I think you should take a look *now*," Marge repeated.

Stu glanced up sharply. His eyes flashed, then faded to a reptilian, heavy-lidded warning gesture. He held the phone out, stared at it, finally slammed the receiver down, grabbed his cane, and followed. "All hell," he warned, "if I miss the director." He meant it. Stu purposefully made sure working relationships were not allowed to grow presumptuous, and that friendship never developed at a pace that could exceed the work itself. Menial tasks were the most common punishment for an understudy who grew too familiar.

His secretary, however, had grown tough over the years. "Maybe you should start working on a vaccine for grumpiness."

Stu grunted. "Where are we going?"

"Biohazard."

They traveled down a series of halls, then across a catwalk from the administrative office complex to the virology lab: Building 15. With eleven separate Level 3 hot suites and additional Level 4 labs confined to a separate wing, accessible via air lock, the Viral and Rickettsial Diseases Laboratory was a structure unto itself, the most sophisticated containment facility in the world, and the crown jewel of the CDC mission.

"We received an anonymous shipment on the dock of the subbasement of Building 1 at 9:15 this morning," Marge continued. "Sam, from Special Pathogens, happened to pick it up, though it was addressed to you. It was in a plain cardboard box with warning labels."

"Like everything else we get around here—"

"Sam thought so, too, until he saw what was inside. Styrofoam shipper . . . metal canister packed in dry ice."

"Vials of blood?"

Marge was cautious. "Nope."

After maneuvering up a couple levels and down two more series of hallways, Marge and Stu reached a dead end—a heavy steel door. This was the preliminary staging area of the containment unit, so both were required to scan their security cards and enter a code. Access to Building 15 was highly restricted to a handful of personnel and monitored constantly with closed-circuit, remote-control cameras. Access to the labs *inside* Building 15 took an act of Congress. It was a fortress, designed at every point to keep people out and microbes in. As if the point needed clarifying, a large, bright sign read: "Infectious area. No unauthorized entry."

The door was big and thick, similar to a bank vault, except that it was outlined in black-and-yellow stripes, with a large red trefoil painted on the door itself, the international warning symbol for dangerous pathogens. After confirming their identities and codes, the heavy bolt inside the door thunked open, allowing entry. Inside the primary interior chamber were some lockers, a stainless steel sink with stainless steel mirror, and two or three stainless steel shelves lined with green scrub suits; also two doors, one straight ahead and one to the right. The door to the right led to a corridor tangled with colored PVC, gauges, and circuit breakers. It was the control room for the containment lab. Inside it were gamma-ray generators, filters, fans, and the compressor system responsible for creating the negative pressure environment of the entire biohazard suite. For each additional layer, each level entered, each line crossed to move deeper towards the heart of the lab—Biosafety 4—the negative pressure increased to assure that airflow would move *inward*, towards the center of isolation, rather than outward, into the world.

The door straight ahead was clearly marked above: "Warning: Biosafety Level 2."

Marge said, "I'll wait outside for you. Our guys are behind the observation plate now." She handed him an envelope, which apparently came with the package, noting dryly, "It's addressed to you."

She departed, leaving Stu to undress. He was still irritable, but sufficiently intrigued to continue. Knowing that to proceed beyond this point required a change of clothes, he grabbed a pair of loose cotton scrubs from the shelf. His bad knee ached, but he shed his clothes, including underwear, packed it all in a locker, pulled on the pants and shirt, tightened the drawstring, and fixed a loose surgical cap on his hairless head. A slight odor of formaldehyde permeated the room, which in younger days used to turn Stu's stomach; he hardly noticed anymore. He scrubbed his hands and arms in the sink for five minutes, placed a surgical mask over his mouth, then proceeded forward.

The Level 2 door made a whoosh as he opened it, evidence of the sucking power of negative pressure at work. Rich blue light flooded the interior of the room, like melting sapphires. Following negative pressure, ultraviolet washes were the next line of defense against viral entities. Viruses exposed to ultraviolet light quickly broke down, like a rock under a sledgehammer, and in the process lost their terrifying genetic ability to replicate. Stu closed his eyes and turned his face toward the light. Even now, he could feel the tingling rush of adrenaline. It had been several weeks since he had visited the containment labs, maybe months. Truth was, he didn't much like to come here anymore; he was strictly a tourist at this point, not because he was denied access, but because an administrator of his rank rarely needed to come, a fact that rankled him still. Standing there silent, he could not help but remember the thrill. Once this had been more of a home to him than his own bed.

He could proceed from here to Level 3, the door straight ahead, and from there to Level 4, maximum containment. Level 3 was called the staging area, where additional latex and rubber and, finally, pressure suits were donned; beyond that, Level 4, with its air-lock door and chemical decontamination shower and tangled strings of air tubing hanging from the ceiling to supply the fill for the suits. Level 4 was the notorious *hot zone,* a maze of rooms filled with banks of animal cages and heavy metal freezers, lockboxes fitted with padlocks and sealed with wide bands of tape, inside each of which was stored thousands of small glass vials containing samples of the world's deadliest known pathogens.

Freezers at the CDC came in all shapes and sizes. If the institution ever lost either funding or mandate, it could immediately serve in simultaneous fashion as an industrial appliance museum, warehouse, and art exhibit for the macabre. CDC freezers were stored everywhere, in every nook and corner of every building—even administration. There were tall, gray, brushed metal Forma Scientific uprights, decades-old double-door Kelvinators, eight-foot-long Harrises, maintained at a cool minus seventy degrees Celsius to both preserve polio viruses and render them dormant at the same time. Deeper still, in arctic CryoMeds, filled with liquid nitrogen, lurked frozen tuberculosis. But pathogens weren't the only things in these freezers and refrigerators. Less specialized units contained a bit of just about anything one could imagine: chemical and biological diagnostic reagents, antibodies, miscellaneous excretions from humans and animals alike, convalescent serum, tissue samples, frozen insects, dolphin kidneys, mashed squirrel brains, necrotic livers, fungus, molds, spores, and all manner of other fascinating, icky stuff.

Stu would not be going into Level 3 or Level 4. The observation plate was available by exiting through a door to his immediate left. Carrying only the envelope Marge gave him, he found himself in a small, narrow room with half a dozen small portholes in the wall. These were triple-layer Plexiglas shields, sealed inside and out with a gooey, rubbery substance

that guaranteed zero airflow. Every ten seconds or so, a pulse of ultraviolet light shot through the portal space just for good measure. Stu pressed
his face to the glass. Beyond, in a small antechamber specifically created
for observation, was a polished, stainless steel table, where two workers in
pressurized blue suits stood beside the table, carefully examining an
object. Strangely, the object was a blue can of deodorant, with cap
removed, sitting upright. Beside the deodorant was an official-looking
cylindrical transport tube, stickered with yellow-and-black warning tape
and the spiked red biohazard flower.

Wordless, Stu took the envelope and ripped it open without looking.
What was a can of deodorant doing here? He glanced away from the port-
hole long enough to examine the contents of the envelope. Inside was a
sheet printed on FBI letterhead, signed by an anonymous field agent:

Sleeper is bigger than we thought. No doubt, in a few days, you would
have gotten this delivery through more official channels, but I don't
think we can afford to wait for protocol to catch up. Needless to say, I'm
violating about a dozen regulations with this break of confidentiality. If
you appreciate the gesture at all, do me a favor and don't hunt me down
or play human resource detective. I have reason to know you're the best,
so thrill me and prove all my fears wrong, because according to the profiles I'm drafting on this group, some major stuff is about to hit the fan.
The only question is, what?

You need to know that the media doesn't have the whole story. Our
boys did pretty good containing the information quickly, if I do say so
myself, at least in the States. Don't know about the global scene.
Problem is, we stopped there, job done, and promptly stuck our heads in
the sand, even though every victim had an identical can, such as I've sent
you. In each case, the cans were empty, with residue evident on the fab-
ric of the backpack. Think the cans were sprayed in the airport terminals? You and I think alike. But why? That's the question, and that's
where you come in. Check it out.

I sent it labeled toxic to be on the safe side, and because I think
these guys were loons. Each one of the suicide notes included an
address: www.globalpurgeplan.com. Sound scary? Wait till you read

their manifesto. The site was supposed to be free access, but we locked it down in less than six hours, and so far have kept the leak from the media. My supervisors are buying the publicity stunt BS. When you visit, you'll see why I was afraid of delaying further investigation. Use the password Lewinsky. Cute, I know. Don't ask.

And don't look for me. You'll screw it up for both of us.

Stu finished the letter, nearly breathless. Staring past the paper, his vision blurred as a dozen thoughts crowded in for attention. He watched for a few more minutes as the men inside transferred samples of the residue from the tip of the deodorant can to sticks for making cultures. Then he exited the room, almost robotlike, stacking up thought after thought, running scenarios in his head. Bad scenarios. *Very* bad. In the locker room, he undressed, still in a daze, dressed again in plain clothes, and exited through the final door to where Marge awaited.

"Belated birthday present from your daughter?" she teased. It wasn't funny and she should have known better. Stu regarded her as if she were an alien. He waved the envelope, his eyes a million miles away. Actually, he didn't even know she had spoken. Crinkling the paper, he dashed off, back to his office, as fast as the pain in his knee would allow. Plopping in front of the computer, his fingers clumsily thumped the keyboard.

GLOBALPURGEPLAN.COM <ENTER>

The CDC had a backbone connection to the Internet, government priority access and secured lines; speed was no problem. Immediately, an FBI splash screen appeared, complete with federal warnings for unauthorized access or tampering of any sort. A small box at the bottom requested a password to proceed.

LEWINSKY <ENTER>

The screen glowed and flickered. The home page loaded.
"GPS," it declared. "Global Purgation Society."
The site was a no-nonsense script, plain text, no graphics. It began:

Not long ago, on October 12, 1999, Earth's population crossed the line of six billion people. Less than one hundred years ago, the world's population was less than two billion—tripling the number in a single century. To grow from five billion people to six billion took a record low of twelve years. With extended life capacities, this "trend" will only continue to accelerate, with exponentially adverse effects.

For generations, the warning cry has risen, to little avail. Aldo Leopold, John Muir, and Rachel Carson artfully defined the problems we face, as well as the value of Earth as a collective unit, an organic reality, from which all life flows. (In this respect, man has evolved very nearly into a predatory role as Earth's natural enemy, no different than the weasel is to the snake, or the lion to the gazelle.) Upon the foundation of these pioneers, a biocentric world-view—as opposed to the anthropocentric paradigm of civilization—has found further nurture in the philosophies of intellectual and spiritual luminaries from Norway, Australia, Canada, and the United States. The cry has gone out. People have rallied. Little has changed. Why?

It is because all the theories remain abstractions of a plan, rather than the revelation of an objective. We have the underpinnings of moral conviction but have lacked, until now, the courage to act with violent and revolutionary purpose, on a scale worthy of our biocentric values.

On and on it went, spouting more blather, more facts, more figures, describing the "woefully inadequate impact" of the NPT Treaty, Montreal Protocol, Basel Convention, Rio Declaration, and Vienna Convention. Included were links to a history of sorts, sprinkled with commentary. Stu clicked on them. The outline revealed the rise of environmental activity in the U.S. and abroad, as well as the relationships between various ecological factions and their divergent philosophies. Hovering in the middle, Stu noted that someone named Jean de Giscard seemed to form the axis around which much of the site orbited. He skimmed the history quickly:

1892: The birth of modern environmentalism. Sierra Club founded by John Muir, propagating the language of modern eco-conscience.

1970: Greenpeace is founded in Vancouver, British Columbia by Irving Stowe, Paul Cote, and Jim Bohlen to protest nuclear testing in the Pacific.

1987: As global momentum stalls, TerraPrime is founded in Manfred, England by Jean de Giscard with the express purpose to "propagate, by any means necessary, profound natural truth." This includes lobbying, lawsuits, letter writing, and research papers, but also confrontation, guerrilla theater, direct action, and civil disobedience.

1991: TerraPrime leadership ousts de Giscard, moves TerraPrime toward mainstream political credibility in the United States, eschewing its activist roots, as well as all criminal acts other than lawful protests. Disaffected members form Independent Earth Assault three months later, embracing the original goal, "by any means necessary."

1993: Brother Monkey, an animal rights group, and Independent Earth Assault publish communiqué declaring solidarity of action, propounding philosophical system dubbed Deep Ecology. Methods employed include monkey-wrenching, ecotage, and strategic forms of property destruction.

1994: IEA ideology deemed insufficient to successfully challenge advancing global structures in a reasonable time frame to avert ecological catastrophes. In response, Global Purgation Society launches, comprised of handpicked volunteers and visionaries—those who understand the martyrdom upon which true redemption is based.

"These," the text declared, meaning GPS volunteers, "are the heroes of the next earth age . . ."

From there the site listed dozens of criminal acts for which a variety of radical groups claimed responsibility, including multiple arsons at U.S. Forest Service Ranger Stations, housing developments that threatened local water supplies, and state universities whose research further pressured developing nations to switch from natural crop plants to genetically engineered varieties. Also tree spiking at timber harvest sites in Oregon, Idaho, Washington, and British Columbia; the release of wild horses from the Bureau of Land Management corrals, of hundreds of mink and ferrets from various laboratories, etc. Total damages were estimated to be somewhere in excess of 250 million dollars thus far, and counting. Rather than gloating, however, the article noted that in spite of such heavy financial losses and resultant press coverage, little had actually changed.

Stu shook his head. Crazy stuff. For some reason he felt a little bit guilty even reading it. At the bottom was a single link: "The GPS Plan."

Stu clicked the link, the last link, and was quickly taken to a final, undecorated page—about 30K of plain text. Labeled at the top, the file was apparently excerpted from a magazine article by Jean de Giscard. It claimed to have been originally published by something called EcoNow Press. The title reeked of self-importance: "Honor Thy Mother: The Significance of Final Devotion in a Culture of Consumption and Depravity." Several editorial reviews accompanied the article, mostly from high-profile figures within the ranks of the environmental under-ground. They hailed the work, calling it Jean de Giscard's "magnum opus," a "signature achievement," the "crown of his life's work."

"This changes everything," one reviewer gushed. "We cannot go back from here, only forward."

Superlatives aside, Stu quickly surmised that the article was *the* point of the whole site, the GPS manifesto, which, hopefully, meant it might also provide a key to deciphering Sleeper, or at least dispel the night-mare scenarios he was already mentally sketching. As he read, though, his gut curled like a fist inside his belly. Jean de Giscard was a prophet. A very mad prophet . . .

All the earth is in transition. Our Mother has been so faithful to give us life, generation after generation, millennium after millennium. But Mother is growing tired. Her children have abused her, stolen from her, cursed her, neglected her. She is weary of the task of bringing forth the old, those who take and give nothing in return. Yet because she is weak, she has no strength to bring forth the new. She has long ago been drained of her resources, stripped naked, prostituted by her sons and daughters, institutionalized, commercialized, industrialized, raped, depleted, and forcibly sterilized of any procreative ability save the furtherance of avarice in the heart of man. She is a feeder of pigs—we the pigs—beasts whose appetites have grown both shocking and insatiable. The noble woman is soiled by our gluttony.

Once, perhaps, we were grateful for her indulgence of our yearn-ings. No more. Nor is there any hope for change. Politics is in perpetual stalemate, a quagmire of hypocrisy and lip service. The world follows the United States, the United States follows the polls, the polls follow the people, and the people don't care.

Now is the time for healing. Now is the time for boldness. Three-and-a-half billion years of life on Earth have come and gone, and never before—not even since the end of the Cretaceous, 65 million years ago—has Mother been so strained. She must be replenished. She must be set free. Let us proudly yield to nature and take up the cause of liberation for future generations of Mother-life. The wisdom that flows effortlessly in the deep roots of the oak, which bellows forth from the throat of the elk, demands it.

(If you have seen the frost sparkle off the bending blades of new buds of green on a cold March morning in the farm villages outside Riems, you know of the wisdom I speak. If you have seen the caribou blow hard breath and lift its call to the moon in north Saskatchewan, you know the wisdom I speak. If you have shouted at the pristine stillness of the stars while standing alone in the middle of the Australian bush, and have heard the silence of your echo, and wept at its awful beauty, you know the wisdom I speak.)

Listen to me. Listen to the wisdom of earth lovers. A midwife is called upon to birth a child. But not always. There often comes a critical point in the delivery when a decision must be made. In that moment, the choice is between the mother or the child. To allow the child to live, continue living, places the mother in irreversible danger. In fact, the mother may die from the strain of supporting the life she has carried for so long. This puts the midwife in a horrific position, but a necessary one.

She becomes, at such a moment, the very arbiter of life.

We, the lovers of the Mother, have determined to allow Mother to live. The child must be aborted. The risk is simply too great to consider any other course of action. But have no fear. As our species sprang from the bowels of the earth, a new race shall surely arise. Mother is able to bring forth something new if we will but summon the will to give her the chance. She has created life in eons past, diverse and marvelous, and will certainly deliver such life again. Perhaps a creature no less glorious than man, but better, more reasoned, more attuned. Such thinking is, of course, pure speculation, but we trust Mother. She may simply allow one of the animal species to come to the fore, with enhanced cerebral function and a soul that truly emerges from the Earth, who is therefore more prone to faithfully protect it. We can only pray the already fixed evolutionary course does not simply yield another race of man, or Mother will likely face the same exploitation in another 100,000 years.

In either case, we cannot allow such predictions to diminish our resolve. Mother needs time now and time is running out. She is tired. Yet by nature Mother is simply too kind to destroy her own children, her most ascended realization of life's potential: humanity. Though they destroy her, she will continue to give until she has nothing left for any form of life. She will give until nothing is alive but greed. If this is allowed to continue, not only one race shall perish, but all, and the green fields and blue waters and snow-capped mountains shall turn to something more lifeless than coal, the atmosphere will collapse, the soil will burn, and our planet shall become a spinning, desolate rock among the galaxies. Millions of years would certainly pass before the hope that even simple life might arise from her bosom again, if ever. Let us not be guilty of such passivity. Let us not surrender to fate and dream silently and wonder from afar. The plan is not hard to envision, the cleansing not too hard to comprehend, nor implement. We shall rejoin you, Mother! We shall be the wise sons you meant us to be! We shall rejoin you, brothers of the field, sisters of the earth, cousins of the sky!

Friends of the earth, the grass and animals and trees need us, one last time. They need us, that they may be free of us forever.

And so we are in transition.

The old must pass away. The new will come. In time, our wisdom will be vindicated. Though no one remembers our names, Mother will.

Long live Mother.

At the bottom was a list of names, the final participants, the "martyrs" of the new earth age. Stu almost skimmed past the list. He had already discovered what he was looking for. The GPS plan confirmed his worst fears. But he skimmed the list anyway, the list of the dead, willing victims of the plan. Name three (in alphabetical order) nearly stole his breath. Gasping, he pushed against the loose skin of his forehead; for one burning moment, he thought he was having a stroke.

Name three was the name of his daughter, Alyssa Josie Baker.

11

His face pale, his skin cold—for a moment, Stu couldn't even breathe. Over and over, his lips formed the same word. *Josie* . . .

Fumbling for the phone, he dialed Century Center Parkway, the offices of the Atlanta division of the FBI. Though he fought for control, his voice trembled.

"Thurman, please."

Agent Thurman was the special agent in charge, a native of Atlanta, a likable guy. He and Stu had collaborated together on a handful of local actions over the years: nursing home illnesses, food poisonings, and the like. Though most of Stu's contact with the FBI was channeled to Quantico, to the Forensic Science Research and Training Center, Stu maintained a reasonably good personal relationship with Agent Thurman. It was the best place he knew to start his search.

A deep, rich voice answered the phone. "Special Agent Thurman."

"Thurman, Stu Baker. Listen, I need an inside track."

"Okay . . ." Thurman replied warily.

"I wouldn't normally try to pull strings, but I've got reason to believe my daughter was one of the participants in this whole Sleeper thing over the weekend."

"What do you mean, 'reason to believe'? Have you been notified?"

"No. Not yet."

"But you think your daughter might have been . . . what? One of the airport victims?"

"I don't know. There's a pretty good chance."

"Pretty good? When was the last time you spoke to her?"

"Seven years. Maybe eight."

"Good grief, Stu! What's wrong with you?"

"I don't need the lecture right now, Thurman, believe me. I need to know whether she's on the list or not. And if she is"—he swallowed, couldn't say it—"on the list, why haven't I been notified yet?"

Agent Thurman exhaled long and slow. "Man, Stu, this is not the thing to start mucking around in. I've heard buzz that this thing may be big."

"How do you mean?"

"Don't know. No one's really talking. That's probably why the list hasn't been released yet. They're probably trying to figure out what's going on before they let us know what they got. People don't coordinate suicide on a global stage for a good string of headlines, know what I mean? Something else is going down. Enough that folks at J. Edgar are getting in on the action. I'm not sure I can do much. This baby is locked up tight."

"I just need a yes or no, Thurman. That's all, at least for now."

"I'm not sure I got the clout to make it happen." He sighed. "What's her name?"

"Josie. Alyssa Josie Baker. Anything you can do, I'm grateful."

They hung up. Stu folded his hands, wiped his eyes.

Josie . . .

The remainder of the day Stu was distracted, troubled. He waited impatiently by the phone for word from Agent Thurman, checked his e-mail for results from Level 4 on the contents of the can. But Thurman had sounded as though his hands might be tied, and residue culture takes time. Stu was left to brood. He made sure no one put new work on him, that most people stayed away. Then he hid himself, fretting, scanning the Internet for any further clues, nervously inhaling half a pack of cigarettes, resorting at last to a couple of shots from his flask to calm his nerves. Nothing worked.

At 8:30, bleary-eyed and worn out, he traveled home. Entombed in the stillness of his home, Stu experienced the loneliest night of his life.

• • •

On the very next day, people began to die.

Nobody knew it yet. The first of the news arrived around ten o'clock via an urgent request for assistance from a terrified chief of staff at a major hospital in Tokyo. Stu didn't take the call, but the report came directly to his desk. The hospital had been forced to set up a makeshift quarantine zone overnight after nearly two dozen people reported in from all over the city complaining of the same symptoms: raging fevers, escalating respiratory difficulty, acute general malaise, and severe aching. The symptoms were severe but could have likely been applied to a half-dozen illnesses. Two things stood out: a hacking, bloody cough and the severe onset of symptoms after an apparent seventy-two-plus-hour incubation period. The victims were literally being carried to the hospital by nervous family members and friends who claimed to have watched their loved ones dissolve in a matter of hours. Only the day before, they were fine, the doctors were told. The next, practically overnight, they were stricken. Old men, babies, pregnant women, strapping young men—all demographics were affected. Worse, the condition of the affected rapidly declined upon admission to the hospital, and medical professionals appeared helpless to stop it, even with intervention. Within a few hours after their arrival, weak and short of breath, five of the affected had slipped into a coma, requiring life support. After ten admissions in three hours, all complaining of the same thing, the hospital responded with standard quarantine procedures, but it had no clue what to do next.

Except to fedex blood samples to the CDC, and wait for the cavalry.

Though the report was sobering, a Post-it note from the director of the rickettsial lab stuck to the corner of the report downplayed concern. Stu read the note: "It's winter here in the States. It's winter in Japan. Sounds like a pretty rough strain of influenza to me, but probably not much more. We're running tests on the blood samples. I'll have results for you later this morning. Don't expect too much."

No, thought Stu. *Expect disaster. It's begun.*

With his heart caught in flux between Josie and the crisis, Stu hesitated, but only for a moment. He instinctively knew that only one of his two primary concerns could benefit from his attention at this point. If his daughter was dead—horrific as that would be—there was simply nothing he could do to stop it. Sleeper, however, was very much alive and, for the moment, so were thousands of its potential victims. Stu settled the issue in his mind. He was on the chase.

"Marge!" he called, not waiting for her reply. "Was the Tokyo airport targeted by Sleeper?"

Marge appeared at the door, sour-lipped. "Dunno. I think so."

"I need you to dig up an issue of the paper from the last couple of days and make a list of every city the Sleeper cult struck."

"U.S. only?"

"Did I say U.S. only? Everywhere. *Every* city. There's something like fifteen, seventeen . . . something. Then I want you to cross-reference the nearest health department in that region. Use official channels if you can, but in the end all I really care about is somebody who can give us some solid answers. I don't care if it's government approved or not. I need you to coordinate all this with Special Pathogens. I want them in on this from the start."

"On what?"

"Sleeper is not a computer virus, Marge. It's biological. I don't know exactly what it is yet, but I know we're about to get slammed. Everyone is about to get slammed."

Marge straightened her back, adjusted her glasses. "What if I get nowhere overseas?"

It was a good question, a common problem. Even for nations with the best of intentions, bureaucracies were notoriously slow to process information. Poorer nations had difficulty even gathering data, much less disseminating it. And where gathering and processing were nonissues, national pride often became an even worse roadblock. Information blackouts were not unheard of in cases where foreign officials proved reticent to admit having a problem beyond their nation's capability or technology.

"If no one at the top will talk to you, then dig a trench underneath. Contact three hospitals in that city directly." He chewed the end of a pencil, thinking. "Change that. Talk to three hospitals no matter what. I want you on the horn all day if necessary, Marge. Clear your schedule. Everything else gets canceled. Got it?"

"Loud and clear. Can you tell me what we're looking for?"

Stu ripped the summary sheet of symptoms out of the Tokyo file.

"This."

Marge took the paper and scanned it. She was ready. This was what the CDC did.

"I'm on it."

"One other thing. Draft an alert bulletin. I want the Tokyo symptomatology, with a warning to use extreme caution. Not isolation—not yet. But get the docs looking for the symptoms. States only."

The phone rang loudly. Stu answered. It was the New York State Health Commissioner.

"Listen, I'm in a delicate situation and I wondered if the CDC might be an appropriate place to find assistance?"

Stu frowned. "Go on."

"I've got a group of nine high-school students who just returned from a school-sponsored trip overseas as part of their foreign language studies. All nine are now at Mount Sinai Hospital. Must have picked up some strange bug overseas."

"What's it look like?"

"Well, from what they're telling me: high fevers, severe aching, and difficulty breathing. Pretty strange, though. Some of them have begun to either cough or vomit blood."

"And there's no variance? All nine? Same symptoms?"

"Pretty much. Which is precisely why we thought it wise to call. The hospital epidemiologist notified the hospital president, who petitioned me for assistance. It seemed like a scenario worth investigating. But *quietly,* if you get my drift."

Stu thought a moment. "What are a bunch of high-school kids doing traveling overseas at this time of year?"

The commissioner cleared his throat. "Let's just say these students come from important families. Ambassadors, senators, etc. It's a private school. As you can imagine, the last thing we need is a highly publicized medical event."

Stu didn't care what the commissioner thought he needed. "Exactly what day did the students return? To the airport. When did their flight arrive?"

"Excuse me?"

"When did they return, sir?"

The commissioner groused. Stu heard papers shuffling. "Apparently, late Saturday night."

"Around midnight?"

"Yes. 12:05 A.M., to be exact."

"I'll have to get back with you. Tell the hospital, quietly, to move the students to an isolation wing, simply as a matter of precaution."

He hung up and called to his assistant, "Marge, first thing, call Mount Sinai in New York City, ask to talk to the hospital's epidemiologist, tell him to immediately send a blood sample of all nine students. I want it here by tomorrow morning."

He dialed Building 15, barking like a dog. "I'm waiting on that deodorant can. When are we gonna know something?"

"I can tell you this so far. Bacterial cultures, Gram stain, and Giemsa stained cytology reveal no bacterial component. We've got a ways to go, but no pathologic organisms have been isolated on culture to date."

"Viral isolation?"

"With cell cultures, I've seen some suggestions of viral activity. All I can tell you is we're working on it."

"Give me a time."

"Later today, I hope. You can't rush the process."

"Take a guess."

"Two, three o'clock."

"Make it one. And give me a tox screen at the same time. I'm expecting lab results from a separate set of blood samples at that time and I'm betting they're going to line up."

"What's that mean? What's going to line up?"

Pretending not to hear, Stu hung up the phone. Last thing he wanted to do was explain what *that* meant. Not yet. Not until he was sure. Even then, how do you explain the worst possible nightmare?

How do you explain global plague?

• • •

Masked and gloved, smocked in white, the young woman bowed over a vial of thin, clear serum, studying the liquid with a tilt to her head. Her name was Mackenzie Faulkner. She was a student at Emory University, a protégée of Dr. Terrance Alexander. Standing in a large, open lab, bright with fluorescent lights, Mackenzie squinted at the vial past two annoying specks of dust clinging to the outer rim of her goggles.

Her present labors were directed towards the hope of a doctorate in oncology. The work was part of her dissertation, intended to build on the efforts of her adviser and boss. It was the fourth time her paper had changed directions (however slight) so far this year, yet Mackenzie remained undaunted. For the most part.

"Matt, hand me that flask of reagent, please," she said wearily, directing her request to her colleague a few feet away. Matt hardly even glanced up, just pushed the flask down the countertop towards Mackenzie.

Peering through a large microscope, she searched for impurities in the reagent solution and found none. She jotted a couple of notes in her notebook and on the charts. Before her, on a large sterilized plastic sheet divided into small square nodes, dozens of common pathogens awaited droplets from the serum.

The laboratory at Emory was highly modern, polished, and clean, equipped with the finest of equipment: biocontainment laminar flow hood, high performance liquid chromatograph, tunneling electron microscope, nuclear magnetic resonance imager, sterilized vials of all shapes and sizes, buffer solutions, computer equipment that specialized in numerical analysis and three-dimensional renderings of base protein structures, and, of course, the standard complement of centrifuges—every lab's bread-and-butter machine.

The test she was about to perform was one of many serologic tests. This particular one was dubbed ELISA, a rather feminized, sweet acronym that stood for "enzyme-linked immunosorbent assay." ELISA was a controlled process by which two substances were thrown together to see how they interacted. The process could be compared to a counseling session for proteins, with a third-party chemical moderator watching carefully to see if the two primary components were hugging by the time it was all over. If so, the third party, a generic reacting agent, would signal with a color change that meant the antibody had bound to the antigen. Otherwise, nothing happened.

Dr. Alexander did not like "nothing." Nothing did not make for an impressive dissertation.

So this was her task. Mackenzie and Matt, another grad student, working methodically down a long list of potential biomarriages to uncover the hidden secrets of multiple myeloma antibodies. Since many antigens were hard to come by, there was little room for error in the trial. It had to go right the first time. Boring work, mostly, apart from an occasional jolt of discovery. Exotic substances that made a student like Mackenzie salivate were simply off limits, reserved for more specialized facilities, due to the nature of the substance itself. But they had some good stuff to work with, common ailments that were allowed wider latitude. Things like herpes, chicken pox, a variety of group A Streptococci, Staphylococci, a variety of cancer cells and carcinomas, *E. coli,* Salmonella, Pneumococcus, tetanus, botulism, Lyme disease, mumps, and rabies.

Too many to count or list.

Mackenzie carefully noted in her charts each step, each time phase, each process and component. The process was fairly simple: Serum, spun down in a centrifuge, equaled blood plasma minus red blood cells. Red blood cells carried oxygen and little more. Blood plasma did everything else. Plasma, then, was the repository of the monoclonal antibodies for multiple myeloma patients. Most antibodies were *poly*clonal, allowing for greater flexibility in the application of a drug, if synthetic, or immunological response if the antibody was naturally occurring. When an invader barged in, pronged with antigen fangs, it attached to certain cells, causing damage. Antibodies worked by searching for those particular fangs and clamping onto them, much like a muzzle, effectively taking not just the bark, but the bite, out of the microbial dog.

Monoclonal antibodies, however, were a different breed. They clamped on, just like their polyclonal cousins, but since monoclonal antibodies were all identical to each other and singular in effect, they could clamp onto one thing and one thing only. Dr. Alexander had verified earlier in the year, through rigorous ELISA sampling on a lupus sufferer, that monoclonal proteins *were* capable of targeting certain cells. Unfortunately, in that case, the cells targeted were beneficial, so the antibodies, rather than helping, inflicted additional, secondary damage. As great as the find was, it was suspected to be rare. Since monoclonals were singular, they were also unique from person to person. By definition, the singular key shape of a monoclonal protein could only match *one* specifically shaped antigen lock—if at all. Therefore, the trick was to discover which pairs of keys and locks went together. Mackenzie's research reflected the expanded hope that a wider variety of pathogens might also match.

The first step in ELISA was to bind a sample of each pathogen onto the thirty-five plastic wells of a microtiter plate at high temperature for twelve hours. Mackenzie had already prepared four such plates. In the meantime, she had also chemically attached a marker enzyme to the monoclonal protein serums from donor patients. This marker was keyed to a third solution, which, like a homing beacon, would only light up if the antibody successfully bound to the antigen and formed a bridge.

It was called piggybacking.

She had tested the serums of two other patients already today, with negative evidence of binding. Three yesterday, as well. All negative. Next on the list, patient C3.

"Here goes nothing," she whispered under her breath. Matt grunted.

Using a sterile dropper, Mackenzie began dropping antibody serum from patient C3 on the tagged materials of the microtiter plate. Drop by drop, she added serum to each of the wells. Then she waited. Nearly every facet of lab work involved lots and lots of waiting. With about fifteen hours of basic prep time put into each plate, it all came down to a final thirty-minute interval, to give potential reactions plenty of time to transpire. After thirty minutes had passed, she added the pure reagent to the wells and put the plate in the lab spectrophotometer. The spectrophotometer would monitor each well for even a slight color change.

Mackenzie glanced at her watch and scrawled the time in her journal. Fifteen seconds passed. Then . . .

Beep, beep, beep.

The light on the spectrophotometer blinked. Surprised, Mackenzie pulled the plate, wondering if she had calibrated the machine accurately. Sure enough, every well was clear except one, which was obviously tagged bright blue. She scribbled furiously in her note, "Positive reaction," underlining the words.

"Dr. Alexander?" she called, marking the time again.

"I think he stepped out for a few minutes," Matt answered.

Hurriedly, Mackenzie grabbed another prepared plate. Tingling with excitement, she added serum to every well, just as before. Just as she was ready to add the reagent, Dr. Alexander strolled in.

"What's cooking, crew?" he asked jovially. He was a tall man, dark-skinned, with a full graying beard and deep wrinkles around his eyes.

"Dr. Alexander," Mackenzie murmured, "I think you'd better take a look at this."

Dr. Alexander was a calm man. He moved closer and peered over her shoulder. Starting at the top, working her way across and down, Mackenzie added the reagent to each well, one by one. No spectrophotometer this time. They would observe the results visually.

Drop, drop.

Negative initial reaction.

Drop, drop.

Negative initial reaction.

On and on she went, down to the middle of the bottom row. Everything was negative, until row seven, column two. Same as the other plate. Slowly, for effect, she squeezed the rubber dropper. Once. Twice.

When the fluid hit the well, the whole thing changed color. Almost instantly.

Dr. Alexander made a low, whistling noise. He picked up the original microtiter plate, studying both it and the follow-up. Then he compared the wells to the master chart to find the name of the antigen to which the antibody had attached. When he did, he raised an eyebrow.

"Fascinating," he said, calm as Dr. Spock. "You better start writing."

• • •

Legs tucked underneath him, Joshua hunched over a coloring book on the floor, painting a rocket blue and gray, blasting into deep, dark outer space. His favorite thing to color was the burst of flame coming out of the tail, so he always saved that for last. He made throaty, rocket sounds as he mashed at the paper with his crayon.

Earlier, he had asked Sylvia when he would get to go back to school. She told him not to plan on it for a while—not until they could better determine how his strength would hold. Besides, Christmas was only a bit over a week away and then school would let out for ten days anyway. Josh complained that he felt fine, which Sylvia longed to believe. Often she fooled herself into believing it. But then he would fall asleep on the couch in the middle of his favorite cartoon—having done nothing all morning—and sleep for two hours straight. He would leave his favorite dinner mostly untouched. He downed water and juice by the glassful.

No surprise, Rick was still there. He had finally owned up to being fired from Tinker, though he tried to play it off as downsizing thanks to broad cutbacks in the military budget.

"Being stretched too thin, that's all," he said.

That *wasn't* all, and Sylvia knew it. Rick had also admitted that his first visit two months ago was prompted by a mandatory probation period imposed on him for unsatisfactory job performance.

Sylvia shook her head, not so much angry as sad at how childish and undependable her brother was. The air force expected more from its employees than he was able to give, plain and simple. They expected military caliber character and a military work ethic, even for a civilian. Maybe the pressure just became too much. Maybe he got careless. Either way, Sylvia avoided outright confrontation on his latest failure, knowing it would do little good. In truth, part of her was glad to have him around. Though Tim had been a bit reluctant to embrace the idea at first, Josh begged and Sylvia found herself agreeing to it. There was no denying that Rick and Josh seemed to work well together. With Tim at work during the day, a playmate for Josh was welcome relief. And ever since he learned of his nephew's condition, Rick seemed content to direct all his attention to Josh's needs.

He sat with Josh now, coloring the rocket. And wonder of wonders, the television was off.

Sylvia loved her brother. She really did. But there always seemed to be something to fuss about when he was around.

Lunch came and went and Josh's plate still had half a bologna and cheese sandwich sitting on it. Sylvia washed a load of laundry, folded another load, then read through the day's mail, amazed how a little bad news can suddenly warm even the most antagonistic hearts. As word had trickled through town of Josh's illness, people were responding kindly. He had received cards—another two today. A couple of Sylvia's former coworkers had offered to bring a meal over. Mrs. Etheridge had dropped by impromptu to take Josh out for ice cream. And Mrs. Tellier's entire third grade class had written him letters, very sweet letters.

Nevertheless, time away from school, combined with all the attention he had received of late, had begun to go to Josh's head. He was starting to get a little cranky, a little demanding, a bit lazy.

"Josh," Sylvia called from his room, "I want you to come clean this mess."

She sat down at the kitchen table to pay bills. She worked through the water, trash, and electricity bills, yet Josh did not respond to her request.

"Josh, did you hear me?"

"I don't want to," Josh replied in the tone of an equal. "I'm busy."

Sylvia stood and walked directly to her son. She did not bend down.

"I didn't ask if you wanted to, young man. Your room needs attention and I want you to give it now. Now get up and move. Do you understand me?"

"Not much."

"What did you say?"

Josh looked up from his drawing. His black hair curled softly over his shoulders, framing a face torn between childish annoyance, defiance, and that low rumble of fear that occurs when you wonder if your bluff's been called.

Rick nudged him. "We can finish this later."

"I'll do it," Josh said. "But I won't like it."

And he did, loudly, defiantly. Sylvia ignored the noise, though she knew he should have been grounded or spanked or something. Rick glanced at her twice, with a question on his face; neither spoke. Except for the pounding, clattering, thumping, and dragging noises coming from Josh's room, the house was quiet. Sylvia checked her numbers twice as she worked through the stack of bills. Now that she was no longer working, the margins were thinner than ever, but it looked as if it was going to work. There wouldn't be much left over for any Christmas presents, though.

I can get a part-time job if I have to.

"Weather looks pretty nice," Rick said at length. "Mind if I take Josh for a walk?"

Sylvia checked the window. She had not yet stepped foot outside, but it appeared bright and crisp.

"Bundle him up good," she said. "Don't be gone too long."

The weather was indeed crisp. It took Josh about fifteen minutes to clean his room, which felt more like fifteen hours. He emerged in a particularly surly mood, shoulders slumped, feeling as though the whole day had been stolen from him. Rick waited with coat in hand. The idea of an outdoor adventure pleased Josh. Together, he and his uncle set off to tromp through the neighborhood, over cracked concrete sidewalks and crunching, brown grass.

Wind whistled through the bare branches, cutting sharply against their skin. The cool burn felt good to Josh. Mom kept the house quite warm— one thing she refused to skimp on was heat—so the change of temperature was welcome, at least for a while. In fact, one of Josh's favorite things about winter was getting to go back *inside* after getting good and cold outside. The walk with Uncle Rick was to Josh a grand excursion, eventually causing him to forget about the complete unfairness of having to clean his room when he's sick.

He and Uncle Rick wandered without purpose, with few words, stopping every now and then only to study trinkets fallen to the ground: a cracked marble from a neighbor's yard, a stick shaped like a pistol, the brittle fragment of a purple water balloon from someone's late summer fun. The crinkled cap tossed from a vanished bottle of beer.

"Why do you drink so much of this stuff?" Josh asked mildly, holding up the cap.

"I don't." Rick winked. "At least not that brand."

"You know what I mean."

Rick shrugged. "I like the taste."

"Does it make you angry?"

"Is this an interrogation?"

Josh shook his head vigorously. "What's interrogation mean?"

"Never mind," Rick replied. "I like the taste. I enjoy it."

"Does it make you happy?"

"I don't suppose," Rick answered. "Clever little boy."

Josh waited for more, observing his uncle as he worked through the answers.

"I don't know what else to say, Josh. I suppose I've been angry about stuff my whole life. The drinking probably doesn't make me angry. It just lets the anger that's already there come out."

Rick's wandering stride came to an abrupt halt. A faraway look filled his eyes. Josh did not know what an epiphany was, but discovered something close to it in Rick's expression.

"Never thought of it that way before," he mumbled.

For Josh, the answer led to another question. An obvious question.

"Why are you so angry?"

Rick resumed their lumbering pace quietly and said nothing. After a few paces, he bent down on one knee, took Josh's shoulders in his hands, and locked eyes with him.

"I wish I could tell you," he said gently. "I've been frustrated so long I don't remember why, or where it all started."

Josh accepted that, not because it made sense, but because Rick seemed sincere. As if to seal the deal, he gave his uncle a big hug around the neck, squeezing tightly. "I know something that would make me really sad, too. For a long time."

"Sad or mad?"

"Both."

Rick stood and began walking. "Let's hear it. What's the scoop."

"You gotta guess. I'll give you three chances. It's something I want to do really bad when I grow up."

"All right, you're on. But this is going to be easy. I only need one chance."

"Nah," Josh said, incredulous. Though his eyes were wide with the thrill of their little game, the mystery didn't last long. Uncle Rick *did* know. He spread his arms, began gliding up and down the sidewalk, sailing like a hawk . . . or an airplane. Josh beamed, delighted.

"How'd you guess so fast?"

"Whoa, there! Not so fast. You have to surrender, and declare me the winner."

Josh giggled at how silly Rick looked. "You win. I want to fly! If I couldn't ever, ever fly . . ." The thought hung in the air like an unspeakable horror. Overhead, Josh caught the streamer of a passing jet glowing in the sky. He pointed. "I want to be right there, above the clouds, looking down. And then I want to jump out and land on a big, fat cloud and walk around and wave to the people below."

"Sounds like a great wish, Josh."

"It's my wish above *all* wishes," Josh repeated seriously. He pulled an airplane out of his pocket, waving it through the air. His voice grew curious. "Why didn't you ever fly, Uncle Rick? Why didn't you become a pilot or something? It's been your dream, too."

"You know the answer, General Josh," Rick said plainly. "Never made it past the physical." His mouth made a tight line and he said no more.

Josh shivered. "Let's go home. I'm getting cold."

They walked a bit, listening to the sounds of winter: cars passing by, dogs barking, papery leaves grown brittle and hard scraping the earth as northerly winds blew them up and down the street. Before long, Rick was carrying Josh piggyback, huffing and puffing. When they arrived home, Sylvia opened the door, saw Josh with his head on Rick's shoulder, resting, and Rick breathing hard from the effort of carrying an eight-year-old for over half a mile. Sweat clung to the skin of his forehead like tiny glass beads.

"I thought you said you were going for a walk," she said to both, smiling.

"Oh, we did," Rick answered. "We walked quite a ways."

"I asked him to carry me," Josh explained sheepishly.

"Did you get tired?" Sylvia asked.

Josh shook his head but didn't answer. Rick thought Sylvia had asked him the question.

"Whoa, I'm not that old!" he grinned, feigning offense. His next words were daggers to Sylvia's heart. "Josh told me his back started hurting."

• • •

A little after one o'clock, a pathologist from Level 4 called with results. Her name was Diane Rieschmeyer; she was a smart, tough cookie. She was quite a bit younger than Stu, midthirties, but Stu had trained her himself. She brought sobering news.

"You aren't going to like this, Stu. It wasn't bacterial, but the residue from the can *is* loaded with pathogens. A sealed reservoir in the bottom of the can held a stabilizing solution for the pathogens, which fed to a specialized hydrocarbon propellant cartridge."

"What kind of pathogen?"

"That's where the news gets worse. Are you sitting down?"

"Go."

"It's definitely influenza. Looks like H1N1, or some variant of swine flu. Only worse."

"Worse?"

"Well, it's strange. The thing looks like the protein equivalent of a ransom note under electron microscopy, with snippets of viral code pasted onto the core. It's got two distinct protrusions. A real hatchet job, pretty scary."

"What're you saying, Diane? Is it influenza or not?"

"Most of it, yeah, but the rest is a slice-and-dice strain I've never seen. I can't help but suspect genetic tampering."

Stu cursed loudly. "Are you sure? Check again."

"I'm not sure of anything, but I've run the gamut and the numbers hold. You can take a look yourself."

"Get it to me," Stu answered, hanging up the phone.

When the results arrived, Stu didn't even bother to study them. He slipped the whole package under his arm, carried it to the rickettsial lab, leaning heavily on his cane with each step.

"Do you have cultures yet?" he asked.

"Yep."

"Compare them to this. You're going to find that they match."

Edgar Bersch, the director, quickly scanned the numbers, nodding.

"Did you happen to take a look at the thing?" Stu asked.

On his computer monitor, Edgar pulled a recent electron microscopy of the virus from Tokyo, compared it to the eight-by-ten photo Stu brought with him from Level 4. Dead ringers. Both revealed irregularly shaped spherical particles, 90 to 100 nanometers, with a lipid envelope. Textbook influenza. Yet the most compelling match were the two unidentified glycoprotein projections coming off each viral body, like claws on a crab. He whistled low under his breath. "I've never seen anything like this on influenza. That double arm is striking. Where'd you get yours?"

"From the original source of yours. A can of deodorant. Similar cans were found in the backpacks of the Sleeper cult . . . in major international airports . . . *empty*. One of them landed in Tokyo."

The director of the rickettsial lab's eyes flew wide, alarmed. "You're joking."

Stu frowned, as if to say, *Have I ever joked with you?*

Edgar protested, "C'mon, Stu. The paper said that was all a computer scare." He held up the eight-by-ten. "No way."

"I want you to get this to Tom Sizemore at the Institute. I want confirmation on whether the virus is bioengineered or naturally occurring. I want the genomic sequence identified. Especially those clawlike projections. Have them use GenBank."

GenBank was a colossal database of nucleic acid sequences, meticulously cataloged, against which scientists could compare sets of known code with unknown strands. This enabled at least a rudimentary method of matching scraps of code to registered code bases. The "Institute," also called USAMRID—pronounced by southerners as "you Sam rid"—was the Army Medical Research Institute of Infectious Diseases, a highly classified facility stationed at Fort Detrick in Maryland near Catoctin Mountain. It stood as the first line of medical defense in biological technologies for the United States military. USAMRID and the CDC often collaborated, especially when the stakes were high. Both contained state-of-the-art Level 4 labs.

"Stu, that makes no sense. It's not necessary."

Stu didn't have time for chitchat. He dropped the rest of the findings from Level 4 in the director's lap, turned, and hobbled out, saying, "Get it to USAMRID. Line up the numbers between you and Level 4 for me; see if there's any variance. And get every last drop of your samples immediately up to Level 4. Use extreme caution. I'll brief you later, probably this afternoon if I can pull it together. In the meantime, don't go anywhere."

He disappeared round the corner and was gone.

Reeling, the director shot back, "I'm leading a team to Mexico this afternoon, Stu!"

A voice echoed down the hall. "Cancel it, Edgar. I'll need you. Don't go *anywhere.*"

When Stu got back to his office, Marge rattled off her findings:

"Only three confirmed outbreaks so far. Tokyo, Singapore, and Brazil. I've only talked to government agencies, of course. Haven't worked the list down to the hospitals yet. And just so you know, I made no contact at all in about half the locales—"

"Keep trying," Stu interrupted.

"—but *I'm going to keep trying,*" Marge finished, eyes narrowing to slits. "Three or four of the officials seemed hesitant to talk, so I don't know what that means. No doubt, the hospitals are where we'll get our answers. I'll hit them this afternoon after lunch."

"I need you on this, not lunch. What's the report from Singapore and Brazil?"

"Same thing. Same symptoms. Two hospitals in Singapore admitted about a dozen people total. São Paulo had fifteen by the time I called. Only Tokyo had quarantined."

"Dependable system?"

"Not a chance. No dedicated isolation rooms. No negative air. No HEPA filters. Half of them were discharged with ibuprofen and instructions to drink fluids before doctors picked up on the pattern."

"Presumptive diagnosis?"

"Strangely enough, flu."

"I need three teams," Stu declared, thumping the table. "I want us in Tokyo, Singapore, and Brazil by tomorrow. We've got three identified hot zones and I want to go face-to-face with this thing before it spreads further."

"If the virus was sprayed in those airports, it's already spread way past any quarantine zone."

"Then we won't have any trouble tracking it down!" Stu barked.

That was enough for Marge. Sucking in air, she sternly replied, "I can't do both. You'll have to assemble the teams yourself."

"Fine, fine." Without yielding an inch in tone, Stu added. "When this is all over, I'll buy your lunch for a week, Marge. I promise."

• • •

The screen door slammed. The front door opened, but Joshua did not rise to greet Tim. Instead, he watched with tired, smiling eyes from the living room.

"How's my boy?" Tim said gently, crouching beside his son, who was lying in a ball under a blanket on the sofa. "How are you feeling?"

Sylvia answered, "He came home from a walk with Rick complaining of *back* pain. I gave him some Tylenol, but it hasn't let up much."

Tim and Sylvia absorbed each other's presence, not listening to words so much as posture, tone. Tim would know what back pain meant; he would remember Sunny's warning. Sylvia looked for fear in his eyes. But he just swept Josh into his arms and cradled him like a baby. The embrace was tender, strong.

"I love you so much, Joshua Chisom," he said, allowing the embrace to linger before laying him down again on the couch.

"I love you, too, Dad."

The phone rang. Sylvia answered and handed it to Josh.

"It's Scooter."

Josh took the phone happily.

"Hey, Scooter!"

Sylvia turned to Tim. Low under her breath she said, "I called Dr. Perkins and we've scheduled another trip to Oklahoma City for tomorrow."

"Tomorrow? I can't possibly pull away from work tomorrow."

Sylvia studied the rough skin of her husband's face. He tried to cover his worry, but it leaked out in his voice. "I know you can't. I figured you could catch a ride with one of the boys. I'll take the truck and drive Josh myself."

Tim bowed his head. Sylvia said, "We don't have a choice, honey. I knew you wouldn't be able to go when I made the appointment, but they're squeezing us in as it is. We'll be fine. Rick can come with us."

"Sorry," Rick chimed in. "Got plans."

Sylvia rolled her eyes. Tim said, "I want to be there. I *need* to be there."

"Mom!" Josh blurted, phone stuck to his ear. "Scooter wants me to come over for a sleepover tomorrow night. Can I? Please?"

Sylvia sighed. Nothing could have been nicer for Josh. "Probably not, dear. Looks like we're gonna be busy tomorrow."

$\bullet \bullet \bullet$

"Frank, I know it seems premature, but all things considered, I believe we should advise the president to close our borders," Stu warned. "If not now, then at least begin drafting the executive action and have it on standby." He was speaking to the executive director of the CDC, who at present sat hunched over a small desk strewn with papers in the suite of the Capital Hilton in Washington, D.C., preparing for a second day before the Senate Appropriations Committee. Asking for more funding, as usual. Given the context, it was no surprise Stu's counsel would be regarded as inflammatory.

"C'mon, Stu," the director snorted. "It's flu season. You can't be serious."

"On the contrary, I'm quite serious."

"You're telling me I should tell the president to seal every border, block all cargo shipments, passenger transportation, and business travel by boat, rail, and air, based on a day's worth of influenza outbreaks *during* flu season on the soil of three foreign governments?"

"You know my record," Stu countered. "Do you really think I would propose such radical measures if the danger wasn't enormous?"

"Yes!" the director roared. "You did it in '76, and again in '93, with legionnaires' and AIDS both. You're always overreacting. You wanted to blockade traffic coming in and out of Philadelphia for a month even though the whole thing was isolated to less than one city block."

"Okay, let's back up," Stu said, breathing deeply. Nothing irked him more than someone failing to keep pace with his deductive insights. "I'm not saying we should turn this decision on a dime. I'm simply saying the evidence thus far looks potentially catastrophic, so I would prefer to be as far ahead of the game as possible. I've got a can full of airborne virus in Level 4 that was released three days ago across seventeen strategic, international traffic centers *and* a matching virus from the blood of patients in at least one of the target cities. These people are crashing quick, Frank. The doctors don't know what's hit them. Say what you want about protocol, but none of this is random coincidence and I'm not overreacting. I'm telling you facts. It *will be* worse tomorrow. This is a bona fide nightmare scenario. I'm sure of it." His voice slowly gained in pitch and intensity as he spoke. Stu hated politics, especially when it hindered effective intervention policy. "The real question is whether or not we will be ready to take action by tomorrow should the worst prove true, or will we need another three days of legislative posturing to make sure enough people die before we're allowed to label it a crisis."

"Don't you dare play the moralist with me," Frank hissed. "I've been sitting in committee for nine hours pushing Congress for more money so that the CDC can do its job. Got it?"

"Frank, the money for next year is great. But we're talking about lives, *tomorrow.* Alive or dead tomorrow."

"Fine, let's talk about lives!" the CDC boss demanded. "How many have died? Tell me, Stu. Has a single person died?"

"Not yet," Stu replied in measured tones. Zero fatalities did not help him make his point. "But thank goodness! I hope the bug doesn't prove lethal, but if it does the stats will go off the charts in a matter of days. I ran a quick penetration matrix, Frank. This thing could go exponential in less than a week. We're already into double digits for comas. I mean, come on, Frank, you know influenza is one of the most highly contagious of all pathogens." He paused. "And there's one other thing."

"What?" Frank sighed impatiently.

"We have reason to suspect genetic tampering."

That was the final straw. "'If' . . . ' perhaps' . . . 'suspect.' It all may be true, but right now it's just speculation, and speculation doesn't make for sound policy. I can't go to the secretary of health or the director of FEMA, much less the president, with anything less than certainties. Your theory about Sleeper may be right, and I've got to say it is alarming, but it's unproven at this point." He sighed. "Are you sending out teams?"

"Three teams. They're in the air as we speak."

"Get back with me after you've got some hard data from the field."

Stu wasn't satisfied. "We'll be days in the field before we know something and you know it. Early containment is crucial."

"I'm returning to Atlanta day after tomorrow. I'll meet with you then. I'm not committing to any course of action until then. That's my final answer. If you don't like that, Stu—if this leaks to the press before we speak—I'm going to assume it's you. I'll have your job, my friend."

He said the last part sweetly, with a hiss, then abruptly hung up the phone, leaving his threat coiled on the phone like a snake ready to strike. Stu slammed the receiver down, fumed, grabbed his coat and cane, and headed for the door. All the way home he fumed; fumed as he stumped towards his front door; fumed even more as he stumbled over a box stuck in the shadows, apparently a delivery from UPS earlier in the day. Stu hauled the box inside, flipped on the light switch, and read the airbill. The handwriting was familiar.

To: Stuart Baker, Atlanta
From: Seattle, Washington

The package was from Josie.

12

For an hour and a half Stu sat in his easy chair, terrified, staring at the box. He tried to watch TV, tried to work on Sleeper. Tried to rest. Nothing. He could not escape the box. He left it unopened, a flat, brown sentinel, a castle wall, daring him to enter. Coaxing, pleading, warning. Defying. He heard it shouting, mocking him.

Old man, it said. *Rotten old man.*

Josie was dead, or so he supposed. He had no reason to hope otherwise. Yet now, here she was, alive in his room. Or at least a part of her, some vital part she felt worth mailing, before all was finished. She mailed it to *him.* For what purpose? Josie hated him. She died hating him. Stu knew that with utter certainty. Perhaps he wouldn't have believed it, could have ignored it—as most parents are able to ignore their children's misspent emotion—if he were not so deeply ashamed, so secretly aware of her fair right to hate him. If ever he had suspected otherwise, those thoughts were appropriately and irrevocably dashed now, as he stared at the brown box addressed in her hand. This would surely be her final judgment against him, delivered in such a way that he could not respond or retaliate or repent. Josie's feelings went much deeper than disappointment. Stu had known it for years, ignored it for years, made himself stupidly unaware, buried in a hole. For years and years! Now, like some hot coil of copper wire unwinding inside his belly, pain burned free.

The truth was this: he had failed his daughter.

As a father. As a man. As a friend.

He pulled out his package of cigarettes, tapping it distractedly against his palm until one of the thin white cylinders of paper and tobacco poked out. He lit the cigarette with a match and watched the tip glow red and crackle. The smell of the smoke brought little comfort. He wondered at the irony of the moment. Even tried to laugh. Josie had probably mailed him a suitcase full of poisonous snakes, hoping they would strike him and he would die, alone in his home, as she died alone in some unknown airport. As she had probably felt dead and alone so many countless nights, when his Palm beeped and told him to call her and he clicked "OK" and ignored it, because he didn't want to have to explain himself or his actions. Stricken as he was, the box might as well have been full of snakes. Chock, slithering full.

What could she have possibly sent? Why would she have done this? Some aggrandizing, final message, a stiletto of words, memorabilia, photos . . . what? Designed to cut him open, lay him bare? A final act of retribution? The suicide note that lives forever in the heart of the surviving family?

Years had passed—years! Stu had not once dealt with the raw reality of his life the way this single, stupid box demanded. Wordless, emotionless, inanimate, it peeled him open as might an electric can opener with freshly sharpened blades. Would there be, somehow, a photo, perhaps, and a letter, and at the bottom of the letter, scribbled in ink pen and wet with tears, a few simple words: "I forgive you"?

Of course not.

He grabbed a pair of scissors and cut the box open, gingerly at first, then with rage, shredding it. Foam peanuts flew through the air, tumbled across the floor. It was not a large box. Inside, there were four simple items: two books, a photo, and a lace doily.

The doily! Round and yellowed from age, it was meant to be a coaster for drinks. Stu bowed his head, picked it up, smelled it. When Josie was eight, he had been assigned to a polio outbreak in Bombay, was gone four weeks, and ended up missing her birthday. When he returned, he found the doily in his luggage, having taken it by accident from the hotel. When he arrived home that night and Josie had run and thrown herself into his arms and tried to kiss him, asking what he brought her for a present . . . what was he to do? He had forgotten her birthday, hadn't called or written, or even remembered upon his return. So he gave her the doily, said it was special, made for a famous Indian princess, and that it cost him a lot of money. Foolish as it seemed, Josie was wide-eyed with delight, and grateful.

She had kept it. All these years. A two-dollar piece of nothing.

He picked up the photograph. It was, apparently, a scene following Josie's graduation. From high school? There she was, in cap and gown and tassel, diploma in hand, grinning. In spite of the moment, Stu found her beautiful. She had her mother's eyes and a graceful, shadowed smile. Stu found the smile curious, compelling, tinged even on that occasion of celebration with sadness. It dawned on him that every memory he had of her smile looked exactly the same, just like that smile. Flipping the photo over—no writing on the back—over again, he studied it further. She stood in a small knot of classmates, her mother standing off to one side. Who was holding the camera? Not Stu. He hadn't attended her high-school graduation. Away, as usual, at work. On site. Somewhere . . . he didn't even remember where. Furthermore, he didn't recognize the photo. With a pang, he realized that probably meant he hadn't bothered to look at it upon returning. From wherever.

He paused, the skin around his eyes wrinkling, brows creased. *Was* it high school? No . . . college. No, he *did* make it to her college graduation. Slowly, the order of things returned. By that point in his life, the pace of things had begun to lessen a bit.

It could have, should have, slowed much sooner.

Then he picked up the books. Not books, actually. Journals. Diaries. *Oh no . . .*

The instant he realized what they were, he set both books down, as if they might leak acid and burn his hands. He couldn't do this. Not now. He rose, staring at the books, wiping his hands on his chest. He stumbled into the kitchen, poured himself a shot of scotch, and downed the drink after swirling it first in his mouth, which had grown numb.

Not now.

With that final thought, he went to bed.

An hour later, he returned to the living room, bleary-eyed and angry.

Sitting under the soft fanning light of a single lamp, journal in hand, he fumbled through the pages, wondering what he was about to find. He hadn't slept a wink, just tossed and turned.

In his bathrobe, cane propped against the chair, he opened both books and adjusted his reading glasses to the proper spot on his nose. The first journal looked older, more girlish, trimmed in little blue flowers, with a Holly Hobbie figure on the front. On the bottom corner, Josie had scrawled, "ages 10 to 17." The second, much more expensive, was trimmed in leather and seemed to cover the last five to ten or so years. Using his thumb and forefinger, Stu stroked the bridge of his nose, rubbed his eyes, and licked his lips. He was nervous.

Randomly, he thumbed the pages. One of the latter entries in the Holly Hobbie journal caught his eye. It must have been when Josie was approaching graduation.

I asked Daddy if I could go with him on one of his trips. I said I was thinking about becoming a scientist, like him. He laughed at me. He told me it would be too dangerous. I told him I would be careful, and be sure to stay out of the way. I've been reading up on the chem suits and know how they work, the panic you can feel when you put one on. So a couple days ago, I decided to practice the feeling with a garbage bag on my head. I didn't panic. Not even close. Plus, I've sent off for an application to Daddy's alma mater. Only problem is, I think I like chemistry better than biology. I won't tell him that just yet.

Anyway, he laughed. Not mean, I don't think. Amused, which made me mad. Like I was some little kid and he was patting me on the head. I told him I wouldn't have to go on one of the high-level jobs. Something smaller. Just he and I. He said being careful wasn't enough. You had to be smart, too. Can you believe it? That's what he said. To my face! He said you have to know what you're doing, and kids aren't allowed.

Kid? I'm seventeen for crying out loud. What does he know? I've already given my virginity away. Twice. And I didn't make either of them use a condom. How about that, Studebaker Boy? That's right, your little girl is grown up, stacked, and giving it away.

Besides, we're long past me caring about being safe.

Anyway, he left for work, and Mom, like usual, immediately got drunk. I

*turned my music way up so I wouldn't hear her and her latest boyfriend in the
bedroom. She yelled at me when it was all over for distracting her, for making
"Thomas" angry.*

I can't wait to blow this hole.

Sitting alone, reading along softly with his lips, Stu felt blood rush to
his cheeks. The only sound, the sound of the refrigerator compressor
turning off, left in its wake a deeper silence than before. Something in
his brain felt clogged, choked. He wanted to gag. Actually, he wanted to
weep. With ironic, clinical efficiency, Stu realized at that moment that
he didn't even know how to weep. He barely knew how to acknowledge
a wrong, and possibly cry for it. But this . . . this deserved *weeping,* or at
least it felt like it did. Perhaps even wailing.

Not Stu D. Baker, though. Instead, all the man could discern with
any measure of clarity was a low rumble, an uncomfortable sensation,
like indigestion. That and . . . nothing more. How do you weep over
what you cannot truly feel? The realization caused a spasm of shame,
but that was hardly the point, either. Shame at this point merely qualified as a surrender to the facts, which was entirely different from the
kind of shame that leads to sorrow. And so, in the darkness of the room,
Stu found himself on trial, doubly accused for sins of commission and
omission. Crippled, not just in his legs, he stood before an unseen judge
and a faceless jury. The final pounding of an immense gavel resounded
in his chest. In the still, soft midnight, a verdict was declared. The only
verdict that could be called just.

"Guilty! On all counts, guilty!"

It was a wrenching moment, one that he could not deny. But it was
short-lived, and soon, by default, for lack of fuel—whether from old-
school, generational male stupidity, or sins so great as to be insur-
mountable—even the shame yielded to the same emptiness he had
always known, always lived from. Shapeless, contorting, amorphous
emotion. True, he felt a great many things, but none were serviceable;
none of chiseled, classifiable content. Old, hardhearted men must have
things spelled out for them. For the first time, Stu pondered whether it
might not be the greatest weakness of all to avoid, at all cost, weakness.

For him at least, it had left little more than a shell of personality from which to engage life. To engage anything.

He flipped back a few pages, a few years. The handwriting was younger, more flowery, the tone more floppy-haired middle-schooler.

Mom insisted we go to church today. I didn't want to go, 'cause I had stuff to do and things like that. Daddy sure didn't want to go, believe me. He got real bothered when Mom even brought up the idea. I think the whole thing is kind of silly. I mean, after all, Dad'll just sit on the sofa and watch TV. Why not sit at church?

So Mom and I went. She dressed me like we were going to a funeral and then drove around until we found this little church on the corner a few blocks up the road. She dressed me right. I did see Stevie Parker there, though. He's pretty cute. We wrote notes back and forth during the sermon, until Mom finally caught on. I thought I was going to be in big trouble, but when I looked at her, she was crying. She tried not to show it. I guess that preacher man said something that made her sad.

When we got home, Mom made sure her eyes were dry and her makeup wasn't running. First thing I did was ask Daddy why he wouldn't let us believe in God. I figured he would just mumble and ignore me. Instead, he pulled me close, looked me right in the eye, and told me God had never once proven he was worth believing in.

I almost thought he was going to hug me.

The dull ache continued. Stu put the older journal down and picked up the most recent. He flipped through the pages, looking for a reference to Jean de Giscard. It did not take him long to find one. The entry was short.

I read a book today. Yesterday, I stood in line for an hour to get it signed by the author. It was the very first day for the book to hit the shelves. I'll never forget it. I met him. Jean de Giscard. They say this book is his finest work, his crowning achievement. I'm only halfway through, but I think I agree. Everything makes so much sense.

In some small way, I think Daddy would be proud of me. If God is dead, then

we must all care more deeply about the Earth. It is, in fact, the only god we have.
It must be watched, served, nurtured, or our lives are lost in the process.
   Jean wrote his phone number in my book. I'm going to call him.

Stu laid the journals down. He couldn't read anymore. He sobbed once, a sudden inhalation and exhalation of wet breath, but there was nothing else behind it. Rising, he shuffled off to bed.

• • •

The next day was Friday, December 18. One week until Christmas. Sitting beside her son in the office of Children's Hospital in Oklahoma City, waiting for Dr. Li, Sylvia could not help but feel afraid. Afraid and small. Nothing in all the world she could possibly do would guarantee her son's life. For a parent, such a realization was the apex of emotional exposure. Nothing left a mother or father more vulnerable, more desperate, more guilty, than knowing their only resource was a cliché, "Pray." When it came to your own child facing a cruel sickness, possibly even death, the elusive qualities of prayer never seemed quite enough. Regardless how valid, or how much faith one possessed.

Then came an echo, a familiar echo.

Healing all over this child . . .

The words of the prophet rang through her head, over and over, like a taunt. They brought no comfort, little hope. He was not healed. He was getting worse.

You know I believe you can do miracles, God. I want to believe. For me, for my son. Prove the skeptics wrong. Show your power.

She glanced at Josh tenderly. On the surface, Josh seemed relatively unfazed, except that he had grown a bit more cranky, a bit more reserved. Yet he had always been such a quiet child, it was hard to tell where one emotion ended and another began. Now more than ever, Sylvia wished she could climb inside his head and know what was really going on.

She folded her fingers around his hand. "Won't it be great when this is all over?"

"Yeah."

Tucking her hands into her lap, Sylvia tried to calm the storm within. She sat uncomfortably in the chair in the waiting room, dressed in jeans and a sweatshirt, hair pulled into a bouncy ponytail. Josh wore a Sooners T-shirt underneath a lined Windbreaker, slumped in a similar chair with legs flopping over, kicking them up and down ever so slightly. The trip to Oklahoma City had been quiet, except for the sound of Josh's gentle snore, and the patchy finger-snaps of scattered showers against the windshield.

After about ten minutes of waiting, out of the blue, Josh asked, "Hey, did you know Dad helped at that building a while back? The one that blew up."

Sylvia was taken aback. "Of course, honey. Your father and I discussed it before he volunteered."

Josh was stumped. "Well, I didn't know."

"You were just a baby, Josh."

"Was it scary, the explosion? Did you see Daddy on TV?"

"Once."

Josh grinned. "What did you think?"

"I was proud. I thought he was very brave." Her eyes dropped. *And how hard it would be to lose a child . . .*

The door opened. A nurse entered.

"Mrs. Chisom, Dr. Li will see you now."

They followed the nurse down a short hall to an examination room with walls the color of fresh milk cream and trimmed in blue. The nurse departed and the door closed; thirty seconds later Dr. Li entered, coughing, with the same nurse following on her heels. Sunny carried a clipboard in her hands.

"Hi, guys," she said in a powdery voice. Her eyes were heavy, glistening. Sylvia thought she looked awful.

"Coming down with something?"

"Mostly jet lag, I think. Probably fighting a cold, too. I woke up feeling fine."

"Maybe you should go home," Sylvia offered, a halfhearted gesture. The last thing she wanted to do was reschedule.

"After lunch I probably will. I wanted to see this young man first. Josh, how you feeling?"

"I dunno."

"Pretty much the same?"

Josh nodded. "My back hurts."

Sunny opened her mouth in mock horror. "How's a kid supposed to run and play soccer if his back hurts? You do like soccer, don't you?"

Josh nodded noncommittally.

"Well, if you like soccer, you would love my home. In Brazil, soccer is *everything*."

"I'm not that good."

"Hey, I'm a lousy cook, but I love to eat."

As she talked, Sunny ran her hands over Josh's shoulders, back, and spine. Josh winced at the pressure the lower down his back she went. With her face to Josh's, she bent down, using her otoscope to peer into the boy's eyes, ears, and throat, but the position must have irritated her throat or lungs. Jerking away from Josh, she let loose coughing, everywhere, though she did manage to grab some tissues and make a barrier with her hand. It was a terrible sound, rising from deep in her lungs—wet, rattling, and fibrous. Worse, the room was small. Each convulsion of her chest shot unseen microscopic droplets of saliva and lung moisture into the air. When the fit finally subsided, Sunny was so fatigued she had to steady herself with one hand.

"That's not exactly healthy, is it?" she said, mostly to herself, shaking her head. "I'm sorry."

Sylvia, trying to think of something funny to say, realized instead that she was sitting very straight, leaning instinctively away from the trajectory of the cough. She glanced worriedly at the nurse, who, though dutiful and quiet, was unable to mask the concern etched on her face.

"Let me get through this quickly so we can all go home," Sunny said. "I sent your original lab results to a colleague in Atlanta. A brilliant man. He wants to see more. With him on board, we are in even better shape. I know you are concerned about treatments, Mrs. Chisom, but I think now may be a good time to reconsider. I would like to draw another blood sample and get an updated snapshot of Josh's condition.

A lot can change in only a few days." She turned to the nurse. "Lisa, why don't you draw some blood while Mrs. Chisom and I wait outside? Let's check his antibody titers and calcium levels."

Sylvia followed Sunny cautiously out the door. She didn't want to catch her cold.

"Smart woman," Sunny said, noticing. "Can't have Mom getting sick. I don't even know where this came from . . ."

"Vitamin C," Sylvia said. "That'll help."

Sylvia had never been paranoid of germs, but to her eyes Dr. Li appeared even worse now than when they had arrived. In fact, everything about her looked *unwell*, beyond the sound of her congestion. What Sylvia did not know, could not have known, was that inside Dr. Li's small body, Sleeper raged. Even as she stared at Sylvia through fevered eyes—breathing the same air—the virus continued to replicate. With frightening speed, it transformed thousands, then tens of thousands, and then millions of cells, each one changed into huge viral factories, churning out even more virus to attack respiratory function and renal function and further infect the bloodstream.

Dr. Sunny Li was dying. She didn't know it. Sylvia didn't know it. But she *was* dying. It all happened so quickly. Sleeper was vicious.

"Mrs. Chisom," she spoke softly. Sylvia could see that it hurt to speak with any volume. "I know you and your husband have wrestled with appropriate next steps. I will admit, Josh still seems to be holding up well. Considering where he is in this thing, especially for what I expect his next blood work to show, he should feel much worse than he does. We won't always have the luxury of saying that, though."

"We don't have a lot of money," Sylvia said flatly; she did not say more.

"Your husband is on the Oklahoma Indian Rolls, isn't he? Comanche?"

"Yes."

"Does Josh qualify?"

"He's one-sixteenth."

"There you go. Indian benefits will cover the vast majority of treatments."

Sylvia closed her eyes, frustrated. "I wish that were true. But Josh isn't registered. We never got around to it. It takes months to go through all the hoops."

"All right." Sunny breathed deeply. "Then Terrance may have the best idea."

"Terrance?"

"My colleague in Atlanta. An old friend of mine, Dr. Terrance Alexander. He's a leading specialist in blood disorders. He recommended clinical trials."

"Trials? You mean like experimentation?"

"No, don't think like that. A trial is a carefully controlled research effort performed within federally mandated guidelines. It's not mad scientists and Frankenstein, Mrs. Chisom. It's medical professionals at hospitals and other institutions. Dr. Alexander matched Josh's particular case to three or four good trials for multiple myeloma currently gearing up across the nation. The goals vary slightly: more effective treatment, fewer side effects, new approaches, etc. That means new drugs, new drug combinations, or things like combining chemotherapy with biological therapy to boost the immune system's response. Josh could probably be accepted as a candidate into any of those programs and it could be lifesaving. Best of all, if they take you, it's free."

"Free?" Sylvia's voice found hope for the first time. Then skepticism crept in. "My husband is proud, Dr. Li. Are these government handouts?"

"Not at all. It's part of the cost of developing new treatments. It's not a handout."

"But . . . we don't really know about any of them, right? That's the whole point: these treatments have never been tried. They could be dangerous."

"In some cases, perhaps, but rarely for this type of disease. Clinical trials usually build on known strategies and techniques. They go in phases. The cutting-edge stuff happens in Phase 1, but as I said, even those are highly regulated. The government has their hands all over this type of thing. Too much, if you ask me."

"I just don't know," Sylvia whispered. "I'll need to talk to Tim. Is there any information . . . do you have anything I could take home?"

"Of course. I took the liberty of submitting an application on Josh's behalf to three of the trials, so I'll have Lisa get you the fact sheets and consent forms. One is at a cancer research institute in Houston, but it doesn't begin for another three months and I don't think we should wait. The University of Minnesota also has a two-year open trial that looks very interesting. But the one I most recommend is a study being conducted by the Myeloma and Transplantation Research Center at the University of Arkansas in Little Rock. I think I mentioned them to you last time. They've had some very interesting results. If it makes you feel any better, MTRC is used all the time by heavyweights like the National Cancer Institute. They're world class. And they're now in a phase to accept additional candidates."

"I just don't know . . ."

"Mrs. Chisom," Sunny said forcefully, "you can't afford to be choosy. Most studies won't even allow children, but these *do*. You are in a position of financial need and limited options. The Minnesota and Arkansas studies are both Phase 2 and Phase 3 studies, which means they've already had some sort of success and side effects are likely known. You and your husband need to decide."

Sylvia stepped back. She didn't like the pressure. "This is my boy. My son."

"We'll get the lab results back tomorrow. Arkansas doesn't start till this time next month. That should give you some time to think."

Sylvia stared at the floor. Sunny stared first at her, then her vision blurred and she looked past her, unable to argue further. She was fading. She could feel it. An hour ago—literally, sixty minutes prior—she had felt mildly tired, easily explainable as travel fatigue since she had not returned from Brazil until late last night. But she had traveled internationally several times before. Jet lag had never felt, well . . . *like this*.

She could almost sense something spreading through her body, as if hydrogen peroxide had been injected inside her veins, bubbling softly, feeding inside her. It *moved*. For the first time, Sunny began to fear. Her body and mind were beginning to feel like separate realities.

I'm falling apart.

Sylvia thought Sunny should never have come to work, or gotten out of bed this morning. A doctor should know better! In twenty short minutes,

Sunny's skin had turned another shade of pale, and when she coughed again, though not as violently, somehow it sounded worse. Sylvia was very aware she stood *near* this sick woman.

She said quickly, "I'll talk with Tim tonight. We'll figure it out."

Sunny nodded wearily, opened the door again to the examination room, allowing Sylvia to enter first. Stepping through, Sylvia noticed several things at once, each of them unexpected: the nurse through the doorframe, standing very still, as if in a trance; her eyes darting around the room, a stunned expression on her face. Lisa . . . was that her name? Lisa held her hands at eye level, staring as if transfixed, like a six-month-old child who has discovered her fingers for the first time. Sylvia saw all that and noticed one other thing . . .

Sunny exclaimed, "Whew! Next time go a little easier on the air freshener, Lisa."

And so it was. Sylvia inhaled, feeling her heart both soar and sink. It was undeniable. As the door swung wide, a sweet, overpowering fragrance spilled out, filling Sylvia's nostrils with a familiar scent: lilacs.

Low under her breath, she heard Lisa talking to herself, repeating over and over, "I don't understand."

"What?" Sunny said, waving her hand in front of her face, nose wrinkling. The scent was intense, especially when trapped in such small confines.

"Well, I don't know. I don't really know." She pointed to Josh. "I was drawing the sample from Josh . . . all of a sudden my head began to spin. I closed my eyes, just for a second. When I opened them, everything was blurry. I couldn't see anything. I—" She brushed at her eyes. "And then . . ."

Still mumbling, she stepped hurriedly into the hallway, staring down the length of tile, reading distant signs for the first time. A small cry escaped her lips. "I don't believe it!"

Sylvia believed. She turned to face her son, searching for the answer in his eyes, drinking the floral perfume lingering in the air as if it were the breath of heaven. Josh, of course, would not return her gaze. Instead, he quietly massaged his arm and kept his chin down. She thought she caught the trace of a smile in the outline of his cheeks. Thoroughly confused and a little irritated, Sunny grasped her nurse's arm firmly.

"What's going on, Lisa? You aren't making any sense. Are you okay?"

"Yes! No. I can *see*," she whispered, pointing at the same time. Dr. Li and Sylvia both followed the line of her finger. On the countertop near the syringe tray, Sylvia found what she was looking for, and Sunny found a riddle: two discarded contact lenses.

"Joshua," Sylvia murmured, breathless.

No glasses. How did he even know?

Sunny, however, was in no mood for riddles. She was feeling worse by the minute, and nothing of the last five minutes made any sense.

"Explain it to me later. Just get the blood to the lab for now, okay?"

"Yes, Dr. Li," Lisa answered, dazed. She didn't linger. She dashed from the room, with blood samples in her hand, her contacts left behind. Forever.

Dr. Li took out a pad of paper and scribbled. "You two head on home. I'll call as soon as we get the results. In the meantime, here's a prescription for the pain in Josh's back. Is he having any negative reactions to the other drugs?"

"No. We've only used them once or twice." Sylvia took the sheet. "Thank you."

Her anxiety must have been obvious. Firmly, reassuringly, Sunny said, "We're going to stay on top of this, Mrs. Chisom. You've got a strong boy, here. I think things look good."

You have no idea what just happened here, she thought. *No idea how special this boy is . . .*

Sylvia wrapped her arm around her only son, held him for love; but she also pinched the skin under his arm to tell him secretly she knew about Lisa. She felt Josh giggle in her embrace. Feeling the tremble of his gentle laughter, Sylvia, for whatever reason, simply could not be anxious. At least not for those few moments. In fact, appropriate or not, the whole thing struck her as funny. A stealth healing. A nurse made well, in secret. She almost started laughing.

"I hope you get to feeling better, Dr. Li," she managed to say, before she and Josh slipped out the door.

Sunny smiled bravely. But as soon as Sylvia and Josh rounded the corner and the door closed behind them, her knees gave way. She sank to the stool, bowed over, breath coming in heavy, ragged gasps. With all her will and might, she restrained another bout of coughing until she knew they would both be out of earshot. A few seconds—maybe ten; it was the best she could do. Then spasms of painful, mucous-filled respiration came interspersed by short, jerking coughs. At length, the wave of pain in her chest subsided. But the fever had only increased. Her skin burned. Her eyes stung. Her body ached. Choking, she hit the call button, could only manage two words.

"Help me!"

• • •

Tim's answer was crisp, terse. "You know I can't help this, Sylvia. We'll have to talk tomorrow." He sighed. "I can probably call you tonight from the hotel. David wants me to go with him to a trade show in Dallas to look at some new cutting equipment. Steve's wife's having a baby, so he can't go, and David doesn't want to shell out a quarter-million without a second opinion."

Stunned, Sylvia stood outside a Git 'n Go on the outskirts of Oklahoma City, shivering in the cold, a pay phone pressed to her ear. Of all people, Sylvia knew Tim didn't like to get pulled away from the quarry during work-hours, but she was nonetheless surprised at his surly tone. He should know she couldn't wait until she got back to Folin. She needed to share and communicate now. Plus, Sylvia knew, however angry he might be at the interruption, a bit of processing time for Tim would help the conversation go more smoothly when they spoke again later.

Only now Tim was telling her there would be no face-to-face tonight. At all.

"What about us? This isn't a good time for us, either, Tim. Isn't there anyone else?"

"Sorry, honey. This is part of my promotion. This is management."

"Tim, I need you. *We* need you."

Tim's voice dropped in the receiver. "Sylvia, you know good and well I would be there in a heartbeat if this was even slightly possible. Now I just got a promotion that may be our only way to carry this whole thing, but my medical benefits don't kick in for the first sixty days. That means the best way I can help Josh is to do my job until the coverage takes effect."

Sylvia scrambled for alternatives. "What about the loan? What did the bank say?"

"We can take out a mortgage. That nets us fifty thousand."

"That's good, isn't it?"

"Sure, and I'll do it. But I don't think it takes long to burn through that kind of money when you're talking about chemotherapy. Plus, good or not, we don't have room in the budget for the extra payment, at least not on my salary alone, so we've got to figure something out. Listen, Sylvia. We can talk about this later. I've got to go . . ."

Sylvia took a deep breath. She trusted Tim and knew it wasn't easy for him, either. Even so, the entire discussion struck her as completely unreasonable on his part. "I'm asking you to please be home tonight, Tim. Ask David to find someone else. He'll understand. He has a family."

"I *won't* have this conversation with you right now, Sylvia. You just told me we won't even know the lab results until tomorrow. I'll be back on Sunday. It's just a weekend thing. Are we going to split hairs over a single day's difference? Did Dr. Li tell you a decision was critical in the next twenty-four hours? Did she say those words?"

Sylvia fumed. "No."

"Then Josh will be fine for an extra day. Besides, why the sudden urgency? I thought we had decided we were going to wait awhile. It hasn't even been a week yet."

"Josh isn't fine," Sylvia said curtly. "He hasn't been fine for months. Do you know what he's doing right now, Tim? He's asleep in the truck. It's the third nap he's taken today. I don't care if it's been less than a week, he's gotten worse—noticeably worse. And I for one don't want to push our luck."

"Oh and I *do*, is that what you're saying? I don't care enough? What do you want me to do? Wave my magic wand? If I had one, I would! I don't know what to do except wait a bit longer. Wait and pray."

For a brief moment, both withdrew. The sound of passing traffic and tires slapping the wet streets replaced their voices. The pause was heavy, full of anger, guilt. Neither wanted it to be this way. The negative momentum had reached a crest, a chance to turn the corner. The abeyance of words offered grace, relief. Sylvia recognized the chance, wanted to take it, to offer it. But the momentum was too great. Something had bothered her for years. Today was reckoning day.

"If you would have gotten him on the rolls like I asked a dozen times, we wouldn't be in this situation to begin with—"

"Don't start with me, Sylvia."

"Am I wrong? Did I ask or not? Over and over."

That did it. Tim's voice grew distant. "I'll call you tonight from the hotel. Good-bye."

Click.

Sylvia squeezed the handle of the phone as if it were an iron pole and she, caught in a windstorm. She wanted to pound the phone and scream; instead, she cried. She knew she had been unfair. But why couldn't Tim have done what she asked? All those years of asthma medication. She had asked over and over. It was the right thing to do, the responsible thing. Why be trapped now, when they needed help the most?

Not fair. This is my son . . .

She sat and stared at the silvery numbers on the phone pad, at the mosaic of her reflection the fragments suggested. It was cold. She got into the truck and stared quietly at Josh. Waves of despondency took their toll.

Not fair at all.

Fair or not, there was nothing to do but head home.

That same night, with Josh in bed, Sylvia nuzzled the phone and whispered into the receiver, her voice drawn thin and small in the open spaces of her home. She stumbled for words, feeling the sting of tears in her eyes. Tim, defensive at first, listened quietly. She hoped he was ready to reconcile.

". . . I didn't mean it. I didn't mean to make it your fault. We'll be fine. I'm sorry."

"Sylvia, you've got to believe me. I hate it that I'm here and not there. I just don't know any other way."

When the apologies were over, Sylvia summoned her courage and asked Tim what he thought about clinical trials. Since they had limited funds, no tribal support, and no insurance on Josh, why not pursue something progressive, potentially more effective than normal treatments, and free? Tim was reticent, as she expected, but he listened patiently. Sylvia read to him from the materials she had, about how MTRC treated more multiple myeloma patients than any other cancer center in the world, approximately five hundred each year. About the thrust of this particular trial, with lots of big words neither of them understood. Tim agreed a clinic like that made the most sense *if* it came down to it, even going so far as to admit that it may be necessary, and soon. Even so, he remained adamant that there was no reason to force a decision until they knew something more definitive from the latest round of blood work. Had Josh's condition deteriorated further in just a few days or not? Was the disease advancing? Were there any other reasonable alternatives?

When it came to Josh's well-being, Tim didn't want the doctors interfering or passing judgment for them. He and Sylvia needed to make the decisions. Listening quietly, Sylvia offered little in the way of response. What could she say that she hadn't said already? She felt increasingly desperate, willing to take action. No one had to explain to her that Josh was declining. She saw it every morning when her son lay in bed well past his normal energetic flurry of motion, well past morning cartoons; she saw it when he sat with toy planes in his lap and stared at the floor, when he only fingered his most favorite foods, and then asked to be excused early. She saw it in his thinning frame. Worst of all, when he moved a certain way, and winced in pain, and then tried to hide it so she wouldn't notice.

But Sylvia did notice.

So Sylvia and Tim talked, but they didn't get far, and neither wanted to push the issue, given the finale of their last conversation. Sylvia veered and took a new route.

"I went to the library the other day to study this clinical trial stuff on the Internet. Thought I'd check out some alternative therapies."

"Still searching for the miracle," Tim breathed.

"Give me some credit, Tim. I actually did it for you, since you're so hesitant about conventional treatments."

"With good reason," Tim reminded her.

"Well, here's your choices. I found all kinds of stuff, all kinds of snake oil. One guy uses mushroom extracts. For two hundred dollars a jar, he'll sell you mushroom extracts. Got that? You'll love this guy, Tim. He said conventional cancer treatments are like bombing a city to get rid of terrorists. You'll kill the terrorists, but you're probably going to kill a lot of innocent civilians, too. Which are—"

"Good, healthy cells," Tim murmured. "Interesting."

"He claims his *mushroom* extracts boosted, let's see," she fumbled for the printout, reading carefully, "specialized subsets of white cells that are highly effective in fighting cancer. Mushrooms. Can you believe it?"

Tim was noncommittal. "Sounds like some Indian cures my grandma used to tell me about. They worked."

Sylvia had hoped to gently use the offbeat and a bit of subtle humor to make a point. It wasn't working. Exasperated, she said, "Let me get this straight. God can't do it. Science can't do it. But mushrooms can. These are our only alternatives to chemotherapy, Tim. Is Josh going to reach a certain point of sickness . . . and then we finally try mushrooms? Are you even listening to yourself?"

"Sylvia, I'm sorry if it bothers you, but I refuse to be motivated by fear."

"Fear?"

Tim sighed over the phone. "I love Josh every bit as much as you. I want the best for him. But I also want to try to find the kind of choices we can believe in. Most of what you're doing right now is because you are afraid."

"Yes!" Sylvia whispered harshly. "And everything you *aren't* doing is because you don't want to fail. What if it doesn't work? What if it causes more problems? What if? Well how about this, Tim? What if, along the way, we just happen to get our son back? Maybe that's faith . . . that first blind step into the darkness. Have you ever considered that?"

Tim did not answer.

"Hold on," Sylvia said, checking the answering machine. Anything to break the flow. There was one message: Rick, explaining how he had to take some time "for myself," get some air, check out the job scene.

He would stop by in a couple of days and check in on Josh. Disgusted, she erased the message.

The conversation never returned to mushrooms, thank goodness. Instead, as she and Tim continued, Sylvia reached for the red-and-white oatmeal tin on top of the refrigerator, popped the lid, and poured the contents on the kitchen table. Thick wads of bills wrapped in rubber bands along with a good bit of loose change dumped onto the wooden surface. Sylvia unrolled the bills and leafed through the fives and tens, an occasional twenty, mostly ones, counting absently. Sitting under the single light of a simple hanging globe, she smiled sadly.

So long. So close.

"I've got almost two thousand dollars in cash spread out on the table," she announced.

Tim gasped. "What did you say?"

"I've been saving up here and there, oh, about three years now. For a new truck. I was going to save a couple more years, then spring it on you." Pleased at the crackling texture of silence coming from Texas, Sylvia pressed her lips together, awaiting his reaction. At the very least, she had managed to surprise.

"My goodness, Sylvia . . ."

"'Course, it's not enough to buy a *new* truck. But we could've stretched a little bit and at least brought you into the nineties."

Tim chuckled. "How would I get along without an extra two quarts of oil behind the seat?" His voice drifted away. "I don't really know what to say."

"Tell me you love me."

"I love you."

"Tim," Sylvia whispered urgently, "I've never wanted anything more than what we have. To be your wife. That's all."

"Now, now. Not true. You wanted college."

"For a while, maybe. But then Joshua was born. I haven't missed a thing."

It wasn't the first time Josh's name had been spoken so far in the conversation. But for some reason, this time, that word—*Joshua*—seemed to hover in the air, dangling from the phone lines between Dallas and

Folin like a phantom, a secret, a covenant ritual. Sylvia was so spent with emotion that his name tasted raw in Sylvia's mouth, felt better *unnamed*, as if too much speaking might bring it to light, away from that delicate cloak of protection afforded by mutual silence. She hoped Tim didn't notice her squeamishness.

With a nervous jitter, she said, "You won't believe what he did today!"

It was a quick retreat, the subconscious reference to Josh as "he," but it caused the immediacy of her son's name to recede, become somehow safe again. The response came from her gut, equal parts emotion and intuition. Perhaps it was the surviving power of denial, though if pressed Sylvia would have elevated her subconscious machinery to a noble defiance of the lot that had befallen her son.

She continued the game. She had to. The distance was not yet safe to be vulnerable again. She spoke in bursts, stream-of-consciousness. ". . . He healed the nurse's eyes. While Dr. Li and I were out of the room, he healed her. Only she didn't know it was him. Who healed her. She just realized she could see all of a sudden. At first I was upset, but then it struck me funny. The room smelled beautiful."

If Sylvia had known how well Tim understood her, she would have relaxed. When he spoke, she heard the sadness in his voice. "I've never been there when it's happened. Never smelled that smell."

Somehow, the simple longing in his voice anchored Sylvia once more, made it safe to go on. "It's the loveliest, most wonderful smell in the world. Sweet and strong. More beautiful than you can imagine."

Tim took a deep breath. "Listen to me, honey. We're going to make it. The Lord is with us."

At that moment, raw and true, Sylvia half believed him. Half didn't. It was all simply too much. Walls could only be built so high and so thick. Given enough pressure, anything could crack. Sylvia tried to hide the tremor in her voice, but no matter how hard she squeezed her eyes shut, how hard she fought her own emotion, she was wrung out. Little by little her fears leaked to the surface, until at length a soft, painful wheeze was wrested from deep in her chest. "I wanted so much to give you another child, Tim. Another son. A daughter."

And then she wept. She could no more stop it, or stem the flow, than she could have held back a crashing wave with a fishnet. Everything inside Tim, every masculine instinct, no doubt rose to the occasion. But he was not physically present. He could not touch her, stroke her hair, hold her. All he could do was say gently, "Sylvia, please don't. We have the most wonderful little boy in the world. Don't do this. You can't blame yourself. It's not your fault."

Sylvia's voice was laced with doubt. "Somehow, it feels like it is."

"We've got to be strong."

"I can't."

"You must."

"What if he doesn't make it?" Sylvia cried. Tim was missing the point. It wasn't whether she could be strong *now*. Of course she could. Anything else was unthinkable. She would fight to the very last! But what about, God forbid, after the disease had run its course? What then? She spoke the obvious, the painfully conspicuous. On the heels of her question, all the nether-regions of dread lurking in her soul came roaring, tumbling down, to the matter of fate. And faith. And fact.

Her thoughts jumbled. She understood destiny, but where was the glory of an early grave for a child? Destinies were given by God. They were not supposed to be punishments. And faith . . . was it something raw, foolish, and extreme, unapologetic in hope of . . . what? For one woman, grasping at the hem of a robe, it was hope for nothing more than a touch. And power was released. Was that the essence of miraculous faith? Or was it something more rational, more subtle—the application of spiritual wisdom?

Then there were the facts. Irreducible, inarguable truth. What was true? That God loved them. That he actually cared for their pain.

That Josh was dying.

"If he doesn't make it," she murmured. "We have nothing."

13

While Sylvia lay in bed, contemplating fate and nothingness, Stu checked a spreadsheet, contemplating fatalities. Lots and lots of fatalities.

He had his own problems.

Namely, Sleeper was loose, though nobody *knew* it was Sleeper, and he, the one man who did know, couldn't tell them. Such was the irony Stu pondered as he clattered away at the keys of his notebook. Though the thought of leaking the news hadn't even occurred to him until Frank mentioned the idea, now it seemed like an extremely reasonable course of action. *Somebody* needed the heads-up; somebody needed to dig deep, ask questions, get the word out. The illness was receiving increasing attention, but until it was tactically associated with Sleeper it would lack an accurate genealogy, which would essentially neutralize the real threat—its pervasive and purposeful release. Worse still, Stu suspected Sleeper soon would prove fatal. Genocide formed the logical terminus of the GPS vendetta against humankind. Comas were only the beginning. From this point on, it was just a matter of time.

Wearing a sweatshirt and jeans, the epidemiologist sat in the restaurant bar of an old Atlanta country club, sipping bourbon on the rocks at around midnight. In the ashtray at his right hand were three discarded cigarettes, burned nearly to the brown filtered end. As people passed by, he didn't bother glancing up, either to greet, smile, or acknowledge, though in this place he would likely recognize many folk. Stu had come here for years to golf before both age and flaring war wounds forced him permanently back to a cane, dismantling what little swing he ever possessed.

Good riddance. He never enjoyed the links as sport, or so he had convinced himself. Pristine emerald carpets of shaven grass? Nice. Sport? Ha! (He still kept his clubs in the garage, just in case.)

This time work beckoned. Whenever he couldn't concentrate at the office or at home, he came here. Laptop open, engrossed in the spreadsheet, he pored over numbers related to Sleeper. In one column were the known facts; then in column after column following, those known facts were filtered through a variety of expectations, possibilities, and projected facts—complex calculations that progressed incrementally according to a wide range of variables, including weather patterns, policy decisions, funding, rate of transmission, incubation period, etc. The spreadsheet was a standard CDC projection tool, not nearly as fancy as the number-cruncher housed on the mainframe, but quite handy in the field.

As Stu expected, even the best scenarios were grim. With only two days of active symptoms on record, the numbers of affected were adding up: thirty-one territorial outbreaks of some form or another in twenty-two nations, three of them in the States—though for whatever reason the U.S. had generally sustained less damage per capita. World wide, over three hundred people had fallen ill. Approximately one-quarter of those had slipped into comas. That was the *facts* column. The projection columns grew rapidly worse. As bad as day two's numbers were, they were wildly deceiving, since the world was going on day *six* since Sleeper's initial release through the airports. Untold numbers of the general population had already been exposed and were carrying and transmitting the disease to others. How long before they began to crash as well?

Even as he stared at the screen, Stu couldn't believe it. Simply couldn't believe it. This was going to be the worst disaster of his professional career. He could feel it in his bones. His field teams were in the middle of three of the hot zones, gathering data, theorizing and speculating. Containment, they said, was a joke. The virus had been released in a way that defied restraint. Crew chiefs reported that they could contain those who happened to show up at the right place with the right symptoms, but otherwise . . .

It's got to be global, Stu thought. *A global effort, nation by nation. The only effective hindrance to the spread of this thing will be city limits and national borders. But nobody's going to listen before it's too late.*

The critical window was already gone. That too was by design. Stu had returned several more times to the GPS Web site. The more he read, the more dreadful the world's predicament seemed. Thankfully, the CDC's executive director would return tomorrow, finally. Budget increase or no, Stu made sure he was number one on the director's list of appointments first thing in the morning. He also hoped someone from the FBI would call soon. Perhaps his anonymous tipper would break the silence—shed a little extra light on the process. Or some news would arrive from Thurman regarding Josie.

The name, the memory, sent him careening.

Josie.

Stu had yet to receive notification of his daughter's condition, whether alive or dead. For that matter he hadn't heard talk on TV about the victims at all. It was as though the whole thing had been quietly forgotten—or repressed as the case may be. But repression implied government intervention, and government intervention indicated official knowledge, and knowledge would surely lead to some sort of federal action toward containment. True enough, but when? Stu knew enough domestic emergency intervention policy to know that FEMA had national quarantine scenarios, but a project on the scale he considered necessary would require all the proverbial ducks to be in a very tight row before a single word was leaked to the public. Otherwise, panic and rioting would ensue, driving the casualty count even higher and making containment not merely a tactical nightmare, but impossible. Thus the tension, to leak to the press or not? Stu absolutely wanted to avoid yellow-sheet journalism, trumping up facts. But the government needed to feel the screws tightening, which might force Frank to allow him to proceed.

Maybe, just maybe, the FBI had already made their case and the big boys were getting some work done behind the scenes.

They've got to move soon. Can't delay much longer.

Stu shook his head, attempting to clear his thoughts. Before coming to work this morning, he had checked the ship date on the box from Josie—stamped two days before the collective suicide. The proximity of time was eerie, as if a time warp had opened, allowing him to hold the very evidence capable of preventing the debacle.

If only I had known. Made the calls, stuck with it, reached her.

It wasn't true, of course—he couldn't have stopped it—but for some reason it felt as if he could have. He had read another couple of passages from the journals, not quite so painful as the first few. Strange, to read your daughter's thoughts, hear what was happening in her head. People always think they want such power. Stu was living proof they didn't. Spent though he was, he was also now driven more than ever to unravel Sleeper and avert catastrophe. Home was no haven. If he returned, the journals were there, waiting to eat him alive.

Sleeper . . .

If initial field reports proved consistent as a model for the virus's behavior, Sleeper was going to prove a terrifying adversary. H1N1 variants didn't just make people sick, and they sure didn't wait for secondary symptoms, such as pneumonia, as was the manner of most flu complications. This sucker did all the damage itself. Any secondary damage was an afterthought of nature.

Mercifully, the headlines hadn't leaked anything alarmist. In fact, at this point, most of the media made no connection at all to Sleeper, though their own language should have given them a clue. On page two of the morning news in Atlanta, Stu read:

STRANGE SLEEPING ILLNESS SPREADS TO EUROPE

With no reported fatalities, the fact that clusters of people were slipping into comas was second-tier news, dumped behind vivid shots of the latest conflagration in the Middle East, dramatic accounts of the destruction of Typhoon Walter off the coast of India, and, yes, the latest round of gains on Wall Street. Even though the media were aware that hundreds were being affected, it wasn't yet deemed a compelling threat to the public at large—especially since most of it was occurring overseas—and therefore didn't quite qualify as news for the six o'clock crowd.

There were exceptions. CNN, National Public Radio, and one other network talked up the dramatic incidence of comas, hinting at speculation in the scientific community that this was not a random occurrence. Evidence, these outlets claimed, was beginning to mount of a "perpetrated contamination," a fact for which Stu was cautiously grateful.

"As the numbers of affected persons continue to climb," wrote one reporter in the *New York Times*, "sources say that it would be unwise to ignore the obvious spread of this sickness. At present, medical officials don't know where it comes from, or how it came to be, or how it is transmitted. Even so, intervention seems to be at the top of an increasing number of health officials' priority lists. At a recent press conference in London, an official at the Royal Ministry of Public Health said, 'Local outbreaks are relatively minor. A regional outbreak is disturbing. But a global pattern of similar symptoms of *anything* is a potentially frightening development.'"

That same reporter was one of two who, earlier in the day, had interviewed Stu by phone, looking for a sound bite, wondering how the CDC was going to get involved, and whether or not the agency was "officially" concerned. Stu answered strictly on the record, nothing anonymous, and diplomatically, meaning he avoided a straightforward answer. In return, he quizzed the reporter for clues. She told him that the scientists and analysts she had spoken with were struggling to piece together everything from cause to transmission. As he listened, Stu inwardly groaned, knowing their efforts would prove fruitless until the FBI released the angle on the deodorant cans—until the connection between GPS and the sickness was firmly established. Without such a vital clue, any investigation would be like trying to set a long jump record without a running start.

Not that easy, though.

Nothing ever was. Too many concerns to juggle. While his libertarian streak resented the FBI holding out, the fact was, effective containment would be compromised if the information was not managed properly, disseminated carefully. The media may need a good leak to get the ball rolling, but practicality trumped principle.

"Stu Baker," a warm, pleased voice intoned from behind.

He turned, folding his computer monitor in a single motion. "Hello, Terrance," he replied, extending his hand. Terrance Alexander took his hand, gripped firmly, and pumped it a time or two. "Haven't seen you in a while."

"Not since you took me for a ride last year in five card draw," Terrance replied gravely, though his eyes twinkled. He wore a jacket and tie.

"Hey, you know what they say about a fool and his money."

"Right. So how come you're doing so well?"

Stu chuckled and sipped his bourbon. Terrance Alexander was one of the few people he liked, a good wit. A real person. He and Terrance met several years back when Stu had been invited to teach a few adjunct classes at Emory. At the time, Terrance was chairman of the Department of Microbiology and Immunology.

"You know, most people come here to get away from work," Terrance said. "I guess such social conventions aren't quite up to par for Stu Baker."

"You know the drill. Always something new popping up here or there."

"Saving the world."

"Hopefully."

Dr. Alexander pulled back a chair. "Mind if I sit a minute? My wife's over there with the golf pro, flirting just enough to try to get him to knock another stroke or two off her game in a five-minute conversation. She's amazing, that woman." Terrance smiled appreciatively towards his wife. "Say, how's Alyssa? Haven't heard a word from her in a while."

Stu didn't bat an eye but took a long, slow drink. "Still out in Seattle." He was antsy to get back to work, more so to shift the conversation away from family. "Anything interesting happening with you?"

Terrance shifted in his seat and pondered the question with a twitch in his lips. He seemed ever to be on the verge of a smile. "Couple things. Got an interesting referral from a friend of mine in Oklahoma. A little boy with a blood disorder."

Stu tried to act interested. "Blood disorder?"

"Yeah. Almost always affects old people, not kids. He's real sick on paper, but not too bad in real life. Something about it's not right, though. Not sure why. We're knee deep in tests right now."

"Knee deep in journal submissions, more likely."

Terrance held up his hands, as if he had no choice. "Gotta renew my funding somehow, right? Not like you CDC fat cats, rolling in dough."

Stu snorted. "Right."

"Actually, I really think we're onto something. This particular disease profile is fascinating in that it produces large volumes of highly specific antibodies. I just got the bright idea to see what those antibodies actually do. Basic lock-and-key stuff, I suppose. Two of my grad assists are taking it a bit further. I'll send you some of the paperwork if you like. Fascinating stuff, right up your alley."

"Sure, whatever. No doubt, all this is gratis for your clients?"

"Research. There's a difference."

"As long as you think so. I'd ask for the money up-front."

"Are you subtly trying to tell me I better pay you to read my research?"

Stu opened his mouth with a retort, but Dr. Alexander's wife strolled by just then, dressed in a floor-length gown.

"Honey, you remember Stu Baker?"

His wife smiled. "Like the car."

"An American classic," Stu said, forcing a pleasant smile. He despised chitchat. "You know, I probably better get back to work."

Terrance rose, patted him once on the back. "Don't work too hard. There's always tomorrow."

Maybe, Stu answered silently, watching husband and wife walk away. *Maybe not.*

• • •

As morning dawned in Atlanta on Saturday, at the corner of Marietta Street and Techwood Drive, a thick crystal veneer of frost covered the sidewalks, tree trunks, windshields, and grass, much like the acid burn of glass etchings, leaving all the colors muted and whitish. In the heart of the city, not too far from the CDC campus, CNN's sprawling, fourteen-floor twin towers overlooked both Centennial Olympic Park and the sparkling frosty surface of the Georgia Dome.

The communications empire was abuzz with the latest revelations. Reporters had been plugging away at a dozen key CDC personnel for sound bites since late evening of the night before, forcing Stu to leave his phone off the hook all night. One reporter still managed to reach him on his cell phone, got nothing, and hung up angry. Stu labored through the night, poring over data, formulating strategies, and reconsidering scenarios. At three o'clock he drifted off to sleep but woke up an hour later disheveled and panicked. Without showering, he headed for the office.

"The mysterious sleeping illness continues to spread at an alarming rate," the anchor of the program *Early Edition* declared. "While the culprit appears to be viral, and possibly flu related, similarities between both samples and symptoms in the different regions have not yet been confirmed, though sources indicate the pattern is unmistakable. Unofficial estimates from the international community place the total number of infected persons somewhere between nine and fifteen hundred, a five-fold increase since this time yesterday morning.

"In that same time period, officials tell us that scores of people in Great Britain, Japan, Australia, India, Germany, France, and Brazil are slipping into comas after failing to respond to medical treatment targeted at core symptoms. Even more troubling, it now appears that in many cases the illness is irreversible. We have compiled scattered reports of dozens of fatalities, though no one we've spoken to is certain these cases are linked, either to each other or to the illness itself. However, in Tokyo, the nation's chief medical officer told CNN that twenty-one fatalities at three major hospitals are presumed to be related, and that a CDC task force is on site to assist in the investigation. CDC officials in Atlanta would neither confirm nor deny a presence in Tokyo. The U.S. Surgeon General's office claims less than three dozen related cases have been reported, and only three deaths have been blamed on the illness, but state coroners are investigating just to be sure.

"Faced with mounting fear and confusion, health officials at the United Nations have taken the unusual measure of calling for calm, though one unnamed source admitted that the nature of the illness could lead to a full-fledged international crisis if numbers continue to escalate. In a press release earlier this morning, the CDC announced they are marshaling all their resources to make this a top priority but warned that the speed with which the illness is spreading does not bode well for a quick solution . . ."

Stu turned from the TV in his office to the computer monitor on his desk and scanned the Web for more. Both Reuters and the *Washington Post* Web sites alluded to rumors that the illness was a virus, and that the virus was purposefully released as part of the Sleeper cult's final action.

"The computer virus was never the point," an anonymous FBI agent warned ominously. "It was simply a prop on a stage, a tool to make a point. The main player was a biological weapon purposefully released on the entire planet, in secret—terrorism of the worst kind. It's out there, right now, and it may well be unstoppable."

"We have hard evidence," another source claimed. "The governments of the world have in their possession a common artifact from the Sleeper cult suicide ritual. I can't say what it is, but the puzzle isn't that hard to figure out if anyone is willing to take a look. Problem is, in today's highly politicized climate, it's not very PC to cast a bunch of green freaks as biological assassins. But like it or not, the facts are there—Pandora's box is wide open."

Stu grabbed the phone and called the rickettsial lab—he needed final assays of the nine students from New York City; he called Special Pathogens; he e-mailed all three Epidemic Intelligence Service teams in Tokyo, Singapore, and São Paulo. He wanted updates in half an hour, no later. He phoned USAMRID. Their analysis of the genomic structure of the virus and speculation as to its origins was due this morning. He couldn't afford for it to be late. He phoned research and actuarials, demanding weather factors. He kept Marge typing nonstop.

"But before anything else, get another bulletin out. Fax it everywhere."

By nine o'clock, Stu was prepared to meet with the executive director. Armed with a large yellow envelope full of data, he prepared for battle.

He was in for a surprise. Instead of being led to Frank's office, Stu was instructed by the director's secretary to join Frank in the conference room down the hall. As the double doors were thrown open, Stu stepped warily into a room brimming with people. Noticing Stu's entrance,

Frank approached him, shook his hand, and drew him privately aside.
The executive director's eyes were narrow, weary, but lacking anger.

"From what I'm hearing, Stu," Frank said, shaking his head, "I'm
afraid you were right on this one from the start." He glanced at the package in Stu's hands. "I assume you're well prepared to prove your case
today, and I hope so, because I think we've already lost valuable time."

"Of course we've lost time! If you would have even—"

Frank waved his hand. "Now don't go and make a scene. I'm con-
ceding as gracefully as I know how. Rather than lose more ground, let's
begin to act in concert. I went ahead and assembled some key folks so
that we can hit the ground running."

Without saying more, he turned, took his place at the head of the
long oak table, and called everyone to attention. Stu stared, open-
mouthed. He had never seen Frank act in such a conciliatory manner.

After convening the meeting, Frank briefly introduced the assembled panel: the Texas state health commissioner, an assistant secretary of Health and Human Services, two advisers from the National
Security Council, the director of FBI counterterrorism, assistant
director of the FBI Critical Incident Response Group, deputy domestic policy staff from the White House, as well as the standard phalanx
of virologists and infectious disease specialists from within the ranks
of the CDC itself, including Edgar Bersch and Diane Rieschmeyer.
Eighteen people total.

"We'll add the director of the World Health Organization's
Communicable Diseases Division, California's attorney general, and
the governor of Texas by phone," Frank declared.

As Stu watched the proceedings unfold, taking his place at the table, all
at once, truth struck him. Though Frank hid his feelings behind administrative fervor, he was actually quite nervous. The meeting now being
staged should have taken place yesterday, if not the day before, and Frank
knew it. He should have requested early leave from the budget hearings
and performed his duties on site. If the CDC was about anything at all, it
was crisis intervention. A day late, maybe two—hours of irreplaceable
value lost—the proceedings would no doubt center on the risks at hand
but were also intended to proffer damage control for his career. By taking

the initiative in gathering professionals and politicians alike, by attempting to win Stu back to his side, maybe, just maybe, he could gain enough personal collateral in the short term to sustain him when the whole thing hit the fan. Because if Stu was right at all, the public would soon demand an explanation for the CDC's slow response time.

It made sense. But there was more. A second realization hit him like a slap in the face with a bucket of ice-cold water. Frank was afraid of more than losing his job. He was afraid, period.

He knows something. Something about Sleeper . . .

"Let's call this meeting to order, shall we?" Frank said, showing his teeth in a thin, grave smile, as the double doors closed and silence enveloped the room. "I know it's the weekend, but we have no time to waste. You've all heard the news reports, I'm sure. Even so, we are about to engage in a discussion of highly sensitive material. Please use your best discretion when our conversation concludes. I trust you at least have made a cursory reading of your briefing materials?"

A few heads nodded. Frank continued.

"Well then, we've got a lot of ground to cover and little time . . ."

• • •

The voice on the phone was male, warm, unfamiliar. "Mrs. Chisom, my name is Dr. Gueverro. I'll be filling in for Dr. Li today."

"Is she still not feeling well?"

"Well, let's just say it's probably gonna be a bad year for colds and flu. Dr. Li was admitted to the hospital last night for dehydration and respiratory difficulties."

"Oh my!"

The line crackled with a burst of static. It sounded as if Dr. Gueverro might be calling from a cell phone. "I'm sure everything will be fine," he continued. "However, in her absence, I have assumed responsibility for your son's case. I've thoroughly reviewed Josh's charts and, I'm sorry to say, the latest lab results paint a very dangerous picture of his current condition. His protein levels are escalating. His blood calcium is way too high. Mrs. Chisom, I don't know what to say, except to confirm the warnings my colleague has given you. In my opinion, Josh's condition is becoming dangerous. He needs treatment."

Sylvia peeked around the corner and saw her son asleep on the couch. She had hoped for better news. "I guess we don't have any choice now."

"Actually, you have many excellent choices. I understand you are possibly ready to admit him to a clinical trial?"

Sylvia murmured her reply, but her thoughts spiraled a thousand miles away. "We were thinking about Arkansas."

"Arkansas," Dr. Gueverro repeated. "I have a note here that says Josh has already been accepted as a candidate. Great news. So I guess you've faxed the necessary consent forms?"

Sylvia was numb. "Not yet."

Dr. Gueverro paused, confused. "I don't understand. Mrs. Chisom, the trial starts tomorrow."

"No. Next month."

"I'm looking at the paperwork right now. Check your consent form."

Sylvia fumbled through some loosely stacked papers on the counter-top, found the consent form, and read a few lines. When she found the date in the top paragraph, she grew angry. The trial very clearly was set to begin tomorrow.

"Your office told me yesterday it didn't start for another month."

"I'm sorry. I don't know how that happened."

Sylvia removed her glasses and rubbed her eyes.

The doctor tried to sound diplomatic. "Is that a problem?"

"It is *definitely* a problem. Why in the world are they starting on a Sunday?"

"Since many of their patients are elderly, they like to get folks settled in before the week starts. Makes for a more comfortable transition. Everyone does it differently, though." Sylvia heard him flipping pages over the phone. "For what it's worth, it looks like an excellent trial. Best of all for Josh, there appear to be minimal side effects. Can you make adjustments?"

Flustered, Sylvia snapped, "I guess I'll have to."

Dr. Gueverro walked her through the steps, instructing her in what the clinical trial would likely look like, telling her to let Josh's school know he would be gone for a while and unable to do homework. Basic details. He had her double-check the map included with her paperwork, showing where the University of Arkansas was and how to get there. He asked if she had reliable transportation.

"I don't know about reliable," she replied. "But we'll get there."

Dr. Gueverro estimated about a six- to seven-hour road trip.

"But you won't need to worry about hotels. They'll have accommodations for you. Oh, and one other small thing."

Sylvia waited.

"The nurse mentioned to me that Josh has long hair."

"That's right."

"It may seem like a little thing. But you might want to give him a haircut. Before you leave, if possible. Psychologically, it may help prepare him for the hair loss that will occur during the trials. You know, soften the blow a little."

It was a straw made of words, and it broke the back. Everything inside Sylvia screamed, *No!*

She didn't have time to react. Just then, Josh shouted her name from the living room. Screamed, more like it.

"Mom! Mom, please, come here!"

She hung up the phone, rushed in, and found him crying, holding his back. He was rolled over to one side, arm outstretched, face contorted in pain.

"I started to get up," he moaned. "It felt like my back was breaking."

Reality set in, numbing Sylvia all the way to her bones. She put her arms around his head, fighting tears, wanting desperately to reach Tim. How? Her mind raced.

This can't be happening.

"It's all right, honey. I'm right here," she said.

"No, Mom. It hurts. Bad."

Her voice was calm, surprisingly serene. "Where? Right there? Okay."

She held him, soothed him, screaming her frustration inside. She felt plotted against, conspired against. The whole thing was so impossible! Reaching Tim was impossible. He would be at the convention until late in the evening. They didn't own a cell phone, and David Tellier, she knew, didn't believe in them. Which left her with only one option. She dialed the hotel number Tim had given her, leaving an urgent message for him to call her back.

She got a glass of water for Josh, propped up his head with a pillow. Then, frantically, she began to pack. One way or another, they were going to Arkansas.

• • •

"Ladies and gentlemen, I read to you the latest correspondence from the chief epidemiologist of my Epidemic Intelligence Service team in Tokyo . . ."

Stu cleared his voice, enunciating each word carefully. He needed to project. This was too important for anyone to miss. Public speaking, however, was not his strength. He glanced up nervously and met the eyes of those gathered around the table. The letter read:

Stu, following standard procedure, we've cultured with throat swabs and transtracheal washes; we've run titers for confirmation and performed the standard battery of chem profiles and CBCs. Furthermore, we've performed autopsies on eight of the twenty-one fatalities here, and have treated nearly as many living in various stages of the illness. We now have a reasonable assessment of the illness.

We face a peracute onset of primarily respiratory pathology progressing rapidly despite all treatment. By our observation, the syndrome appears suddenly with little to no known prodromal or premonitory symptomatology. Patients complain of extreme malaise and, upon examination, are routinely febrile, with temperatures ranging from 104 to 106 degrees Fahrenheit, variably cyanotic, with a pulse oxygen of 35 to 55 percent even on supplemental oxygen. Patients are often dyspneic, and orthopneic with great respiratory effort and O2 hunger. Hemoptysis is a common finding. Lumbar and large muscle myalgia is also noted.

Artificial ventilatory support has been mostly ineffective and only palliative. Radiographs reveal a massive pulmonary interstitial infiltration that rapidly (within two to three hours) progresses to a form of

Acute Respiratory Distress Syndrome, which to date has proven to be irreversible despite all efforts. In advanced cases, we see neurologic sequelae such as seizures, immediately preceding the patient going comatose. This is the final precursor to death.

Autopsies have revealed massive pulmonary infiltration and consolidation, marked cyanosis, multiple pharyngeal petechiae and hemorrhages along with ulcers of the larger airways. Thus the coughing blood. Severe pulmonary edema is also noted. The pathogens seem to jump from the meninges right to the spinal cord and central nervous system, causing encephalitis. As a result, we have noted significant subepidural and meningeal hemorrhages as well as evidence of meningeal inflammation, meningitis, and chorioretinitis. Histopathology of the lungs reveals a massive cellular infiltrate composed primarily of polymorphonuclear cells, macrophages, atypical lymphocytes, and numerous Type-II pneumocytes.

Treatment thus far has been entirely supportive and ineffective. No antibacterial or antiviral agents have had any noticeable effect. The morbidity of this disease is defined as 100 percent of known exposures with a 99 percent mortality to date.

Stu folded the letter, allowing the silence its proper effect. When he spoke again, he spared nothing. "Ladies and gentlemen, you have all heard the reports on the news. You have your briefing materials. What the media have not yet figured out is that the symptoms we are seeing worldwide are not accidental, but purposeful. Almost six days ago, a bizarre suicide ritual was played out in the world's major international airports. We now know that ritual was not merely a suicide, but a sinister attack, an extermination attempt. We are facing an authentic, global biological crisis, and it is already out of control."

A moment, a half-second of utter calm followed. Then the room exploded into clamor and argument. Every corner of the conference room walls echoed with voices, pencil tips tapping the wooden surface of the desk, papers shuffling. The voice of one of the two advisers from the National Security Council rose above the fray.

"I want to know what the devil you are talking about," the man demanded. "I didn't understand half of what you just said, except that something ugly has hit Tokyo. Now why should we make the leap to global crisis from that?"

"If I may, sir," the director of counterterrorism for the FBI interjected, standing to his feet. "I believe I can shed some light on that."

Stu sat down. Slowly, the crowd hushed, as the director explained in near monotone how, several months prior—in fact, stretching back as far as three years—counterterrorism informants had begun to whisper off and on regarding what seemed at the time to be completely unrelated rumors. In various forms, these rumors suggested a biological attack on an unknown world city. Predominantly, the information centered around an alleged infiltration of a classified research project in Norway, where a group of scientists had successfully exhumed the bodies of three men who had died of the influenza pandemic of 1918. The biological samples from these men would represent the only known specimen of the actual virus that had destroyed millions. Stu confirmed that no other agency or organization in the world had ever claimed possession of the actual 1918 pathogen—certainly not the CDC.

The FBI also told the assembled panel about a separate group of rumors, centered around a shadow organization that operated under several aliases both in the States and abroad. Although it used an environmental activist facade, it was classified by the federal government as a terrorist organization. For the last five years, the group had apparently made sporadic inquiries towards acquiring biological pathogens, including smallpox. Rumor suggested a theft of materials from the Norway project. Some additional information from Chechnya that suggested black market procurement of advanced British aerosolization equipment now seemed relevant, though hardly so at the time. In fact, no connection between each strand of information ever materialized, nor were the rumors able to support any real weight of their own.

"It all definitely lacked a sense of cogency, we felt," the director explained. "This group actively dealt in misinformation and propaganda. In other words, they knew how to cover their tracks. At least the leader did. The French government clued us into this guy: Jean de Giscard. That name is one of the aliases we had. He was with French intelligence for a while and was the cult's mastermind. French authorities positively identified his body at the airport in Paris the night of the suicide, with an empty can in his backpack and a broken cyanide pill in his mouth."

But that was all hindsight. At the time, FBI personnel decided the information was too vague, the sources too unreliable, and the theorized conclusions too sensitive to pass on reliably to the Department of Health and Human Services or state health departments. Ironically, the director explained, just three days before the Sleeper cult struck, FBI informants again reported rumors that something major was about to happen. They just didn't know where, what, or how.

Someone snorted. "You're telling me that all of this is the result of that computer cult? From just a few days ago? The suicide loonies?"

"Sleeper. That was the virus."

"A *computer* virus."

"No. The computer virus was a warning and a distraction. Sleeper, the real virus—as you just heard—puts people to sleep. First into a coma. Then permanently."

"And this thing was released on the planet? From the airports?"

Another interjected, "What is the virus? Ebola? What?"

"Not Ebola," Stu answered. "At this point our best guess would be to call it a superflu, possibly even a genetically enhanced version of the extremely virulent 1918 strain. Our preliminary findings are consistent with FBI intelligence in that regard. But yes, all over the planet is exactly what we're saying. Listen, folks, I've been doing this for over twenty years. I've been up to my elbows in deadly, deadly stuff." He exhaled slowly and shook his head. "But what we are uncovering here scares me out of my wits. This is a nightmare scenario like I have never seen before."

The governor of Texas, joining by phone, was incredulous. He appeared to have hardly heard Stu. He was enraged at the FBI. "You had information, at least suspicions . . . and did nothing?"

"Sounds like negligence to me," agreed the California attorney general, like a snake hissing; he also was on speakerphone. "If this gets very bad here in the States, you might have a class-action lawsuit, Mr. Director. You should have notified HHS, plain and simple. You should have notified WHO. God knows who else."

The assistant director of Health and Human Services shook his head. "Happens all the time. We're always the last to know."

"*We* knew," interjected the director from WHO haughtily, in an unmistakably clean South African accent. "We needed time to confirm. You don't run your mouth on something like this unless you're quite certain. Are you going to sue WHO, as well?"

Frank stood. "Please, please! Listen. We have a lot of ground yet to cover. We are not here to bicker about what might have been, or should have been. The fact is, this thing is real. It is not a matter of *if* it hits the States. *It already has.* Texas, California, and New York, minimum, and that does not account for infected travelers crossing metropolitan and state lines. The question we have been assembled to answer is how to tackle this thing with sufficient vigor and unified purpose to stem the tide as much as possible. Folks, we must view this as if the United States of America has been attacked. We are now fighting a biological war."

"Wait a minute, wait a minute!" growled the White House staffer. "I will be the first to admit this is serious, assuming your data is accurate thus far. But these are absolutely wild projections. I mean, if all this is true, why aren't we seeing more outbreaks?"

"Every virus has an incubation period," explained Stu, "a time when the virus lies unseen, like a bear hibernating in a cave. Remember, it was only two days ago that the first symptoms appeared, and already we see high rates of infection, broad exposure, and an exponential increase in reported cases. Exponential, ladies and gentleman, means growth factors *multiply*, rather than merely add. But the unseen story is that the virus has been spreading, person to person, for almost *six* days. These first occurrences are likely individuals who directly crossed the paths of the Sleeper runners and therefore inhaled concentrated amounts—"

"But you don't know for sure."

"No, that's true. Unfortunately, in my job, success or failure involves a lot of speculation. If we are right, though, and choose instead to wait to have the scope of this thing confirmed by the number of body bags we must manufacture, then I can guarantee you we have absolutely no hope. You and I might as well pick out our body bags today if that is the case. Because based on very sound diagnostic principles—principles we work with every day that make a difference between life or death for scenarios drastically smaller than we now face—we can easily project rampancy in the next two to four days."

"For crying out loud, who is this guy?" the White House staffer demanded.

"He's the best we've got," said Frank calmly.

"Well, I don't care if he's channeling Einstein, let's calm down and be rational! Body bags? What are you talking about? I'm not about to report to the president that we should close the borders because a few people in the States have died of a flu during flu season. Or that a group of dead hippies started a biological war."

Another agreed. "The news this morning said only three dozen cases have been reported, and only three deaths from that. That doesn't sound so bad."

"That's intentional," Frank said evenly. "I've been in contact with the FEMA director on this. He has coordinated an information blackout with the National Security Council." Both NSC agents glanced sharply at each, eyebrows spiked. Frank acknowledged their irritation. "Obviously, you gentleman weren't in the loop. I'm sorry. Actually, I'm not sure why you were chosen as council representatives, but you'll have to take that up with your boss. At any rate, as much as possible, actual death rates have been suppressed and/or withheld from the media until we can get our act together. To reduce panic."

That's what you knew, Stu thought, disgusted.

"How much?" someone asked. "How skewed are the numbers?"

"I told them to take the real numbers and divide by three."

"My office has been getting calls all day, from all over the state," agreed the Texas health commissioner. "We've probably had three dozen calls this morning. All similar symptoms to what Mr. Baker read from the Tokyo field report. If this is a superflu—if anything they've said so far is right, well . . ."

"If, if, if!" roared the Texas governor. "Give me facts."

And so the CDC team laid out the facts—a stream of facts, terrifying as they were. Viral identifiers. A precise chronology of events. The fact that blood samples from nine students in New York not only matched one another, but also precisely matched samples from Tokyo, which further matched virus specimens from the deodorant can, one of which was found in the backpack of every dead Sleeper cult member, contents fully expelled. The CDC virologists explained how small a virus is, how a million viruses packed together were about the size of a speck of dust, that many hundreds of millions could be contained in a single drop of liquid, not to mention the seven ounces of liquid that were diffused into the air for literally thousands of internationals to inhale as they wandered the terminal. Due to the extremely fine aerosolization, it was very likely, they speculated, that each airport terminal remained infectious for four to six hours on the fumes of the aerosol alone. Worse still, airport ventilation systems would likely have spread at least trace amounts of the vapor to other terminals beyond the targeted terminal. Those that boarded a plane after being exposed likely immediately infected a significant portion of the passenger list. In typical, painstaking CDC fashion, they went so far as to factor in regional weather patterns around each airport both the day of, and three days following, calculating rainfall, temperature, prevailing wind direction and velocity, and proximity to other metropolitan areas. It did not take long for projections to go geometric, with loss factors into the tens of millions, and becoming much worse, at least in the United States, if containment scenarios were not immediately put into place on a state-by-state basis.

"That's bare minimum," Stu said in a gravelly voice, allowing no contradiction.

Facts. More facts. It was further explained to the panel that in a typical year, plain old garden-variety flu had a mortality rate of only .01 percent. A low figure, indeed. Yet in a typical year, an average of 20,000 Americans died. How? The cold reality of those two figures meant that up to 200 million cases of infection were occurring. Each winter. For a plain old garden-variety flu.

Sleeper was not a plain old garden-variety flu.

Sleeper was aggressive, eminently airborne, genetically modified, deadly and, worst of all, had shown no response to known treatment modalities. That was the real problem, the scary problem. While flu viruses in general often underwent minor genetic shifts in their surface proteins, shifts that made treatment a real chore, those caused little worry.

Major genetic shifts, however, usually led to full-blown epidemics, because in essence a major shift made the virus essentially unrecognizable to the human immune system, leaving a virgin population ripe for attack.

There was no cure for influenza, Stu reminded the crowd. The only treatment possible was a vaccine, and all a vaccine could do was send a signal to the body to produce a highly precise antibody. Antibodies couldn't kill influenza. Rather, they attached themselves to the little vermin, preventing them from infecting other cells and producing more viruses. It was like a policeman training the K-9 unit to a new scent. Once the dog knows what to look for, everything is fine. Vaccines gave the human body the right scent to look for. Natural immunology did the rest. If an identified virus entered the system and attempted to co-opt the machinery of a cell, to turn it into a virus factory—boom!—the body already had the scent and could produce a specific antibody that could sniff out that virus, clamp onto it, and block its ability to bind. If a virus couldn't bind, couldn't attach, it couldn't replicate. If it couldn't replicate, it was eventually flushed. No damage done. But vaccines were highly specific. It took years to develop inactive ghost viruses, the kind that carried a scent but were incapable of replication.

As such, the specific 1918 virus, known to be a derivative of H1N1, but unseen for nearly an entire century and never sampled or studied, would be like placing thousands of Attila the Huns and Genghis Khans on each continent with massive, fully equipped armies . . . and then unleashing them. Indeed, having been released *en masse*—not in one location, but in seventeen major travel destinations—the virus had likely spread from there to a minimum one hundred other population centers, if not five hundred, within just two days. And those were conservative estimates based on limited destination projections assembled from three sample airport schedules. Now, it was just a matter of time before the incubation period ran its course and the virus became active in untold numbers of unsuspecting people.

"I don't believe what I'm hearing," the White House staffer said, pale faced. "You're talking about some sort of plague. A freaking epidemic. You're telling me we could easily see 200 million people *in the United States alone* contract this thing. Is that what you're telling me?"

"In 1918, the virus killed approximately 30 million. That was *without* mass transportation as we know it today," Stu replied.

"What the—? Why are we even talking about this? Let's vaccinate everybody! We have flu vaccines."

"Not for this. Not even close."

"Well then, what *can* the CDC do? Anything? What are you guys here for?"

Stu ground his teeth together. "We have the world's most sophisticated containment labs. We deal with Ebola, Marburg, hantavirus, Lassa fever, smallpox. The world's worst diseases. I'm telling you, nothing—none of those—compares in lethal capacity to a superflu. With influenza, you touch an infected doorknob, you breath the same air, and you've got it. With a killer flu, you combine maximum infectiousness and maximum virulence. And, in the case of Sleeper, massive early deployment. All that remains is the destruction."

More diplomatically, Frank said, "If it were limited to one, maybe two locations, we could do a lot. This is going to require a much broader, more stringent effort. I fear a recommendation to close the border must be placed on the table. Possibly citywide quarantine zones."

"What?" roared the California attorney general. "You want to make a quarantine zone of New York City? L.A.? You might as well start World War III."

Edgar Bersch agreed. "It can't be done. Impossible."

Frank said, "It *can* be done. FEMA has the plans. The president has the authority. The military has the force, if necessary."

"Now you're talking martial law."

"In many areas, it may be necessary. Folks, I'm not saying people are going to accept this readily. But I don't think we have a choice. It's early, yes. But this is a matter of survival."

"Oh, my God."

The room grew still, faces haggard.

"We aren't at that point," one breathed softly. "Show me, please! You haven't shown me anything to make me believe it's anywhere near that scale yet."

"*Yet,*" Stu repeated, ominously. "Three days, tops, it will be."

14

A little before noon, while the CDC panel pondered measures both reasonable and drastic, Josh sat at the barbershop, watching blankly as great clumps of his hair fell to the floor to the metallic rhythm of cutting scissors. He didn't flinch, didn't blink. Just watched. Sylvia had no idea what he was thinking, whether he was upset or merely tired. Ever since the disease had set in, it was harder to tell; he spoke so little anyway. She watched carefully for signs of sadness, surprise at his new look, anything. But Josh only stared at himself in the mirror.

In the end, he gained a cute little haircut, one that completely changed his appearance. Ever since he was just a little boy, Josh had had long hair, and Sylvia always loved it. Long and curly. Now, with a short bowl cut, he looked more serious than ever.

She paid the barber and they strolled into the sunshine together. To a mother, the effect was striking. Was it the haircut? The light? She didn't know, but Josh looked shockingly pale. Pale and thin, and stooped in the shoulders. When he walked, his feet dragged along. Sylvia bit her lip.

Is this what happens? she wondered. *Is he just going to waste away?*

They strolled along slowly, for Josh's sake. Since she could not help but feel as though he was trying to figure things out, she tried to set his mind at ease.

"It looks great, Josh. You look real nice. I think it was time for a change."

"Okay," Josh said. And that was all.

They drove back home and finished loading the truck, then sat and waited. Tim hadn't called yet, must not have gotten the message. The rest of the day passed in fits. She called the hotel to see if he had arrived and left another message. The concierge assured her both messages were properly logged in the hotel's voice-mail system. As soon as Tim returned from the trade show for the day, he could retrieve them. Sylvia then called Mrs. Tellier to ask if perhaps she had heard from her husband. In case Tim might get a message somehow through his boss first, she left word with her, as well.

When Sunday morning arrived and the call had not come, Sylvia had no choice but to begin the journey. She called a few friends, hoping to catch them before church. Most had already left for morning services, so she had to content herself with a few teary messages on answering machines, asking for prayer. Josh watched her thoughtfully through out. She explained to him how they needed to make a trip together, all the way to Arkansas.

"It's time to try to help you get better," she said.

Josh asked a few questions, which she answered as vaguely as possible. On the kitchen table she left a handwritten note with the number of the clinic and a brief explanation of recent events, then took about five hundred dollars in cash from the oatmeal tin and stuffed it in her purse. Josh grabbed his favorite plane, the F-16 Falcon from Uncle Rick. Together, they set off.

In the truck as they rolled down the road, Sylvia fiddled with the AM radio, flipping from station to station repeatedly. She was obviously agitated. It did not help that the reception was mostly static. Josh watched her.

"I'm sorry I acted snotty the other day."

Sylvia touched his newly shorn hair. "I know."

"I guess Christmas this year isn't gonna be too good."

"Oh, we'll make the most of it."

Neither said much after that, for a good long while. After about an hour of mostly silence, Sylvia asked a question.

"Josh, how did you know that nurse had bad eyes? She wasn't wearing glasses. She didn't ask for help. Did she?"

"I think maybe she did," Josh answered. "She just didn't know to say the words."

Sylvia shook her head, amazed. After all, that was everybody's problem, wasn't it? Finding the words . . . asking for help?

"Is that what holds you back, Josh? Are you afraid?"

Josh shrugged.

Sylvia pressed gently on. "Do you need to know the right words to say, to talk to God?"

But Josh, a private person, turned his head away. "I don't really want to talk about that stuff now. Please? It's embarrassing."

"That's fine, honey. Just fine. But until you're ready, I always want you to remember: Jesus loves you, Josh. Even if it doesn't make sense."

Josh murmured, "But I *want* it to make sense."

After that, he slept. In Norman, Oklahoma, she stopped at a convenience store, bought a Coke and peanuts to help her stay awake. One of her favorite things was to pour peanuts into the bottle of Coke, then take a swig and munch on the peanuts. Josh slept. The hours dragged on; the day wore on; the truck, thank God, held up. About an hour away from Little Rock, Josh woke up, hungry. They ate at Taco Bell. As usual, Josh didn't finish his meal.

How can a little boy with a gift of healing be so sick? she asked herself, hoping God would answer.

For the final stretch of highway, Josh was wide awake. The sun was setting. Darkness rapidly overtook them. Josh took the opportunity to pose his own question.

"Tell me again why you and Uncle Rick don't get along."

Sylvia locked her eyes on the road. Opening her mouth to speak, she thought better of it, finally said, "Josh, we've been through that already. It's a long story."

"But I don't get it. I want to understand."

"Well, sometimes things get messy. I don't know why. Brothers and sisters don't always treat each other as nice as they should."

"Is that why you didn't have any more kids?" he wondered aloud. "Because you figured me and them might not get along?"

"Not at all, dear. I was *lucky* to be able to have you. God answered our prayers. Like I told you before, my tummy hasn't always worked as well as it's supposed to—"

"How? How's it supposed to work?"

"Well," Sylvia said slowly, measuring her words. "It's supposed to be able to bear children."

"So why doesn't it? Other moms have more."

Sylvia smiled, a mixture of sadness and secrecy. She had made her peace on this issue, believing as she had since the day he was born. Every mother considered her children special, Sylvia knew. But Josh was different. "It's my destiny. Your destiny."

Her words might as well have been lemons. Josh's face soured. "Not that again."

"It's true, Josh. Before you were born, or I was born, or even before Meem was born, God had a special plan for each of us. There are things you were born to do that nobody else was ever born to do, or will be again. *I* was *born* to have *you*. That's destiny."

He had heard it plenty of times. Even so, something about this time seemed to click with him, Sylvia thought. Trying to act aloof, offhand-edly, he said, "So maybe I was born to like planes?"

"Kind of like that."

More softly, he asked, "Mom, was I born to get sick?"

Sylvia shuddered and bit her lip so hard it might have drawn blood. "Okay, let's get back to Rick and me. I'll make you a deal. I'll try to explain the story, but if I do, if I try, you have to let me end it when I think I should, whether you understand everything or not. That's the deal, all right?"

"All right."

Sylvia took a deep breath and began slowly. "When I was a little girl I wasn't treated right."

"You mean when you were a foster child? After your parents died?"

"That's right."

She wished Tim were with her. He would be silent, but make his presence felt, maybe with an arm around her, or around Josh's shoulder. He would let her know he was there, engaged.

Josh said matter-of-factly, "I heard at school one time about a girl who was attacked by her daddy. The other kids laughed at her, but one night her and her mom took off and never came back."

Sylvia swallowed hard. Josh was only in the third grade. "It was kind of like that, yes. And it messed me up inside. I wasn't sure I would ever be able to have even one baby."

"But then came *me,*" Josh said proudly. "Destiny."

"Then came you." Sylvia smiled.

"So what about Uncle Rick? Was he mean to you?"

Sylvia touched his hand. "Honey, Uncle Rick never hurt me. For a long time we were the best of friends, and Rick needed me, especially as a little boy. But when our mommy and daddy died, we were put in separate foster homes. The one I was in was not a nice home, pretty mean. That was where I had the daddy that did not treat me nice. I got hurt a lot. One day there came a chance for Uncle Rick to move in with us, and he was very excited because we had been separated for quite a while. But I didn't want Rick to move in and be treated mean, too. So I acted real ugly towards Rick and made a fuss with the foster parents and the social worker . . ."

Her voice trailed away.

"And that's why you all don't get along now?"

"Sort of. It hurt Uncle Rick's feelings. He didn't understand. After that, things changed. Even after we got back together a few years later and were finally adopted, things were different."

"Why didn't you just explain it to him?"

Sylvia didn't answer. The question lingered in the air.

"I don't know, Josh. It just became easier to fight, I guess."

"See," Josh said, point proven. "It doesn't make sense. Nothing adults do makes sense."

• • •

In times of crisis, there was no such thing as a day off at the CDC—even on Saturday. By the end of the day, the death toll had risen from less than one hundred to more than fifteen hundred, while the number of cases reported had skyrocketed from around five hundred to roughly six thousand, best guess. In Stu's office alone, the CDC had logged 722 calls from referral physicians and clinics in the States, not to mention hundreds of international inquiries, asking for confirmation of symptoms. Stu expected another tenfold increase in the next twenty-four hours. The media didn't have those figures yet, of course, but information blackouts would become pointless after tomorrow. The whole thing was about to crack open like a smelly, overripe melon.

Frank's hastily assembled panel had concluded earlier this morning with a few guiding principles. Admitting to precious time lost, the vote was taken to recommend an aggressive posture and ask forgiveness later, if need be. Better an active stance than to falter along and risk losing whatever thin containment borders could be utilized—namely, major metropolitan areas. The plan was dependent on presidential approval, since it would require an executive action to set the thing in motion, but Frank, the FEMA director, and the director of HHS were flying to D.C. tonight for an emergency consultation with both the president and the secretary of state. Following that decision, the panel was advised by phone that the president had already begun conferring with other heads of state to determine the most effective course of action. High-level conference calls between CDC, FBI, HHS, the National Security Council, and FEMA were to continue throughout the day and into the night, laying the groundwork for a smooth and decisive transition to medical containment.

Since it was reasonable to assume that the targeted cities—New York City, Houston, and Los Angeles—would have a significantly higher concentration of affected persons, pending approval, those cities would be designated as quarantine zones in the next thirty-six hours. Dividing each city into quarantine grids was discussed—vehemently—but in the end it was decided, with CDC pressure, that attempts to localize further, such as to certain city blocks or to certain hospitals would be to lose control of the virus. At present, 75 percent of all reported cases in the States came from those three cities. California's attorney general screamed about civil rights, and everyone understood why. If entire cities were placed under the ban, the cold reality for both governors and FEMA was the tragicomic irony of modern society: while the virus itself may be better contained, the city could be gutted in the process.

But the problem of massive looting and a disaffected populace paled in comparison to the problem of a dead populace. Monumental as the task would be, every single CDC projection tool said the loss factors were heavily tipped towards sealing off primary exposure areas. So the National Guard would be called out, and Federal Emergency Management Agency crisis management teams would be deployed. By dawn, day after tomorrow, no traffic in or out of those cities would be allowed, by rail, air, automobile, or seagoing vessel. Such an undertaking would require mammoth deployment and tight coordination between federal officers, military, and local police forces. But that's why FEMA existed: to put the plan into action. Detailed, longstanding scenarios for this level of disaster were on the books, coded to the nth degree.

Even so, as Stu contemplated what tomorrow and the next day would look like, his mind reeled.

An expanded panel was scheduled to meet again tomorrow in Washington, D.C., to review data and confirm all decisions. This time it would be the big boys, not the assistants. Stu wasn't invited and didn't want to go anyway. Instead, governors of affected states, their health commissioners and state epidemiologists were flying to D.C., where a vast army of federal agents and cabinet-level officials would begin coordinating the massive shutdown of three major U.S. cities. Locales of the other 25 percent of cases reported would be subjected to a scaled down containment effort, but addressed with the same vigor.

The entire project was given a code name: "Project Resurrection."

Media alerts would follow a precise schedule. On the day Project Resurrection was set to launch, if all went as planned, the president would address the nation at noon. The purpose would be to inform the nation of the bioterrorist attack, to urge calm in spite of a few days of obvious difficulty, and to fully cooperate with health authorities. Prior to the national address that morning, localized, simultaneous addresses comprised of each state governor, health commissioner, and city mayor would attempt to show solidarity within the affected states, and prepare the public incrementally for the president's address. Any decision to close the national border would be tabled until initial impact could be determined and resources allocated as necessary. Stu vigorously argued against the decision to delay. If they managed to seal L.A., New York, and Houston, as well as isolate the other 25 percent scattered beyond, they *might* be in pretty good shape. But if they didn't close the borders also, it would be like closing the front door to get rid of summer flies, but leaving the back door open. Besides, sealing the national borders would be a far easier task than sealing the cities. He was overruled. The border would remain open at least until there could be a reasonable assessment of both damage and containment thus far. Sealing the national border was relegated to half a dozen backup plans; also additional citywide shutdowns (as evidence of Sleeper infestation appeared) and state-by-state border enforcement. Again, as needed.

Armies of legal teams had already begun preparing piles of briefs to handle the flood of litigation that would be unleashed. If at all possible, the panel wanted to avoid martial law and the suspension of civil rights, but that depended entirely on the voluntary civility of the affected populace, and also the panic factor that the announcements would generate. Riot police were to be dressed and ready, and additional units from the army reserves would be put on alert status.

Meanwhile, the CDC *had* its funding. That much was absolutely settled. Whatever they needed, they had. Priorities one, two, three, and four were to be Sleeper and nothing else. Every available employee was to be devoted to the task of discovering a cure and strategizing containment. On this front, the CDC bore the weight of the world, not merely the nation, though it was reaffirmed in no uncertain terms that the welfare of the United States was its top priority. As a result, the CDC national healthcare network was to be alerted at the proper time, with coordinated support efforts from the National Institute of Health. Health officials—state by state, county by county, town by town— were to be faxed or e-mailed detailed briefings of symptoms to watch for and procedures to follow. Every hospital with an infectious disease unit was to be charted and mapped for referrals from surrounding areas. Though conversion was not yet required, all hospitals and clinics were to immediately develop a plan for converting 10 percent of available floor space to isolation units, until such a time as was deemed no longer necessary.

In each state, but especially those reporting even a single confirmed case, the state epidemiologist was to immediately establish a statewide surveillance and case investigation system. Stu knew that by tomorrow, the 25 percent overspill that seemed so hopeful today would likely jump to 40 percent or more, and be scattered across a dozen additional states. Efforts to develop a registry of all face-to-face contacts of severe influenza patients, therefore, needed to be put in place today, ready to hit the ground running, along with a network dedicated to monitoring all contacts for fever on a daily basis. Anyone reporting a fever greater than 101 degrees Fahrenheit was to be isolated, at home if possible, and be tracked for further symptomatology. A massive public education process would begin airing on TV and radio to inform communities of proper procedures, allay fears, maintain communication, and instruct individuals in how to proceed should they suspect they've contracted the virus. State health departments would activate a prearranged phone tree to query all hospitals and walk-in clinics in the state about similar cases, and to counsel immediate isolation of all suspected patients.

Reeling from the enormity of the task, Stu had to sit for a moment and catch his breath. *This is crazy,* he thought, over and over. *Crazy.*

Crazy or not, it was real.

This nation, the whole world . . . stands on the brink.

A little before six o'clock, the phone rang. It was Frank, calling from the air phone aboard one of the private government jets used to shuttle important people like him from place to place.

"Stu, I want you to head this effort up," Frank said. It was a pristine moment. Stu had no right to feel so satisfied considering what was at stake. But he had been waiting years to be invited back into the game. Since about 1993—his first promotion out of the field.

"I want you to form a prime team," Frank continued. "This is the team that will be the brain for every other team. I want you as lead man, and I want you to crack this virus. Pick whoever you want or need. Shed the administrative overload. Don't worry about it; I'll get people on it for you. If you need to get in the field, go. I want you on active duty. Got it? Just like the old days."

Stu's heart pounded. *Just like the old days.*

"I'm on it." He hung up and called out, "Marge!"

Marge was already frazzled, ready to go home. It had been a long, long day. "What?"

"Before you go, phone Diane Rieschmeyer. And Edgar, at the lab. Tell them I want to meet in fifteen minutes, my office. And see if you can get Tom Sizemore on the line."

Grumbling, Marge complied. Stu shuffled through papers on his desk he hadn't checked in about three days. Hadn't checked his e-mail in nearly as long. He hated paperwork. Underneath a pile of yesterday's mail was more mail from the day before. On top was today's mail. Stu shuffled through and found a package from Terrance Alexander, marked in the upper left corner with the distinctive Emory University logo. He didn't need the distraction but opened the package anyway and pulled out a paper-clipped file probably twenty pages thick. A Post-it note stuck to the front was from Terrance.

"This is from my grad assist, like I mentioned. Interesting stuff."

Stu read the title of the work: "Antigenic Specificity of Monoclonal Antibodies Present in Multiple Myeloma: a paper in progress for the doctoral dissertation of Mackenzie Faulkner."

Thumbing through the report, he found the names of five patients included in the study. Apparently, as a follow-up to Dr. Alexander's original research earlier in the year, assays had been expanded to discover whether the naturally occurring antibodies of other multiple myeloma patients might indeed target *other* pathologies. Having run a broad assay, Ms. Faulkner had made interesting discoveries, blah, blah, blah. Stu scanned the names, found the one unique case, the positive match. A boy named Chisom, from Oklahoma. Eight years old. Must be the one Terrance had mentioned at the country club.

Joshua Chisom.

Joshua.

The name "Joshua" triggered unbidden, unstoppable thoughts of Josie. Bitterly, Stu recalled that Josie was only eight years old when he gave her that stupid doily. And so the whole thing crashed around him, again. Fortunately, the phone rang. It was not the call Stu was expecting.

"Stu, it's Agent Thurman. Listen, I can't tell you any more than this, but I have found one thing out. Answer me this: how many airports were struck?"

"Seventeen."

"Right, and one victim was found at each airport. Don't ask me why they aren't releasing names. It makes no sense. But I can tell you this. *Eighteen* tickets were purchased."

Stu gulped. "What do you mean? What does that mean, eighteen?"

"Well, to me it means *someone didn't sail.* I don't know if it was your daughter that chickened out, or someone else, so don't get your hopes too high. It may have been the ringleader for all I know. But someone bailed at the very last."

The room spun beneath his feet. Far away, Stu heard a light tapping coming from his door.

He coughed and tried to focus. "I owe you big time, Thurman."

He hung up. Diane cracked the door open and poked her head through. "Hi, Stu."

"Come . . . come in, Diane. Edgar should be along shortly. Have a seat."

Clumsily, he pushed the research file from Emory aside. His heart raced. No time for casual reading. The planet was dying and he needed solutions. *And Josie might be alive!*

• • •

By the time she and Josh were settled in their room at the Myeloma and Transplantation Research Center, Sylvia was not feeling well. She recognized it easily enough. Anytime she came down with a fever, her back started to stiffen, and then she got a throbbing headache. Not wanting to mention anything to Josh, she took an aspirin and tried to ignore it. Although they arrived late to the clinic, the staff was gracious and quickly accommodated them. It took two hours to fill out all the paperwork.

Nothing was ever easy.

Eventually, paperwork concluded, they were escorted to their living quarters, where they unloaded their luggage and set about making the small, private suite as homey as possible. Not too difficult; the suite was much nicer than Sylvia expected. On the ground floor, it had two single beds—one was a hospital bed, with IV racks and EKG monitors ready—a phone, a purple vase with fresh-cut flowers, and two abstract prints, framed and hanging on the walls. A TV was mounted at an angle, hanging from the ceiling. They were told it had cable, which excited Josh to no end, since they didn't have cable at home.

"Please, Mom! Can I watch Nickelodeon?"

"Yes, dear. But not now. Let's get settled first."

Josh tore through his suitcase, stuffing all his things in two dresser drawers. Sylvia calmly unpacked, appreciating the small touches as she went along. An area rug on the tile floor kept the room from feeling cold and too much like a hospital, and the small sofa and easy chair were comfortable enough. For clothes, they had a simple cabinet system, like a dresser, with a little desk built into one side. A tiny room adjoining the main one served as a kitchenette, with sink, dishes, a half refrigerator, and microwave. Next to the kitchenette was the bathroom. And in the middle of the far wall, two big windows overlooked what in summer and spring would surely be a beautiful grassy lawn, shaded by large, leafy sycamores.

Not surprisingly, the suite wasn't located in the hospital proper, but in a separate clinic facility adjacent to it. MTRC was an integral part of the Arkansas Cancer Research Center, which fell under the larger umbrella of the University of Arkansas for Medical Sciences. Most research and treatment would occur from this building, though some might be required elsewhere. Josh was assigned a nurse, a smiling young woman with a sweet Arkansas drawl who cheerfully volunteered the fact that she was still in nursing school. The lead researcher on the project, she told them, was Dr. Alexis Coleman, but she would not make rounds until tomorrow. However, the nurse did go ahead and draw blood and take a urine sample as well as x-rays. In the morning, they would be briefed by Dr. Coleman as to what to expect. Following that, the trial research team would spend a day or two analyzing each case—fourteen people total had been accepted—and a treatment schedule customized to each person would begin. She told them this would be a Phase 2 pilot study of the effects of suramin on both multiple myeloma and Castleman's disease.

Josh, they were told, was the only child.

The first thing Sylvia did when she unzipped her luggage was pull out a couple of candles she brought from home and artwork of Josh's that once hung on her refrigerator. Also a photo, a favorite photo of Josh running, arms outstretched like wings, pretending he could fly. These she placed around the room, lighting one of the candles at the same time. Soon, the tingling smell of cinnamon and pumpkin spice wafted through the air, and things started to cozy up a bit, as much as possible. The staff had decorated the suite with touches of ivy and holly—a Christmas wreath on the door and a bit of garland at the foot of each bed—adding a fresh, seasonal tone. Josh took the whole thing in stride. For now at least, the clinic seemed like nothing more than a big adventure. He set his plane on the nightstand near the bed that was obviously his.

"Can I watch TV now?" he begged.

Sylvia acquiesced, flipping on the TV. The NBC affiliate in Little Rock was broadcasting a special news bulletin. Sylvia realized she hadn't watched TV at all for nearly a week. Tom Brokaw's face was solemn, his voice, if possible, even more sedated than usual. Sylvia flipped the channel, only to discover Peter Jennings in the same mood.

". . . can confirm that earlier this morning, Carson Mitchell, the two-time all-American center for the Boston Celtics, after requesting treatment this morning, has slipped into a coma. Carson Mitchell's symptoms are consistent with the illness that has been cropping up all over the nation over the last two days. The culprit has been positively identified in many of these cases as an unusually strong strain of influenza."

The report flashed to an M.D. with the National Institute of Health, repeating the fact that the virus had been positively identified as influenza, but further explaining that they really don't yet know why it is suddenly everywhere, and so severe, rather than exhibiting the typical creeping effect usually seen in the spread of a flu during flu season. He concluded with a warning that flu season might be rough this year, and that people should be careful to wash their hands often and stay away from crowded areas as much as possible.

Peter Jennings then continued: "But is it really just a bad flu bug?

Many think not. Sources have begun to call the virus 'Sleeper,' after last week's infamous computer virus. Allegedly, the same group responsible for the computer virus released a toxic spray into the air at the seventeen airports in which they killed themselves. These rumors, though speculative, do corroborate the stories of sources close to the FBI, who tell ABC News that the federal government will issue a statement sometime tomorrow to address the situation. Meanwhile, a spokesman for St. Elizabeth's in Boston confirmed that Mr. Mitchell, at six foot eight and 260 pounds, admitted himself after complaining of high fever, difficulty breathing, and weakness. A bloody cough later developed, which seems to be a telltale symptom for this particular illness. We go now live to Los Angeles, where Reggie Tucker is standing by."

Reggie, a young black man with round spectacles, dressed in a light overcoat, stood in front of a group of demonstrators who held signs and chanted, "We won't go; we want to know! We won't go; we want to know!"

"Peter, behind me is Century City Hospital in West Los Angeles, where a group of eighteen kindergarten students have all fallen sick in the last twenty-four hours with a hacking, bloody cough, dangerously high fevers, and extreme fatigue. Parents report that their children suddenly and without warning experienced great difficulty breathing, after which everything turned sharply worse. It is extremely important to note here, Peter, that every single child complained of the same symptoms at roughly the same time. A spokesman for the school declined comment, but on further investigation, ABC News has discovered that the teacher of that kindergarten class is actually now in a coma, after herself suffering the *same* symptoms, *and so is her husband,* who only five days ago returned from a business trip overseas, healthy and well. Although the children appear to be in stable condition, parents and friends are irate at the lack of dialogue from both school and medical officials. But as a physician I spoke with earlier explained, it's not that they are trying to keep things secret; they simply don't know what to say. This has got them all stumped. And that may be the most frightening thing of all. Back to you, Peter."

"Mom," Josh urged. "This isn't it."

"Shhh."

The camera cut to Peter Jennings. "Reggie, is there any speculation as to whether the illness these children suffer from is the same as what appears to have attacked Carson Mitchell and so many others?"

"Peter, we don't know. What officials are telling me is that if they had to go to court with this one, there would be plenty of circumstantial evidence to make a winning case. At present, a team of physicians from Century City, St. Elizabeth's in Boston, and Mount Sinai in New York City are sharing information and comparing blood samples. They all know it's influenza, and the symptoms do line up, but they haven't yet confirmed if it's the same influenza. However, a hospital spokeswoman told me that one of the physicians would probably release a statement tomorrow to announce their findings. What has a lot of people scratching their heads here, though, is why we aren't hearing anything of note from the CDC and other federal health organizations. Back to you, Peter."

"All right, to summarize the best information we have at this point, although many of these reports are conflicting, we can safely say that hundreds of cases have been confirmed in the United States over the last two days, and thousands worldwide. Stay tuned to ABC News as the story unfolds. Now back to our regularly scheduled programming."

20/20 came on, with Barbara Walters describing the lead story for the night, about a "Christmas miracle" along a Michigan waterway, where children helped clean up a polluted freshwater stream. Sylvia flipped the channel again and finally gave the remote to Josh. The nurse appeared at the door, smiling.

"Mrs. Chisom, your husband is on the line."

She hurried down the hall to the reception area and took the receiver. "Tim?"

"Sylvia, I got your note. What in the world is going on?"

"Tim, what happened? I tried to call you in Dallas. Did you get my messages at the hotel?"

"No," Tim said bitterly. "I found out this morning that their voice mail's been screwed up."

Sylvia bowed her head, fighting tears. "I didn't know what else to do.

I tried and tried. I left word. After the doctor in Oklahoma City reviewed Josh's tests, he said a treatment plan was urgent. Then Josh started screaming from back pain. And then I found out the clinical trials started today, not next month. I made the decision and brought him here. I'm sorry. Please don't be angry."

She heard Tim take several long, measured breaths over the phone. "I'm not angry. Is Josh okay?"

"He's in the room now, resting. The place is very nice."

"All right, here's the plan. I'm on my way. I'll catch the next flight I can from Oklahoma City. I should be able to get there by tomorrow morning."

"Use the money from the oatmeal tin. The red-and-white one on the fridge." She paused, thinking. "How will you get to the airport?"

"Jackson owes me a favor. I'll have him take me."

"I love you."

"I love you, too. Don't worry, I'll be there by morning."

"Okay. Oh, and Tim . . . bring the camera with you. It may be awful, but we'll want the memories."

Tim's voice changed. "Are you feeling okay, Sylvia? You sound raspy."

"I'm a little clogged. I think I'm catching a cold. No big deal."

"Well, get some rest tonight. And try not to get Josh sick."

They said good-bye and Tim hung up. Sylvia held the phone to her face just a little longer, a lingering moment. She wanted to tell him again, so she breathed it into the phone, so soft he couldn't have heard even if he had been listening.

"I really do love you."

And then she coughed.

15

The ride to the airport early Monday morning was long and dreary for Tim. Light flurries danced in the air and the wind was bitter cold. It was early. The sky was a gray wash of clouds, no sun. The forecast called for snow. As the countryside blurred past—sparse, rocky, with scrawny trees jutting naked in the air, and field after empty field stitched with thick layers of dried grass husks—he said a prayer for his family.

Tim's feet were sore. A few days ago, he had bought a new pair of boots and they still weren't broken in. Last night, he had not slept well, not at all, had risen early, packed economically, grabbed some money, and departed. Jackson, being a man of few words, spoke none of them now, a fact for which Tim was grateful.

But silence was both more and less than he truly wanted. He flipped on the radio, knowing Jackson wouldn't mind. U2 sang "One Tree Hill." At the top of the hour, news:

"Panic and rioting today in London, Munich, and Sydney. This is the third morning of what is now being called the Sleeper virus. With only four days before Christmas, the shocking death toll now stands at eleven thousand on this . . ."

Tim jerked fully awake. Jackson turned the radio volume up.

"Sounds like what Carson Mitchell's got," he mumbled.

". . . in addition, several nations across Europe and Asia have announced the dramatic step of closing their borders, including Great Britain, Germany, Switzerland, India, and Japan, citing public health concerns. Other nations are said to be considering similar options. In the United States, several hospitals have begun to complain of inadequate facilities and limited room for the suddenly burgeoning population of people, all complaining of Sleeper-related symptoms. In Houston, Texas, the governor's limousine was surrounded downtown by a group of some five hundred protesters, demanding answers, as Houston seems to be one of the cities hit hardest by the illness. Reuters News reports that hospitals in Los Angeles and New York are also struggling to handle the increased caseload, which is clogging emergency rooms and, quite possibly, spreading the disease further. An official estimate this morning from the World Health Organization says over fifty thousand people have contracted the illness worldwide, though it warns those numbers probably do not include persons in remote or outlying areas, especially in Third World countries. Nevertheless, a spokesperson for WHO says people should remain calm, as a coordinated effort is being mounted by world governments to tackle the problem, evidence of which can be seen in the decision to seal the borders until the spread of the virus is halted . . ."

Jackson shut the radio off.

As he listened, Tim found himself more glad than ever to live in small-town America, away from big city problems. Ever the man of few words, Jackson had but one thing to say. On this occasion, Tim could think of nothing better.

"God have mercy."

• • •

Sylvia staggered to the bathroom, half awake, coughing fiercely. It was early morning, maybe five o'clock. Tim, probably on his way, felt far away. Josh was still asleep. When she turned the light on and caught a glimpse of herself in the mirror, she nearly cried out, recoiling at the sight of her own face. Her skin was pale, eyes sunken, her hair flat and waxy. After tossing and turning all night, she finally awoke to sheets wet with sweat, and she, shaking with chills. Staring at her reflection, she realized she hadn't seen anyone look this bad since . . .

Sunny.

The thought triggered a fit of coughing, or seemed to. Sylvia clutched her chest, fist to mouth, but couldn't stop. She coughed so hard she bent over double, with her face in the sink. Something in her throat seemed to peel away, slip free. It burned. It almost gagged her. She spit and looked.

Dear God.

Blood.

She spit again. In the heavy, bubbled mucous of her saliva were thick streaks of bright red. Sylvia collapsed onto the flat toilet lid and covered her mouth. She found it hard to breathe.

Oh please, no . . .

Her first thought was of Josh. Her second, Tim. Acting on impulse, she grabbed a clean washrag, covered her mouth in a makeshift filter, and wandered out into the hallway towards the reception area, hoping it was staffed around the clock. The lights were on, but no one was there. Up and down the hall she searched for movement, wandering a few feet each direction, increasingly frantic. On the countertop of the receptionist's station was the same phone she had used last night to speak to Tim. She picked it up and dialed zero, hoping it was part of the hospital network.

Fortunately, it was. The hospital operator answered.

"Umm, hello," Sylvia whimpered. As much as she tried to fight it, she started to cry.

"Hello?" the operator said. "Are you all right?"

"No, no. I'm not. My name is Sylvia Chisom. I'm in the . . ." she fumbled for the right words. "I'm sorry, I can't even remember the name of this place. I'm on campus. In the building near the hospital. Where they do myeloma trials."

"All right, yes," the operator replied. "MTRC. Go on."

"I need to speak to a doctor, please. Any doctor."

"Well, what seems to be the matter?"

"Just get me a doctor!" Sylvia sobbed.

The operator put her on hold. A moment later, a different voice answered.

"This is Dr. Ludlow. Can I help you?"

Sylvia labored for control of her words. She could not stop thinking about Josh. What in the world was he going to do now? Without her? Had she kissed him? Breathed on him? She couldn't remember.

"My name is Sylvia Chisom. My son is taking part in the cancer trials at MTRC. We just arrived, but I think I may need to be moved away from here. Soon."

"I'm sorry," the doctor answered slowly, confused. "Why is that?"

"Well," it seemed almost impossible to say. "I don't want to get anyone here sick. I think I've come down with that virus. Sleeper."

It took thirty minutes for a team from the hospital to arrive at the clinic. Sylvia sat alone in the hallway near the entrance, bawling in the flickering light of the TV, as CNN droned on and on about how terrible Sleeper was, how deadly, how dreadful. One hundred percent mortality, they said in low, monotone voices.

After that came a rerun of a talk show on another station. Conan O'Brien joked that Sleeper was like trying to talk to his old girlfriend: both put you in a coma. He also had his own statistics to share, describing the findings of a recent Gallup poll: 68 percent of Americans disapproved of how the government was handling the job.

"You know what this means," he smirked. "The other 32 percent think it's really, you know, *okay* that all these people are dead."

Ba-da-boom clanged the drum and cymbal. The crowd laughed and clapped.

Sylvia couldn't watch anymore, nor could she return to the room with Josh. Not yet. Curled on an uncomfortable chair, she drowned out the noises clanging through her head, the statistics and TV voices, and instead traveled thousands of little roads and memories, each one full of joy and sadness. Drifting into fog and mist and uncertainty, the paths were supposed to lead gently into the future, where she and Tim grew old and Josh, magically conquering his disease, grew up.

A fairy tale, it seemed.

Grieving, not so much for herself, but for all that might yet be, Sylvia summoned what courage remained and decided that she wasn't dead yet. She flipped off the television, steeled herself, and waited. Courage or no, a haunting truth confronted her as she sat in the darkness. More than surrendering herself, she realized she must surrender Josh—all that he could be, was meant to be, things she might never know if Sleeper had indeed become her fate. She had always held him so tightly.

He was never mine, anyway.

When the intervention team arrived, dressed in masks, caps, gloves, and scrubs, Sylvia spoke through her rag, asking one question: If she did have the virus—if—would she be able to see or touch Josh again? No, the answer came; if she had contracted Sleeper, she would be isolated. No further direct contact would be allowed.

Sylvia could not bear such news. She broke down, begging. The lead physician, who was actually the hospital epidemiologist, finally recanted. Given the unusual circumstances, with her son and all, perhaps they could arrange a unit for her, under a plastic bubble, that might allow limited contact. No promises. She accepted that. What about Josh, though? He was asleep. He would have no idea. Who would watch him until her husband arrived? She was assured all would be taken care of.

Good-bye, Josh . . .

They gave her a mask and gloves and asked her to sit in the wheelchair. Not yet. Not yet. She could not just leave, not like this. She turned and walked slowly, step by step, each footfall an ache, a dream, a failure, down the hallway to their suite. Inside, the room was coated with the soft drizzle of light from the bathroom door, left ajar. She had not turned off the switch. It fell on Josh's face, which was almost hidden beneath the covers. Carefully, Sylvia peered for the best view, but she could see very little. She did not dare enter further, could not get too close, just stretched out her hand as if she might touch him. Perhaps touch his dreams if nothing else. Yes, that would be nice. In whatever he dreamed—of heaven or baseball or chocolate, or running free through the fields and not hurting or being laughed at— Sylvia prayed God would make these dreams, the final signature of this one single night, some of the sweetest memories of Josh's life. Somehow . . .

"I'm so sorry, honey," she murmured, wiping at her tears. "Daddy'll be here soon."

With that, she turned, not knowing what else to do, and crept back along the hall to where the intervention team awaited her.

At ten-thirty Sylvia awoke from a drug-induced sleep and found herself peering through a veil of clear plastic into the face of her husband. Tim stood alone, wearing a mask, gloved hands resting on the plastic, watching her. The fear and pain in his eyes was obvious. He opened his mouth to speak and closed it, jaw muscles clenched. Yet he would not take his eyes off her. Deep and brown and piercing, they also shone unspoken with years of love.

"Oh, Tim," she wept. "I'm so sorry."

"Shh . . ." he said with difficulty. "Don't speak."

She lay in a bed, connected to an IV bag with a saline drip. Tim explained that she was receiving dosages of rimantadine, which should slow the spread of the virus, if indeed she was a carrier. Carefully, Sylvia let herself absorb her surroundings. She was in a specialized infectious disease wing of the hospital, in one of several isolation rooms. Her bed was enclosed inside a protective barrier membrane, a Trexler negative-pressure plastic isolator. He described how they were pumping oxygen into the bubble for her, with internal pressure stabilized to a level below that of the surrounding climate, thereby preventing contaminated air from seeping out. Inside the canopy of transparent film, the air Sylvia breathed was then recirculated through HEPA filters, high-efficiency particle arresters, and released back into the atmosphere outside the isolation chamber.

"Where's Josh?" she said at length, suddenly alarmed.

Tim pointed. Sylvia rotated her head ninety degrees to her left and gasped. Beside her bed, a few feet away, another bed with plastic isolator was set up. Inside lay Josh, sleeping soundly.

Apparently, after charting Sylvia's symptoms and checking the latest CDC update on file, doctors conferred and agreed that the safest measure would be to isolate both her and Josh, and run blood work on both. Results should arrive later in the day.

"Are you all right?" Sylvia asked.

"No," Tim answered.

Sylvia could only imagine. Freshly arrived from the airport, expecting nothing, the sight of both his wife and son under plastic bubbles, surrounded by soft-spoken nurses padding along on quiet feet as if working on cadavers, wearing masks and warning him against violating the barrier tent in any way, was surely a devastating experience. She felt sorry for him, perhaps even more than for herself.

Tim forced words to come out of his mouth. "After they brought you here, they sedated you so you would sleep. Do you remember that?"

Sylvia barely shook her head. She was hot, sweaty. "A little. Not much."

"They went back for Josh after that. Since you both have shared the same air for several days and were exposed to the same people, they decided to monitor him, also. It's procedure. Part of effective containment, they said."

"Is he . . . sick?"

"No, no symptoms. But they have to play it by the book. Apparently this thing is pretty wild. Sleeper, I mean."

Sylvia felt awful, but she was reasonably alert and coherent. She struggled to put all the pieces together.

"How long have you been here?"

Tim replied, "About forty-five minutes. They updated me in the waiting area. Asked about a million questions. They weren't going to let me in at first."

"I guess it's good you went to Dallas, huh?" Sylvia whispered and meant it, but had no idea the words would sting so badly. Eyes open, bloodshot, Tim pressed his fist to his lips.

"I'm not so sure."

Sylvia raised her hand and touched it to the inside of the plastic, toward Tim's chest, pressing outward. The plastic bulged and creased. He responded in kind, matching his fingers to hers. Her skin was too hot to feel the warmth of his hand through the material.

"It's like a big, ugly condom," Sylvia said, eyeing the membrane, forcing a quick smile before a fit of coughing overtook her. Tim snorted, tried to make a laugh out of it. She had caught him off guard with her sense of humor. Sylvia was pleased.

"I wouldn't know," he replied.

"No, I guess not," she agreed. "We never had that problem, did we? All we wanted to do was have babies, not avoid them."

"We got one, didn't we?"

"Most certainly we did. The finest I've ever known. I think he'll be as fine a man as his daddy, one day."

"You did it Sylvia. It's always been you."

"C'mon, Tim. He has your eyes. Your smile. Your walk. Your strength. He's every bit your son. I just got to enjoy the ride."

Tim couldn't bear it. "Sylvia, please—"

"Tim, you have to be strong now," Sylvia whispered urgently. "I've got this thing. I can feel it. My lungs feel like a mess. I feel like Dr. Li looked that day."

"No . . ."

"And if I *do,* I don't know how much time I have. Have you listened to the news?"

He nodded. Seeing herself through the pain in Tim's eyes, Sylvia knew she looked awful. Her strength ebbed.

"You've heard the reports, then, right? They don't have a cure for this thing. It kills people, fast. Listen, honey. I'm *so* glad you weren't there, or you'd probably be in here with us. Hopefully, Josh won't get it. It seems like if he was going to get it he would have started having trouble about the same time as me, but he's not. That means you and he have to keep going on. No matter what."

She coughed again, loudly. In the next bed, the sound caused Josh to stir and awaken. For a split second, all he could do was stare at the ceiling and the bubble around him, in confusion. Next, he bolted upright, terror in his eyes. When he saw his dad, he calmed, but when he saw his mom, laying under a bubble as well, he started to cry.

"What's going on?" he cried, eyes darting furtively. "Why are Mom and me underneath all this stuff? Mommy, are you all right?"

"I'm fine, honey, I'm fine," Sylvia tried to reassure him. "I got a little sick and they wanted to make sure we're both okay. Are you feeling okay, Josh?"

"I don't feel anything," Josh said. "Nothing different than usual, anyway. My back still hurts."

"No fever, no trouble breathing?"

"Mom, what's going on? This is scary."

It *was* scary, for all of them. Tim strode over to Josh's tent. "It's okay, Son. I love you. We're all here together. We just have to figure some things out. You've got to relax."

Sylvia started coughing again.

• • •

While the Chisoms awkwardly tried to be a family, the hospital epidemiologist scurried around in an ever-increasing state of agitation. Time was ticking. A high contagion immediately set a cascade of hospital policy and regulation into motion. While he was not yet prepared to declare a contagious disease emergency, another update from the CDC had arrived last night, confirming H1N1 variants as the bug to watch for and recommending immediate isolation for those complaining of symptoms who also tested H1N1 positive. Given the previous CDC update on file that outlined the symptoms, and obvious media saturation, the epidemiologist insisted that contact be strictly limited to the father alone. It would only take a couple careless mistakes, and this would become not only an emergency situation, but a public relations nightmare.

At the top of the policy cascade, infection-control nurses were ordered to begin interviewing clinic staff to determine who was in face-to-face contact with Sylvia and Josh during the admissions process. But he couldn't wait for that process to be completed. He called the chair of the department of medicine and the hospital vice president of medical affairs and broke the news to them.

Within half an hour, he was in a meeting with the infectious disease physician, the chair of the department of medicine, the vice president for public relations, and the hospital's general counsel. Joining them by phone were the city and state health commissioners. After a lengthy discussion, and an additional ten-minute consultation by phone with a CDC official, the group decided to secure the clinic. Mercifully, Sylvia and Josh, the only suspected viral carriers, were immediately and appropriately isolated, with zero extraneous contacts made inside the main facility. Since the clinic maintained a separate staff, tracking potential developments was greatly simplified. Once secured, no one would be allowed to leave—patient and medical personnel alike—until the full range of contacts for each person was identified.

By the book. It was all anyone knew to do.

• • •

While many rumblings continued through administration, inside the isolation room, Tim stood between his wife and son, whispering love. As Josh calmed down, the family rallied to one another. Sylvia asked a strange question.

"Josh, honey, did you have any dreams last night?"

Josh had to think only a moment before a broad smile split his face. Tim had not seen him smile like that in many, many days.

"How did you know?" Josh asked.

"Would you tell me about it?"

Josh closed his eyes. "All I remember is that I was flying. That was the whole dream. It was wonderful. Just me flying. High above the clouds, looking down."

Sylvia smiled. Tim saw her move her lips. *Thank you.*

A little after one o'clock, another doctor entered the room and spoke softly. "Mr. Chisom, could I speak with you for a moment?"

Tim caught Sylvia's eye before he followed the man outside, around the corner.

His name was Dr. Kemper, and he murmured in a low voice, "Mr. Chisom, I have some very difficult news to convey. Your wife's blood sample has tested positive for an especially virulent form of influenza."

"It's the one on the news, isn't it? Sleeper?"

"It looks very likely. We're asking for confirmation from the CDC, but I thought you should know as soon as possible."

Tim took a deep breath. "All right."

"One other thing. When we first transferred your wife earlier this morning, she had a pretty clear mind, so we tried to get as much information from her as possible to build a case history. One thing she seemed adamant about was that she had likely contracted her sickness from your son's referring physician in Oklahoma City. Dr. Sung Li. Does that name ring a bell?"

"Sure. She was the specialist that arranged for Josh to be a part of this clinical trial."

"Well, I wanted to make certain. Because if that's true, I'm afraid the news gets worse. As part of our investigation on your wife's behalf, we called to check on the status of Dr. Li. Mr. Chisom, I'm sorry to tell you, Dr. Li is dead." The news was like a jolt of electric current. Tim staggered backwards as if pushed and ran his fingers through his hair. How could this be happening? The doctor continued. "She died yesterday. Apparently several other nurses and physicians who worked closely with Dr. Li, as well as some of her patients at Children's Hospital, are also gravely ill. At least five additional people have gone comatose. It does not look good, sir. I'm sorry."

"My son," Tim said emphatically. It was meant to be a question.

"We'll continue to monitor him. He looks fine, now. That's all I know to say."

"How long for Sylvia? Isn't there anything you can do?"

The doctor shook his head. "We'll increase the rimantadine, but it doesn't seem to be doing much. I really don't know. In all my years, I've never seen anything like what we're hearing about this virus."

"How long, please. I need to know."

"Based on anecdotal evidence, given her current state, I would guess you have the rest of the day, maybe tonight, before she slips into a coma. From there, who knows? I'm terribly sorry."

There was nothing more to say. The doctor touched Tim's shoulder and walked away, leaving him alone with his thoughts. Tim slumped into a padded seat in the waiting room. Alone under the fluorescent lights, the acidic, chemical aroma rising from the freshly polished tile floor burned in his nostrils.

"I can't do this," he whispered to no one but himself. Half a dozen loose thoughts intertwined, tangling through a mesh of undefined emotions, unraveling at the same time in his head. *I've never walked this road. Never thought I'd have to.*

It was the type of journey every spouse feared, every parent dreaded.

Am I supposed to just sit here and watch them die? My son to cancer? My wife to disease? At the same time?

He thought of Job and felt ashamed. A simple, desperate confession came choking to his lips.

"I want to believe, God. I want to . . ."

They're being punished because of me.

It was a foolish thought. Another followed, rising to the surface of his brain like a hot bubble sputtering from the depths of some primeval tar-pit. He knew better, knew it wasn't true. But his heart was too weak to fight hidden shames, fears, and pride. The failings of humanity lurked in his soul, creating fault lines for crisis, snagging his conscience.

I'm being punished. I doubted God would do miracles. So now he won't. My family is being taken from me to prove me right, because it's all I was willing to believe.

"No!" he argued with himself aloud. That wasn't how God worked. Not his character. *Or is it?* Maybe Tim had been singled out to prove a point: Don't mess with God.

The only answer was silence. Tim shook his head. It was one thing to struggle for money when bills came due, or to hold devotion and find faith in an hour of stress and testing. It was quite another to watch your family be suddenly uprooted, victimized by nature—which was under God's providence, wasn't it?—to watch them suffer towards an early grave.

And still find faith.

Another question gnawed at Tim, one he was loath to admit or consider. Yet its persistence battered him. It was an indictment of God's motive and virtue.

Why didn't he stop them? That cult? How could he have allowed this to happen? God must have known the plague would reach all the way to Tim's family, to the innocent, the undeserving. To millions of others who had done nothing to warrant a curse of this magnitude.

He wrung his hands together and pulled at his hair. Tim had always been a strong man. Always knew what to do. Had always done the right thing. Yet now, all he knew to do was surrender.

I can't walk this road alone.

"Come with me," he whispered to the unseen God. "Don't leave me."

• • •

An otherwise uneventful afternoon was transformed into a spectacle in the middle of downtown Little Rock—a microcosm of the tumult rocking the nation. The epidemiologist called the Arkansas state health commissioner, confirmed that the virus was Sleeper, and requested assistance in sealing MTRC. The health commissioner then called the FBI branch office in Little Rock and asked for an FBI special agent to be dispatched to help coordinate the securing of the clinic. Forty-five minutes later, the FBI agent was on the scene requesting a dispatch of four police squad cars to help maintain order and ensure that no patients, staff, or visitors left the facility.

Although not directly affecting the hospital, the scene drew quite a number of gawkers and onlookers, especially since no explanation was given for the containment to staff, visitors, or the police. Rumors abounded, the chief being that a crazy woman broke into the clinic, coughing Sleeper on everyone before collapsing on the ground; other rumors suggested that a terrorist wanted by the FBI was hiding in the building. A fight erupted between an old man trying to leave the facility and the police. Since the hospital was part of the University of Arkansas, a small knot of students quickly formed, picket signs in hand, looking for a cause.

Local television networks were soon on site, reporting outside the hospital for the noon news edition, explaining that sources inside the hospital pinned the blame on a woman and her son.

A hospital public relations representative calmly explained on camera that the lock-in was temporary. "This exercise will only last long enough to gather the names and addresses of potentially affected individuals, so that they can be further contacted and treated should a suspected, unnamed, contagious disease be confirmed," she said.

Nobody needed help figuring that one out. The word *Sleeper* whispered through the crowd, the city. People watched the news and began calling the hospital, complaining of a cough, certain they had bumped into a woman and child earlier that day at the market, the gas station, the bank. A flood of ghost symptoms gripped the city.

As the day wore on, the mayor and state attorney general's office were contacted by the health commissioner. The hospital's general counsel was included, with the question being, did they legally have the right to impose quarantine? Fortunately, by midafternoon, most of the data gathering was complete. Only the receptionist, radiologist, and nurse had been exposed to either Josh or Sylvia. They were detained, questioned, and placed under observation for seventy-two hours. The big scare, at least for everyone else, ended there. Crowds dispersed. The FBI departed the scene. And hospital administration, over and over, thanked their lucky stars only the clinic had been affected.

• • •

Sylvia was growing weaker. After confirmation of her illness from the doctor, Tim had sat in the hall and wept, deep guttural sounds that leaked from his chest, pitiful noises, mainly because of the strain he employed to suppress them. It was agony like he had never felt before.

Sylvia was going to die. Maybe Josh, too.

At around 4:30 P.M., he reentered the room with face washed and no tears remaining. It didn't matter. Sylvia would know the truth, would recognize it in his eyes, despite his efforts to hide and be casual and brave. He didn't have to say a word.

"Tim, I want you to do me a favor. Call Rick. Tell him what's happened."

Tim nodded. At the nurse's station, before making the call, he asked that Josh be moved to another room. He didn't want him to see his mother die in pain. The nurses told him the order had already been scheduled. Tim dialed the only number he had for Rick in Oklahoma City, hoping his brother-in-law had found a new rental, but kept the same number.

Now's not the time to be at some new job, he thought as the phone rang.

"Yeah," a sleepy voice answered.

"Rick, it's Tim. I want you to listen very carefully and don't inter-rupt . . ."

Then he told Rick. Everything. At the end, Rick had only one question.

"Little Rock?"

"The university hospital."

"I'm there."

Click.

Tim stared at the receiver, mildly surprised.

When he returned, Josh was crying, for they were about to transfer his bed to another room. Underneath the plastic, he was sitting up in bed, pushing his hands against the plastic towards where Sylvia lay.

"No, stop it! I want to stay here, with Mommy! Dad, tell them. Tell them not to move me."

With a heavy heart, Tim moved beside his son, shuffling along as the bed rolled. He could only whisper, "It'll be all right, Josh. This is for the best. You'll be fine . . ."

But Josh was not fine. Tim was not fine. Sylvia was not fine.

Nothing was fine.

• • •

Motionless, Sylvia felt the life drain from her body, the sharpness from her mind. She struggled to remain conscious, drifting in and out. In, from pure force of will. Out, from exhaustion. Every scrap of thought or feeling came with tremendous effort. Her body felt dense, pressed into the mattress; then a moment later, feathery, drifting, as if she had been separated from herself, soul from flesh. As her awareness failed, objects and memories and emotions blurred together, like differ-ent chunks of colored Play-Doh rolled up into a single senseless, mis-shapen mass. She couldn't move, couldn't even blink.

Near the edge of her vision, however, she could see a familiar face floating above the plastic shell that sustained her and protected others. He was someone important. Tim?

A spasm of violent coughing seized her. Then a voice penetrated.

"Sylvia . . ."

It was Tim.

This is what it's like to die, she thought, laboring for breath.

Like a gurgling current flowing downstream, fragments of thoughts bounced off the pebbles and rocks of countless other random fragments, making noise in her head, intermingling. In her delirium, cogency only broke through on occasion. When it did, raw panic struck.

Dying . . .

She had followed God to this place, in search of a miracle. No, that wasn't true. She had searched for a miracle elsewhere, begged for one. As a last resort, she had come here. Now her son remained, and she was passing on.

As if from a great distance, she heard a voice. Tim praying. She could barely make out his throaty whisper, full of pleadings.

"Sylvia, please. I don't want to lose you. Hang on." Then, more fervently, a spattering of words. "Please, God. I don't care how. Forgive me. Heal her. Don't punish her because of my lack of faith. I can't make it without her. Do you hear me?"

Sylvia tried to speak. Her lips twitched.

Tim.

She wasn't sure if she had actually spoken, or only thought she had. Either way, he must not have noticed. He kept praying, "Please don't let her die. Please . . ."

A thought struck, like the weak spark of flint and steel. Soon as it came, it fled; she almost lost it. But some part of that spark stuck to her brain, burned, and left a mark, surprising herself with the force of its conviction. Her conviction.

There's a reason, she thought.

From deep in her being, a few brief moments of utter clarity clutched her. She had come looking for the hand of God. How now could she deny his answer? Perhaps her miracle yet lay ahead? For her. For Josh. He had never been hers to save anyway. Or keep. He was chosen by God, for God's own purpose. Perhaps she would never see the miracle, or understand. Did that diminish the truth, that God was present in the affairs of men, causing wonders unseen to grow in the most unlikely places? It had ever been that way. Victory snatched from the most desperate circumstance. Tragedies turned to triumph.

Always a reason.

With every ounce of strength and focus she could muster, she twitched her finger, flicking at the plastic bubble.

Tim's whispers stopped. "Sylvia?"

Her lips moved. No sound came out. She saw Tim's face lean further over the edge, far enough that she could see his face. The image of her husband at that moment was the most beautiful thing she could have imagined. Brown and weathered, cheeks streaked with tears.

I love you! Sylvia tried to shout, and her heart nearly burst. Just as quickly, her thoughts began to scatter, as clouds of nausea and weakness threatened to drag her under. She felt her conscious mind grow dim. But there was one more thing to say. She had to let him know.

Tim!

Through the plastic, their eyes met. One final moment, one last touch. She forced her lips to move, her throat to form words. Tim leaned in as close as he could, pressing his face against the clear cellophane. Tears welled in Sylvia's eyes and slid down her cheeks. She wrapped the words as best she could in a thin ghost of a smile.

"I . . . still believe."

Tim sat in the lobby, hollow, as if his spine and bones had been ripped from his insides, as if someone had come along and found his skin and muscles lying in a heap and taking pity had propped him into a sitting position, awaiting the final strokes. He was utterly spent. Ringing through his head, over and over, three simple words: *I still believe.*

The words haunted him.

What was she trying to tell him? Was it a final, defiant declaration of unswerving devotion to God, even in the midst of failure? Spitting in the eye of death? Or did she think she would survive, after all? A sudden reversal of fortune, baffling the doctors. Or was it that Josh would overcome his myeloma, somehow live to a full age, have a family of his own—every mother's dream? *I still believe.* Tim wondered. Was it some gentle reminder, that in spite of all that can be seen and known, her miracle was yet to happen?

At the last, nearly broken, he had joined her in her simple request, one he had previously found distasteful, or weak, perhaps even immature. Standing beside her bed—whether true or not—he had asked for every sort of miracle possible. Alone with his thoughts, Tim had to confess a mild sense of irony and amazement, perhaps even sadness, at how much circumstance could affect one's theology. There was nothing worse than to reach a point of need, and then be imprisoned by your own belief system.

Everyone has a God box. Everyone.

Tim knew in that instant that to the very last man, no matter how brilliant, no matter which seminary or life journey their boxes came from— the boxes were all too small. When the shock of discovering his wife stricken finally subsided even a little, Tim suddenly felt willing to ask for all the things he previously had the luxury to dismiss as unessential. Willing, but timid. Timid, but determined. Aloof positions safely ratified in the confines of his head had become as valuable to him as foam anchors in a storm—insufficient for the demands of real life. Now he felt trapped, on unfamiliar ground, like Dorothy from Kansas, with no way home, wandering aimlessly in search of the favor of the Great Oz.

But what was the trick? Was it in how one phrased the request? How did one drag faith through the mud of real life and not get soiled in the process? More than anything, Tim wanted to click his heels and go home, taking his son and wife with him, healthy and well. But how? How was a person supposed to believe, really believe, in a way that makes a difference, when it wasn't just a promotion at work or a new car on the line, but life itself?

Tim had followed Christ much longer than Sylvia and usually considered himself the stronger of the two. If such things could be measured, then in all fairness, he probably was; she would have agreed. But with those three little words, he had seen something in her fevered eyes that shocked him. Sylvia, having stared into the spectral face of death for herself, with her son dying in the next room of cancer, without flinching, without batting an eye, had buried a stake in her own heart, raised the flag, and proclaimed . . . faith.

Against-all-odds kind of faith. Absurd faith. A heavy iron anchor that plunged the depths and held fast.

After saying those words, her condition had rapidly declined. How ironic. The cough grew worse, if such a thing was possible. Within the hour, she had quietly faded to an unconscious state, which the doctors warned was likely to be the beginning of a coma—that, as a result, she might not ever see consciousness again—though for now she still had brain activity. Tim would've remained with her. They forbade him from that point on.

Shifting in the uncomfortable seat, he tried again to rest. He wasn't yet ready to face Josh. He sat and watched TV. By the end of the day, the six o'clock news was only reporting the death toll. Accurate infection statistics were anybody's guess. Twenty thousand people were dead, that was all they knew for sure. That, and the fact that the president would address the nation tomorrow. Waiting in the lobby, Tim didn't care to watch more. He switched the TV off.

Feeling empty, he sat with Josh for a while, arranging a checkerboard outside the tent. Josh told him where to move, which pieces to jump, and beat him two out of three games. Neither of their hearts were in it. Josh asked about Sylvia. Tim told him she was sleeping. Soon, Josh grew sleepy, too. Not the same. In fact, Josh still showed no symptoms whatsoever. Tim felt safe leaving him to rest.

For Tim, sleep was a long time in coming.

• • •

The next day at the CDC was the most ferocious, backbreaking day in the history of the organization. People were literally sprinting up and down the halls, just to move information, samples, and other data along a bit quicker than walking would allow. Meeting after meeting was held. Teams were assigned. Duties divided. Priorities established.

No solution, no methodology, was off limits.

No idea was a bad idea.

The goal was singular and clear: supply Project Resurrection with an effective medical response to the plague. To accomplish this, the CDC needed to create or discover a means to prevent Sleeper from binding to cells inside a host and thus replicating. Their best hope was a protective antibody. Someone mentioned the sports metaphor: the best offense was a good defense.

But the effort wasn't easy to organize. Several rounds of fiercely debated meetings were held. In the end, no less than seventeen separate teams were established, each allocated with the necessary support personnel. These seventeen teams were further clustered along lines of specialty: the Prime Team, Communications, Field Tactics, Field Surveillance, Gene Therapies, Vaccine Solutions, and Alternative Treatments.

The Prime Team would be composed of Stu, Diane Rieschmeyer, and Edgar Bersch, with Tom Sizemore directing a similar group on a parallel track from the labs at USAMRID.

One team would strictly be a Communications hub, responsible for both assimilating and disseminating information between the eleven other CDC teams, along with USAMRID and other international facilities: Antwerp, Porton Down, the National Institute of Virology in Sandringham, South Africa, NIH labs, a dozen or so universities with virological specialties, etc.

A second large team, Field Tactics, would serve as the strategic and tactical information center, gathering reports from the news and the field, plotting the spread of the disease, charting geographical saturation as well as available resources, tertiary influences, and the success of various containment efforts. This information would be vital to effectively targeting the disease if and when a solution materialized. At the very least, the burden of containment and, ultimately, survivors fell to Field Tactics. Working in conjunction with the World Health Organization and other continental health consortiums, this group, sanctioned by WHO, would be the brains behind the global containment effort in terms of policy recommendations to governments both foreign and domestic.

Field Surveillance would be comprised of five teams, each with three EIS officers. The CDC made arrangements for military transport and escort for each of these teams, as they would need to travel great distances in a matter of hours, and be subject to all manner of hostile populations.

Field Surveillance were the young guns, renegades, and speed freaks, the men and women that thought extreme sports were for sissies. They were usually cocky, extremely observant, often brilliant. Stu had once been one of them. Armed with mobile labs and orange Racal portable pressure suits, they would serve as a roving band of highly mobile strike forces, transferring from hot zone to hot zone to gather information, dispense treatment as it developed, assist in containment of difficult areas, and provide firsthand analysis of the impact of the virus from region to region, in hopes of staying ahead of any possible mutations.

A mutation in a virus like Sleeper would be an almost unthinkable scenario. Disaster stacked upon disaster.

Two teams would comprise a long-shot solution, dubbed Gene Therapies. Thanks to their unlikely chance of success, they were soon being snickered at as the Gene Dream Team. Through various genomic deconstruction techniques, such as polymerase chain reactions, the Gene Therapies group would attempt, essentially, to declassify the secrets of Sleeper's blueprints, including its surface shape, thereby allowing the team to isolate the location of the binding antigens. Not only was it a difficult task on short notice, but an improbable one; it was given little hope from the get-go, mainly due to the length of time required to produce anything useful. Decoding the genetic substance of the virus would be difficult enough, but to then reassemble that code again in the correct three dimensions, blind, would be next to impossible. It was like a plumber trying to install pipes for a house with four bedrooms and two baths without ever having looked at the plans. How many possible four-bedroom, two-bath house combinations were there? Thousands and thousands. Pipes could land anywhere: in the garage, the dining room, the bedroom. But only one pipe mattered, the one that connected to the right fixture in the home. In other words, substance wasn't enough. For example, if that single pipe was the antibody—the piece that fit the flange on the toilet—then it mattered a great deal where in the foundation the pipe emerged if it was ever going to connect at the right spot with the toilet or, in this case, the teeth of the virus. Shape was the critical mystery, because shape determined where the fangs of the virus were placed on the viral body, and unless you knew where the fangs were, you couldn't stop it from biting. Genomic deconstruction could only reveal substance in the short term at best. It would likely take months for that route to succeed.

The world did not have weeks, much less months.

Still, the possibility had to be pursued. *Every* option had to be pursued. No idea was a bad idea, because the CDC had so few ideas to begin with. Two teams maximum, though, were allowed for that dead end.

A third cluster of teams, four in all, would explore vaccination. While still difficult, the Vaccine Solutions group had the most likely chance of being the heroes. Flu vaccines were a known quantity in a general sense. They could be mass produced, once the proper formula was discovered. And they could be deployed in volume. Plus, there was an ample supply of methods and technologies to move things along at a good clip.

Methods varied. One track, a good place to start, was to expose primates to the virus, in search of a species with inherent immunity. That was virology 101. Another, crossing the virus from species to species, was also known to cause surface mutations to a virus. Theoretically, such a mutation could render Sleeper harmless, yet remain similar enough to the original to trigger an effective immune response. The neutered virus would then make an excellent vaccine. Ultraviolet radiation also broke a virus, possibly leading to vaccine candidates. All of this required extensive testing, however, and guaranteed nothing. Especially since there was no evidence that Sleeper itself, much less a vaccine, was triggering the proper antibodies.

The Alternative Treatments group, another cluster of three teams, would investigate the impact of radical drug combinations, as well as seek emergency clearance from the FDA of developmental drugs for accelerated testing on human subjects. New experimental antiviral drugs were ever lingering in pharmaceutical labs all over the nation, awaiting years and years of trials before being approved for prescription. Information on many of these was readily available. Some claimed to prevent binding for a broad spectrum of antigens. Others made the audacious claim of actually preventing replication, postbinding. Some of the early ideas thrown out in the brainstorming session included combination drug treatments with varying dose levels of amantadine and rimantadine, megadosing with Vitamin C, even chemotherapy.

Each of these teams was to be staffed in such a way that they could work around the clock, no downtime.

From five o'clock Tuesday morning to seven o'clock that night, the CDC revved up every operation, drafting policy sheets, updating bulletins, making the labs dance with furious bursts of activity. Televisions were tuned to CNN or MSNBC or C-Span in each office, each lab, each room, listening to the death toll rise. By the end of the day, twenty-two thousand were dead. Tomorrow, Stu knew he would have to form yet another group to provide procedural support to the hospitals and health clinics that were already beginning to strain under the burden of treating Sleeper's victims. For now, the only thing he could tell them was the same thing he had in another bulletin e-mailed and faxed everywhere, across the globe: to keep people alive on respirators and concentrate on supportive rather than therapeutic care. He told them to basically just maintain vital functions as victims went comatose—and quarantine rigorously.

Every CDC phone rang off the hook. All day.

When Marge came, blouse tousled and hair mussed, looking more than frazzled, to tell Stu—surprise!—he had a phone call, he almost didn't answer.

"Sounds important," Marge said. "Someone's not getting sick with Sleeper."

At first, Stu was so preoccupied her words didn't register. When it finally soaked in, he nearly dove for the phone, guessing as to what it meant.

"This is Stu Baker," he said. "CDC."

The voice on the other end was high for a man, slow and alto, with a heavy southern drawl. Considering the things he was describing, he seemed as calm as a summer breeze. "Mr. Baker, my name is John Kemper. I'm the infectious disease physician at the University of Arkansas for Medical Sciences Hospital. How are you doing, sir?"

"As you can probably imagine, I've done better."

"No, I can't imagine, to tell you the truth. Here's the deal. We have a boy here whose mother is dying of H1N1. Confirmed, mind you. We have taken the time to track down her original viral source, as well as others affected by that source. All have contracted H1N1 and, in the last thirty-six hours, have either died or gone comatose. Fourteen people in all. In a matter of hours I suspect the mother will go into a coma as well. Now, Mr. Baker, I'm no CDC hotshot, but this boy was also exposed to the original source, as well as remaining in close confines with his mother during the maturation of the virus in her system, leaving him originally exposed as she was, and fully exposed in ongoing fashion. She is dying. He is not. I thought that might be the kind of information you folks would be interested in."

Stu tried to keep a level head. "It definitely is, Dr. Kemper. However, children have so far proven a bit more resilient, at least in terms of length of incubation. Do you think that could in any way account for his health?"

"Well, sir. Like I say, I'm no hotshot. We've got him in isolation, under observation, and will continue to do so. But this little boy has a disease, a form of cancer, something altogether unrelated to H1N1. And that's what's most unusual, because this particular disease profile usually suppresses the immune system and creates a heightened sensitivity to all manner of infections . . ."

Destiny was about to happen. The next few words would forever change Stu's life.

"If anyone should be getting sick," Dr. Kemper drawled, oblivious, "out of all the people affected by the source, it should be Joshua Chisom."

Stu gripped the balled handle of his cane so tightly, his knuckles whitened.

"I'm sorry. Could you say that name again?"

"Joshua Chisom. The boy's name is Joshua Chisom."

Stu coughed. "I need you to hold on a minute, please."

He punched the hold button on the phone, began riffling through his papers, found the envelope from Terrance, ripped it open, dragged out the latest dissertation sample, page 13, and scanned the names. There it was.

Patient C3. Joshua Chisom.

What was it about Joshua Chisom? What was this assay about? He couldn't even remember. His stomach was in knots. How could he not remember? He flipped to the title page and read again: "Antigenic Specificity of Monoclonal Antibodies Present in Multiple Myeloma."

He didn't have time to read the whole thing, just scanned the summary paragraph.

"All nine serological samples failed in each assay of twenty-four sample reagents, with one notable exception. The monoclonal antibody serum of patient C3 tested positive against a sample of nominal virulent influenza, strain H1N3. This result was confirmed on two subsequent tests . . ."

Stu gulped. The words kept going, flowing, but he could barely breathe, much less read. The boy was *not* getting sick. Of all people, he should be getting sick, because his immune system was depressed by disease. Instead he was quite well. And tests showed his body produced an antibody.

For influenza.

Stu had never considered something so fantastic in all his life.

He punched the phone and spoke excitedly. "Dr. Kemper, is this boy suffering from multiple myeloma? Is that the disease?"

"Why, yes, in fact."

"Is he from Oklahoma?"

"Yes again. Do you know this boy?"

"No, sir," Stu replied. "But I think it's time. I will arrange immediately for a secured military transport from your facility to the CDC offices here in Atlanta. If you'll hold on the line, I will have my assistant make all the necessary arrangements."

He didn't wait for reply but slammed the phone down and yelled, "Marge! Get me a transport. The nearest military transport to Little Rock. We've got an immunity!"

16

Josh got to fly. At long last, he was above the clouds, looking down.

Tim had no time to think, to figure things out. Suddenly, there was Dr. Kemper, marching into the waiting area, explaining the "situation"—how extremely significant it was to find a person with demonstrated immunity to an epidemic-level infectious disease. He said the CDC had requested permission to examine Josh further to find clues that could maybe crack Sleeper open.

Sylvia was unconscious; Tim wanted to remain with her.

No, they told him. No time. The chopper would arrive soon for his son. He had to go with Josh. There was nothing he could do for Sylvia. She was beyond help, they said, which made him angry. It might well be true, but he didn't like being pushed. He needed time. Did they have any idea what they were asking of him? It never occurred to him to wonder how the CDC discovered Josh.

Before he left, all Tim was allowed to do was touch his hand to the clear membrane surrounding Sylvia's bed, look into her face, hope that somehow she could understand. And forgive him. Forty-five minutes later a helicopter landed, and they whisked Josh away to Barksdale AFB near Shreveport, where they boarded a C-9 Nightingale medical plane.

Josh, forgivably—though upset at leaving his mother—was soon overwhelmed by the noise and people and commotion; the fuss they made over him; the camouflaged military men, the white-coated doctors; the sound of the chopper blades, the vertical thrust, the sensation of soaring; then, after transferring to the medical transport, the awesome power and roar of the jet engines, the sinking, giddy feeling in his stomach as the plane curved into the upper atmosphere, lifting from the clouds, with nothing but stars overhead.

Josh kept his face pressed to the glass the entire time. His mouth never closed.

He was eight years old.

And flying.

"Whoa," he said, at the sight of the earth as it fell away, of twinkling lights below. Low to the horizon, the sun was shredding with orange and vermilion brilliance, like a block of cheese sliding down a grater, the tattered remains slowly yielding to the soft, crushed velvet of night.

"Whoa," he said again, as a pillar of dark clouds rushed past, gray and flaming in the half-light of the fading sun. He murmured again, at the rumble of turbulence, kept saying it, saying nothing else, in a small voice laced with wonder.

"Whoa . . ."

Heartbroken, Tim watched his son's wonder. He knew Joshua didn't understand where he was going. His son had never heard of the Centers for Disease Control. Neither of them knew what would happen when they got there. But etched on Josh's face was one thing, one clear truth.

He was flying.

• • •

Not twenty minutes after the helicopter had lifted from the hospital helipad, Rick pulled into the parking lot on his Honda Shadow and rushed inside. They directed him to the isolation wing, but security detained him, catching him by the leather jacket as he came running by. Traffic in and out of isolation wings, by design, was tightly monitored.

"She's my sister," he said. He had ID. He had a photo of them together, in his wallet. Sylvia would have never suspected a photo of them to be in Rick's wallet.

"Please . . ."

They let him through. He was required to sterilize, don scrubs and mask and gloves. They prepared him for the severity of her condition.

Gingerly, he stepped into the room. Saw her beneath the plastic bubble.

Nothing could have prepared him.

"No. No, Sylvia . . ."

He took a careful step towards her. She couldn't see him or hear him. Her eyes were closed. The EKG beep was faint, slow. Her breaths came in thick, rattling bursts, clogged from the fluid and mucous building in her lungs. She would cough and her body would shake, but she wouldn't stir. The monitor showed a thin, weak pulse, low blood pressure, raging fever.

Rick closed his eyes, bowed his head.

"Sylvia, what is this? What's happened to you?"

He didn't know what else to say, didn't think he had the words.

"I've spent a lot of my life running from you, Sylvia. Probably hating you. But I never wanted this. You gotta believe me. I never wanted this."

He sat down on a stool and drifted into silence. Nearly half an hour passed. Presently, with rare bravery, Rick just started talking. Things he had wanted to say a hundred times already—and should have said. Years and years earlier.

"Do you know what the worst thing in the world is, Sylvia? It's to not be wanted. That's what I've felt like most of my life. Mom and Dad didn't want me. I was always causing problems. Our real parents died to get away from us. I know that's not true, but that's what it's felt like all these years. And I've hated it. I've lived every day hating that feeling inside. With everything that's gone wrong in my life, that's exactly what it feels like."

He stopped, tilted his head to line up with the angle of her face. Her skin was pallid, practically lifeless. The EKG beeped . . . beep . . . beep.

"I've tried so hard to be my own man. For a while I thought I was making a pretty good show of it. I even thought I was going to be a pilot at one time. I was going to surprise you with that one, when I joined the service. Then the doctor screened me and told me my vision wasn't good enough, that pilots aren't allowed to use contacts. That knocked the wind out of my sails, you know?" He paused a moment. "It doesn't matter. Nobody's fault but mine. God knows, I've screwed my life up real good on plenty of other occasions. Can't blame my eyes for that." Rick forced a laugh and shook his head. His eyes burned. The saliva in his mouth thickened with grief. "But you know, I think I could have handled it all, all the stuff that would happen to me, that did. I think I could have played my bluff, if you know what I mean. Except for the day I discovered you didn't want me, either. I don't know how to say this, Sylvia. But when I finally figured out I wasn't supposed to be a part of your world, I started hating you, too. I hated it that you didn't want me. You were all I had at that time. All that mattered. Nothing hurt me more than when *you* didn't want me, Sylvia. It's like, something inside me knew the rest of my life would be a fight for every single day, every scrap of respect, every ounce of joy."

He sniveled and tried to wipe his nose. Hard to do with latex gloves. He took a seat on a nearby stool and rolled it to her bedside.

"I believe I'll just sit here with you, now, if you don't mind, Sylvia. Just sit here. Until the end if that's what I need to do."

He folded his hands and stared around the room, unsure what to focus on. Then the tears came. He could not stop them.

"Please, Sylvia . . . don't leave me again."

• • •

By the time Josh arrived, it was late in the evening. Workers had converted a large office in Building 6 to the rough equivalent of a hotel room for Josh and his father, complete with beds, dresser, private phone, microwavable popcorn, sodas, and Sony Playstation, among other things. Although Stu didn't personally pick them up at the airport, he was waiting for them in the room when they arrived.

Gesturing across the room with his cane, he said, "I hope this will be comfortable for you. It's far from home, I know, but we would like to keep Josh on site for ongoing surveillance. I hope you understand. My name is Stu Baker. I'm the director of one of the primary divisions here at the CDC. I'm overseeing the drive to discover a solution to the influenza epidemic."

Stu extended his hand, which Tim accepted, cautiously.

"I'm a little bit uncomfortable with all this," Tim said.

"I can only imagine. I'm very sorry to hear about your wife."

He didn't sound sorry. He didn't look sorry. He looked like he was ready to peel a grape with his eyeballs, if that would amount to a cure. His eyes lingered on Josh. Tim didn't like him.

"And you must be Joshua," Stu continued. "Are you feeling well?"

Josh shrugged.

Stu turned to the lady beside him, "Diane, let's take Joshua to the lab and get a quick serum sample from him. Put it together with the virus, and see what happens."

"It's been a long day," Tim said, putting his hand on Josh's shoulder. "There'll be time for tests later. I think I'd like my son to be able to rest now."

Immediately, Stu seemed irritated. "I know you have both been through a lot. And I truly am sorry. But time is something we don't have. Your son may well hold the key that will enable us to reverse-engineer a solution."

"He's my boy. I'm his father. As long as we're here, I'll determine what's right for him."

"Just a sample, say 10 ccs? Make that *two* draws . . . that's all for tonight. How's that? Then you can rest, a good full night hopefully. At least that'll get us started. We've got teams working around the clock. It might give us a jump-start."

Tim considered. "Fair enough. And don't get me wrong, I want to help. And Josh does, too. We talked about it on the plane. If he can be part of the cure, to help others, we're all for that. But he is still my first concern. It won't be long and he'll be all I've got left."

Silently, the four marched together down a short hallway to the lab. CDC staff had strategically renovated a room near the lab, for the Chisoms' convenience as much as their own. Standing beside Stu, Tim watched as they drew two syringes of blood from the arm of his son. Josh had gotten used to needles recently, but he still flinched, still fought tears. All the while, Stu explained to Tim what was happening. They were going to spin down one of the samples to separate the serum from the red blood cells, and then take the serum up to a lab in Biosafety Level 4, where they would put a few drops of the serum together with a sample of serum from the blood of a victim who had died of Sleeper. That sample would be infested with the virus. The hope was that Josh's sample was full of a matching antibody. The final stage would occur when virologists put both serums together in a cell culture—one in which the virus had consistently proven to replicate. If that virus then did *not* replicate, Josh's antibodies would be confirmed as a match. An effective block.

"It would be a bona fide miracle," he said. "This is the nastiest virus I've ever seen."

The other vial would be sent to the Vaccine Solutions group. Other teams would have to wait their turn. Since it was going to take a couple of hours to run the tests, Josh and Tim were escorted back to their room in Building 6 and encouraged to rest. Tomorrow would come early and Stu warned it would be quite stressful. He wasn't good with kids, but when he mentioned stress, he bent down to Josh's level as well as his knees would allow. For the first time he stared deep into the boy's eyes. Tim observed the encounter protectively but didn't intervene. His son was expression-less, unflinching, leaving questions to dance across the older man's face.

Stu managed to mumble a few words. "This is going to be hard on you, very hard. You're going to have to be brave. It's probably going to hurt, because we're going to have to use that needle several times. We don't have a choice, though, do you understand? People are dying. And you may be their only hope."

It was a lot to dump on the shoulders of an eight-year-old.

Josh said, "I'll try."

Stu said, "Thank you. I'm sorry it has to be this way."

Trapped in Josh's eyes, Stu's tone *had* changed, however slight. Tim was a witness to it. He watched the older man limp away, leaning on his cane, and found himself believing that perhaps in some small way, this time, Stu truly was sorry.

Tim still didn't like him.

• • •

At an eleven o'clock session that night, the Prime Team was deep in review, tossing out ideas in the midst of minor celebration. Test results were in, and Josh's blood had proven positive. That a ray of light could shine so brightly and so suddenly upon the monumental search for a cure was cause for clinking glasses. Stu had purchased a bottle of champagne just in case.

"We've got a golden child," Diane said happily, as they toasted one another.

"To protective antibodies!" Edgar said with a flourish. And they all drank. They weren't quite jovial, but certainly happier than when the day had begun.

With one exception. Stu thought Terrance Alexander seemed a bit ill at ease with the celebration, although he was present at Stu's request. After receiving the call from Little Rock, Stu had phoned Terrance, briefed him, and asked him to consider joining the Prime Team should Josh's antibody prove effective. Terrance's familiarity with Josh's disease could prove essential to the effort, since the health of the host was now a factor. Plus, Terrance was great with kids. He would make a much better liaison to the family than Stu. Terrance had been hesitant at first, forcing Stu to coax and cajole, both of which he did poorly. But one thing was on his side.

"I *do* want to meet this little boy," Terrance admitted. So he agreed. Tonight was his first encounter with the Prime Team.

Champagne finished, the meeting was called to order. The real challenge lay ahead, Stu told them. The fact that an antibody had been identified meant a restructuring of at least half the teams and groups. As the four of them took their seats around the narrow table in the conference room, laptops open and pad and pen in hand, Stu dialed Tom Sizemore, who awaited their call from Frederick, Maryland. On the walls were huge marker boards, scribbled with notes and flowcharts.

Stu started with a simple question. "What's next?"

"First thing, we should leave Communications, Field Tactics, and Field Surveillance alone," said Edgar. "Fold Gene Therapies and Alternative Treatments into a new unit, which can divert all resources to the rapid development of a stable host culture. We can run trials with trace amounts of Josh's bone marrow. From there, once something sticks, we'll farm out production to other labs."

"Regular serum draws," Diane said, her mouth full of a honey bun.

She washed it down with heavily creamed coffee. "We need to begin control groups and trials to gauge the actual impact of the antibodies on real people. Which means we need to do animal testing and primates first."

"That'll put a strain on the boy. Terrance?"

"I'll want to keep a close eye on his health," Terrance agreed, adjusting his seat. "But before I say anything else, I want to remind us all of something very important. We are interrupting a potentially *lifesaving* series of treatments that this child was scheduled to receive and couldn't, because his mother is dying. Now this is only my first time with you folks, but I don't get the feeling anyone in this room fully appreciates that fact. Has anyone even talked to Mr. Chisom to find out how *he* wants to proceed? I mean, this may in fact be an international emergency, but let's at least do him the courtesy of making sure he is agreeable to *our* decisions."

His voice dropped off abruptly, waiting for an answer. Edgar lowered his head. Diane stopped chewing. Terrance had one more thing to say. "Joshua Chisom is *not* your golden child, Stuart. Do you hear me? I will not have any part in this if he's just going to be a factory for you to work from."

"We are all appropriately chided, Terrance," Stu muttered, unimpressed. "Since you seem to have claimed the moral high ground here, caring for this boy while we lowly thugs and charlatans care for the world, I will allow you to make your point with Mr. Chisom tomorrow as emphatically as you desire."

"And if he walks?" Terrance asked.

"He walks. Is that satisfactory?"

"It is. As to Josh's health should he choose to stay, I will want daily monitoring of his protein and calcium counts. Standard chem profile, CBC, and urinalysis will be sufficient. There will be unusual protein spikes in the urine and two protein spikes in the blood, besides albumin. I'll need to keep on eye on those, and check his titers. He's on medications now for nausea and back pain."

"What about weakness? Fatigue? We're going to need to draw a lot of blood."

"Well," Terrance said. "The best place to start is to figure out how to get the most out of every drop. Recycle what you can for other purposes, other tests. Be efficient. We can also give him iron supplements. If worst comes to worst, we can add growth factors."

"Colony stimulators? Interferon?"

"Things like that, yes. But in his particular case, that's a dangerous course—"

"Can we at least take him off Prednisone?" Stu interrupted. "That's an immune suppressant. Like it or not, Terrance, we need his body to produce a lot of antibody. That's why we're here."

"But you don't understand. That's what's *killing* him. We have to walk a very fine line here, folks. Adding growth factors and removing Prednisone will cause the multiple myeloma cells to increase and, yes, with it monoclonal antibodies. While that may be great for curing Sleeper, it's bad for Josh. Increasing production of those things in his system is going to accelerate renal failure and the risk of secondary infections other than influenza. Remember, this is not a healthy child."

The room grew quiet as everyone mulled the circuitous route they must take. Stu watched their faces, attempting to read the mood. It wasn't hard. The fact that all their hopes were pinned on a weak, fragile child had suddenly sunk in a little deeper, turning the tone from celebratory to reflective—even burdened. Edgar, Stu knew, was single; Diane was a divorced mother of two; Tom had grandchildren. They had all gotten a bit carried away early on, and Terrance had come along and pricked their conscience. Now they could empathize. That was a good thing, humane. But it could also weaken their resolve.

Stu changed the subject. "I think we should fold Vaccines into the pot as well," he said, pouring himself a second cup of coffee. "If we get far enough, a vaccine may not be too hard to squeeze out of it. But I don't think we should waste our time chasing riddles when we've got an answer."

"I agree," echoed Diane.

Tom chimed in, in a voice thick and sticky as tar. Tom was ancient, about ten years past retirement, gray and wiry. He was one of the old guard, the legends around which virus-hunting lore had formed years ago. "One bit of good news from our labs. It may not seem good at first, but we've tried to get this thing to mutate in every way possible. We've run it cross-species, through about a hundred chicken eggs, even contaminated cell cultures. Everything. It won't budge. Now, while that would be bad news if we were still hoping to make a vaccine, I think it may actually be good news for avoiding field mutations. Whoever patched this thing together probably intentionally dialed it down to the hardest setting and then stabilized it there to wreak maximum havoc. Mutations can be bad, you know, but they're also unpredictable. It could have gone in our favor, instead. They obviously didn't want to run that risk."

Diane was disgusted. "Who would have possibly conspired with them on this? I mean, I know it doesn't matter now. But didn't they get it? If we don't solve this, they might as well have written their own epitaph."

Tom countered, "I doubt if they knew at all. They were probably paid well and told a lie."

Edgar jumped in. "I hate to let go of a vaccine attempt altogether, Stu. I think we might get caught with our pants down if we have trouble culturing. And why not keep at least one team working on a chimeric antibody? Maybe we can reverse-engineer the one Josh produces and build our own."

"Yeah, but you've got the same time constraints as if you were trying to reverse-engineer the virus, Edgar. Sure, we have the real deal now. But we're just going to face the same problems from a different angle. I don't see how it's worth the manpower to shoot blind like that."

"But we aren't blind anymore. Not with Josh."

"He changes things dramatically. I agree. But you still have to face the problem of redundancy in the genetic code. Each triplet, each amino acid, each protein could take literally weeks. *Each* one. We would need a pure DNA sequence of the antibody, a reasonably accurate idea of tertiary and quaternary structure, and a sound understanding of how the antibody binds. By the time we got there, there would be about a half-dozen people left to save."

"But we know the virus seems to concentrate on the host's respiratory epithelium. That gives us a pretty good clue, doesn't—"

"It was a dead end when we started it the first time. We all knew it. It's no different now."

"One in a million," Tom agreed by phone. "Maybe ten million. Maybe a hundred. And the vaccine won't work, either, Edgar. Sorry. I think we've got to recognize a difficult reality here. So far, all indications are that we are dealing with passive immunity. The population is not able to produce their own response. Even if we could figure out a trigger, I'm not sure it would work on a scale to be worthwhile."

"Which means we really need the cultures to succeed," Diane said. "One eight-year-old can't possibly produce enough serum."

"As I see it, we have one other possible course of action," Stu interjected, tapping the table with his pencil. "Until we have the serological complexities of Josh's antibodies figured out, I think we could divert a team or two to trying to neuter those two claw arms coming off the body of the virus. The hanta code. What do you think about that, Tom?"

Tom growled softly. "Well, not bad. You and I both know we have trial vaccines we've been developing for years, good ones, based on the actual antibodies of folks who've survived hanta. We could pull those out of the freezers, run some tests, see if it looks doable."

Edgar said, "At the very least, it might buy us some time. The extreme respiratory response of this illness looks as much like hanta as flu, I think. 'Course any swine flu variant would be bad enough all on its own, I know, and the airborne nature of influenza is what makes Sleeper so infectious—"

"But if we *could* trim away some of the ARDS symptoms, we might give each victim a few more days time. That may be all we need."

Tom said, "Even if it works, we have no volume at present. I'll try to put together a network of labs with sufficient equipment and resources to turn production on a dime if we decide to go that route."

Stu wrapped it up. "Make the network global, Tom. We'll need it everywhere. Edgar, you tackle developing a stable culture, with high yields. We've got to have both or the whole thing folds. Diane, you work on immunization and serological antidote testing. Tom, you tackle trimming hanta out of the picture. We'll get you whatever trial vaccines we've got here that are different from USAMRID stores. Agreed?"

Everyone in the conference room nodded. Tom saluted by phone.

"Great. Diane, I want seven day projections from Field Tactics first thing in the morning. Let's go for it."

As Stu predicted, morning did indeed come early. The headline for the Wednesday edition of the *Atlanta Constitution* was framed with big, black letters and told a grisly tale.

DEATH TOLL APPROACHES
QUARTER MILLION WORLDWIDE

On his desk, seven day projections only went up from there. Tomorrow, Christmas Eve, three million people will have died. Then ten. Then twenty-three. Then forty. Then seventy-six. Then one hundred twenty. Then two hundred. Stu speculated if the present rate sustained, the earth would suffer losses approaching one billion in the next ten to twelve days.

Hard as it was for Stu to fathom, such numbers revealed the nature of a true epidemic: explosive growth; frightening, geometric rates of infection.

Worse still, those numbers included relatively successful international intervention, cooperation, and containment. Stu chewed each word bitterly. How was he supposed to speak of "containment" with any credibility when losses were projected to nearly a billion? The very concept became a parody of itself.

Still, Stu reminded himself, losses would be far worse if containment were not a goal.

Marge appeared at his door and handed him a cup of coffee.

"Gotta love the holidays," she said dryly.

Stu grunted. He unfolded the paper to read the rest of the story. He didn't need to, but he read it anyway. More nations were sealing their borders. Most of western Europe was now closed, as well as scattered portions of the Far East. Muslim nations quickly ground to a halt, denying all traffic except the kind that made money, namely, oil exports. Protests and demonstrations had taken place through the night in Paris, Madrid, and Moscow. The winter in Russia was particularly severe, and

Sleeper was spreading like wildfire. In the States, New York, L.A., and Houston were no longer isolated cases. Philadelphia, Oklahoma City, Cleveland, Boston, and Seattle also made the news, struggling under the load of hundreds of cases, along with dozens and dozens of small towns and communities from coast to coast. Canada announced a crisis in Toronto—all of Ontario, actually—but only sealed the province itself, not the nation. Ontario had established quarantine zones outside her major cities, to which victims would be shuttled as identified.

Stu knew in his gut the American response was too timid. Based on the numbers he was looking at, he felt recommendations to the president should be dramatically revised. He phoned Frank, urging him to get on the horn with the director of FEMA and talk it through one more time. Sleeper was spreading way too fast. Original projections of relatively tight containment in New York, L.A., and Houston were now worthless. It was going to take a much broader effort; they needed to go state to state, right from the start. Frank listened, didn't argue, said he would take it under advisement. Stu didn't know whether that was a promise or a facade, but he didn't have the authority to do more than make his case. If the ground war was in the hands of other generals, he at least could still win in the lab. He phoned the newly converted office/home of Joshua and Tim Chisom in Building 6. After four rings, Tim answered groggily.

"Good morning, Mr. Chisom. We need to start the day. I'll be there in thirty minutes to escort you and Josh to the laboratory."

He hung up. Gathering some papers into an attaché, he prepared to leave. But then a timid voice greeted him. He looked up, shocked to see a vaguely familiar, slender figure standing in the doorway.

"Hello, Daddy," Alyssa said.

• • •

Early that morning, in Little Rock, Sylvia slipped officially, quietly, into a coma. Rick was asleep in the waiting room when it happened. A doctor woke him and conveyed the news. They would not allow him back into the room. During the night, five other Sleeper cases were admitted. The need for security and isolation increased. Fudging on the rules was over. To Rick's ears, that basically meant Sylvia was being forced to die alone. He contested but didn't have strength for the argument. For an hour, he sat on the waiting room bench and stared. Stared at nothing, unmoving. What now?

The staff had previously informed him of Tim and Josh's whereabouts and how they had been relocated to the CDC.

"Your nephew may be a miracle boy," a nurse told him.

"I know," Rick answered.

He had no job, no ties—nothing to hold him back.

"Good-bye, Sylvia," he said. He left the hospital, mounted his Honda, and headed east, along the winding roads of Arkansas. Towards Atlanta.

. . .

Stu wasn't ready for the sight of his daughter.

Even after hearing from Agent Thurman, he hadn't dared to believe. He was one of those people that preferred to keep his negative column firmly in sight. That way, false hopes were rare. And small. Braggarts were kept humble. Success was genuine or not at all. In short, it kept Stu in control. He considered it realism more than pessimism, a means of mastery over the wild swings of emotion and circumstance. It's what made him a good scientist, a great researcher, a lousy person.

Facing his only daughter, none of the clean lines with which he preferred to segment his life mattered. As if to prove the point, both his good knee and bad knee had gone weak at the sight of her. He would have surely fallen if his feet had not felt heavy as concrete.

Josie stood unmoving, as well, holding at her side a bulging green canvas bag that looked as though it could have been a soldier's standard army-issue backpack. She wore a fairly stylish overcoat, unbuttoned, and a wide scarf that wrapped around her neck, hiding the bottom of her face (partly why he hadn't recognized her instantly). She was dressed in tight jeans and tight shirt, her exposed midriff revealing a glistening metal loop curving through her navel. Her hair was dyed and scraggly—the kind of color that looked black, except when the light fell on it from certain angles, which brought the deep burgundy highlights to the surface. Her makeup was dark, severe, and appeared to be about three days old; her eyeliner had obviously run several times and been wiped clean off her cheeks.

None of that mattered. For the first time in Stu's life, it simply didn't matter.

His lips formed her name without sound. Then he was moving, nearly falling over himself, his cane, stumbling forward, taking her in his arms. He squeezed; no, he clutched at her. Seesawing between outrage, fear, and delight, he embraced his daughter ferociously, speechless. Each time the seesaw went up or down in his chest, the motion caused him to squeeze tighter.

"Josie!" he cried. He could not contain himself. His voice shook. "I thought . . . I thought you were dead."

Josie stood stiffly in his arms, unresponsive. After all the years, she was someone else. He was someone else. But as Stu's body trembled against hers, as she heard his voice crack and stumble over each word he tried to speak, her body gradually melted into the contour of his embrace. They had a long way to go.

She loosened her scarf and pulled it away. "I don't feel well, Daddy."

Stu pushed her back and studied her. "Are you sick?"

"I think maybe so."

"What happened?"

Her story was simple, a concise little tragedy. "I guess you know by now. I'm sure you do." She shook her head, as if sweeping thoughts into piles. "I was scared to death. I hitchhiked here all the way from Seattle." She twitched her head again, once, twice, tried to start over. "When it came time to board . . . that plane, I couldn't do it. I just couldn't. So I ran. But I couldn't stay in the city, either. I knew what was about to happen. I didn't have any money. I didn't have any time to try to make some money. Jean was gone. So I hitchhiked." She swallowed and didn't bother to glance away. "I slept with all of them. Everyone who gave me a ride. I didn't care at that point."

Stu could feel the fever in her skin. He didn't know if he had breathed her same air yet. He did know she had to get out of the CDC building.

That much was critical. Her illness may or may not be Sleeper. Could just be a cold or fatigue. Or, from the sound of it, venereal disease.

"Have you talked to anybody or coughed? Has that scarf covered your mouth the whole time you've been in here?"

No, no, and yes.

They were probably lucky then. Either way, she had to get out.

"Let me take you home," Stu said.

• • •

The sudden appearance of his daughter turned Stu's day on its ear. With him out of the picture for at least the rest of the morning, Tim was gratified to find that Diane had assumed responsibility for his son. A female touch would be gentle, he hoped. Terrance joined them shortly, in the lab. He introduced himself to Tim and Josh and explained his connection to Dr. Li. He told them that the provost at Emory had agreed, in view of the crisis, to allow him to devote as much time as necessary to Josh's well-being. Tim decided not to tell him Sunny was dead.

After a couple of hours and a little minor surgery, a shunt was placed in Josh's arm—a merciful move. No more prickly needles for blood draws. As she worked, Diane tried to make small talk.

"So, Josh. Did you play Nintendo last night?"

"Playstation," Josh corrected.

"Oh, of course. Did you play Playstation?"

Josh nodded eagerly. "Dad let me play for a whole hour!"

"He's been asking for one of those things for Christmas for months."

"Well, perfect," Diane offered. "Tomorrow's Christmas Eve, you know."

Up until that point, Tim hadn't given much thought to the season, except to buy a pocketknife for Josh while he was in Dallas. The whole thing seemed anything but perfect, however. Shaking his head, he thought of Sylvia, lying in a bed, alone. He ran his fingers through Josh's hair.

Merry Christmas, Son.

They withdrew a half pint of blood, the safest quantity Dr. Alexander would allow at present. Dr. Alexander gave Josh an iron pill but refused to begin growth factors until they were absolutely required. After that, he queried Josh, attempting to build some rapport.

"Josh, or Joshua?" he asked.

"Josh."

"Sounds good to me. Are you feeling okay, Josh? Are you sore? Your back sore? Do you feel tired? Anything?" He bent down to Josh's level. Josh glanced away. Terrance continued, more softly, "Are you afraid at all, Josh? This is a pretty big deal. A pretty scary place."

"I miss my mom," Josh answered.

Dr. Alexander carefully took the little boy's hands between his own big hands and held them tight. "I don't know why your mommy got sick, Josh. I wish I did. But sometimes there's nothing we can—"

Midsentence, he stopped, eyes wide, fixed on a nowhere point. Tim felt his heart skip, wondered what was going on. Abruptly, Terrance stood, pulled Diane aside, with his back to Tim. Tim strained to hear their conversation. He thought he heard Terrance whisper, "Why *isn't* there something we can do?"

"What do you mean?"

"Well, think about it. You're preparing to test antidote serum drawn from Josh's blood, right?"

Diane nodded.

"And how long will the tests take? Mice and monkeys first, I know. When on *humans?*"

Diane started to rattle off an answer and froze. Tim saw comprehension dawn on her face, just as it dawned on his own. Josh, distracted with some piece of lab equipment, fascinated by the green digital numbers, wasn't even paying attention. Terrance pressed his point. "This boy's mother is about to die. She may be dead already, I don't know. Either way, she has absolutely nothing to lose."

Diane tried to think through the ramifications. "I'll have to clear it with Stu. And we'll need Mr. Chisom's permission."

"You've got it," Tim announced boldly, surprising them both. "It's worth a shot."

They turned to face him, looking guilty and relieved at the same time. Terrance said, "I agree, but I wasn't sure how you'd react. If it's all right with you, I'd like to speak about some other things in private, anyway." To Diane, Terrance said, "Let's move fast."

She spun on her heel and started to walk away. Tim caught her elbow and whispered his own secret in her ear.

"Don't explain any of this to Josh," he said. "Not yet. I don't want him to get his hopes up."

· · ·

Sitting in a diner on the outskirts of a little town called West Helena about twenty miles from the border between Arkansas and Mississippi, Rick thawed in the heat coming from the wood stove and watched TV. He had ordered a burger and fries, but when it arrived he discovered he wasn't really hungry. Another talk-TV freak show was on, but he could hardly hear it. The diner was noisy with conversation, the ringing bell when the front door opened and closed, the ceramic rattle of plates slipping on trays being hauled to the kitchen for cleaning. It was almost one.

The ride thus far had been cold, bitter cold. Rick had bundled up well, but the skin of his face was chapped from the wind. Sometimes one can get so cold it's hard to get warm. Sitting alone, he picked at his fries, dipping them in ketchup, staring with disgust at the blood-red tomato sauce.

No, he wasn't hungry at all.

It would be a long ride from here to Atlanta. He planned to ride all night. As he sat, watching, the talk show ended and the credits rolled. Instead of a soap opera or something else, a special news bulletin flashed on screen. The president's face appeared, sitting in the Oval Office. He had a studied look on his face—gaunt, concerned.

"My fellow Americans, I come to you today with difficult, sobering news. I beg your full attention for the next five minutes, for I speak of a greater crisis than you can imagine.

"As most of you are aware, in the last three days a strange illness has appeared seemingly out of nowhere. Some of you may know it by the name 'Sleeper.' In reality, it is a very dangerous form of influenza . . ."

All noise in the diner stopped, as if someone had flipped a switch. As one, each person turned to face the TV. Old men chewed their tooth-picks thoughtfully. Old women fretted. The cook wandered from the kitchen, grease smeared on his apron. In three seconds, the only remaining sound was the faint sizzle of beef patties, left untended.

The president continued: "This virus was purposely released over the entire planet by cult members eleven days ago, right before they killed themselves. From internal documents we have discovered from this group, it is now clear that their intention was to decimate the world's population.

"Such a despicable act is beyond comprehension for all of us. I can-not ask you to try to understand their motives or their cruelty, since I do not understand it myself. Many of you may have already suffered or lost a loved one to this dreaded illness. I do not tell you any of these things to incite fear or panic, but rather to appeal to your best nature, that we might join together, as Americans always have, to conquer what would seek to divide or destroy us.

"So far, 250,000 people have died. While that may not sound like a cri-sis to many of your ears, you must remember that four days ago, as far as we knew, Sleeper did not exist. To date, thanks to the sinister manner of its arrival, there is no known cure. The illness has proven lethal in every case. Medical experts, doctors, and leading scientists describe what could become a national and global tragedy if we fail to act decisively in our best interests as a nation. Therefore, as of this hour, I am authoriz-ing the Federal Emergency Management Agency to intervene in sys-tematic fashion to halt the spread of the infection. The United States of America has no choice but to close our international borders to all and, I repeat, *all* traffic and commerce, by rail, sea, and air. Furthermore, upon joint recommendation by the CDC, FEMA, the Department of Health and Human Services, and the National Institute of Health, the federal government is asking each state to enforce a zero traffic policy state-to-state. All major highways will be closed and blockaded.

"Please listen very carefully. The chief and prevailing concern, even before we address treatment, is to *stop the spread of the virus*. Right now, many thousands of people are carrying the virus, yet show no symp-toms. They won't know they are sick for another one to three days. If we do not limit travel, those thousands will infect tens and even hundreds of thousands more. At present, we have no accurate way to measure how many actually are infected. Our only option, therefore, is to contain the virus by limiting individual movement as much as possible. Certain major metropolitan areas will be placed under further restrictions, as they are at greatest risk of spreading the disease.

"It is my sad duty to convey these facts to you today. I am deeply sorry for the inconveniences this will cause, and the lives that may be lost to this virus. However, please know, these restrictive measures, and any additional measures required in the days ahead, are being performed on behalf of the American people to limit the damage as much as humanly possible and will be lifted completely the moment medical officials consider the situation safely under control. Also, beginning today, regularly scheduled health advisories will air on every major network to inform you how to best care for yourself and your family.

"In closing, I urge each citizen to demonstrate calm and to cooperate fully with law enforcement and health officials in your local communities. This will be a trying time. We must carry on with the normal course of affairs, in business and industry, as much as possible, with civility and respect for all we encounter. We must guard against rash reactions that will only further the cause of chaos and deepen the suffering of others. If we allow this challenge to fragment our resolve, and if our character yields to base impulses during a time of national need, then I fear the greatest sickness is not medical, but of the soul. I plead with you, my fellow Americans, let us demonstrate to the world exactly why, whether in times of blessing and prosperity, or faced with adversity, trial, and difficulty, America remains a nation of ingenuity, perseverance, and goodwill, united for the common good, under God's watchful eye. May God bless you and keep you safe. And may God bless America."

Rick rose quickly and left the diner, heading east on winding US 49. He didn't have much time.

17

Wall Street crashed. Stu knew it was destined to happen. Though the market dipped and dived through the midweek as governments announced sealing their borders, each time it managed to climb back up again. Following the president's speech, the bottom fell out.

Stu reeled at the reports. He owned stocks, mutual funds. He wasn't wealthy by a long shot, but most of his retirement had a Wall Street address. He should have pulled and he knew it. After all, he knew in advance about the president's address.

It had concluded yesterday at 2:15 P.M., Eastern Time, with instantaneous reaction. By 2:30, the Dow Jones Industrial Average had plunged 9 percent—severe, but not enough to trigger the standard U.S. stock market circuit breaker sequence for single-day declines. The problem was, stop-loss orders failed to protect the highly leveraged, margined high-tech stock holdings. And since the Dow was the only measured factor that could throw a circuit breaker, tech-heavy NASDAQ—where most of the new economy money was stored—was free to plunge nearly 24 percent before the Dow finally crossed the trigger line of 10 percent. Once that happened, a thirty-minute halt on trading was imposed, freezing all markets, including the New York Stock Exchange, NASDAQ, and AMEX, while panicky floor traders and investors chewed their fingernails to the nub. By the time trading resumed, no daily time constraints remained, allowing a further 18 percent drop in the Dow before the bell rang at 4:30, shutting down trading for the day.

When morning dawned December 24 and the bell clanged again on

Wall Street, stocks immediately plunged 10 percent, triggering another halt. Composite losses in a twenty-hour period of time cut the value of the stock market by nearly half. Congress intervened, refusing resumption for the next round of trading, silencing the floor for the remainder of the day. Otherwise, Stu had no idea how great his own losses might have been. In Japan, the Nikkei, which had survived its own border closing, could not bear the weight of the sell-off in U.S. markets. Reeling from the shock wave, it dropped below 10,000 for the first time in decades.

Between NASDAQ and the NYSE, nearly 14 billion shares had traded hands.

Trillions of dollars . . . vanished.

Rioting broke out in several major U.S. cities, random criminal acts bearing no connection to the failing stock market. In the wake of the presidential address, the nation had remained in a stunned state of relative calm. But as the day progressed and darkness fell, night brought out fear and wildness. Riot police were called in Miami, L.A., Chicago, St. Louis, Houston, and New York City and responded better than expected, though the logistics of coordinating the cooperative efforts between hundreds of local precincts and thousands of National Guard troops caused nearly as much mayhem as the messes they were trying to control. Denying traffic from entering or exiting a city the size and complexity of New York—especially on Christmas Eve—began to seem like a foolhardy idea at best. Nevertheless, zones were established, command posts erected, and the law enforced. Overcrowded jails had no room for the extra thousands of arrests that followed. Detainment camps sprang up in public parks, open-aired courtyards, and housing projects.

Predictably, petty instincts rose to the surface, even among those who were supposed to be helping. City and state agencies competed for jurisdiction, dragging their feet if required to recognize a contrary authority. Flurries of lawsuits from private citizens immediately clogged the courts. These caused little damage compared to the rash of litigation from corporations suing the government for loss of revenue, unfair trade restrictions, and illegal intrusion into matters of commerce. Employees were given extended holidays without pay. Companies demanded the freedom to ship product and receive inventory. But how could they? Trucking lines were shut down. Railways shut down. The U.S. Post Office refused to cross state lines. Only mail within each state traveled. In fact, that morning's public service announcement asked the public to rely on e-mail for state-to-state communication, rather than letters or even phone lines, which had already experienced critical loads as families tried to contact one another.

After all, it wasn't just a crisis. It was also Christmas Eve.

Also on the heels of the address, phantom symptoms began cropping up everywhere, making a farce of containment projections. Emergency rooms ballooned as a jittery populace begged for admission, making treatment difficult to obtain for legitimate Sleeper victims.

To enforce state borders, troopers manned blockades. Hundreds of arrests were made in a matter of hours, many composed of families— husband, wife, and children—who loaded their minivans and SUVs to abandon the urban nightmare.

Stu rolled his eyes as he read the paper. Even the media were suing the federal government, claiming their collective Second Amendment rights were being violated. Such an alleged violation of rights didn't seem to crimp their style too much. Commentators continued to speculate ad nauseam on every facet of the crisis: social, economic, legal, medical, and governmental. Of greater concern, HMOs began protesting to the Department of Health and Human Services that they could in no way afford to isolate every patient complaining of a fever at facilities in their network. After the president's address, HHS had generated a universal one-page form that was now required if a hospital attempted to refer a patient to a secondary quarantine zone. A minimum of half of all available hospital units was required for Sleeper treatment before any transfer would be approved. Hospitals complained that they were being overrun. State governments fielded calls all day, demanding reimbursement for associated quarantine costs. Faced with the possibility of crippling legal obligations, states began pressing U.S. congressmen and senators to pass legislation freeing emergency federal funds to handle the crisis.

Then it happened. According to presidential mandate, Sleeper qualified as WMD: a weapon of mass destruction incident. In response, the National Domestic Preparedness Office began the behemoth task of interweaving all federal efforts, including those of the Department of Defense, Federal Bureau of Investigation, Federal Emergency Management Agency, Department of Health and Human Services, Department of Energy, and the Environmental Protection Agency.

By midnight, just twelve hours after the president's address, only eleven states did not yet have at least one confirmed case of Sleeper inside their borders.

Sleeper was a bona fide national disaster.

• • •

Holed up in Level 4 on Christmas Eve, Diane Rieschmeyer kept in contact by phone with the infectious disease staff at the University of Arkansas Medical Center. She spent the remainder of the day and all night in a Chemturion suit, double-checking her math, appropriate serum-to-weight ratios, and tracking titers on Gracie, a 125-pound female baboon. Gracie was also in the advanced stages of the illness and slipping quickly. Diane administered her best estimate of dosage, then watched and waited. She was sacrificing much to be there—there, instead of with her own children—who were now in bed, having celebrated the holiday with Grandma around the family tree, minus Mom. But it seemed a reasonable gift to Josh and his family. Using a phone inside Level 4, she had spoken with her children earlier in the evening and told them how much she loved and missed them. Afterward, she called Arkansas again.

Sylvia was barely holding on, they told her. Officially, the doctors gave her less than twenty-four hours to live. But they had a serum sample ready to administer as soon as word arrived. Diane had drawn a sample from Josh yesterday. A CDC hematologist had volunteered to make the overnight delivery to Arkansas. Before leaving, he was given two orders.

"Call for confirmation of dosage before administering the serum," Diane had told him. "I hope to get a better idea of the impact of this thing, if possible, while you are in transit. Delay as long as you think you can, until tomorrow if she remains stable. The last thing I want is to cause a reaction that could kill her even quicker just because we administered it incorrectly."

The other restriction. "Only, and I repeat *only*, administer the serum to a patient named Sylvia Chisom. No one else."

He departed with a National Guard escort. Since the ban did not apply air travel restrictions to military and/or vital government operations, he boarded a military jet at about four o'clock and was on his way. When he landed in Little Rock, he called to ask for dosage. But Diane didn't know yet. She needed more time. He was told to wait—monitor Sylvia's vitals, keep them informed, but delay a few more hours if possible.

Meanwhile, she remained with Gracie, watched her, drew blood, and ran tests all night.

Just before dawn, Christmas Day, Diane found herself screaming. Screaming so hard the faceplate of her Chemturion suit fogged up. After a transtracheal wash and examination under microscope, Diane clearly noted less inflammation and a dramatic decrease of inclusion bodies, macrophages, and neutrophils . . .

In other words, the virus was losing.

She decontaminated and peeled out of that suit faster than ever before. Gracie was breathing easier and required less oxygen supplementation. Her fever had dropped three degrees.

"Twenty-five ccs!" she shouted into the phone to the physician waiting by Sylvia's bed in Little Rock. "That should be more than enough. Repeat, 25 ccs."

• • •

Morning was filled with tension. All that was left to do was wait for news from Arkansas and run more tests on Josh's blood. But they needed a lot more blood than the preliminary draws. Tests were only increasing, not diminishing. Primate experiments required large amounts of undiluted, virgin serum. Worse, early word was that efforts to culture had produced mixed results. Without cultures to create serum artificially, Josh remained the lone source.

Hardly anyone noticed it was Christmas morning. Tim presented his son with the pocketknife. Josh drew his dad a picture of an airplane.

So much for the Christmas.

Around ten o'clock, with consent from Terrance and Tim, Stu ordered a second sampling of bone marrow, as well as nearly 600 ccs of blood for expanded testing,. For a child, that was a significant amount of blood to lose. Not dangerous, but still requiring an immense amount of energy and physical resources to replenish, not to mention the dull, throbbing ache of bone marrow removal. Josh was placed on constant fluids and nutritional supplementation via IVs. He became bedfast, hooked up to everything: EKG, pulse-oximeter, blood pressure, IV infusion. They even made him wear an oxygen mask. All of it, Tim was told, was necessary to sustain him at an appropriate level for additional serum samples.

But that wasn't the worst of it. To achieve such levels for more than a single day would require transfusion, given his condition. In a transfusion, blood was drawn, serum was removed, after which Josh's own red blood cells were then transfused back into his system through an IV.

They had no choice. With the pressure of mounting fatalities, Terrance finally agreed to growth factors to maintain the supply. That night, Josh's titers spiked. His body's production of monoclonal antibodies was responding as anticipated to the growth factors. The cancer which ravaged him was now being fed.

Though extremely weak, Josh tried not to show it. Tim knew better. Though he did not have a singer's voice, he hummed his way through a couple of Christmas songs to lift Josh's spirits. He tried to get Josh talking, to tell his favorite stories of Mom. To laugh and remember. It was difficult to see his son in such bad condition. His eyes were sunken, with dark circles. Tim had made it very clear to Terrance that aggressive blood sampling would only be allowed for two or three days, maximum, just enough to provide plenty of serum for research and marrow for cultures. Josh's life was not to be put in jeopardy.

And then we're done. We're going home.

At the same time, Terrance informed Tim of Sylvia's condition. His wife had received a dosage slightly larger than what Diane thought was necessary—just to be on the safe side. The antidote had by now been in her system for several hours. Since the dosage was based on his best guess of her weight at the time, Tim worried whether or not he had given the right amount. Either way, it was time to tell Josh.

"They gave your mom some of your blood," he said, sitting in bed together in their room, playing video games. Josh was winning. "Your blood has stuff in it that seems to be the only thing that works against this disease. You understand that, don't you?"

Josh's eyes were wide. He dropped the Playstation control pad. "Mommy's still alive?"

Tim had not considered that Josh might think otherwise. But then, why would he? When they left, she was nearly dead. "She's alive, yes. At least for now."

Josh was nearly breathless. "And she might make it?"

"Might. No guarantees."

"I'll give more if I need to."

Tim rubbed his son's hair. It felt as short as it looked but was thick and soft.

"I know you would, Josh. I know."

• • •

Wet and cold, Rick arrived at the CDC a little after noon, surprising Tim and delighting Josh.

"Managed to get across Mississippi before blockades went into effect," he told them, "but a patch of freezing rain in Alabama turned the roads slick. I shacked up in a hotel, but the roads weren't much better yesterday. Rode all last night to get here—long, slow, and cold."

"On Christmas Day, no less," Tim observed, impressed.

Rick shrugged, even seemed embarrassed. Turning his attention to Josh, he attempted a casual wink at his nephew, but was unable to hide his shock at what he saw. Josh appeared severely depleted. Rick said, "Are you *okay*, General?"

Josh offered a faint nod, said nothing. Rick glanced at Tim.

"What about the Georgia state line?" Tim asked, purposely avoiding the silence. "They should have had blockades up by the time you were there."

"Well, here's the thing. About five miles from the line, I realized how much I've been wanting to do some off-road biking. Get the picture?" Quietly, he whispered to Tim, "You're all the family I've got left now, you know—you and Josh. Sylvia's not going to make it."

Tim knew otherwise. He updated Rick on the miracle of Josh's blood. Sylvia had received a treatment, he told him. It had cured a baboon named Gracie.

"We don't know, but it may just work. There's hope."

Rick listened carefully, eventually dropping his gaze to the floor. Tim wasn't sure what his brother-in-law was thinking, except that he seemed strangely unsettled by the news.

"That's *good* news, Rick," Tim mumbled, a little perturbed.

"It's great news," Rick agreed. "I just shouldn't have left her. I shouldn't have given up."

Tim heard the ache in his voice and was surprised at his own response. "There was no way you could have known. Besides, I'm glad you're here with us."

Obviously, Josh agreed. They tried to relax and allow Rick to settle in. Tim observed the two of them together. Rick's presence immediately created a small bright spot in Josh's day. Rick, however, struggled to keep a firm and steady smile on his face. No doubt, Tim realized, he had never seen Josh so sick, pinned up with tubes like a marionette on a string. After a few moments, he pulled Rick into the hall to explain.

When he mentioned the growth factors, Rick blew his top.

"Have you lost your mind?" he whispered hoarsely. "You've got to stop all this right now. Tell me you're going to stop it."

Tim took a deep breath, "It's not what you think."

"He's your *son*, for crying out loud! Not some laboratory experiment!"

"You think I don't know that? You think I want this?"

"How would I figure that out, Tim? I wonder?"

Tim showed his teeth, clenched his fists. "You don't know *anything*. The blood samples are for two days, three at the most. They just need enough to run trials."

"Trials!" Rick scoffed. "Am I supposed to feel better now?"

Tim took a deep breath. "I appreciate you being here, Rick. I really do. It says a lot about you. But let me make something crystal clear. I'm *living* this thing. Up until this point, you have just been an observer. Got that? If you would shut up and think for just a minute, you'd realize that everything up to this point may be what saves Sylvia. Josh's serum may actually save his own mother's life. That's not all. He may be able to save other lives. Maybe millions. I told him we could leave anytime. This is what he wants to do. It's his decision."

"It's not his decision!" Rick hissed. "It's yours. You are the father. He is an eight-year-old boy."

"Who is *also* dying," Tim bit off each word as if it were a rancid piece of meat. "There is no cure for his disease. His only option is pain even worse than this."

"Bah, excuses! One little boy can't save the world."

Rick had meant his words to be a cry for justice; Tim took it personally. The words sliced him open at his most vulnerable, in his role as defender and champion. Every muscle twitched, stiffened, demanded a response—a shout, a fist to Rick's jawbone. Anything. Instead, he stood paralyzed. The impact of his decisions loomed as a crushing weight. He had tried so hard to accommodate the wildly changing circumstances of the last few days in a rational manner. To balance compassion with his natural desire to protect his son. Implied or real, he feared Rick's accusations were right. Standing outside the room, alone with Rick, he cupped his hands together, buried his face in them, and tried to hide. Men don't like to be seen when they cry.

But he didn't cry.

"They say they can grow his antibodies," he explained, raising his head enough to be heard. "The ones that cure Sleeper. They say they can grow enough to stop this thing, maybe. But they have to draw bone marrow."

"Bone marrow!" Rick exploded. "Is that what's happening? Not just blood serum? No wonder Josh looks like he's about to fall apart. Tim, do you have any idea how much it hurts to have your bones *scraped?*"

"Please," Tim whispered. "I would trade places if I could. I'm in agony, Rick. Please don't add to it for either Josh or myself. Dr. Alexander is monitoring everything. He knows my limits. I've told him. He knows Josh's limits. Put yourself in my shoes. What would you do? Millions of people, Rick . . ."

Rick didn't hesitate. "I would take my son and leave."

• • •

December 25 limped by, barely recognizable as a day of cheer and goodwill. The holiday spared the stock market another day of losses, but cost the nation two million lives. Two million dead in America since the outbreak began. Nine and a half million dead from around the world.

A story leaked that the president, vice president, cabinet, and prominent members of Congress had received a special vaccine and, furthermore, that emergency military vaccinations were currently underway. The news inflamed Washington, D.C., leading to outbreaks of violence and protest. In the middle of the furor, the mayor died of a massive coronary. When the dust settled, the source was proven false, or at least misinformed. High-level officials *were* scheduled to be among the first to receive a treatment as soon as it became available, simply because the engine of government had to keep going or all would degenerate into chaos. That was the cold reality of life. As yet, the CDC had released nothing.

The explanation failed to appease the general public. That privilege and entitlement might determine medical priority—a fact that most had not considered up to that point in the crisis—triggered a rash of class warfare rhetoric, conspiracy theories, and further suspicion. Both the White House and CDC were immediately flooded with calls from furious governors, mayors, and health commissioners, demanding an explanation. The lieutenant governor of Tennessee called, because the governor himself was in a Sleeper-induced coma. Meanwhile, weary epidemiologists, nurses, and other volunteers worked around the clock to interview patients, trace the chain of infection, place contacts under surveillance, and isolate those with symptoms.

Everywhere, people begged for a cure.

Desiring to appear heroic, or at least busy, senators and congressmen from both parties worked the holiday, pledging vigorous bipartisan cooperation loudly on camera, then immediately plunging into a fruit-less round of oversight investigations into the epidemic. Accusations were brought against the FCC for failing to provide adequate airport security checks. Congressional investigations of when the FBI actually knew something and what it was, who knew it, and with whom they talked were ongoing. Emergency legislation was passed to both remu-nerate the millions of dollars spent thus far by states on the epidemic—including establishing quarantine operations, paying for added public health personnel, and overtime pay for police—and also to equip more strident measures of intervention. A ten-billion-dollar appropriations bill flew through both Houses and was signed by the president late Christmas Day.

Inside the offices and labs of the CDC, though work continued at a fevered pitch, morale was sinking. The entire staff, from secretary to scientist, desperately needed a break, having put in several back-to-back days of sixteen-, even twenty-hour shifts, then sleeping four or five hours before rising again the next day. Most had missed their families entirely. At this point in the spread of the virus, nearly everyone had family or friends that had been hit. Stu made it clear that traffic in and out increased the risk of Sleeper getting inside the building. Atlanta was one of nine other secondary metropolitan regions that had begun to lock down. Bodies were beginning to stack up.

Josh was kept under continual surveillance. Stu requested that guards be placed outside his doors for security reasons, but Tim forbade it. The cruelty of science was enough: poking, prodding, drawing blood, and additional bone marrow aspirates. Five in all so far. Josh had little strength. He would sit, breathing oxygen through his mask, and attempt to read or play a video game. He never lasted more than fifteen minutes. The shunt hurt. He was uncomfortable. Meaningful amounts of sleep became increasingly difficult. His bones literally ached.

The problem was simple: serum was a final product, an invaluable source of antibodies, but was itself useless for creating *more* serum, *more* antibodies. Serum could not culture the monoclonals, because serum con-tained fully formed proteins, rather than the DNA that told the proteins to grow. In other words, what was drawn from the vein was what was gotten, nothing more. On the other hand, bone *marrow* was the human body's repository of precursor cells, an assembly line for plasma, the base component of blood. A scraping of those cells planted in a cozy new artificial home would allow the antibodies to grow *outside* the body—exact duplicates of the materials the disease was producing inside the body.

"Anything from Antwerp?" Stu demanded, standing in the middle of the war zone in Atlanta. "Porton Down? We sent them samples of Josh's blood two days ago."

"Five failures, sir," a member of the Communications group responded. "So far. Out of eight cell lines."

Edgar's team was struggling. Josh's bone marrow was proving difficult to culture.

"We're going to need another aspirate," he said.

Terrance shook his head. "Too much. I won't allow it. He's already in a lot of pain."

"Then we're stalled," Edgar sighed. "Either we get high yields or we get a stable culture. We've tried everything, Stu. We can't have it both ways."

Stu didn't take the news well. "Grow it on a block of mozzarella cheese if you have to! We *must* have it both ways. If you people would have an original thought, you might just save a few lives. Or haven't you heard the news lately?"

Edgar let out a warning growl. "I've got men and women that haven't slept in two days. We're trying everything we can. Back off!"

"I haven't slept, either, and you don't see me complaining."

"Well, by all means, go take a nap. A nice, long nap."

Terrance stepped in. "Cool it down, guys. The troops are watching."

"Fine," Stu snapped. "Just give me a rundown."

Edgar didn't budge. One of his assistants volunteered the latest information. "It seems everything is great on Josh's end. His titers are ridiculously high. As a result, theoretically at least, only small samples should be required for dramatic yields." She was tired, nervous. "I don't really know what this disease normally looks like, but this kid's marrow is *packed* with this stuff. Just packed."

"So what's the problem?"

She lowered her head, puzzled. "It *should* be good. But we've got twenty or so cell lines running. They either produce like crazy for three generations and then die, which benefits us very little, or we have slow-growing cultures that seem to be in it for the long haul, but couldn't produce enough antibodies to save your mother-in-law."

Stu frowned. "I don't have a mother-in-law. Not anymore."

"It was a joke, sir."

Edgar exhaled, "Look, Stu. I'm as baffled and frustrated as you are. I don't know why it's not working—"

"You've added growth factors?"

"Sure we have. A variety of them."

"Ph? Nutrients? Hormones? Tried different media?"

"Truckloads, all of them. Stu, why are you doing this? You know how fickle culturing can be. It's just not working. Not according to original expectations. We're going to have to go for a middle-road compromise."

Stu tapped his cane on the ground. "What are you thinking?"

"Well, for starters, about ten generations. Minimum."

"Impossible. That'll only last, what, three days? We've got to be able to transport these cells to labs around the world that can then culture them for an extended period of time, for antidote development in their region, on their continent."

"I said minimum! Minimum! Ten generations at near high yields."

Diane strolled into the lab, wearing the same clothes she had worn yesterday and the day before. A smile lit her face that could have blown fuses. "Ladies and gentleman," she announced. "I have three little words for you, compliments of the serological testing teams . . ."

"Let's have it," Stu grunted.

"Cell-mediated immunity," she proclaimed, bowing at the waist.

Edgar dropped his jaw. Stu followed suit.

"You're joking."

"No, I most definitely am not joking. The antibodies trigger cell-mediated immunity. We not only have a confirmed defensive weapon that binds to new viruses, but that same antibody is also an offensive weapon that attacks the infection itself."

A spontaneous, joyful roar erupted from the rickettsial lab staff. Under the circumstances, the noise was both strange and wonderful. People suddenly clapped as if it was a famous person's birthday party, or the conclusion of a virtuoso performance by some great symphony. They slapped each other on the back. Hugged. It could have been a replay of the command center in Houston when they brought Apollo 13 home safely.

Cell-mediated immunity would give their fledgling efforts a significant advantage in the field. CMI meant that the antibody in Josh's blood would not only bind to free-floating viruses—viruses that had not yet infected a cell—but also that it sought out *infected* cells, forming a bridge that the body could then recognize and send reinforcements across. At present, Sleeper was winning, not because people were fighting the battle inside their bodies and losing, but because their bodies were not able to fight at all. The human immune system was blind to most invaders. It had to be given eyes to see them, to fight back, to attack. CMI was the equivalent of blowing a bugle and raising a flag on the battlefield: it marked the point on which to rally other forces, namely, killer T cells, the marines of the white blood cells.

Killer T cells could get the job done, if they were just given a commission, and a boarding pass.

Immediately, Stu saw further impact. "That's going to affect dosages, right? It should drop it? Give us more to work with?"

"I'm way ahead of you." Diane beamed. "We gave 25 ccs to Sylvia Chisom. I now think that we can get by with 15 ccs for the average-sized adult, 140 to 190 pounds. Less for children."

"If it works," Stu cautioned.

Diane shrugged. "True, but I can't imagine why it wouldn't. However, if we can't get cultures, it doesn't matter anyway. That little boy can only produce so much serum. By himself, he couldn't treat enough cases to clear a single hospital."

Edgar wrung his hands together.

"Let's go, people!" he bellowed. "It hangs on us!"

Stu took a break in his office to drink some more coffee to stay awake. He had used CDC showers to clean up a bit and had an extra pair of clothes in his locker, which helped. Josie was resting at home. Their home. She had been confined to her own bed and instructed not to leave. Stu made it very clear: if she was sick, she could *not* leave. He needed to be sure of what was causing the sickness.

It didn't take long. Classic signs soon developed. Her fever progressed. Difficulty breathing. Then the bloody cough. Sleeper had infected his daughter. No doubt she got it from some trucker she slept with on the road who was probably long dead by now.

Never in his life had Stu felt like more of a failure. He tried his best to care for her, watch over her, give her space; and best as he knew how, show her a little love. Problem was, he couldn't stay with her. He was needed at the CDC.

He called her from the office. It was around noon. She had taken another turn for the worse.

"We're making progress, Josie. Okay? I'm going to see if we can get you well."

"Daddy, nobody gets well from this. We made sure of that. Jean made sure." She coughed, wincing at the pain. "It feels like I'm on fire."

Stu wanted to say something comforting, didn't know how. He never had. "We're working on some things here, Josie. We're getting closer."

Half true, half a lie. He agreed with Diane, but the fact was, they still didn't know for sure if the serum had worked on Sylvia Chisom or not. They didn't know if it would work on humans at all. Josh's mother was still in a coma. True, she should have crashed by now, perhaps even died; instead, she remained in critical condition. While that alone bode well for success, it did not prove anything. Proof or no, Stu had determined he would inject his daughter with an antidote sample before Sleeper could progress further.

"I'm not going to lose you again," he told her.

Her reaction was unexpected. "Don't you get it, Daddy?" she wailed. "I don't *want* to get well. I did this. I caused this! I was one of them."

"No, you walked away. In the end, you made the right choice."

"But I could have told someone. Alerted the authorities. Stopped it . . ."

"You're alive. That's all that mat—"

"It's not all that matters!" Josie screamed hysterically. "I'm guilty. I'm a murderer. Give my cure to someone else."

Stu didn't have time to convince her. "Stay in bed. Keep drinking fluids. You have my number if you need to call me. Things will change
when I get home tonight."

He left the office, crossed the catwalk to Building 15, swiped his ID
card. The air lock opened. Diane was inside, just about to suit up.

"How close to human trials?" he asked.

"Very. The serum's 90 percent effective in mice and rats, 80 percent
in a wide range of primates in various stages of the disease. Cases like
Gracie are the norm. We're seeing immunity for new exposures, and
gradual symptom reversal for those already infected. Prophylactic treatments are staying in the system, not getting flushed. I'm giving large
dosages right now, so when we finally thin the mix, results will likely
take a bit longer."

"We'll need to. It's going to take a lot of this stuff. Any amantadine
or rimantadine combinations that improve the efficacy?"

"Nothing. I gave up on them. Nothing else works, plain and simple."

"Then let's move on it. We don't have time to finesse this one. I want
human trials finished by the time we've settled on the best culturing
media possible."

Diane nodded. "I'll start working with area hospitals today. We'll set
up a procedure. Control groups. I'll get you what you need."

"What I need," Stu said, and he did not try to hide the sadness in his
voice, "is a syringe of 15 ccs. For my daughter."

18

The morning following Christmas much of the East Coast and several southern states lay under a heavy quilt of thick, fluffy snow, the first snowfall of the season. Trees and gutters and railings were trimmed in clean, white lines, up to four inches thick in Atlanta. It should have been beautiful, and it was, hopeful and fresh. For those who had most reason to care, the snow was far more than lovely. It was fortuitously strategic, functional, especially further north, where they called it a blizzard. There the snow forced people inside, shut down traffic, and in the process, probably bought the CDC a little bit of time.

Stu returned home in the wee morning hours; he would wait until morning to attempt the serum treatment on Josie. Suspecting resistance, he placed a mild sedative in her morning tea, which he brought with toast on a tray to her bed. They spoke briefly, with palpable tension—Josie looked dreadful—but soon the drug overcame her. Stu quickly rubbed a topical anesthetic on her arm, slipped a thin, silver needle into her vein, and drained 15 ccs of Josh's blood serum into her bloodstream.

Now we wait, he thought as he departed.

The first depressing bit of work was to confirm the accuracy of the original seven day forecast: thirty-eight million people dead worldwide so far. Stu didn't bother listening to the media's numbers anymore, though he reluctantly acknowledged the accuracy of their estimates relative to internal projections. No matter. At this point, everyone's numbers were nothing more than wild guesses based on the estimates of international observers. Field Tactics and Field Surveillance teams were running themselves into the ground gathering data. Stu didn't give them any breaks.

"Sleeper is now officially the worst epidemic in modern history, surpassing the death toll of the infamous 1918 Spanish Flu, with no end in sight," explained the haggard anchor at CNN. Journalists weren't getting much sleep, either. "City streets look like war zones, as looters take advantage of every opportunity to steal. In many areas of Chicago, impromptu youth crime syndicates now monitor activities around the homes of known Sleeper victims. After the coroner departs with the body, they strike. Police say they have no manpower to spare to halt petty theft, as their own forces are being thinned dramatically by constant exposure to Sleeper carriers."

Another story detailed how survivalist groups, ridiculed for years for sitting on stockpiles of food and ammunition, were openly firing on men, women, and families as they attempted to flee from urban to outlying areas, especially in the rural Northwest. Militia groups did not dare allow infection to creep in.

In Japan, a lucrative black market for false antidotes had sprung up. Likewise, rumors of miracle drugs flew through the United States, many fueled by a media desperate for good news, further provoking the populace. Droves of people turned to ancient remedies, holistic medicine, rare herbs, wicca, and crystals. They died, like everyone else. Street-corner prophets waved their Bibles, warning of judgment. Apocalyptic communities sprang up overnight. People begged for God to save them.

Following one such story, the television flashed to a reporter for CNN, standing outside the CDC front office with breaking news. As snow fell lightly around his face, the reporter announced rumors "of a little boy who has proven to be immune. Sources tell us his body produces the right antibodies to beat Sleeper."

Stu couldn't believe it. He slammed his cane against his desk, shouting obscenities. But the damage was done. Within the hour, a frenzy of inquiries battered the CDC. The official response was carefully scripted, purposefully vague.

"We are exploring all known solutions," CDC spokespersons repeated time and again.

One fact became clear to Stu. The news story punctuated the truth of it: the CDC was nearly out of time. Possibly, Edgar's teams could continue refining culture yields in transit, but the facts were plain. Infections had nearly reached a critical phase—a point of no return in the spread of the disease.

Stu called the rickettsial lab. "What's the best we've got, Edgar?"

"Nine generations. High yield. But we've finally got another cell line that's showing promise for even more."

"Go with the nine for now. Collect all previously cultured antibodies and prepare them for distribution. I'm going to announce a press conference for noon today. We're going live with the human trials Diane's been working on. People need a little bit of hope."

"You're going to need armored tanks if you plan on transporting serum down city streets," Edgar warned.

Stu called Tom Sizemore. "I want to announce vaccinations. Where are we?"

"I've got about thirty laboratories around the world that have the right equipment, or at least the know-how if we can ship equipment to them. About half have been mass-producing hanta vaccine for nearly four days."

"I want to release it all. Keep them going, but get the word out. I'm holding a press conference today at noon. Let the labs know we're close to sending culturing materials, as well. Do we have enough equipment?"

"I've lined up some manufacturers. They're even willing to donate."

"Good."

He paged Diane next. No answer. He paged again. An unfamiliar voice answered the phone.

"Where's Diane?"

"Her daughter has contracted the disease, Mr. Baker. She thinks her son and mother have likely contracted it, as well. They were all together for Christmas. Diane is home taking care of them."

This is insane, Stu thought. For the first time since his sister had died, years and years ago, he considered prayer reasonable. All he knew to think, to feel, was, *God help us.*

He phoned CNN to announce the press conference.

• • •

Terrance stood with Josh by his bed, checking the latest CBC, chem profiles, and urinalysis. Protein spike, 69. Calcium, 12. Normal levels for stage 3 of the disease, though he would have expected the protein to be a bit higher. Josh's titers, the density of the monoclonals in his blood, remained off the charts.

Tim sat quietly in a chair beside the bed. Since his conversation with Rick, he had become increasingly withdrawn. For the first time ever, he didn't dare look into Josh's eyes.

"I don't want any more bone marrow drawn," he announced suddenly. "Do you hear me, Dr. Alexander? No more. Not for a couple of days, at least. I want my son to be able to rest, and not hurt."

Dr. Alexander nodded. He reminded Tim of a simple fact. "We can stop this anytime."

"I'm okay, Dad," Josh protested weakly. "I can handle it."

"Josh, I'm not going to allow much more, do you understand? This has *got* to end. It was supposed to be over already, but it keeps dragging on."

Josh lifted his head off the pillow and shook it emphatically. His words were slurred and groggy with morphine. "That's not what you and Mom used to tell me. Remember? Everyone's born for a reason . . ." He lay back again. "Maybe this is my reason."

"No," Tim said in a flat voice. "The virus is not your fault, Son. It's not your job to fix."

"I know it's not my fault. It's my—" He waved his arms so that the tubes dangled underneath. "What's that word again? Mom explained it to me . . ."

Tim knew, or at least had a guess. *Destiny.*

"You need to rest, Josh," he said. "No more talking."

• • •

The news conference was broadcast around the world. For the first time, Stu considered it fortunate to have CNN's headquarters in Atlanta. With the red light blinking on top of the camera, he announced that approximately five thousand samples of an experimental antidote serum were being distributed to critical areas in a four-state region, based on the findings of a smaller trial currently being completed under tight security at a local hospital. He cautioned the media and the public that it would take time for the effectiveness of the antidote to be fully assessed, but declared ample reason to hope.

"These are the first shipments we have yet made," he announced. "If the trials go well, many more will soon follow."

He thumbed to his second page of notes.

"I would also like to announce that a limited vaccine is also being distributed, as of this hour, to hospitals, clinics, and quarantine zones around the world. This vaccine targets a portion of the virus believed to cause the most severe of the respiratory symptoms. While we do not claim this vaccine is in any way curative or complete, we believe with mass vaccination programs we can at least slow the spread of the disease and extend the lives of those already affected, until we are able to produce the actual antidote in sufficient volume as well."

A cacophony of questions from the assembled reporters followed.

"Dr. Baker, is it true a little boy is the source of this antidote?"

"Yes. It is."

"Can you tell us his name or anything about him?"

"No, I will not. For matters of privacy, I will simply confirm that the boy has demonstrated immunity to the disease. Therefore, we are examining the antibodies that his system produces and are basing our antidote on those findings."

"Has anyone at the CDC contracted Sleeper?"

"No."

"Is the boy in any danger in these proceedings? Is he healthy?"

Stu didn't want to answer a veering line of questions regarding Josh. It was a no-win scenario. "We have hopes for both the vaccine and the antidote trials. That is all. Thank you."

The world received the news with cheer and solemnity. The assistant to the general secretary of the United Nations called to discuss fair distribution to the international community. Doctors clamored for samples. Movie stars, entrepreneurs, and billionaires offered tens of millions of dollars for a single treatment. No stratum of society was left untouched by the news.

One day slid into another. Reports from large regions of Africa, India, and Brazil revealed decimated populations. Much of Europe, meanwhile, lay under a heavy layer of snow, and while border closings there were proving to stem the tide, it was the weather that had begun to help the most. Russia, by turn, had become a pioneering nation in macabre solutions. Officials there were creating, not quarantine zones, but "Dead Zones"—cities so badly hit that the dead from other locations were being shipped, sometimes by the truckload, and dumped, even while the living struggled on in the city. The policy was readily acknowledged as a moral outrage, even by the Russian officials who enforced it; to millions of Orthodox, it was sacrilege. But they had no choice. There were not enough coffins or gravediggers. The dead were piling up in the streets.

Seventy million, worldwide.

Of all the states in America, California was hardest hit, followed, not surprisingly, by New York and Texas. Hundreds of thousands—perhaps millions, no one really knew—were dead in those states alone. Simultaneously, millions more were slipping into comas. Large industrial incinerators were converted to crematories, and entire assembly lines were dedicated to eliminating contaminated corpses.

The question was raised, "Are the ashes safe?" No one knew the answer. But the fires continued to light.

• • •

Edgar's team landed a cell line with fifteen generations and high volume. It was the best they could hope for. While cell lines routinely extended for hundreds, if not thousands of generations, the end result was completely dependent on the material being cultured. In that respect, Josh's antibodies—miracles that they were—were highly uncooperative.

Stu ordered for the necessary lab equipment and cell lines to radiate through the international network, and begin revving up production for regional distribution. Representatives from WHO and Field Tactics strategized the best means of deployment, as well as the most critical regional lines to hold for the sake of containment. Until multiple cell lines developed, they would have to make the best of limited supplies. The minimal bone marrow samples they possessed—representing all the pain Tim would permit Josh to bear—would allow perfunctory gains at best. Especially since the cultures didn't last long. A large, initial, high titer deposit of bone marrow was like kick-starting the whole process, allowing for dramatic multiplication over fifteen generations. Small starter samples yielded anemic totals in comparison.

Knowing this, Stu took it upon himself to beg Tim for more bone marrow. It was within reason. Dr. Alexander concurred. Josh's body could handle it. But Tim wouldn't budge. His son was in tremendous pain. The numbing effect of the morphine had already begun to plateau.

Dawn of the following day revealed an America mired in chaos and rebellion. Having held off as long as he could, the president had finally declared martial law under cover of night. Citizens awoke on December 27 to a temporarily military state. In many regions, social order had all but collapsed anyway. Provisional guarantees of the Bill of Rights were suspended, including the writ of habeas corpus. Universities, school gymnasiums, civic centers, and municipal auditoriums were converted to local quarantine areas. In Florida, Louisiana, south Texas, New Mexico, Arizona, and southern California, where winter temperatures were less a problem, tents and outdoor compounds were used as well. In towns of less than fifty thousand, physicians were urged to avoid allowing admission for Sleeper victims and to care for patients in their homes, instead.

Still they died. Young, old. Babies and their mothers. Black, white, red, yellow. Heterosexuals. Homosexuals. Christians, Jews, Muslims, Buddhists, Taoists, Confucianists, Scientologists. Rich and poor. Technogeeks and athletes and bodybuilders and paraplegics and old men on respirators. They all died the same way.

Coughing blood.

• • •

Josie, however, improved. Since Stu had intervened relatively early in the disease, her system responded vigorously. The cough lessened. Her lungs opened.

Stu welcomed the news with relief. Yet sitting in his office, exhausted, there came a particular moment as he watched the news and witnessed images of coffins stacked three and four deep up and down the streets of New York City, and looters dumping the bodies at night so they could steal a coffin for their loved one instead, that he became enraged at his daughter. He tried to fight it, suppress it; but he could not help the sense of rage he felt. He dialed the phone, and when Josie answered, he didn't bother to say hello, just began shouting.

"What were you thinking, Josie? Tell me! Make sense of this! Are you even watching the news?"

"I already know what they're saying," Josie replied. "Jean promised us it would look this way. Just like this."

Her answer was incomprehensible, only served to enrage Stu further. Whether he had royally messed up her life or not, somebody had to call her to account. "How could you have ever followed that man? What about this plague could you ever be made to think is remotely right or just?"

"Nothing. Not a single thing. I see that now."

"*Now*," Stu gasped. "Are you *now* free of his spell? Is that what you're saying? Thank goodness, because I read your diary. You said he . . ." Stu threw up his hands, mocking the word, "*captured* you."

"I can't explain it."

"Try."

He could hear his daughter searching for words. "He wrote a book. Eight years ago he wrote a book."

"And that's what did it?"

"I think so. At least for all of us who joined him. I'll never forget the day. I stood in line for an hour, just to meet him. It was on a Monday. September 17."

"You're telling me a book is killing the world?"

"I'm telling you ideas have consequences. Look at my life, Daddy! You wonder how I could ever believe such a thing? What else did I have? What did you ever give me to believe in?"

Stu was disgusted. "Watch, Josie. Turn on the TV and watch. Rub your nose in the consequences. At least give these people the dignity of your attention."

"It won't change anything, Daddy. I can't undo what's been done."

"Done? Josie, this virus is nowhere near done! Your boyfriend's little plan might kill us all yet."

He slammed the phone down and stormed out the door. Trudging to the lab, in the midst of his anger, fear struck him. He felt vindicated, but that was not the source of his fear.

Have I driven her away?

• • •

Another day passed. And another. Nobody went to work. Nobody bought a Happy Meal. Newspapers shut down. The major networks managed to keep a skeleton crew going, especially CNN, but large blocks of time were left empty on the air, with nothing but a blue screen showing. The media were staffed by people whose job it was to report, face to face, a contagious death to which they were not immune. Clusters of ham radio operators flourished again, though they could only reach each other. In many places, phone lines were dead. With no one to maintain them, many Internet servers crashed, causing chokepoints on the backbone of the World Wide Web.

Australia could claim the most success at containment thus far. Geographically severed from the world, the government had taken no chances, moving rapidly to secure Sydney. It had worked. Elsewhere, isolated villages and hamlets scattered around the Third World also demonstrated a natural resistance through cultural containment. For them, little traffic in or out was a way of life.

Major cities in Third World nations, however—populated in the shanty towns and underbellies of cities like Calcutta, Mexico City, Dhaka, Shanghai, the five hundred thousand trapped in Cairo's "City of the Dead," Lima, Jakarta, and others—were the worst of all. No running water. No toilets. Streets of mud and open sewage. Living quarters mired in filth and contaminants. These suffered most cruelly from Sleeper's unchecked ravages.

By comparison, dictatorships fared well. Because they were used to controlling the people—often through brutalities, yes—they experienced less difficulty than more technologically advanced societies.

As a whole, though, the world was brought to its knees. In many places, the crisis ignited mankind's better angels. Where Sleeper devoured in darkness, compassion kindled a flame. In the quarantine zones, brave volunteers fed Sleeper victims soup, at risk of their own lives. Military and CDC officers labored in the mud and grime wearing pressure suits, breathing clean air from the tanks on their back, or more often, relying on face masks alone. Kindness remained possible: a cool rag on the brow, a hand squeezing a hand. Though the gestures did nothing to save the body, each and every touch wafted through the soul, offering grace to those who otherwise would die feeling very much alone. Most did die alone.

As in war, containment lines spanning dozens of maps eventually grew distinct. Some territory the troops were forced to surrender. New York was lost. L.A. was lost. Houston, nearly lost. Hold them tight, the command said, but concentrate on new areas. In other words, expand the lines, abandon certain geographies, form a new flank, reinforce emerging strongholds as quickly as possible, and hope the antidote arrives soon. The one bit of good news was that in more rural and agricultural states, though the raw numbers soared, home isolation was proving adequate to slow the spread of the virus.

And so the world gasped its way through another day. Secondary diseases from decomposition began creating an additional logistical nightmare. Worse, the medical industry was losing physicians and nurses to the disease *en masse.* Jean de Giscard's plan was proving as brilliant as he had hoped. The earth was being systematically purged of her human occupants.

Two hundred million, dead.

The very number seemed surreal, defying either comprehension or belief.

• • •

The morning of December 30, CDC physicians performed a rather large bone marrow aspirate on Josh, the first in three days. They gave him morphine, of course, and it numbed him. Nearly enough, but not quite. He could feel it, deep inside. Literally, in his bones. Pain.

Tim sat beside his son in the operating room while doctors worked to remove the marrow. He held Josh's hand, rubbing his fingers through Josh's hair.

"Don't leave me, Dad," Josh said, as the anesthetic closed his eyes. "I can do this as long as you don't leave me."

Tim squeezed his son's fingers and stayed by his side.

When the procedure ended, Dr. Alexander had to perform a second blood screening. His routine was two a day, morning and evening. Fortunately, Josh was no longer transfusing blood. The antidote had proven effective in the expanded trials, so all efforts had been diverted to culturing. No more large serum samples. That meant at least a couple fewer machines, a couple less tubes. Tim held Stu to his word: enough to supply the trials, no more. Once Edgar got the cultures going, he and Josh would head back to Little Rock, and then to Oklahoma—with Sylvia, they fervently hoped.

Josh had given enough. More than enough.

Barely lucid, Josh rolled his arm to expose the shunt for the draw. His eyes, so rich and deep all his life, were now fallow sockets, vacant and dull.

"I'm so sorry, Josh," Dr. Alexander said as he departed for the lab. Half an hour later he returned with a curious expression on his face.

"I didn't want to say anything this morning," he explained. "I felt we needed at least another test. But there it is. They're changing."

He held up Josh's chart, reading aloud a set of numbers from three days ago, two days, then yesterday and today.

"What do you mean?" Tim asked suspiciously. "What's the problem now?"

Dr. Alexander let him read the numbers for himself. For several weeks now, protein levels had held steady. Over the last few days: 69, 72, 74, 73, 72, 71.

Today. "Sixty," Dr. Alexander said. "And just now, 53."

Calcium, he continued: 11, 11, 12, 12, 11, 12.

Today. "Ten. And then nine."

He told Tim the lab had run a hemoglobin, too, another facet of the daily routine. It tracked antibody levels by establishing a ratio of plasma to red blood cells. The process was called Packed Cell Volume, PCV.

Josh's red blood cell count was *rising*, according to the PCV. That could only mean one thing: the monoclonals, which typically crowd out red blood cells, *were beginning to diminish*. Josh's PCV had hovered around an average of 29 percent for days.

Today it was at 33. A huge jump.

"No problem at all, Tim," Terrance explained with glee. "It may be rare, but it's definitely not a problem." He shook his head in wonderment. "What a unique little boy you have."

Tim rose from his chair. "Are you telling me what I think you're telling me?"

Dr. Alexander nodded. "I don't know how else to explain it. Your son's multiple myeloma, sir, appears to be going into remission."

19

By two o'clock, the Prime Team had convened an emergency meeting. Diane joined by phone from her home.

"What are our options?" Stu asked.

"Vaccines are proving to be of limited benefit," Tom said flatly. "In probably 40 percent of the cases we've been able to track, we are seeing a nominal decrease in respiratory pathology."

"In other words, don't count on it."

"Pretty much. We've only begun to treat large groups of people, but I'll be surprised if it makes a dent."

"Terrance?"

"I'll know more about Josh tomorrow. But I feel very confident in predicting remission. His titers have dropped in half."

Edgar said, "Could the numbers be skewed for any reason? A reaction to the bone marrow aspiration? Anything like that?"

Terrance shook his head. "You would have to remove a lot of bone marrow to affect these numbers. However, I did allow for those factors. Either way, his protein and calcium levels are still dropping."

Stu clenched his fist. "That puts us back at square one. We've got to find an alternative culture. One that's stable enough at high yields to go a hundred, maybe *two* hundred generations."

The room grew quiet. Edgar, grim faced, was the first to broach the silence.

"I don't think it's gonna happen, Stu."

Tom's voice rose from a chest as deep as a cavern. "We're looking at half a billion people dead in two or three more days. We can't afford to start at square one."

Diane searched for a more hopeful angle. "Most curves on this thing are going to show the virus starting to slow a little bit in major population zones by virtue of its own success. It is going to run out of people to kill."

"But it's still out there. We can't possibly rely on the virus to self-terminate. I don't even want to try to imagine the damage . . ."

"We're losing our only source," Edgar sighed, holding up his hands. "This thing may just have to run its course, and we all take our chances. Either way, I'm all out of ideas. We can culture what we have and hope for the best."

"Unacceptable," Tom, the old war horse, growled. Even though he was a grandfather, he was a fighter first. "You're sealing not just our fate, but the fate of the planet. We have to consider the unthinkable."

Stu knew instantly what he meant. He had been thinking the same thing but had not wanted to be the one to say it. Looking into Edgar's eyes, he knew Edgar was thinking it, too. Terrance, however, had to first experience the horrible weight of the silence that followed—that nearly sucked the air out of the room—before he understood.

"I will not be party to this," he announced, jabbing his finger. "Take it off the table. Don't even consider it."

"We must consider it, Dr. Alexander," Tom countered. "It is our duty."

"You have no authority. No right. I will report you—"

"To whom, sir, if everyone is dead?"

Terrance kept shaking his head, more insistent. His answer sputtered from his lips, "No, no, no. For God's sake, no."

Edgar jumped in. "With the network in place, we can maybe play with the numbers. A boy Josh's size, knowing his titers—if we had 100 percent of his aspirate to work with, we could produce massive amounts of antibodies. We might even be able to divert 10, maybe 15 percent of it away from the fifteen generation cell lines, and grow it instead in one of the three or four generation hyper-cultures. May get a bit more that way once an operation is going full steam."

"You will *kill* him! That's what you're saying. You know that's what you're saying."

"Dr. Alexander," Tom said. "Has it occurred to you, that if Joshua's multiple myeloma does go into remission, that he too will become susceptible to Sleeper?"

The very thought stole the breath from Terrance's lungs. Everyone in the room could plainly see he hadn't considered it. It didn't matter. "You don't have the right."

"No," Stu said. "We don't. But Tim and Josh do."

• • •

It was a joyous occasion that afternoon. Though trapped in his bed-shaped prison, a part of Josh felt as if he was floating, the best kind of floating, from the inside out, where your heart soars. He was sure it wasn't the drugs. Dr. Alexander seemed sure he was getting better and that made him very happy. He insisted on at least sitting up (though an upright position typically triggered serious nausea). His dad and uncle joined the minor celebration staged around the bed, supplying chocolate bars and Coca-Cola from a CDC vending machine. Josh was especially pleased at how much more relaxed his dad seemed.

"I was getting afraid," he whispered in his dad's ear. "I felt so sick."

Tim squeezed his hand and said nothing.

"Beat you two out of three," Rick challenged, holding up the Playstation control pad.

Josh shook his head. He wanted something a bit different.

"How about I Spy?" Tim offered. "Or gin rummy?"

"I want Uncle Rick to tell a story," Josh decided.

Tim said, "Something brave and triumphant."

Rick screwed his face shut, searching for a suitable tale. Finally, he stood and made a sweeping bow with arm extended, like a courtier to a king. "In honor of my courageous nephew, I shall tell the story of . . . Johnny Rogers, the man who wouldn't give up."

Josh grinned. He loved the story of Lt. Johnny Rogers. It was one of his favorites.

Rick began: "Lt. Johnny Rogers was the son of a poor dairy farmer, the third of nine boys. Eager to get off the farm, Johnny decided to join the war as a combat pilot. He enlisted in the Marine Corps in June 1942, ready to fight, except that he had a girl he loved. On the day of his commissioning, she was the one who pinned on his silver wings and gold bar. Even though he was poor as dirt, Johnny gave her an engagement ring that day, purchased by deeding his military life insurance policy to the jeweler. He loved this girl that much and planned to marry her. As soon as he was assigned to his F4 Wildcat squadron, he named his plane Lady Laura, after his best girl. That's how Johnny Rogers went to war."

Josh loved the way Uncle Rick told stories. Alternating in tone and tempo between the hushed, the sacred, the dangerous and daring, ever soaring to the verge of triumph or total defeat, he spoke as much with his face and arms and hands as he did with his lips. Josh listened, breathless.

"Johnny lived big, talked loud, and when he walked into a room, everyone would turn to see who it was. He carried a rabbit's foot on his plane and never walked the ground without a big, fat cigar in his mouth. On the last mission of his career, Johnny was in the South Pacific, high in the skies above Guadalcanal, surrounded on all sides by quick little Japanese Zeroes. In all his service, Johnny had gained twenty-four confirmed kills, nearly the equal of the famous Eddie Rickenbacker from World War I."

"I remember him!" Josh said proudly. "You've told me about him, too."

"That's right," Rick said. "So Johnny was hoping for number twenty-five. But today was not Johnny Rogers's day. Two Zeroes tailed him, and he couldn't shake them. *Bam, bam, bam, bam!* The wing of Johnny's Wildcat shredded with lead. His plane went into a dive. The entire mission was failing. Other American planes were also in the air, attempting to dive bomb a Japanese battleship below. Now this battleship was crucial, because it was hammering the coast where marine battalions hid in foxholes. Johnny knew he had only one chance to help them. He pushed the stick and fell into a steep dive, way too steep, aiming straight for the belly of the battleship. Then he radioed the bombers to follow his lead. The maneuver was so dramatic, so terrifying, the battleship immediately concentrated their fire on Johnny's single plane, fearing he was about to crash into them. If he were a lesser pilot, Johnny probably would have crashed. But at the last he pulled up, his wing nearly blown off. The bombers came in range, dropped their payloads, and the battleship was destroyed. But Johnny had to bail out. His Wildcat was too torn up."

"What happened to him?" Josh exclaimed. Asking was part of the fun.

"Well," said Rick, dragging out the drama. "Old Johnny was captured by the enemy and taken to camp as a prisoner of war. He wasn't treated well, as you can imagine. He was roughed up a lot, and only given boiled cabbage and stale bread to eat. Other prisoners were treated badly, too, only they couldn't stand the pressure. Over and over they tried to escape, but none of them ever made it. Old Johnny knew he had to buckle down and hold tight. He knew he had to survive."

"Why?" Josh whispered. This was the best part. Even for an eight-year-old boy, this was the best part. "Why did he have to make it?"

"Because he had a girl waiting back home!" Rick exclaimed loudly, as if the answer were obvious. And of course, it was. "When other soldiers grew weary and afraid, ready to give up hope, they would ask Johnny how he held up, and Johnny would always tell them, 'I've got a bride waiting for me, fellas. And I intend to marry her.' And he did. It took another whole year before he was freed, and by then he was weak and battered. But he won the day. He married his girl and they had a whole bunch of kids," Rick swiped his nephew on the head, "just like you, Josh."

Out of the corner of his eye, Josh saw Tim smile. It was a good story, well told, and the silence that followed seemed laden with promise. He shifted his position to watch the snow swirling outside his window. The ground had become a rolling blanket of pillowy drifts and glistening flat spreads.

"Looks kinda like the cotton fields back home," he murmured. "Only whiter."

They drank hot cocoa, compliments of Marge. Without speaking aloud his thoughts, Josh wondered secretly about his mom; wondered, too, if Rick and his dad were also thinking of her. Presently, the phone rang. His dad answered. A moment or two later, he seemed to have withdrawn a bit.

"Can this wait?" Tim spoke low and cautious into the phone. Then, "Okay, I'll be down in a few minutes."

He rose and left without another word.

His dad seemed agitated. After he left, Josh turned to Rick, his face full of questions.

Rick didn't try to answer them. "You've put up with a lot here, General. I'm impressed."

"What would you have done," Josh asked, "if it were you?"

"Gone home. In a heartbeat." Rick snorted unapologetically. "That's what I do best. When the going gets tough, Uncle Rick leaves."

Josh didn't flinch, didn't challenge him. Didn't take his eyes off Rick.

Rick turned away. "Stop it. Don't do that."

"Do what?"

"You know what I'm talking about. With your eyes. You just . . . I don't know, *do* something. You look at people a certain way and they want to run and hide."

Josh knew what Rick meant. He didn't see it that way.

"I'm just looking at you," he said innocently. "I guess people are afraid I'll see something."

Rick leaned back in his chair, closed his eyes, and yawned. "You are awfully old for an eight-year-old kid. I don't know how you do it."

It was obvious Tim wasn't coming back anytime soon, so they played a game of gin to pass the time. Rick won but was dragging by the end. He had not slept well in several days.

"I'm just going to lay my head on the bed, General," he said, stretching his arms, yawning again. "If that's all right with you. Probably ought to grab a little nap for yourself, too."

Josh laid his hand on Rick's head. "Mommy told me something about you."

"I can only imagine," Rick said dryly.

"She explained why you all don't get along."

"I think I'd rather just sleep now, okay, Josh? We can talk later."

"Don't you want to know what really happened?"

Slowly, Rick sat up. He frowned. "What do you mean?"

"You know, when you were a foster child. She was trying to protect you. She didn't want you to get hurt."

Ever so slightly, Rick edged forward in his chair. "Josh, is this a joke?"

"No, Uncle Rick. I promise."

Josh told him everything he knew. Young as he was, he didn't really understand what it all meant—how exactly Sylvia had been abused. That sort of thing. But he did understand that in spite of what it looked like, his mother had been guarding Rick, and Rick had never known that. The more Josh revealed, the further he went, the more Rick seemed to shrivel. By the end, he sat staring quietly into the open air, at nothing. Josh wondered if he had upset him, or made him angry.

"No," Rick said softly. "Far from it." He refused to say more, laid his head back down, and closed his eyes. The sleep he fell into was deep and peaceful.

Josh stayed awake for a long time after, running his fingers through his uncle's blond hair. He had an idea, something he had wanted to do for a long time. Something for Rick. He wiggled into a better position, carefully adjusting his tubes and electrode wires. Just as he was about to begin, the phone rang loudly, jarring the stillness. Unsure whether to answer—not wanting to wake Rick—he picked up the receiver.

"Hello?"

"Hello," an unfamiliar male voice answered. "I'm looking for Tim Chisom, please. The CDC switchboard sent me to this number."

"That's my dad. He's not here."

"Then this must be Joshua? Is that right?"

Josh felt nervous. "Who is this?"

"Forgive me, Joshua. My name is Dr. Kemper. I'm your mother's doctor here in Little Rock. We met once a few days ago, but you probably don't remember."

"I remember," Josh replied. "Is my mom okay?"

"Well, that's why I'm calling. I have some very good news. Your mother's vital signs are improving. Her condition is still serious. She's weak and can't really talk. But she's alive. Your mother is going to make it, Joshua." He paused thoughtfully. "The amazing thing is, she has you to thank for it."

Josh didn't know what to say, but in the darkness of his room, he grinned from ear to ear.

Dr. Kemper said, "Could you let your dad know I called, Joshua? Pass the word along. He can call here anytime for an update, day or night."

"I'll tell him," Josh said. "Thank you."

They hung up. Josh closed his eyes, still smiling. He would have fallen asleep right then and there, except he knew his dad would be returning soon, and he needed to act fast. Josh preferred to be secretive; he had been planning this gift for a long time. First, he made sure Rick was sound asleep. A bit more strength would have been nice, but he couldn't afford to delay. This chance might not come again. Gently, as if Rick were a little wounded bird, Josh laid his hand on his uncle's cheek. From some hidden place inside, his gift broke open. From God to him. Josh had never suspected otherwise. The muscles in his arm twitched slightly; he scrunched his eyes.

Suddenly, the smell of flowers blossomed in the room.

"Uncle Rick," he whispered, eyes glistening. "Now you can fly."

• • •

Fearful and ashamed, Josie finally did as her father had instructed. Two days after the fact, she turned on the TV. While Joshua and Rick rested, while Tim's world collapsed beneath him in the span of a single, closeted conversation, CNN ran a story. And Josie watched.

". . . has been living at the CDC with his father for several days. We can now confirm that the child is eight-year-old Joshua Chisom, from a small town in southern Oklahoma. High-level sources inside the CDC tell us that Joshua's body is beginning to slow its production of the materials required for antidote development. Without the building blocks of the antidote that Joshua alone seems able to provide, no further cure remains in sight, and vaccination attempts have proven only moderately helpful at best. Medical experts conversant with the details tell CNN that any attempt to harvest the bone marrow would be so drastic, Joshua Chisom would not survive the process."

The news exploded around the world, from CNN to the BBC, to satellite uplinks and through the foreign press. The Internet lit up with reaction. Though millions were cut off from regular communication, the public responded. Many were horrified, but the loudest and most vicious immediately demanded Josh and his father make the noble choice, the right choice, for the good of others. Debate raged, but nations were ragged and desperate. Government leaders called to put pressure on the United States government to sacrifice the boy's life if no other viable options remained. Better that one die than hundreds of millions. A Web site quickly polled for opinions. Should Joshua Chisom voluntarily forfeit his own life if it would save the lives of millions and stop the spread of the virus?

A photo of Joshua Chisom flashed on-screen, obtained from Folin school records. His third grade picture. Joshua was a sweet-faced, timid looking little boy, with a crooked grin and hair as black as tire rubber. Josie stared in disbelief until she could watch no more. Her stomach turned. Gagging, she ran to the bathroom and vomited into the toilet.

Bent over, choking on guilt, she pounded the linoleum floor with both fists. One question demanded an answer: Was *that* the little boy that had saved her?

• • •

When Tim returned to the room, the mood was calm and peaceful. Standing in the doorway, he felt as if all his life and spine and muscle had been sucked out with a big hose. After hearing the Prime Team's desperate proposal, he had wept like a baby for an hour and a half, curled on the floor of some anonymous, darkened office in Building 6. The best he could manage at present was to stare at his feet, and ask over and over and over, how? Why?

Strangely, the room smelled of flowers. Tim drank in the scent, tasted the sweetness of it. Josh had done it again. Deep inside, Tim knew it. It smelled the way he imagined it would, the way Sylvia had described it. The smell of miracles. For whom? Rick?

They were both asleep, Rick and Josh. Evening had come. Tim collapsed on his own bed, staring at the ceiling through the darkness. If a thousand knives could have been driven into his skin, one by one, the pain could not have hurt any more; he could not have bled any less.

They had asked him for Josh's life.

At first Tim laughed at them. Indignant, he had stormed out. He would unhook Josh then and there and drag him out of this God-forsaken place. Rick had been right all along. The audacity! Spineless, bloodsucking, soulless scientists. As he stormed away, the last thing he heard echoing down the hall was Tom Sizemore's thick voice, "Nobody said it would be easy, Tim . . ."

It sounded like something Meem would have said, holding his chin in her hand when he was a boy, pointing to the candy in his pocket that he hadn't paid for, the evidence of the sin he must confess to the owner of the store. That memory triggered another. A memory of long ago; the words of a silly moppy-haired waitress, at a time when Tim was learning to be a man.

. . . I don't think the whole world hangs on one moment for you, Tim . . . but if it does, chances are you won't drop the ball next time people need you. You'll remember this moment and you'll make sure all is right.

Such memories had nothing to do with anything. Stupid bits of nostalgia. Yet it awakened a sense of responsibility in his heart, a call to duty. In one translucent moment, the burden of the world became his burden. After all, he *was* a father. He knew that pain. What would it be like, then, to lose not one child, but two, three, four? Millions? In spite of himself, in spite of every instinct he knew as *Josh's* father, as a person, as a human being, the man Tim Chisom found himself turning around in that hallway and walking back to finish hearing what the Prime Team had to say.

Now, as he lay on his bed, he could think of nothing but the legacy he would carry, not in the eyes of the public, but in his own heart, if he failed to intervene on behalf of the entire world. And with that, yes, the question also lingered: How could he live among people he himself had chosen to let die? Either way, he was making a choice for someone to perish. One or many. Perhaps even himself.

Such a severe, unthinkable decision, of course, *should* be left to Josh. He was the one who would be asked to give the most. But that was exactly the problem. More than any other thing, Tim dreaded, feared, already knew, exactly what Josh was likely to say.

In some small, undefinable way, his son had carried this burden all his life.

Destiny.

Tim could see it so clearly now, in ways he never had before, and he squeezed his eyes to keep from being blinded. Stretching into the past, the old soul within his son called out to him, eyes that carried the depths in which the stars were born. Tim saw the color and shape of the mystery, the depth of destiny woven into the whole story. If this moment had never come, Josh would no doubt have grown into a fine man. But having now arrived, for whatever reason lines of fate intersect, he knew because he knew, his son would see it for what it was, surrender to the weight of it, lift it upon his shoulders, and walk that final road to where he alone could go. And the world would live or die based on his willingness to go there.

Time, Tim cried. *Please. More time.*

In that moment, Tim realized with a shock what was actually being replayed in his own life. He was Abraham with Isaac. He was Father God, surrendering his own Son. For redemption. To save many. It was the story of the ages, the timeless tale of history itself.

I'm not that strong.

But Tim too had been prepared for this moment. Deep in his bones, he knew it. Hated it. Bitterness burned in him like vinegar in a mouth full of open sores.

There must be another way.

No other way. No more time. Tim knew what would happen. If called upon, Josh would first grow still, solemn. Then, nodding without words, he would accept, almost as if it were expected of him. As if he had no choice. Tim saw the whole thing play out in his mind as he lay on the bed. In his gut, he just knew. He also knew it would wound Josh to the core that his father would even ask such service of him. Yet even then, Josh would likely voice nothing. And so Tim wept all over again at the thought of the silence that would come from his son when the cruel words at last were spoken. His mind raced down a dozen other, far happier possibilities. If he ran, if he took Josh and ran, and didn't tell his son anything, then none of this would have to happen. If he simply told the Prime Team no. If Sleeper would just magically go away. Why couldn't *that* happen? Why this? God, why this?

I trusted you! I believed! Where is the miracle!

Such was the burden of faith. For Tim, it was a summons to duty. For Josh, it would be an invitation to sacrifice.

He could not help but think of Sylvia. What would she say? What would she do? Strength and duty raged in her, even when she felt weak to the task. But she also prized Josh above all else, and would protect him to the last. No, the plain fact was that Tim was alone now, would have to face this alone. No grace. Not this time. Her wisdom and strength, the solace of her nearness—all were denied him.

Most dreadful of all, if she survived, how would Tim even begin to tell her the awful truth?

Nobody said it would be easy, Tim.

Nobody said it would be this hard, either. The Prime Team, at least, had agreed that no one would speak a word to Josh except Tim alone. That gave Tim the option to say nothing. Forfeit the decision. Walk away. Perhaps with shame in his heart. But he would have his son.

Or would he? *Shame will accompany either path,* Tim realized.

He glanced out the window and saw the splashed cream glazing left by the moon on piles and drifts of snow all around the CDC campus. Stately old trees stood as mute sentinels to the truth: time and seasons will go on and on, one after the other. This, the barren time, the time of stripping and coldness and weariness—this was the season of sorrow. Next to come, green and free with life, spring . . . what would it look like? Would any children be found swinging on an old tire hanging from a rope in the backyard? Would husbands and wives lie down together and in naked embrace conceive another generation? Would new books be written, new songs sung, new masterpieces created from the genius of the human mind? What about the guys at the quarry? How many of them would die, were dead already? How many would suffer through watching their entire family die, and then, if they survived, turn to see Tim walking along . . . with his son?

Come spring, would there be anything at all?

No time. No time to know. What's right. Necessary.

If he ever needed to hear God's voice, to get an answer to prayer or know what to pray, this was the time. But in spite of the need, the pressure, Tim felt only blankness inside. He didn't have the words, scarcely a muted groan in his spirit. The Prime Team made clear to him that a swift decision was critical. They had maybe twenty-four hours, at the most, if morning blood tests continued to demonstrate remission. Otherwise, the density of antibodies in his marrow would begin to thin too much to produce in culture the massive volume required. They had fifteen generations of culture to work with, and every moment that ticked away with Josh's disease in remission meant less and less from each generation, until there would be nothing at all.

Only in a dream, or a dreadful comedy, could the best possible news for Josh become instead his death sentence. Staring out the window, Tim barely caught the half-moon, tucked in the upper right corner of the sky, wet with light. Around it in perfect symmetry, the multitude of winking stars lay cold and unfeeling to his plight. What did they care? The vast sapphire sky hardly gave pause to the small rock of Earth, that spinning ball of blue and green in a far-flung galaxy. Nothing too impressive there. What was Earth that they should care?

We live here, Tim found himself answering. *Living, breathing people.*

Abraham had looked at those same stars. He had heard the voice of God, telling him he would one day have as many descendants as the stars in the heavens. He was given a son to prove the promise true. For the world, it was the beginning of faith. Then Abraham heard the voice of God again, telling him to murder his son. And Abraham thought of the stars. What about the promise? It was a mystery. How could it happen? How could a father be brought to such lengths? How could he raise the knife above his own son? It didn't make sense. And that was the truth of it.

That was why it was called *faith*.

For the first time, Tim saw the horrific high-dive resident within the act of faith. At heart, faith was a burning desire to touch God, to be found and known by the unknown. Such a radical pursuit couldn't possibly be made subservient to forms and fashions of logic. It seemed foolish to Tim to have ever thought otherwise. Faith colored outside the lines, would always do so; its entire essence was given to redefining the picture according to the pleasure of the power it served. But knowing those things did not make the leap any easier. Beneath Tim, a great chasm of utter darkness suddenly opened, and now, positioned on the edge, he was being told to jump.

He knew what had to be done. Though he might hate himself for the rest of his life . . .

"Josh," he said, rising from his bed, touching his son lightly on the shoulder. "Josh, we need to talk."

• • •

Opinion polls required little deliberation. In a matter of hours, the public had decided Josh's fate. Ninety-two percent of people thought he should die if it meant they would live. They would gladly accept the rare, curing power of his blood. "Give it to us!" they cried, in unison, until their collective cry became a mighty roar. The government did not dare ignore such cries. Congressmen and senators, the president, foreign ministers and dignitaries pressed the CDC to act with force if necessary. Of course, they themselves would cast no vote, nor lift a finger to cause his death. Commandos would not dare storm in to seize him.

No stain of questionable ethics would be allowed to harm anyone's career.

Across the world, a few intellectuals rose to the challenge, decrying the barbarism of the plan. The pope denounced it. The Dalai Lama, confirmed as a carrier, nonetheless refused to accept an antidote treatment. Philosophers spoke of irreparable harm to the moral self. They were brilliant in their position, morally justified, full of righteous offense. In newspapers and on the Internet, they pledged "not to partake of the antidote, nor to join this blood ritual," even if it meant their deaths. They stood on principle.

They would die on principle.

Nobody lived without the blood.

Other intellectuals argued differently. They postulated a mathematical reality that, by virtue of sheer numbers, was rubbed clean of moral discord. If one died, many lived. A phrase from *Star Trek* was soon elevated among pop cultural references to the status of anthem: "The needs of the many outweigh the needs of the few. Or in this case, the one."

Repeated over and over again, it only took a few hours to generate a huge groundswell of conviction that Josh must die. For the common man, a pithy Hollywood phrase was all it took to make sense of the scandal, to rationalize the deed. Posters were plastered on the walls of the CDC building. "The needs of the many . . ." some of the signs read. Other posters, neatly printed, asked a frightful question: "Will there be a New Year without Joshua Chisom?"—except that the artist had cleverly scratched out the word "Year" and scrawled the word "You" in graffiti-like red letters.

Will there be a new you without Joshua Chisom? it asked.

The sound bites worked. Police in riot gear were called to guard the doors of the CDC, to deny a growing mob of citizens from gaining access. In response, the mob shouted louder, demanding a cure. They used the word *justice*. Justice for the world, they said.

Nobody mentioned justice for Josh.

Other voices were strangely silent. In the halls of academia, at the Darwinian core of society, Josh should have found numerous, vociferous advocates. After all, the plain truth was that Josh alone was evolutionarily qualified to survive, a fact that should have been trumpeted among the elite. Some few brave souls—the more honest among them—tried. They were summarily silenced, drowned by the larger noise.

Doesn't apply here, the rebuttals argued. *Different biological construct. Extraneous factors. Not the same.*

Tim knew nothing of what had recently transpired in the opinions of the outside world. He didn't even know people knew about Josh. Josh didn't know, either. They were in a different building, away from the mob. But as they talked that night, as Tim bled words and tears, begging for Josh's forgiveness as he asked the unthinkable, as he held his son and wept, the mob took up a chant that echoed down the hill, bouncing off the walls of other buildings. As more desperate people joined it, the chant rose higher and higher, until it leaked through the walls.

"His blood! His blood! His blood!" they cried.

Faintly, it reached all the way to Josh's ears. And Josh, hearing them, said yes.

To his father.

20

After they spoke, after Josh said yes, his dad unhooked him from all the machines and left him to himself.

"I'll be here waiting for you," he said. "If you want me."

Josh didn't answer. He didn't know what he wanted, didn't know how to think. Rick remained sound asleep. Josh didn't want to stay in the room, crippled by the silence. So he wandered the hallways, away from people and noise and activity, seeking dark corners and other lonely places, places that tasted and smelled and felt as he felt. He wanted to cry but felt numb, strangely calm, as if he had been detached from the entire affair, then called upon to observe his own inner workings. He roamed without purpose, lost in the murky half-light of empty CDC corridors. At the end of one hall, he found a window positioned at the right angle to see the mob three buildings distant, standing in the cold night under street lamps and parking lot lights. They couldn't see him, but he could see them, their fists raised into the air. They were angry, denied entry by police holding Plexiglas shields with billy clubs raised. Josh watched them shout his name, barely heard their faint voices.

What will it feel like? he wondered. *Do they even care?*

He slid to the hard tile floor with his back to the wall, wearing only the gown he had worn for days, and began to cry. His own father had asked him to die. His own father . . .

It was cool in the building. Josh was chilled and felt goose bumps tracing lines on his skin. Knees propped up, unmoving, he found his attention drifting down the long dark tunnel to the halfway point, where the ceramic tiles smudged shadows and reflections together. There was a faint, faraway fluorescence coming from the end of the hall. Muted grays in between. White, at the far end. Dark near him.

And that seemed right, just about then, to be enveloped in darkness. He wished the shadows could come alive and swallow him. He wished the hall was a cave, and he could hide and never be found. Clutching his knees to his chest, Josh huddled in the corner for nearly an hour, rocking slowly back and forth. No one saw him. No one passed by. Until work resumed tomorrow, the wing was deserted.

Tomorrow. The last day of his life.

At length, spent, he rose, returned to the room. Tim sat in a chair, staring at the door, waiting for him. It was dark in the room. Only one light.

"I don't have to do this, do I?" Josh asked. He had not yet mentioned the phone call from Little Rock. If his dad knew Sylvia was improving, was going to make it, what then? He could find out later.

Tim shook his head. "No, Son. Not at all."

"But more people will die, right?"

"Many, many people, Josh."

"Maybe everyone?"

"Maybe."

"That means you would die, too?"

Tim swallowed. "I don't know."

A tear slid down Josh's cheek. It all came down to one question.

"Do you want me to do this?"

Tim said, "No, Son. It's *not* what I want. Not in a million years. I would rather die myself."

"But you can't. Only me. I'm the only one that matters."

"Yes."

"So whether you want it or not, it's what you think needs to happen."

Tim met his son's eyes. "Yes."

Josh lowered his head, suddenly very afraid. "Will you be with me? I won't do it if you won't be with me."

Tim nodded. "To the very end. I promise."

Josh climbed into bed, pulled the covers over his shoulders, and curled up. "I want to sleep now."

Tim turned off the light.

• • •

New Year's Eve arrived, sparkling with new snow and sunshine, making diamonds of the world. It was painfully bright. Compelled by what she had heard on the news, Josie visited the office. Her fever was completely gone. She was well.

"Daddy, you can't do this," she told Stu, standing resolute in his office. "You can't allow it."

Stu knew what she was talking about. He had seen the news, the polls.

"It's our only choice. Besides, they made the decision. He did, Josh. And his dad. No one forced it on them."

"It's wrong and you know it. It's no different than what I did."

"It's very different," Stu cautioned, removing his reading glasses, peering down his nose at his daughter. "The actions of your group took life. This decision will save lives."

"You're trying to justify yourself. They both murder someone."

Smoldering, she stalked out, asked staff for directions along the way until she located Josh's room.

Knock, knock.

Tim answered the door and peered at her without recognition. He looked haggard, on the verge of collapse.

"Please go away. Whatever it is, it can wait."

"I don't think it can," Josie pleaded. "I *have* to see him."

He began closing the door. "No, you don't."

"It was me!" Josie blurted out. "I did it. I'm to blame."

Tim stopped, stared at her.

"Please," she said. "Just a few minutes."

Josh peered timidly around the corner. Josie saw. She pushed her way inside. Josh stood with his arms dangling uncomfortably from his side because his gown didn't have any pockets to hide them in. His hair was dark, cut short. She looked straight into his eyes and tried to catch her breath.

"I'm Josie," she said, her voice cracking. "And I need to tell you something. Something awful. I'm one of the ones that spread the disease. I was with that group. Have you heard the stories?"

Josh nodded.

"I was one of them." The confession was simple: guilty by association. Even so, the reality of her own words doubled Josie over. She dropped to her knees in front of Josh, and words spewed out like a torrent, as fast as she could think them. "It was me, Joshua . . . or might as well have been. The others, they're all dead now. I ran. In the end, I didn't do it. But I might as well have. I helped them. I believed what they believed." She stared at Josh through glistening eyes, unsure whether it made sense or not, uncaring. All she knew was that an innocent child should not have to pay for the gross stains of her soul. "I'm so ashamed. You don't have to do this, Joshua. You shouldn't." She looked up to his father and stood. "Mr. Chisom, don't let him do this. Joshua has got his whole life ahead of him. Maybe they can beat Sleeper some other way, I don't know."

Josh stood straight, still, patient for her to finish. Tim was too exhausted to respond, much less hate her. She deserved his hatred, no doubt. If her story was true, he should destroy her right there on the spot. But he couldn't. He had no strength.

"You should leave," he said. "I want you to leave now."

"It's a horrible mistake," Josie begged, sobbing. "You'll regret it."

She clutched at Josh's arm. Tim intervened, tore her loose, his anger rising. She continued to sob.

"But it's not fair! I have your blood, Joshua. Don't you see? I was going to die, too. I had Sleeper and my dad gave me some of your blood. You've already saved me once." She grabbed fistfuls of Tim's shirt with both hands. "Don't let him do this. I can't bear it."

Tim started to shove her out the door, raging. What right did she have to come here at a time like this, to try to absolve her guilt! It was everything Tim could do not to pour his fury on her. Josh stepped in between his father and Josie and touched the girl's face.

"Go do something else," he murmured to her. "Do something better. Pretend you're someone brand new."

He wiped a tear from her cheek.

"Please forgive me," she begged.

"I do," Josh said.

Tim felt the anger drain away. He wanted to hate this woman—this foolish, stupid woman. But he realized if Josh, of all people, could forgive her, then he must as well. He pulled Josh back inside the door and stepped away. He left the door open but didn't look at her again.

"Go away, please," he said. "I want to spend time with my son."

• • •

Nothing could wake Rick, no noise was too loud, until nine o'clock. Gradually he stirred and wiped his eyes, tasting the film in his mouth. At first he didn't seem to be aware of all the doctors in the room. Tim watched him squint and try to focus. Terrance drew fresh blood for a final test. He and the other docs had arrived an hour or so ago. Josh was back in bed, hooked up to more machines. More tubes in his arms. He was quiet.

"My eyes are all blurry," Rick mumbled, brushing at his face with both hands. Tim glanced at his son. In spite of the terror of the day, Josh smiled faintly.

"Maybe you took your contacts out last night," Tim said with a heavy voice, trying to play along.

"I sleep in them," Rick replied, confused.

He put two fingers to his eyes, pinched, pulled one contact out, blinked, and tried to focus.

"What the—," he mumbled, removing the other. A simple, stunned declaration followed: *"I can see."*

He repeated it, louder. "I can see!"

His joy was short-lived. Finally, he noticed the unusual activity in the room. "What's going on here? Why all the docs?"

Tim dreaded the next ten minutes. He motioned quietly to Rick and led him slowly to another room down another hall. Once the door was closed, with several walls between them and Josh, he explained the decision that Josh had made.

"It happens today," he ended. "In just a few—"

He was not allowed to finish. Stunned at first, Rick now cried out, threw a doubled fist that connected squarely with Tim's face. Reeling, Tim tripped over a chair and dropped to the ground.

"Rick!" he begged.

"Shut up!" Rick screamed, incredulous. "You can't do this! If you don't want him, I'll take Josh myself. Do you hear me!"

Hunched and angry, he aimed for the door. Tim gathered his wits, leaped to his feet, and tackled Rick, grabbing him from behind and wrapping his arms around Rick's chest. Rick roared and flew into a frenzy of arms and legs. Tim took another blow to his ribs from Rick's elbow. He grabbed at Rick's jaw with both hands, twisting, and threw him against the wall. Rick gasped for breath as his lungs deflated. He didn't wait but dove on Tim, cursing, clamping his hands around Tim's throat.

"He's your son! How could you even think—"

Tim kneed him in the groin. They rolled and turned and warred for several minutes, until both were finally exhausted.

"You fool!" Tim wheezed, rubbing his throat. "I don't want this at all!"

"Then get him out of here, today," Rick gasped. "Today!"

"It's not that easy, Rick. You can hate me if you want. I don't blame you. But it's not that easy. People need Josh and he knows that and he is willing."

"To hell with them!" Rick spat. "To hell with the whole world. That boy is one of the only good things I've ever had in my life. I won't let you. For God sake, Tim. You're talking about killing your own son!"

Tim wasn't going to go through this again. He had traveled this road over and over all through the night. He never slept. He had made his decision.

"If you need to leave, leave. If you can't make that decision yourself, I'll have you escorted. But you aren't going to get in the way and cause even more pain. I won't let you upset Josh."

Rick's eyes bored a hole through Tim's skull. He spat his words. "You are the worst kind of father I can ever imagine." With that, he stood, straightened his clothes, and stormed out of the room.

• • •

All the preparations were made. The only thing that remained was to get the final test results, to confirm the remission that would seal Josh's fate. The specialists recruited from nearby Northside Hospital departed, allowing Tim and Josh a few final moments together.

"Dad," Josh said. Hearing his son's voice, Tim labored to control his emotions. He was so proud of him, so fearful, so bruised to his very core by the inevitability of their decision together. Josh continued, "I think I understand now."

Such a simple phrase, but Tim's spirit broke under the grace of it. He pulled Josh to his chest.

"You amaze me, Joshua Chisom," he whispered, nearly choking. "I'm so proud of you. I hate it that the world is so cruel, so messed up. I'm so, so sorry."

Josh did not passively receive the embrace. Instead, he clung to Tim's neck.

"I don't want to die," he said softly. "But I don't want to be the only one to live, either. When I was sitting alone last night, I kind of figured maybe that's how Jesus felt."

"Maybe so . . ."

"For the first time, it makes sense to me. Before it always seemed so wrong. So unfair."

"It *is* wrong, Josh. It *was* unfair."

"But it saved people, Dad. Saving people is very right."

Tim squeezed Josh tighter, rubbing his hand over the back of Josh's head. Josh said something Tim had longed to hear.

"I want to be sure and go to heaven, Dad," Josh said. "I'm ready."

He was asking for help. Tim readily gave it. In his own heart, Tim feared judgment for what he was allowing, cried out to God for mercy. *Save us all,* he thought. They said a simple prayer together, because Tim could not manage more. Josh responded, receiving an offering of life he himself did not deserve as he prepared to surrender to the world his own.

"Tell Mom I love her," Josh said, refusing to explain. No more words were spoken.

When the lab ran the numbers, they confirmed the worst possible truth. In any other time, for any other life, on any other day, such news would have sent cheers through the room: cancer in remission. Josh *was* in fact getting better. His titers had dropped by half yesterday and were dropping still. Today there were no cheers, only solemn preparation. Everyone understood the gravity of the moment. No light conversation was allowed. No questions asked. They had to move quickly.

The procedure would be short, painless. Tim was assured over and over that it would be painless, at least as far as Josh was concerned. No medication invented could block the kind of pain Tim felt, would likely feel the rest of his life. The plan was to anesthetize his son completely. Josh wouldn't even know what was going on. They would surgically remove every last bit of marrow from his bones, and blood from his body. The process would kill him. His marrow would be iced, divided, stored in sterile canisters, and flown by jet to labs for immediate cultivation. The CDC had determined that 40 percent of the marrow would be held in the States. The other 60 percent would be shared internationally. At the very least, their projections showed such a concentration would enable the United States to survive, as well as several other critical regions in the world. The human trials had revealed breathtaking results. From 100 percent mortality, to 100 percent recovery. Even for victims in the latter stages of the coma, like Sylvia, Josh's blood had proven effective.

Surgical oncologists who specialized in bone marrow transplantation were recruited from nearby Emory, scrubbed and waiting in the wings. The team of physicians and specialists from Northside would assist to assure the longevity of the marrow once removed. In the meantime, Edgar had contacted the international laboratory network, briefed them, and told them to be ready. All the important people were alerted, including the president. No call came to step down; no reprieve was given.

They prepped Josh, led him to a sterile operating room not eighty feet down the hall from his makeshift living quarters. The room was usually reserved for animal or human autopsy. As his bed wheeled down the hall, trailing the lights overhead in succession, Josh held his father's hand. Tim walked beside the bed the way a man might walk to his own execution. Neither he nor Josh spoke. It was the most excruciating eighty feet of Tim's life. As he moved, he could not help but turn his face towards the ceiling, hoping to break through, to the clouds and beyond. To wherever God was. Wherever he seemed to be hiding.

Tim had been asked to raise Abraham's knife. He had obeyed. It was raised.

Where is the ram? he pleaded. *Show me the way out.*

For Josh, staring into the face of his father—etching in his memory the lines of pain and love he saw there—he found comfort. It didn't make it easy. That morning, in the soul of an eight-year-old boy, a mighty battle was waged. A battle more fierce than ideas, than emotion, than getting beat up one more time on the playground. It was a battle Josh knew he could lose if he wanted. It could have ended right then and there, and might have, but Joshua chose, again, as he had done many times before, to stand his ground.

Today, the fight must go on. Now, it was the world that needed him.

He said to his father, again, "Don't leave me."

Tim squeezed his hand.

Inside the OR, they put a mask over Josh's face and began pumping anesthetic into his air supply.

"Breathe deep," the anesthesiologist told him. And Josh did.

No angel stayed the hand of death.

No voice from heaven congratulated Tim for his faith.

No power intervened to rescue his son.

The halls of the CDC were quiet. Nobody worked; nobody tried to fix anything or figure anything out. Men and women alike stood in shocked silence. Many cried. A few waited outside the OR, peering through the glass: Rick, Josie, Stu, Terrance. Though none of them could really see what was going on, each understood they had nowhere else to go, nothing else to achieve. Everything that mattered was right there, voluntarily strapped to the lonely confines of a surgeon's table.

No one took this life. Josh was giving it. An eight-year-old boy.

Stu bowed his head, mortified. Yet he neither moved nor ordered a halt to the proceedings. Rick, moaning softly, pressed his forehead to the glass, palms flat on the cool surface. Inside his brain was an empty hole, where everything logical and right was stored, a place that refused access to the memory of this moment. Eyes vacant, flat as two stones worn smooth in a river, he found himself breathing moist lung air on the glass, tracing in fog the words of a poem by Ralph Waldo Emerson—a poem quoted in one of his many war books.

So nigh is grandeur to our dust,
So near is God to man,
When Duty whispers low, Thou must,
The youth replies, I can.

Inside, in surgical mask and scrubs, Tim ran his fingers through Josh's hair and rocked back and forth.

"I will always love you," he said; he did not try to stop the tears. "You will always be the most important person in my world."

Josh could barely hear his father's voice. The drugs made the sound of it seem so far away, as if the words were floating down a long corridor with no doors, swathed in piercing bright light. His eyes rolled back in his head as he fought the cloud of anesthesia coagulating in his mind. With great effort, he tried to speak. Tim leaned over and put his ear to his son's lips, straining to hear.

"Don't . . . cry," Josh whispered.

The feel of his breath sent a jolt through Tim's system more powerful than electric current. His entire body stiffened. In his son's voice he heard the one thing he could not fathom, nor bear: trust. Quiet, innocent, coming not from a great distance trapped in bitterness or drug-induced lethargy, but near between them, as close to Tim as his own name. Josh was trying to give his father a final gift. Never had a gift cost more. Tim began to shake. The price was far too steep to bear. It was too much. He could not endure any more.

The surgeons took knives in hand, preparing to cut. There would be blood. Much blood. Tim's heart pounded harder, harder. Bile began rising in his throat, causing him to retch. His airway constricted. Faint as the brush of feathers, Josh squeezed his hand a final time.

Tim nearly broke. He could not possibly watch, could not find strength to stay in that room a minute more. He turned.

Josh's eyes fluttered open, saw his father turning.

"Don't . . . leave me, Daddy!" he groaned. "Please don't . . . leave me."

Tim froze, knew he could not possibly leave. As a father, a human being. Somewhere between grit and honor and a crushed heart, courage arose. A gentle, farewell smile came to his lips, as he surrendered to gravity, forcing himself to remain in the chair. Stroking Josh's forehead with his first two fingers, he said, "I will never leave you. I'm right here, Josh. Right here."

Josh's brown eyes glistened, but the drugs were too strong. Tim watched helplessly as the life drained from his son. He did not dare look away, would hold this moment forever, cruel as it was. They stared into each other's souls, knew one another. Josh swallowed, tried to speak, couldn't.

Then the end came.

Tim imagined he was running. Running, but never arriving. It was his heart that fled. Far as it could fly. Trailing each step, like ghosts that would haunt him for the rest of his life, Josh took two last, long, slow breaths through the mask.

Then closed his eyes.

Epilogue

The father sat alone on one of several benches, facing a tall, bronze statue of his son. It was high noon and deep summer. Pigeons bobbed and scratched on the ground around his feet, waiting for crumbs. The day was as humid as July should be, but a fresh breeze from the northwest kept it cool as June. People were everywhere. Power players, personal aids, and policymakers on their way to important staff meetings; beggars and street musicians; moms dragging toddlers on phone cord leashes.

People. Alive. Well.

At the very least, the survival of the planet was providential. Some called it luck. While failing in the original objective, early efforts towards containment *had* established dependable communication and supply lines, enabling rapid and effective antidote deployment. To this end, at least in the U.S., state disaster plans had proven invaluable. Quarantine zones, though hellish, allowed mass immunizations. Tens of thousands were treated every hour, region by region, city by city, all over the planet. Boosting the outcome further, approximately half the labs reported stretching the number of culture generations to nearly thirty, some even more.

Luck? Of all people, Tim knew better.

It took two weeks to immunize everyone struck down by Sleeper, but only the first four days to immobilize the spread of the disease and begin achieving reasonable containment goals. Many regions were simply empty of the living. Medical intervention teams, United Nations task forces, and military escorts discovered entire villages and even cities where Sleeper had claimed every last life. Rescue workers recounted horrors to the press for weeks and months, even after the tide was turned. Scores of workers required therapy to avoid breakdown.

Tim had no trouble remembering these events. The final report on the epidemic had been issued three months ago by WHO. It revealed staggering losses: 1.2 billion worldwide, including an estimated 50 million lost to secondary infections from contaminated water supplies and unsanitary living conditions. An additional six months was required to clean up the global mess, dispose of the dead, rebuild infrastructure, and assess damage. The cost to the global economy was undetermined. In America, the Dow hovered around 5,000.

No wonder the world was quick to hail eight-year-old Joshua Chisom a hero—in every sense of the word, a savior. Noble, they said. Selfless.

His memorial was erected in Washington, D.C., almost immediately, in a ceremony attended by heads of state from fifty-nine nations. The world witnessed the dedication on TV. Businesses closed for the day. Half a million people attended. They wept. They prayed. The president declared September 17 to be a perpetual day of remembrance for the duration of the nation's history. Never would they forget the awesome sacrifice, and as proof of their gratitude, the memorial was designated a national shrine, on a par with the Lincoln Memorial, or the Tomb of the Unknown Soldier. It was further given the rare honor of an unflinching honor guard, posted twenty-four hours a day. Other governments swiftly erected similar tributes in their own national capitals, agreeing upon a common name for the collective effort.

"Spirit of Life" the memorial was called in English. *Zoe Pneuma.*

Dozens of nations participated in the memorial project. *Zoe Pneuma* would be everywhere, all over the planet. Anywhere a person went, the spirit of life would be there. At the dedication, a single dove was released into the air, took wing, and darted away.

Tim smiled at the memory, so proud of his son. But his heart ached.

The day after Josh died, Tim was informed for the first time of his wife's improving health. A week later, he flew to be with her, explaining the dreadful choice he had been forced to make. Sylvia wept uncontrollably for days, was an empty shell for weeks after. When by chance they discovered that Josh had actually known of his mother's improving condition and yet remained silent, both were overcome all over again. As the months wore on, their marriage nearly fell apart. After all, Sylvia had taken her son's blood and lived. Had that in some way driven Josh to his decision for others? For Tim, the fact that Josh *knew* and wouldn't tell him was almost too much. What had gone through his mind those final few hours? Did Josh know Tim would have waited, stalled?

Most dreadful of all, had their son died feeling abandoned?

Even a year and a half later, the wounds were still fresh. In the end, though, Tim and Sylvia did the only thing they'd ever done, ever known to do, which was cling to one another—and God. Tim didn't expect her to understand or forgive. But he loved her. And they both loved Josh. Somehow, through it all, healing came. Books were written. Tens of thousands of letters poured in from all over the planet, praising Josh, thanking the Chisoms, telling stories of families saved from pain and death, of men and women doomed, alive today because of Josh. It was like getting a second chance, they wrote. Being reborn.

Months later, Tim and Sylvia finally felt inclined to visit the memorial. Arriving yesterday, they spent a restless night in the hotel, silently searching for anchors for the emotion tomorrow would surely bring. They tried to talk but could not find the words, settling instead for a stiff and hungry silence. When morning came, they still were not ready. But by early afternoon, they summoned their courage and made the journey together to this sacred patch of ground. The nearer they came, the more slowly Sylvia moved. As the monument came within sight, she nearly stopped altogether, hunched over, her gait timid, dragging along as though her feet were shoeless and the concrete were shards of glass. As the top of the statue appeared over neatly trimmed rows of trees and manicured shrubs, she stopped.

"You go on," she murmured, fighting tears. "I can only do this a little bit at a time."

Tim squeezed her hand. "Sylvia, we can come back tomorrow."

"No, really. Go on. Please. I'll be along."

He hesitated, but she nudged him. Tim also felt like retreating, but the need for closure beckoned him. Inside the wide ring of trees, he stared into the fading blue sky, to the top of the monument, having no idea what to feel. A depth of emptiness and loss dropped straight through him, into the earth, where it lay like a flower, rare and beautiful, waiting for a name. He had no name to give it, only grief. But as he sat under the shadow of the great bronze reminder, he smelled again the fragrance of Josh's flower, sweet as lilacs, and he bowed his head in awe.

The statue had been crafted from a photograph provided to the memorial committee by the Chisoms. It was Sylvia's favorite image of her son. There was Josh, silhouetted like a T, back straight, hair trailing in the wind. Arms outstretched to either side.

Like he was flying.

The artist had done a fine job. It managed to capture a bit of the personality and depth of his son in nearly every respect. Except for the eyes. It was impossible to capture that, ever, in any medium.

The setting was lovely, trimmed in carefully sculpted shrubs, plush grass, perennials, and cobblestones, shadowed at all times by the circle of trees, which visibly marked off the hallowed ground. Cautious, watchful, Tim observed the manner in which people approached the shrine. Many seemed fearful, or ashamed, as if it might hurt them. Others, with great reverence, stood with head bowed, reading the story of Josh's life on the markers beside the statue, of the miracle of his blood and the courage of his final days. One father bent down beside his son, pointing up at the statue and whispering in solemn tones. The boy would have been about Josh's age. He blinked, mouth open, eyes wide, asking questions, listening. An old woman bowed at the waist and kissed the bronze feet. Some strolled by casually, but in the wide periphery of the shrine, there was silence.

Tim was pleased. He glanced beyond to the sidewalks where life continued apace, hustling and bustling, buzzing on cell phones, dashing to meetings. On the fringe, folks reclined on benches, reading, talking. Giggling tourists, with friends or family members snapping a photo of them by the nearest landmark, posing with goofy grins.

The dichotomy between the sacred and the casual struck a deep and sorrowful chord in Tim. Would Josh one day also become a fixture of the landscape, an icon belonging to history? For a moment, as a father, he could not help but wonder that everyone did not throng to this place, that anyone could be so cavalier, so callous, as to continue their lives without daily tribute. No doubt they passed by here every day on their way to work or lunch, didn't they? In the initial wake of their own personal second chance, hadn't they made sure to nod their heads, or lovingly stroke the feet, as the elderly lady still did? Why not now? Tim knew that for the most part the salvation of the planet was still fresh in the collective memory. The media referred to him still. A big director in Hollywood was making a movie. But how long would it take? How long—months, years—before the memorial became merely an obstacle on a walking path, no different than a tree or a bush?

As the father beheld the face of the son, he did not see an obstacle. He saw a likeness he knew all too well. Memories of a life—astoundingly short, but powerful. This was his son! And he had sacrificed everything to spare not only those who took time to honor the sacrifice, but those who had resumed life unaware, content to absorb and largely ignore the immensity of the price.

My son! Tim cried silently. He wanted to jump onto the base of the statue and shout from the top of his lungs to those who passed by. *Look at my son! Look at what your life cost him! How can you just walk by?*

Many didn't. But many did.

"It's beautiful," a voice said softly beside him. Turning, Tim found Sylvia beside him, staring into the face of the statue. "It's not Josh, but it reminds me of him."

He started to reply, but at that moment a mother passed by with her teenage daughter. Though they spoke in low voices, Tim could not help but overhear.

"Mom, I have his blood *in* me. I'm here looking at him . . . and his blood is in me. Isn't that strange?"

"It's why you live," reminded the mom. She said more, but they moved on and Tim lost their words.

Sylvia heard them as well. Tears streamed down her face.

"I need to be alone, Tim. I think it's best if I just go back to the hotel for now."

Tim searched for her eyes. "I know it hurts, Sylvia. I'm sorry."

"Don't be. I'm glad we came. I'd like to come back with you tomorrow." She smiled and kissed his cheek. She started to walk away, turned around, and said, "I know it was hard. I can't imagine anything harder."

Tim watched her go but could not leave. For many hours, the father simply sat. He sat and watched as hundreds of people stole a few moments to enter the sacred circle and gaze upon the spirit of life. His son. The memory of his son. He was moved to see the expressions on their faces, the tears, the crooked, humble smiles. They left notes and flowers. Nineteen months later, the place was packed with tokens of gratitude. The people came from everywhere, a mishmash, walkers and strollers and joggers, milling about, bumping into one another, cursing, snorting with laughter, traveling in twos or threes or alone, dressed in suits, shorts, leather, spikes, tattoos, noses pressed to a folded copy of the daily news or sipping coffee from a Styrofoam cup, walking hand in hand with dreams in their eyes, living their lives as they had always lived—but when they entered the circle, they paused and grew still, if only for a few moments. He knew that he could not hate them. Nor could he hate those who did not bother to stop at all. Ignorant as they were, the more he observed, the more they became to him something precious. How could he possibly balance within himself judgment for the very lives his son had purchased, and still cling to love for his son at the same time? At the end of the day, what was to be gained? All that was left now was to love those Josh had saved.

The whole world had been given a gift.

He would revel in that gift.

Absurd as it was, his son had chosen the darkest path, and the world breathed and lived in light because of it. And that was the greatest miracle of all.

Evening came. Standing, the father turned in a slow circle, absorbing every trace of humanity around him. He shook his head, amazed. Amazed!

Live, world, his heart cried, washed by a strange and fierce torrent of love. *Live!*

afterword

It is only fitting to acknowledge the spark of the idea behind the story you just finished. Sometime in late 1999 and on into early 2000, an anonymous tale burned through chains of e-mail all over the world. It was a simple parable, approximately thirteen hundred words long, but it stirred the hearts of many people, including mine. In response to the drama of the tale—a plague sweeping the world, a little boy with a cure, a father's crisis—I undertook the effort to craft the book you hold in your hands, composed of the same basic elements. To my knowledge, the author of the original idea has preferred to remain nameless (we have never met or spoken). Other than rudimentary similarities, mine is a wholly original work and should not be construed as an attempt to finish what that person started, but rather to give the tale a broader stage and a larger voice. Wherever the author of the anonymous piece lives, if he or she should stumble across this effort, I hope it will be enjoyed, and in some small way serve as a tribute to the power of creativity in the Christian community.

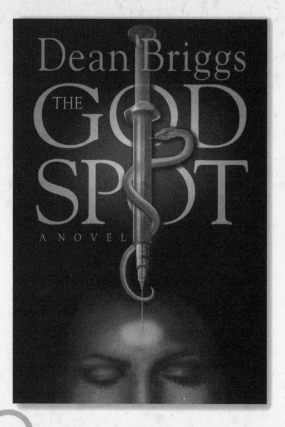

O the edge of the most shocking medical discovery of the past 2000 years, neurosurgery resident Hank Blackaby has no idea the chain of events he is about to unleash or the peril he faces. Pulled from today's research and tomorrow's headlines, Dean Briggs's scientific thriller weaves espionage, genetic research, and murder into a riveting, unforgettable tale.

WORD PUBLISHING